A CADE REARDEN THRILLER

MIDNIGHT ZONE

By
JK Franks

This book is a work of fiction. The characters, incidents, and dialogues are products of the author's imagination and are not to be construed as real. Any resemblance to actual events or persons, living or dead, is entirely coincidental.

Editor: Debra Riggle
Cover Design: Tom Edwards

eBook ISBN: 978-1-7326144-6-8
Paperback ISBN: 978-1-7326144-7-5
Hard Cover ISBN: 978-1-7326144-8-2

Email the author at author@jkfranks.com
Friend him on Facebook at
facebook.com/groups/JKFranks
Visit the author's website at www.jkfranks.com

A portion of the profits of this book are going to support the following Marine charities: Ocean Conservancy (oceanconservancy.org) and Oceana (oceana.org).

Second Edition

v. 2020-0910

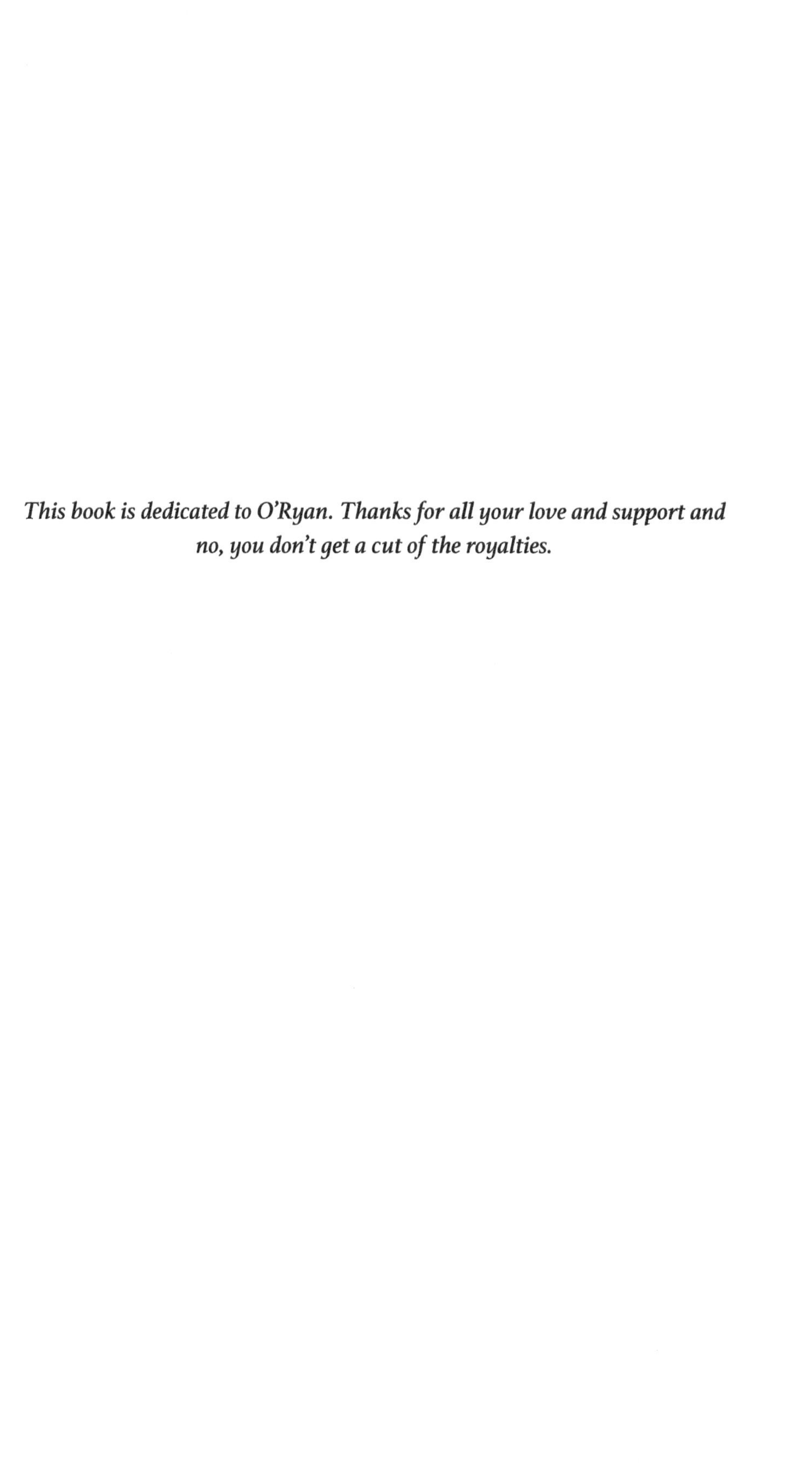

This book is dedicated to O'Ryan. Thanks for all your love and support and no, you don't get a cut of the royalties.

"Beware that, when fighting monsters, you yourself do not become a monster...for when you gaze long into the abyss, the abyss gazes also into you."

— Friedrich W. Nietzsche

1

MEDITERRANEAN

1155 Hours, June 7, 1967

The ship slipped quietly through the black Mediterranean waters. The two Cleveland diesel engines were capable of 500 horsepower, but the captain was not interested in speed this night. At a mere 177 feet long, it barely registered as a ship of war. In fact, the only weapon it carried was a twin .50-caliber machine gun mounted amidships, just under the bridge. The *USS Liberty* was a light duty vessel based on the Victory ships of WWII. Officially, it was an Environmental Research Ship, but everyone aboard knew it for what it really was, a signals intelligence gathering vessel. Instead of weapons, the top of the squat, somewhat ugly ship bristled with antennae masts, multiple receiving arrays, and more even less identifiable equipment.

The few lights from Rafah, Egypt, could be seen about eight miles away as they passed to the north. The nearly invisible port of Ashdod would be just inland off their starboard side. Ahead, the sky shone a faint, telltale yellow as Tel Aviv was just coming into view. The captain ordered the *Liberty* to cut speed as they cruised to within five miles of the coast. Most of the two hundred-man crew were asleep in their billets or at duty stations below deck. The bridge crew tonight was mostly senior officers. Two armed sentries patrolled the ship and acted as lookouts. These were dangerous waters, possibly only slightly less so than the area five thousand miles away near Vietnam.

Two weeks ago, the *Liberty* had been stationed off the Ivory Coast before a quick port call in Spain where they picked up three new people and an assortment of odd-looking cargo cases. They had made top speed to the current location. Captain McGonagle was a thorough leader and a capable officer with more than twenty years' experience. The mission tonight was relatively routine; it required them to be at the rendezvous point at the precise time.

The skipper checked his watch, then eyed the charts laid out on the table. He'd crewed in these waters before, but the eastern Med was new to most of his men. Although captain of the *Liberty* for just over a year, he ran a tight ship and trusted his officers to carry out commands with haste. He would have liked to have fully briefed them all, but he had his orders. Naval intelligence oversaw this mission.

A call came from one of the sentries up near the bow, "Reports of an explosion and gunfire just south of the city, Captain." Tensions were sky high here, but McGonagle and his crew were safely outside any areas of risk. That did not necessarily mean they were welcome. America was never completely welcomed in another country's back yard.

"Thanks, Chief," he answered, still checking the time. Eight minutes later, the captain eased up to the helmsman and quietly ordered, "Full stop." The sound of the engineer bringing the engines to idle sent a brief shudder through the boat.

"Sentry reports small craft in the water approaching fast, Captain. Should we man the guns?"

"Negative, Lieutenant. Recall both sentries." Turning to a man standing in the rear of the room, he nodded. "Mister White, you're with me." The two officers walked briskly out the door to the aft section of the ship, leaving a bewildered senior staff on the bridge.

* * *

Hours later, the sun-baked coastline shimmered in the distance as the two men talked. "Hell, Adams, I don't know. She ain't making any sense, you know. Talking about free love and why we shouldn't be bombing Cambodia and shit."

The other man made a sound, maybe a laugh. He kept working the handle on the grease gun.

"I swear to God I ain't making this shit up. The same woman who has no idea where the fuck Vietnam is, now has an opinion on why we shouldn't be in that war. Now she thinks we are just out here having the time of our lives cruising around the Mediterranean." A pair of fighter jets flew low overhead, surprising them both. The aircraft veered away just past the ship, heading south toward Gaza. The sound of the passing jets arrived several seconds later.

"Those ours?" Pete asked, holding his hand up to shield his eyes from the morning sun.

Adams stood up, shrugged, and wiped the grease from his gigantic hands with a rag, then used the same rag to wipe sweat from his forehead. "I don't know, our carriers are a few hundred miles away, I think." The *Liberty* was loosely assigned to the *Saratoga's* carrier group. The *America* was also stationed nearby, supposedly. The commitment to Israel was, if they were attacked, to be able to provide air cover within fifteen minutes.

The men moved to the next in a long series of grease fittings along the boat's mechanical equipment. The saltwater and ocean air meant that maintenance was almost non-stop. The sailors aboard all knew they would likely never be involved in an actual battle. Like its sister ship, the *Pueblo*, the *Liberty* was assigned to hotspots around the globe simply to monitor growing escalations.

The situation here in the eastern Mediterranean definitely qualified. It was a powder keg, and everyone knew it. While the United States as a whole was focused on Vietnam, a divided nation with admittedly little direct domestic impact, tensions here had been growing heated between Israel, one of the country's top allies, and an Arab coalition that included every one of its neighboring countries.

"Nasser seems hell bent to wipe out the Jews. That's what my pops says," Adams said.

"Who the fuck cares? Hitler tried—he failed. Besides, whose idea was it to just give them a country right smack dab in the middle of all these Arabs?" He said it like two words, *A-rabs.*

A claxon sounded from high overhead. "What the fuck?" both men seemed to say at once. The two jets had returned, circling the ship several times before leaving. None of them had any markings. "They damn sure look like ours," Adams said.

"So why are we going on alert?" the other man asked, buttoning up his tools and stowing them out of the way. He noticed other sailors rushing to uncover the twin guns, and uncrating ammo belts. Over the next several hours, various planes came and circled the ship. The American flag and U.S. Navy markings were clearly visible on this ship. They heard from the bridge crew the skipper had requested a destroyer escort or permission to evade. The *USS Liberty* maintained its patrol now off El Arish, Egypt.

Even before the battle stations was eventually sounded, the two friends had already taken up positions in different parts of the ship. Adams was topside, assigned to fire control, and Pete's assignment was additional security outside the massive radio room.

"Multiple small craft approaching from the port!" a sentry yelled from atop the bridge. Adams felt his insides go watery. This damn sure was beginning to feel like the real thing...like battle. The port would have been Israel, though, Ashdod probably. That was good.

Two unmarked delta-winged Mirage jets reappeared; this time they were not circling, but lining up for a firing run. From his position, Adams couldn't see what was coming, but heard the panicked shouting. The fire control suit he wore was heavily lined, and he was baking in the midday heat. The twin guns opened up on something just before incoming missiles took out the gun mounts, followed by explosions near the ship's antennae and bridge.

Six minutes later, three other unmarked jets attacked with a menacing combination of napalm and rockets.

McGonagle franticly had his radioman attempt to contact Sixth

Fleet, but the radio room report circuits were jammed. The air attack lasted twenty-two minutes. The badly damaged *Liberty* was burning and had already lost nine men with another sixty seriously wounded. Adams lay half in a hatchway beneath the bridge. Singed flesh covered one arm; the other was completely gone. Blackened bits of meat and bone and dried blood covered the right side of his body. The entrance to the radio room twenty yards away was now just a gaping black hole billowing toxic smoke. Adams was fighting to keep the darkness away, unable to even wonder about his friend as the attack finally subsided.

"Torpedoes in the water!" Consciousness was leaving him as he heard someone screaming, "Why would they do this?"

Why indeed? he wondered. He'd seen markings on the last wave of attacking jets, the five-pointed symbol more commonly referred to as the Star of David. *Goodbye, Pete,* he thought as his eyes closed one final time.

2

CARIBBEAN – PRESENT DAY

He heard them long before he saw them. Glancing up, he saw tiny brown legs running through the marsh grasses.

"Doktè, you must come."

He didn't want to move; he was comfortable, and it was his day off from the health clinic. How in the hell had the little ones even found him? He pulled the brim of the hat even lower and closed his eyes, willing them to respect an old man's siesta. It was not to be.

Several little hands shook him as they pleaded, "Doktè, please, we found something. You must come now."

He tried in vain to ignore the little ones, but he knew it was futile. Whatever curiosity had their attention, it now enveloped him as well. Rising unsteadily and packing away his fishing pole, he allowed himself to be led toward the nearby beach.

"Come, come...you see dair," they urged.

He recognized only one of the children but was nearly certain he had helped deliver them all. Many of the parents still refused to bring their offspring into the clinic for anything except the direst of situations. "Ricardo," he called out to the one he knew. "What are you going on about?"

The boy just grinned and nodded, pulling him steadily to the water. He could see through the grasses a small group gathered on the beach. In a few steps more, the stench hit him. The smell of rot and decay was a constant in the tiny village, but this was far worse. He removed a tattered handkerchief from his pocket and held it to his nose, his steps slowing as he drew closer to the group. Probably a beached dolphin, maybe even a small whale, although it would be early for one of those to be near the island.

Murmurs of concern echoed through the small group as he politely eased his way in.

"You see, you see now, Doktè?"

He heard Riccardo's tiny voice as he broke into the inner line. His eyes stared at what lay in the sand. It was definitely not anything he'd expected. Easing around to what obviously had been the head, he gasped in disbelief. "No, no...no. This cannot be."

* * *

Several hundred miles away, Kissa watched as his girlfriend glided through the crystal-clear Caribbean waters. Thera was a natural; her swimming was a rhythmic ballet, whereas his own was more often described as creative drowning. Where she glided, he fought the water like a warrior. At the end of the hour, she would be rejuvenated, energized, and ready for the rest of the day. He, on the other hand, would be winded and exhausted from the exertion.

Both of them were from the tiny town of Ampala on Isla El Tigre in the Honduran Gulf of Fonseca. Today's dive trip to the nearby island of Guanaja was to monitor several of the large whale sharks recently spotted in the area. He loved being an oceanographer, almost as much as he loved Thera, but recognized his inadequacies in both specialities.

Climbing back aboard the small boat, Kissa waited for her to resurface. The water was clear enough to see her silhouette thirty feet below as he lay back against the hull and let his eyes drift closed. He could trace her line of bubbles. Thera was no scientist but had a love of nature, and the ocean in particular, that easily equaled his own. This part of the Caribbean was known as the Miskito Coast, named after the indigenous Miskito Indians who settled here. While once the coast was considered inhospitable, development was starting to creep in. Here on Guanaja, that would take a while, as over ninety percent of the land and surrounding waters was protected as part of the 450-mile Mesoamericana Barrier Reef system, the second largest in the world. All development was tightly controlled, unless you knew who to bribe of course.

"I will get your certification revoked," she said as her head broke the surface. "Never leave your dive partner—right?"

He grinned and nodded, eyes still closed, feigning sleep. "I'm tired, woman," he said in a deliberate tone perfectly pitched to set her on edge.

"Woman? Woman?" she yelled just before splashing him with sea water.

"Come on, get out, girl. We still hopping the ferry to Utila tonight?"

She ignored the question but was leaning over the gunnels rummaging around in her gear bag. "Come back down with me, something I want to check out, but I need my lights."

"I'm tired, Thera, I'm not as young as you."

"Come on, we're both twenty-nine, Kissa. It's near the bottom, you know the rules."

Bottom depth here ranged from thirty to sixty feet, but neither ever went that low unaccompanied. Good dive discipline had been drummed into them both since being open water certified in their late teens. The difference was, Thera had gone on to become a dive instructor and then an adventure dive guide among her other accomplishments. Today, off in the calm, relatively shallow water was not even a test of her skills, but still, no one went to the bottom alone.

"Girl, we are already down to our spares," he said pointing to the tanks strapped together in the boat's bow.

Thera was already removing her nearly empty tank. "Come on, Kissa, it won't take long. Something is down there. I still have thirty minutes on my tank."

He took his regulator off the almost empty tank and strapped it onto one of the spare bottles. Screwing on the hoses, he looked at

Thera again. She was incredibly beautiful, and he was powerless to refuse her request. Quickly checking the low-pressure connection and then the pressure gauge, he took a couple of test breaths before fastening the rig on his back and rolling backward into the water.

Kissa watched as she hung in the water twenty feet below, impatiently waiting for him. He angled down, adjusting his buoyancy compensator as he dove. The surface water was crystal clear, but he could see below was murkier. Sweeping his head from side to side, he didn't understand what his girlfriend could have spotted. Several small coral outcroppings and related bottom structure dotted the landscape and the normal assortment of parrotfish and black grouper, but nothing they had not seen for most of the morning. Following her down even farther, the natural light faded. When she finally cut the spotlights on, he suddenly saw what had Thera's attention.

The bottom structure in this part of the Caribbean was normally rather boring. The relatively shallow water and regular storms made it difficult for more substantial plant life. There were few rocky outcroppings nearby except around the more volcanic island. Occasional outcroppings of coral reefs and the even wreckage of small craft was about all there was to see. To be honest, despite the gorgeous, crystal blue water, it was somewhat mundane even to an oceanographer like him. Other than to spot the whale sharks that congregated here, neither of them would have deliberately chosen this particular area.

Thera was about forty yards ahead and seemed to be circling an oddly colored mass he took to be some sort of sea grass. He assumed it was another patch of dead sargassum. Actually, a type of algae instead of a true seaweed. The brown mats were common all over the Caribbean, often clumping together into large floating mats. Over time, these mats inevitably would wash up onto beaches where they were despised. The sight and the smell kept tourists away, and so most coastal villages had eradication methods working constantly during heavy blooms. No one was exactly sure of the cause. Kissa himself had worked on several projects investigating it. He believed it was a combination of global warming and increased fertilizer runoff from the large commercial farms inland.

His girlfriend, however, wouldn't normally be interested in something that mundane. Her own field of expertise didn't focus very heavily on plant life. Still, she was intensely interested in the patch of seafloor ahead. Her powerful dive lights cast a yellow circle of illumination. What he had taken for rippling grass was beginning to seem like something else. Like the pattern was on the object itself. He wished again their department budgets could have sprung the extra money for the dive gear with wireless comms. As it was, they had to rely mainly on hand signals to communicate underwater.

Kissa had covered about half the distance when suddenly, Thera backed away from the object. She looked directly at him. *What was that expression*? he wondered. *Fear, panic, shock?* She held her right arm out to him palm facing up. A clear signal to stop. He slowed…but didn't fully stop. *What have you found, love?*

A sudden and intense burst of blueish light flooded the area. Simultaneously, he was filled with an intense headache, quickly joined by a disquieting sense of dread. He wondered if her dive lights had exploded, but the glare was still there. He held a hand up to shield his eyes from the brightness. It was definitely coming from where his girlfriend was…or had been. He could no longer see Thera.

Kissa's head was pounding; his mind was fuzzy. Was he running out of air? He couldn't look directly at the object, which now seemed to be slowly moving. It seemed to be hovering atop the light. Several times in his peripheral vision, he thought he saw ropes or *shit, maybe even snakes* burst out from underneath the object. Something was coming out of the light, coming for him.

Panic rolled inside him as he scanned again for Thera, then, guessing what she might have done, he began swimming for the surface high above in long, deliberate strokes. Thera had to have gone back up to the boat..she had to be there.

3

SITE 21

Oily dark blood dripped from every surface of the room. Like some macabre tableau of horror. There was a coppery smell, something that let him know what happened here was very recent. "Jesus, Mary, and Joseph," the man said in a voice with a pronounced Austrian accent. His legs wobbled, and he reached out to steady himself. His hands grabbed for a greasy, iron pipe affixed to the wall. *Not grease*, he realized, jerking his hand away. His fingers rubbed together feeling the gritty bits of residue he knew to be bone...saliva. He should not be in here. Turning in a full circle, he took in the space. This was a scene from a horror movie. His heart pounded in his chest as he tried to force his legs to move him back up the ladder to the hatch above. Fear kept him frozen in place.

The dark water rippled slightly against the far wall. The pool occupying most of the space was almost fifty meters across. A grinding sound rose up from beneath the deep water. It traveled through the walls, the floor, and into every dark space in the man's soul. It was loose, it was feeding, and it was coming for him next.

In despair, his mind went to his precious Hannah. He always saw her as a precocious fourteen-year- old. Those days that his mind had captured as the perfect snapshot of his only child. He and Lea, his late wife, had held off too long on having children. Hannah would never have brothers or sisters. His work with the university, then later as a full-time research scientist, had given him little time with his child. She was grown now, expecting her own child. She lived in...

The sound came again cutting off the brief memory. A new sound, not the creature. This was from somewhere else, somewhere up above. His eyes remained intensely focused on the surface of the water. The face of a man shouted from outside the barred door. Flashing, yellow lights illuminated the man's face in a stop motion staccato.

"Doctor, open the door! Do not terminate the experiment!"

The 'experiment,' had just terminated his two assistants. It was their blood, their viscera, their lives that now decorated the habitat. *I should have known,* he thought. Humans were never meant to unlock the ancients' secrets. What avarice it had been to seek the treasure. His help in unlocking the human genome should have been enough. Sadly, he'd missed out on winning the Nobel Prize. That academic slight had been enough for him to pursue this. To chase this dream, to unlock the secrets of the angels. The human genome project, by comparison, was infantile.

A dark rope-like tongue flicked from the water five meters away. Then, an enormous spike-covered tentacle reached for the ledge. It did so delicately, almost gently. The long rapier-sharp, hooked claw dug into the hard floor leaving a gouge several inches deep as it pulled the rest of its iridescent body slowly up from below. The man saw remnants of hair and what might be a human eyeball drifting in lazy circles around the beast.

An enormous eye, nearly eight inches across, came into view atop a bulbous head nearly four feet wide. A radiating pattern of blue and green bands rippled from the head down the squat body and out each of the six tentacle legs. The doctor knew this was a warning visual, a predatory response. Despite his fear, a tiny whisper of pride tinged his thoughts. This was his, he'd unlocked the secrets, he'd given life to this creation. The banging on the door increased. Glancing away from the approaching leviathan for a moment, he saw the man above, his boss, his patron, watching horrified, no doubt knowing what came next.

The doctor managed to get his feet moving and backed slowly away from the animal. 'Animal' would not have been precisely accurate, but the genus and taxonomy of the life-form were irrelevant now. His breathing accelerated, the panic not entirely his own doing. He could feel the waves of hostility emanating from the creature. *Oh, meine engel, what secrets you could have told us,* he thought as his left hand found the plastic cover. Flipping it up, a new alarm began to ring, this one inside the pool chamber.

Yes, the creature would die, as would his creator. In seconds, the water would drain away from the massive pipes, and fire would rain down from the ceiling. The intense heat would incinerate every bit of living tissue in the space. The shouts from the man above had quieted; no doubt, understanding what had to be done. The containment procedure was an emergency protocol, one that he, the chief scientist, had insisted be put in place.

The creature's snake-like tongue whipped out like a bullwhip. Tiny barbs lined the muscled tentacle, which delivered a deep and horrifying cut to the doctor's outstretched arm. The cut burned from a toxic protein in the creature's saliva. If left untreated, he knew the arm would be lost. That would not make any difference now. Quickly, he stabbed his other hand at the red button, depressing it fully into the recessed slot in the wall. He braced himself, and—nothing happened. The creature stepped closer, the two middle tentacles now also on the ledge. The failsafe had been a ruse, they never intended on letting him kill their pet. In his final thoughts, he knew he'd been the part of the experiment that was expendable.

The creature's maw opened to reveal thousands of squeezing tentacles surrounding hard, grinding plates lined with razor-sharp teeth. Like an enormous version of cilia, they were designed to propel food into the mouth. The doctor knew the creature preferred its food alive. The claw-like tentacle arms swung in unison trapping him like prey. One hand fell disembodied to the floor as he was lifted into the air. A scream tried to escape his mouth, but the tentacles already were dragging him in and down.

4

CARIBBEAN

"Adriano!"

The young officer pulled the headset away from one ear just long enough to hear the man next to him. "What, Pitre?" he asked, glancing at the radioman to his left. The Tridente class submarine was the pride of the Portuguese Navy, and they were on patrol several hundred miles north of the coast of Venezuela. As the acoustic weapons officer, Adriano 'Bugs' Bilbao was responsible for identifying and classifying every object in the immediate area emitting an acoustical signature. From surface traffic like the small, but rowdy, dive boats coming from the various Caribbean islands, to the occasional pods of humpback whales or other 'biologics.'

Shifting his eyes from his computer screen to the radioman sitting next to him, Adriano saw Pitre was making the face again. He had to admit his crewmate could do a good impersonation of the XO. He fought to suppress a smile. His ears picked up something, and his focus immediately returned to his screen. Even before the computer tried to classify the noise, he knew this was something new. On the ship's display, the underwater sound was visualized by a series of fuzzy lines. The computer displayed 'Desconhecido,' unknown, over the acoustic signature. The sound faded almost as soon as it had occurred. The signal lines quietly fading back to nothingness.

Adriano replayed the sound many times, adjusting the speed, volume, and other settings. Water distorted sound waves and not always in predictable ways. His job was to know what he was hearing; was it a threat, was it alive? Leaving it listed as 'unknown' was not something he often permitted himself. With only two submarines in the fleet, he was one of the very few men to hold this seat. His excellent performance reviews and career track had confirmed that he was also one of the best. For the rest of his shift, he continued to monitor his scope but also kept replaying the sound, manipulating, analyzing, and comparing it to known signals.

While the U2809 was primarily a defensive vessel, they carried a considerable amount of research equipment to monitor various oceanic conditions. Portugal still had strong ties to the sea, and its Navy, which had once been the strongest in the world, now had a more modest mission, but still important. With the recent troubles in the United States, that mission seemed more vital than ever. While the U.S. still maintained the largest military in the world, they seemed much more concerned with domestic matters now. That was good news for most of the other world governments. While Portugal had allied with many countries in the Caribbean and South America, it was nice to not worry about Uncle Sam quite so much.

"Entering the Cayman Trench," the executive officer said.

Adriano glanced quickly at Pitre knowing the man would be mimicking the XO's face again. "Scope is clear," he said, offering his station report. As the boat left the relatively shallow waters to the 7000-plus meter depths, and as they neared Cuba, he could relax. More depth meant more space to maneuver. Few vessels traversed these depths, and even the sea life here was widely scattered. The trench, also known as Bartlett Deep, was an almost straight scar at the bottom of the sea. Water temps at the bottom were near freezing. Volcanic vents dotted the floor of the rift miles below. The entire landscape was an anomaly, out of place here in the shallow sea surrounded by an archipelago of thousands of islands and reefs.

For several hours, he watched and tagged various craft, including what was an oil company ROV, exploring well into Cuban waters. His commander would pass the incident and location on to his Cuban counterparts. Like most days, Adriano stared at his screen, wishing it somehow was a window into the world outside. What mysteries of the sea passed just inches away from where he sat?

"Entering Bathyal Zone," the navigator called out. Also known as the 'Midnight Zone,' this was the region of the ocean that sunlight never reached. From 3000 meters down to around 13,000, it once was thought to be devoid of sea life. Not enough oxygen, no sunlight for plankton to survive. All that changed when more capable research vessels began to explore the depths. First, unmanned ROVs and later, manned exploratory craft found an abundance of strange creatures and a diversity of life beyond anything they expected.

"Bugs is in his happy place," Pitre called out for anyone to hear.

Adriano couldn't argue that he never tired of listening to the ocean here. It was a virtual cacophony of unique sounds. From active lava vents spewing molten rocks into the icy dark water, to a vast orchestra of cataloged, but still unknown, biological origins. Most manmade sounds faded into the distance nearer the surface as the U2809 passed three miles below.

Reflexively, he yelled out, "Contact," even before his mind registered the sound. Instantly the XO was at his shoulder, also watching the scope.

"Sonar," the senior officer called out.

"Sonar clear, sir," came the near immediate response.

"Tell me what it is, Bugs," the man said calmly.

Adriano adjusted his sensor array so the external microphones could pinpoint the location. "Bearing 185," he said with a note of uncertainty. "Moving, sir, moving fast." He did several quick calculations on his notepad. *Too damn fast.*

"Sub? Drone, biologic?"

Adriano shrugged, fixated on the sound. It was back. He knew this was the same as he'd heard earlier. That one had been a faint echo compared to now.

"Is it on our path, Bugs? Do we need to adjust course?"

"XO, I have something, possibly cavitation. It is changing course. I believe it is manmade, not a whale."

The XO stood back up, looking toward the bow. "Sonar, what do you have?"

"Scope still clear, XO," the voice called out.

Adriano knew it was there. He flipped the switch to allow the sound to play through the speakers. All submariners were used to the various sounds of the ocean. Some of which, like the mournful calls of blue whales, you could occasionally hear right through the hull of the ship. This sounded like nothing any of them had ever heard. The rhythmic pulsing offered none of the typical sounds of a propeller craft, nor did the sound resemble the newer induction drives that pulled water in and jetted it out the back. "I don't know what it is, sir, but it is approaching us fast. Recommend evasive maneuvers."

"Collision alarm, wake the captain," the XO bellowed before giving the pilot a new heading and depth. Leaning down, he spoke again, voice just above a whisper, "Bugs, you need to be sure what it is and where it is going."

Adriano had no idea; they were too deep, nothing should be here. Yet this object had been close almost a hundred miles earlier and thousands of feet closer to the surface. Had it ever really gone? Was it some sort of echo of their own audible signature? Various layers of water could essentially mirror signals like sound, but no, this was not an echo. This was something else, something malevolent. He was certain. He plotted a new position on the sound, clicked off the timer and calculated the speed of the target. Looking at the number, he gasped; it must be a mistake. Nothing could travel that fast underwater.

"Russian Shkval?" the XO asked, eyeing the speed of 355 kilometers per hour.

The Russian-made Shkval, or Squall, supercavitating torpedo could reputedly travel that fast, but they had an existing sound profile on those. They were a noisy beast, and whatever this was, it was whisper quiet but just as fast. Adriano rechecked his numbers again;

this whisper of sound was closing fast. "Less than two thousand meters, sir. It has matched our course change."

"Captain on the bridge!" the COB called out. Seeing his XO engaged, the chief of the boat quickly brought the commander up to speed.

"Options, XO?" Captain Willmonte demanded.

"Sonar ping, evasive maneuvers, sir."

Resorting to sonar was the captain's worst option. While going active on the sonar would give them a better picture of what was out there, it also would pinpoint them to everything else for miles. Subs operated by being invisible, stealth was the greatest weapon, and announcing where they were went against every bit of training. "Make it so, helm come about 245, make depth 9000 meters. Flood tubes one and two."

The routine patrol mission was quickly escalating to full combat protocols. "All hands, all hands to your battle stations!" the XO called into the ship-wide comms. The sonar ping was so loud it reverberated through the speakers and bulkheads.

"What's out there?" the XO asked sounding nervous.

The sonar operator's voice sounded tiny in the claustrophobic space, "Nothing, sir. Scope is clear."

"Three hundred meters," Adriano said, seemingly in defiance of what the sonar man had said. The pulsing sound was now so loud they could hear it without the speakers. "Closing fast, one hundred, fifty..." the sound was so deafening he didn't hear the captain's orders to fire. In the end, it didn't matter. The sound from outside suddenly went silent. Fear etched the faces of all the sailors as a rending metallic sound was heard coming from just inches away. It was from the outside hull plating. Their fate was sealed, and death would come to each of them swiftly here in the Midnight Zone....

5

Kissa reached, fumbled, missed, then finally grabbed the handgrip to climb onboard the small boat. His heart pounded, bile was churning up from his stomach, and as quickly as possible, he removed his mask only to see the boat was empty. Quickly, he checked around the gunnel. Perhaps she was hanging there, resting, waiting to board...but no. She hadn't surfaced; she was still down there, down there with that thing. He'd never let fear control him, that would have been suicidal growing up, but somehow, now when he needed courage the most, he felt fear's icy grip. Almost reluctantly, he stuck the respirator back in his mouth. His primary was empty, he needed to swap tanks to go back down.

Uncertain what to do next, he placed both hands against the side of his aching head as he frantically searched the deep blue waters for his girlfriend, praying, begging...hoping for a miracle. So far offshore, out of the shipping lanes, and without a decent radio, no help would be coming. An inquiry, questions, and then, very likely retribution from his girlfriend's family. She was one of the primary breadwinners. That made her loss intolerable in a nation with so few opportunities. "Oh, God, Thera!" he moaned.

Something on the surface caught his eye; an irregularity on the otherwise smooth surface, as something silently rose from the calm seas. It was small, dark, and mostly round, almost like a human head, but not really. Kissa guessed the distance to be sixty meters away. On some deeper level, perhaps his more ancient reptile brain sensed more than anything that most of the 'thing' lay hidden beneath the waters. 'Object,' he quickly decided was the correct word as nothing about it seemed to be natural or even living. The bulge didn't move, twitch, or vibrate, and he had the distinct opinion it was somehow watching him.

The pain in his temples finally beginning to fade, his clarity, closely followed by anger and then resolve, once again stepped forward. Slowly, he reached a hand for the speargun and then his dive mask. If he could slip into the water, he might get a glimpse of what this was. Could it be what had taken Thera down below? Stories had long persisted locally of monsters: Encantado, El Hombre Caimán, and the Blue Hole Creature from just up the coast near Belize. That one, he was sure, had simply been a rare but misidentified oarfish. What he was seeing resembled none of those creatures though. Slipping the dive mask on, his eyes never left the object which maintained its distance and position relative to the boat. Sliding over the gunnels and back into the water, he firmly grasped the speargun and went hunting.

Heart pounding, Kissa forced himself to take long, normal breaths. Hyperventilating would only make his mind foggy, and he needed to be sharp. He knew this was likely his only chance to get answers, possibly to find his Thera. The surrounding water seemed to literally be vibrating. He felt more than heard a near-constant hum. Another thought occurred to him. Absolutely no other fish of any kind could be seen. The rich biodiversity they had seen earlier was completely absent now.

Both had known the telltale signs of large ocean predators. As a trained oceanographer, he could identify nearly every known creature they encountered. Thera could do that one better by also being an expert in most extinct ones as well, yet here was something neither would be able to get a handle on. Perhaps it was a monster, something new and dangerous that rose up from the cold, deep ocean to feed upon the unwary inhabitants of the warm shallows. A cryptid, something new, something ancient and thought extinct. It had happened before, many times.

The discovery of the coelacanth fish off the coast of Brazil, something they now called the living fossil, was an example. Not to mention the giant, ribbon-like oar fish or the almost mythological giant squid which had only been captured on film about a decade earlier. With over seventy percent of the earth covered in water, with an average depth of two miles, he knew less than five percent had ever been explored. The truth was, Kissa and the experts had little idea what actually lived in the deep ocean.

Still, something like this...or any large predators that came up to shallow waters, even occasionally, couldn't easily stay hidden. Fishermen would have caught them, carcasses would have been found. He dismissed the idea. Even beasts of the pelagic realm of the deep ocean that were capable of something like this were few. Those known species that would knowingly attack an adult human were incredibly rare. Despite numerous movies and television shows, sharks were not the biggest ocean threat to man. He knew, in fact, that if you looked up the top ten most dangerous sea creatures, only one shark, the Great White, would likely even make the list.

Something months ago had triggered Thera's near obsession in solving a puzzle. He and Thera had been following a pod of whale sharks which were acting strangely. Around that time, a series of seemingly random events across the enormous Caribbean had piqued her interest, and she'd easily convinced him to help. The whale sharks, the largest fish in the sea, were being hunted it seemed; other large sea life was as well, creatures that would rarely be considered prey. It had been a curiosity at first, for him at least. Mainly, it was an excuse to spend more time with her. Lately, though, it had become something more... something serious.

They'd been hunting for months now. What had begun as a casual interest had blossomed into a full-blown obsession. Something was lurking in the normally tranquil waters of his homeland. Something that now may have claimed the love of his life.

Kissa's head slipped silently beneath the surface. Kicking the oversize swim fins, he propelled himself down and toward the spot they'd seen the mysterious creature. Carefully, he followed the bottom structure. From above, his dive suit would blend with the coral below, rendering him nearly invisible. Despite the incredible water clarity, the sun was in the wrong position for him to make out anything but a blurry shadow above. After years of looking up at dive boats above, he could make a reasonably accurate guess on the size though. It was big, not enormous, but big. The shape couldn't have been mistaken for any species of shark, and some were pretty common in these waters. It lacked the normal fin profile; the body proportions were all wrong, and frankly, it only vaguely looked alive. He adjusted his buoyancy compensator and ascended about three meters. The mysterious subject, which he was increasingly thinking of as a creature, seemed to silently drift away, maintaining its distance. It was just too smooth, too perfect to be natural.

His time in the Honduran special forces, called TESON, had provided excellent training and grueling discipline. While he'd left all that behind years earlier, once again, he felt the adrenaline pumping and the training kicking in. He quietly descended back down to the coral bed. The reef here was immense and here, at least, teaming with life. Hand over hand, he slowly crawled along the rock in the direction of the shadow above. Thoughts of Thera were overwhelming him, and he was convinced this thing had something to do with her disappearance. Was it connected to everything else as well? He paused briefly to get his heart rate under control. While not deep, he still had to maintain regular breathing. The object was nearly directly overhead now. Focusing hard on the blurry shadow, he made a mental outline. Rounded and larger in front, tapering toward the rear. Several protrusions, but not symmetrical, no tail fin or any propulsion device he could see. This was not the same thing he'd seen on the prior dive.

Deciding to be bold, Kissa planted both feet on the rocky surface and crouched down. He checked his arm sheath to make sure the dive knife was still there. He sprang from the seafloor like a gymnast uncoiling from a somersault, his taut muscles unleashing all their energy in one move, propelling him straight toward the surface. In seconds, he had covered half the distance. The object was much clearer now. He could even see the bottom half was a lighter color than the top. Then he heard a high-pitched sound unlike anything he could recall. The surrounding sea erupted in a brilliant light. Not a yellow light of spotlights, but a pulsing, blue-white light.

Abruptly, he ceased rising, eyes clinched shut while his hands uselessly were covering his ears. The headache was back along with the persistent vibration in the water. After a minute at most, the sound and light began diminishing. Slowly opening his eyes, he saw the object was already a hundred meters away and picking up speed. Suddenly, it began speeding up at a phenomenal rate, so fast Kissa wanted to rub his eyes to make sure it wasn't just an illusion. Perhaps the light had blinded him or something, but no...the object or creature was gone. Something else, he realized he was trailing blood. Touching fingers to his ears, they came away reddened. Looking back, he saw a swirling, red drifting lazily behind him. He'd seen enough. It was time to go.

6

THE COVE

"Captain Rearden, are you okay?"

"Huh? Oh, ummmm..." *Shit, what was her name?* "Uh, Doris, I don't know." He fell into a table, chairs skidding away in various directions. Even the furniture seemed afraid of him.

The bodiless voice came again. "Clearly, you are in distress, Cade."

He stood more or less upright, looking around the home's tasteful interior. Muted grays and blue accents detailed a kitchen any chef would be proud to own. Countertops that looked and felt like Italian marble, but were a composite material molecularly more similar to the polysteel used in the tactical armor his Talon Teams used.

"I think I just had too much to drink." It sounded stupid, but he was used to being stupid.

"Cade, the CommDot's bio-sensors detect no alcohol in your system. It does show highly elevated levels of stress hormones, respiratory, and heart rate. You are not drunk, you are frightened."

Cade hated how literal the super-advanced AI was sometimes. Having her voice words that he refused to acknowledge even to himself was unnerving. "I'm fine, Doris. Really, I am. Just leave me alone, okay?"

Doris would not leave it. "You are part of my senior staff, Cade. You are also what I would call a friend. Should I take it that the sessions are no longer helping?"

For months, Doris had been working with him to possibly reintegrate his multiple personalities back together. Clearly, the other 'travelers' inside his skull didn't appreciate that potential loss of autonomy. The bio-feedback technique Doris had devised relied, in part, on the ReLoad instant learning process she'd invented. Early on in the sessions, it had allowed him to communicate more freely with the internal entities, but the more Doris tried to merge them into a single version of Cade Rearden, the more they resisted, or maybe it was just him.

"Sorry, Doris, I don't know what is going on in here." He tapped at his head.

"The visions again?" she asked with a perfect tone of sympathy. "The memories, the panic?"

He nodded reluctantly. He hated admitting weakness. Being broken was an embarrassment, one he'd decided to try to remedy with the super-computer's help. Right now, though, it seemed to be making things worse. She'd suggested he try again to sleep inside his own home. It had been an enormous step for him. Something most people would view as routine, yet for him it took Herculean effort.

"Awful things happen in houses. Bad people...bad stuff." The memory surfaced again. He'd been about twelve when he was talking to yet another caseworker. He couldn't recall if she'd been from foster care or child welfare. It never mattered, they were all well-meaning but overworked, over- regulated, and operating in an under-funded system that was well beyond its capacity to offer hope, much less real care.

"What happened with them? The Thompsons?" the woman had asked. "Cade?" He'd ignored the question. The mental picture of blood sprayed along the wall, vividly painting the interior of his shared childhood bedroom. He remained quiet; he'd never shared what happened on that day so long ago, not even to the doctors who'd poked around his head after he'd been freed from a terrorist prison camp earlier in his military career.

Inside his head an internal battle raged. "They're fighting back," he said to the empty room. "I think I'll do better sleeping outside again." A flash of lightning and a roll of thunder sounded in the distance. Rain began pelting the windows.

"I don't think that would be very restful tonight," Doris said, a touch of sadness in her voice. They'd made some progress early on. The barbarian personality, the one Cade called Brutus, seemed to be totally dormant now, maybe reintegrated. And Gus—his voice of reason— was now speaking to him in his own voice, something Doris indicated was a positive sign. The analyst, though, he was another story. He went by Ace now, and if anything, seemed to grow stronger and more dominant. "None of them have a problem having a home or sleeping all night in an actual bed, Cade. This is all you."

He filled and drank a glass of water from the tap before nodding his agreement. "I know. I just can't."

"It's okay, we will keep working through it," Doris answered.

"No, Doris, I think we should stop. At least for now. Something about all this seems to be making me different, weaker....you know, somehow less of what made me good." He knew he was doing a lousy job describing how he felt but hoped she'd get the message. The anxiety and night terrors were just two of the manifestations. Lately, there'd been other, more tangible problems as well. Interference with the ReLoad knowledge packets. Information that should have been there when he needed it not being available to him. It was in there; he could sense it in there, but it seemed to be walled off to him, existing just out of reach of his conscious mind.

The soldier part of Cade knew he had to stay sharp. Maybe it was nothing critical. What happened if...or when...that changed? He had people who depended on his being sharp, being the best. What happened when he wasn't? While he'd not spoken openly to Doris about it, he felt sure she knew. Through her network of sensors, layer upon layer of pattern recognition, and a uniquely insightful intellect, she didn't miss much.

As if expecting some of his fears, she said, "I will not mention this to the director. I have to rely on you to make the call on how mission-capable you are, Captain. We both know your other personalities are probably more of an asset in your professional life. It is here in your private one that concerns me. How long do you think you can keep everything balanced on this knife edge of reason?"

He shook his head now, wishing he'd reached for something stronger than water. "I have no fucking idea, Doris. I'm screwed in the head, have been since I was a kid. Maybe it's just who I am." He put the glass down on the white counter with a bit more force than was needed.

"Lack of sleep can make you crazy," she said, "...and irritable."

"I go to sleep that way, lady. Too late to worry about any of that." He walked through the French doors to the covered patio, the night sounds of crickets chiming in the night breeze, rain pattering, and tree frogs singing their ancient song. Thunder rumbled again, echoing down the river valley. The house Doris had given him was one of about two dozen in the neighborhood. All very upscale with luxury touches in all the right places. It was a dream home, yet, out here was where he spent most of his down time.

Looking at another house about fifty yards away, he noticed an upstairs light on. It was often on at this time of night. The occupant of that house was having trouble sleeping, too. "How is she doing?" he asked the darkness.

The darkness answered him with a steadfast reassurance, "She is coping, Cade. Jasmine still feels a lot of guilt over her fiancé. She feels like she failed her mission commander on Snowbird as well."

Jasmine Kline was a brilliant scientist who Cade had brought to The Cove a year earlier for her own safety. Since then, she had become a valued member of the command staff. Cade knew Jasmine felt responsible for the apparent disaster aboard the Air Force space plane, even though she'd been relieved of her position and escorted out of mission control before it had happened. He felt responsible for her. Not just because her fiancé, Tim, had been his commander on his last special operations mission. The one where he'd been the lone survivor. No...it was more than that. Cade had dragged Jaz here to Georgia without telling her anything. He just wanted to keep her safe, and this had seemed like the best plan.

"Cade, is it possible you are developing feelings for Jasmine?"

He ignored the question. He refused to answer it, even to consider it. Not just to Doris, but to himself as well. She was his dead friend's love. He owed the man at least that much respect, that level of basic human decency. That was what people outside the military never seemed to get. *We don't go into battle because we feel vindicated in our belief. We don't go to try and vanquish evil. We go because it is our duty, and we stand our ground and possibly die to protect that soldier beside us, not for any idealistic, bullshit speech, or even orders from the back lines. We do it for our brothers; we fight, we laugh, and fuck, yeah, sometimes we die.*

Possibly sensing his inner thoughts again, Doris broke in, "What about what *she* might want, Cade? Do her needs not rise to the same level of care?"

Cade had never really known love and never really missed it. Most of his life he'd viewed it in the same vein as he did having a home. It was an attachment...a failure point, a weakness. "She can do a lot better than me. I'm BSC, remember?"

Doris chuckled, "Oh, yes, 'Bat-Shit Crazy.' Remind me again, is that more severe than 'Bug-Fucked Nuts', or is it less?"

Lightning arched across the sky, striking at a bit of high ground on the ring of tree-lined hills nearby. Cade laughed, "Doris, you are getting quite the sense of humor." She really was amazing, not just for a computer, she was an amazing creature. He watched as the light in Jasmine's bedroom went off. Lying back on one of the cushioned lounge chairs, he sighed. "Put me back to work, Doris. Somewhere with open spaces."

7

SOUTH TEXAS – U.S.

"We've got a problem, Boss."

Captain Cade Rearden, watching from the low roof, shook his head; problems were not on his agenda for today. He tapped at the nearly invisible, yet complex, communication system on his cheek. "What?" he growled.

"Sorry, Nomad," the man said, using Cade's official combat call sign. "Greg says the Tangos are not alone, and they are coming from the opposite direction."

Greg was one of the five genius kids he'd been working with at The Cove for much of the last year. They'd met as a super AI, known as Janus, was wreaking havoc all over the U.S. Cade, with the help of Greg and the others, had finally managed to defeat it. If Greg said it, you could count on it being true. What Cade had just been told meant that all of his team was deployed in the wrong direction and....*Well, shit.*

Cade stood, arranged the tactical goggles back down, and looked directly behind him, down a short tree-lined street to the two-lane highway beyond. He followed a trail of dust being kicked up on the seldom used road by something moving fast. The goggles instantly offered up the speed and alternate views from the closest drone. None of that helped; they had positioned the drones to the south, toward the border—that was the direction you would expect a Mexican drug cartel to come from. Near his leg, Cochise was on full alert. The dog understood fully what was going on.

All it seemed they had been doing since the Janus events, something now colloquially referred to as The Troubles, was putting out criminal brush fires like this. In America's weakened state, corruption was rampant, inflation was out of control, and most police forces had their ranks decimated. The vermin had moved in almost overnight like a bunch of cockroaches snatching crumbs. Unfortunately, these cockroaches had the money and the manpower. They'd been declaring war on border towns across three states.

"Greg, get those drones repositioned. Hammer, shift your position, please." Cade missed his friend, Charlie; they worked well together. But his friend and former XO, call sign Deuce, was training a new team, WarHawk. McTee was now his new second, and Everett 'Hammer' Harrison was now the man on overwatch.

"Dee, what the fuck is that I hear?"

The nearly invisible CommDot high on his cheekbone had lots of unique capabilities, including a super-sensitive microphone and a built in AI assistant he called Dee.

The crisp, slightly British voice calmly said, "I believe it is a human infant, Nomad."

"A baby? Someone brought a baby to a fucking stakeout?"

"I am unsure if that is a rhetorical question or not. Do you require a response?"

"Forget it," he growled, zooming in on the approaching convoy. Maybe staying home trying to sleep in a bed wasn't the worst thing. Many large SUVs were heading straight toward the little town. "McTee, please tell me that isn't you crying like a baby?"

The response was a little slow in coming. "Umm, sorry, Boss. The informant said she had to bring him...it. Umm, not sure which or what."

The informant was a seventeen-year-old Hispanic mother who looked too young for any of this. She had agreed to provide the intel on this op. They were targeting an offshoot of the ruthless Sinaloa gang. For the information, she and her family were getting protection and a new life here in the U.S.

Venturing this far inside Texas was well beyond the gang's normal hunting grounds, but these were strange times. Since The Troubles, the southern border was more porous than ever. To be honest, this mission was not the usual for a Talon strike team. Drug runners and gangs fell under DEA or Customs & Border, but the intel suggested a potential national threat, an organized terrorist attack, something clearly in The Cove Project's current operational mandate.

Cade had assumed the baby daddy was one of the gang-bangers and hadn't stepped up to the plate the way the new mother had hoped. *But shit...bringing the baby with her? Whose job was it to make sure that didn't happen?*

"That would be your job, dumbass," one of his internal voices said out loud. Cochise gave a gentle whuff, apparently agreeing.

"No time for this, Gus," Cade said in response to his near constant inner-monologue. *Okay*, Gus acknowledged internally. *But...the girl could be playing us, that's all.*

Gus was one of three distinct personalities, all inside his crowded skull. Gus was the one gifted with common-sense, though. Cade agreed, something was definitely off; had the girl signaled the cartel somehow? No reason they should approach from the north. Would she give them away in the next few minutes?

She's a kid, a new mother, and she's been wronged by her boyfriend, Gus replied. *So, yeah, pretty volatile I'd say.*

"McTee, get the mamasita and her baby out of here. She's now a liability more than an asset," Cade ordered. They wanted the girl to identify the leader so they could question him. That had been part of the deal, but now all that seemed unlikely. The baby cried again, even louder than before. "McTee, do you copy?"

Cade knew the man heard him. Their comms equipment always worked; they could talk from anywhere on the globe. But his second in command didn't respond. "Hammer, you got eyes on?"

The man's deep voice echoed what Cade feared, "McTee is no

longer in position. He appears to be...ummm, well, in pursuit of the asset."

"Nomad, I have surveillance if you want."

No, Greg, I do not want to watch my super special operator, former SEAL buddy, chasing down a young Mexican mother. Those were the words he wanted to say, took everything he had not to say, but he held it inside. McTee would have to handle this himself. "Negative, Greg, stay on target."

Once again, Cade questioned the director's logic in putting the teams out here for a mission like this. Shit, even the ATF was better at law enforcement than his team. Talon were soldiers, now just one more group of private military contractors to the U.S. government, but they were not cops. Even the real cops here in this town had been of little help. They were outgunned in every way and had been barely competent in vacating the downtown under the guise of a potential gas leak. Now they, too, were nowhere to be seen.

He clicked his goggles, enabling the new digital zoom feature. Still not as good as his old-fashioned binoculars, but like most of his team's gear, pretty damn impressive. A red square appeared over a small running figure. Obviously, the girl was carrying the baby in a carrier and heading past a parking lot toward the main road. "Fuck," he growled.

The approaching convoy was less than a mile away. "Cochise, target, stop, non-lethal." The dog at his side took off at once, understanding the complicated commands thanks to some ingenious upgrades he'd received at The Cove. The large German shepherd was down the metal stairs and in pursuit of the girl in seconds, the animal's black and brown fur a blur of movement against the neighboring storefronts.

"Sorry, Nomad," McTee's strained voice registered in his ear. "She got the drop on me, hit me with something heavy and got away before I knew what had happened. I do have a shot."

"Negative," Cade said bitterly. No way they were shooting a young mother, even if she had set them up.

The digital assistant, Dee, offered, "Nomad, your man could use non-lethal rounds to subdue the subject."

That had occurred to him. Back at The Cove, one of the other super-smart kids, Riley, and her R&D team had also made significant improvements to the weaponry and ammunition. One problem all the squads had with the originals was, they felt unfamiliar. A soldier's relationship with his weapon has to be instinctual, even though ReLoad, the near-instant learning process they had, could provide you the knowledge needed for almost anything, including guns. That did not match the level of experience that a soldier earned through months of carrying, caring for, and shooting thousands of rounds through his weapon. Most of the guns they carried now looked very much like those of the military, M-16s and H&K subcompacts. They weren't, but they felt like it. The ammo, though, was anything but ordinary. Each magazine contained traditional rounds, smart bullets, and non-lethal, all of which could be chambered by a mere thought or done remotely by the shared live-fire AI command systems.

"She's carrying a baby," Cade said. "We stun her, she could injure the child." He knew Dee wouldn't get the fact that an uninjured infant was one of the mission objectives but, *well fuck*, that's why they were human and not a team of robots.

"And being attacked by your K9 unit is less damaging to the child?"

"Well..." *Shit. The goddamn computer has a fucking point,* Gus quipped. Cade furiously used hand signals to Cochise. These would be translated to sensors placed in the dog's tactical vest. He watched as the dog bit at the girl's heels, then darted in front of her, bringing her to a stop. A piercing sound joined an ultra bright, flashing strobe emitted from Cochise's collar. She sat the baby carrier on the ground as she covered her ears and eyes. In seconds, the takedown was over, and neither baby nor mother were injured, although the intense wailing cries of the child could be heard throughout the downtown.

"Nomad, be advised we now have vehicles approaching from the south as well."

Wow, Cade thought, *this just keeps getting better.* "Team-2, focus on the new targets, McTee and Hammer, stay on Tango One." His teams only totaled six soldiers, seven if he counted Greg, which he did. He eyed the drone feeds coming into his tactical goggles. Now they were facing nine vehicles and God only knew how many thugs. "Greg, any way of knowing which group the primary is in?"

"Negative on that, Nomad," Greg responded from his hidden position a half-mile away.

A female voice said, "Team-2 back in position. Looks like the convoy is splitting up, trying to flank us."

Cade tapped his cheek and directed, "All Talon Teams, we are blown. So much for covert. Weapons free at the first sign of hostilities. We are out-manned, and they obviously know we're here. Let's not give these guys any other advantages."

He then opened a private channel to Greg. "You and Dee have about thirty seconds to identify the primary. Otherwise, we are lighting all of these fuckers up."

An alert signal began flashing in his goggles. Cochise was signaling a problem. Cade focused on the dog and saw the girl attempting to stand while waving her arms wildly at the approaching SUVs.

"Weapons, north side, second car," McTee yelled just as Cade saw the young girl's head explode in a cloud of red mist and near-simultaneous sound of a shot.

8

"Light 'em up!" Cade ordered.

Dee spoke calmly, "It appears they are going after the infant. I have instructed Cochise to protect."

Cochise's idea of protecting was to assess, then attack all threats by priority as they came into range. A car slid to a stop near the downed girl, and two men jumped out, guns aimed toward the dog who was already moving at blinding speed toward one of the men. The second man dropped as a round from Hammer split his throat apart and lodged in the car door behind. Cade was at ground level and sprinting for the baby before he had time to think. He used the auto-targeting feature built into the H&K style sub-compact to lay down a withering barrage of suppressing fire while he ran. Dee was using the KillPoint scope to pick targets for him, all he had to do was hold the trigger.

Distant gunfire confirmed that the other team was also now fully engaged. Cade emptied a clip into the lead car, which burst into flames as the fuel tank erupted. He slid down beside the baby carrier like a baseball player stealing second base. His hand wrapped firmly around the carrier as rounds began pinging the dirt around him. This was a stupid move, he was well aware, but that was sort of his thing. He darted for cover behind several cars in the nearby lot. A side window shattered, showering him with glass. He looked down to see the baby, a dark-haired little boy, now silent and grinning up at him. He dusted a few bits of broken glass away from the child and gave him a little tickle under one arm.

"Cochise, patrol wide," he ordered the dog. He was now able to switch his view to that of a camera mounted on the dog's vest to see all the hostiles. "McTee?"

"Go ahead." The former SEAL's voice still sounded strained.

"You got two Tangos hugging the sidewall of your twenty. Might want to say hello." He sent the video feed to the man's visor. The location, or 'twenty' as they called it, was indeed too damn close.

"Roger that, Nomad," McTee answered, followed closely by, "Frag out!"

The massive explosion rocked the car Cade and the baby were behind. "Hostiles down," came McTee's voice as another volley of rounds peppered the parking lot.

"Primary identified," Dee stated flatly as an image of a man holding a weapon in one of the SUVs near Cade displayed briefly.

"He's mine!" Cade yelled as he leaned over the hood and took aim at the black SUV that Dee had lit up brightly in his goggles' overlay. Cade squeezed the trigger just as a round impacted the hood of the truck he was using for cover. Shards of metal cut through his nose and cheek. Blood was flowing freely, but he felt nothing but rage. Cade knew Brutus was coming. *Gus, calm him down, I don't need the barbarian.*

He thinks you do. You're letting them shoot at you, so...I kinda agree.

"Fuck all of y'all," Cade said angrily. "Dee, can you get some doves over here to take out some of these Tangos?" The 'doves' were a general-purpose bird-sized drone. They had defensive, and even some offensive, capabilities and could be used in swarms to engage an enemy force. She acknowledged as the whisper-quiet drones appeared overhead and began circling the other two SUVs.

"Deploying incendiaries," Greg said, now in control of the drones. They began dropping small objects on the cars which immediately began to smoke before igniting in a bright white phosphorus fire. This would eat through the metal roof of the vehicle and any humans beneath. Screams of agony echoed across the open ground.

"Primary is bugging out, Nomad," Greg said. "Too fast for our doves."

"Assist Team-2, all assets!" Cade yelled. *I got this asshole.* How he was going to pursue was another matter. Both of the teams' vehicles were parked well away from the town. The plan had not been to engage in a full-on firefight and car chase, but like most battle plans, this one had gone to shit at first contact with the enemy. "Dee, scan plates, best option," he ordered.

His digital assistant had learned a lot about him over the last few months, and cryptic commands like this now needed no other explanation. He was in a parking lot full of cars, the AI would take various drone images to scan the tag numbers of each, match that to a serial number in one of a multitude of data files, and discover which was potentially the best choice for vehicle pursuit. All of this was done in seconds.

"Vehicle is three rows back and two over," she replied.

"Great!" Cade took two steps, about to break into a run, when the baby let out a cry. *Oh shit*, he thought. *The baby.* With the rest of Team-1 moving south to fight alongside Team-2, he had no one to take the child. Deciding quickly, he grabbed the carrier and raced to the selected car. "Looks like we're going on a ride, little man."

And what a ride it was. "Damn, Dee!"

He took his SmartCom, the agency's highly specialized smart phone, and triggered the key fob icon now blinking on the screen. Dee could clone any digital key just from the serial number. Through the main AI, Doris, she had access to even the manufacturers' secure databases. The supercharged, special edition Dodge Hellcat fired up with a throaty roar. This was simply a beast of a car with a massive motor capable of over a thousand horsepower. Cade felt sure he'd wet himself a bit.

Dirt sprayed for nearly a hundred yards as he peeled out of the lot and onto the blacktopped highway. In the backseat, the baby carrier slid from one side to the other, the infant giggling loudly now. *Probably should have at least buckled that in,* Gus said smugly.

"Well, yeah, but I was busy, okay? And if you want to really be helpful, tell me before I do something stupid, not after."

"Primary Tango is nearly a mile ahead of you, Boss," Greg said.

"Dee, can you disable his SUV?" Cade asked. He wasn't sure how she did it but had seen her do that before.

"Negative, Nomad, they have disabled onboard computers. Probably didn't want the car's tracking system ever used against them."

Cade floored the gas pedal, feeling the power surging through the car. He wasn't exactly a 'car guy,' but behind the wheel of this thing you had no choice. It was a bucking bronco, and he was glad just to be hanging on. From the cheerful sounds in the backseat, his passenger felt the same. Shame the little guy would have to grow up without a mother, but she'd chosen stupid over motherhood. Cade wouldn't mourn her. His own mother had essentially abandoned him as a child after his sister's brutal murder, and he felt his life was actually better because of it. She was unfit, uncaring, and unwilling to do the basic minimum requirements of motherhood.

He could see the car ahead; the Hellcat was gaining on it fast. It appeared that the target was turning onto a main road heading back south. "Hang on, Compadre, going to be a bit of a ride here." He arced the Dodge through the left turn at ninety, the back wheels losing traction several times despite the track-mode software compensating for the crazy man at the wheel. Cade steered with one hand as the other held tightly to the shifting baby carrier behind. Another giggle confirmed the child was still enjoying the ride.

"Nomad, town is secure, all hostiles down. Do you need an assist?" McTee called.

"Roger that, track my twenty. Target is heading roughly south, deploy to intercept." He thought briefly about who all he'd left behind. "One of you grab Cochise, we may need him on this as well."

Cade caught up to the fleeing SUV, then eased to the driver's side. A window in the backseat rolled down and the barrel of what looked like an M4 slid out. If he'd been in one of three tactical vehicles, it wouldn't have mattered. They offered unprecedented protection from small arms fire, but this Dodge didn't. He slowed slightly and slid in behind the big Cadillac SUV.

The road ahead widened, and he eased up on the passenger's side. Holding his pistol out the open window, he fired several times into the tires before slowing to fall back.

"That model is equipped from the factory with run-flat tires, Captain," Dee said.

"Well, great. Again, you guys, this info is much more useful before, not after." He thought for a few minutes. All I have is this *massive car*. "Can I successfully do a PIT maneuver?" PIT was now standard training for most law enforcement. It stood for Pursuit Intervention Technique and involved nosing the front side of your car into the rear quarter of a lead vehicle to spin it out then accelerating on through. It had some dangers, not the least of which was flipping one or both cars in the process. Also, it tended to work better when you had multiple cars in pursuit, since the action wouldn't put the target car out of commission. Typically, it just caused them to be banged up and facing in the opposite direction. If they took off again or jumped out shooting, then he wasn't a lot better off.

"You are currently driving at 163 miles per hour. PIT would likely be fatal to all involved at this speed."

"I am going to take that as a no, then?" Cade said questioningly. "Give me some options, guys. Greg, you have anything?"

"Time to intercept team is fifteen minutes. Time to the international border is ten," Dee said.

"Nomad, get your car in front, then brake hard. This should cause him to stop, or he'll crash into you, damaging the cooling system, which will put him out of action."

"Greg, let me get this straight. You want me to let him crash into me at 160 miles an hour? That's the best you have? Okay, you and Miss Wizard have got to come up with some better toys than this. I need to be able to spray oil out the back of the car or launch rockets or something."

"We have all that and more, Nomad," Greg answered with a touch of humor in his voice. "You just didn't take the right car."

"Point taken, but you should see this thing. It's freaking awesome, man." Both cars were still traveling south at something that felt close to light speed, yet when he punched the gas, the Hellcat jumped forward like it had just been unleashed from its shackles. The back end twitched slightly as Cade swerved to go around the big SUV. *Man, this thing is a monster,* he thought as the car screamed past the gang leader.

Cade lined up the grill of the Cadillac in his rear view mirror. He hated to deliberately crash the Dodge but saw no other good options. Just then, a stream of rounds stitched over the roof and across the dash beside him. He stomped the brake just as he thought about the innocent baby in the backseat. He reached for the carrier and missed as the impact of the larger car drove his body forward and into the steering wheel. Tearing metal and the smell of burning tires assaulted his senses. Then the sound of the baby crying brought all of his awareness back online.

We got this, dude, a recognizable voice said. *You just sit tight and babysit the kid.*

Shit, Cade knew he was not the one in control of his own body anymore. A hand, his hand, gently placed the baby back upright on the backseat. Another hand opened the car door and stepped out. Cade watched through his own eyes as more of a passenger than a driver now. The scene was total chaos with both cars in pieces and locked together like an unholy marriage of Detroit excess.

A limp arm dangled from the Cadillac's passenger window. A starburst impact shaded in blood on the SUV's windshield suggested that particular hostile would not be a problem. Gus, or most likely it was Brutus, literally jerked the crumpled door off of the huge SUV and grabbed the back of the head of the dazed driver. In one violent motion he drove the man's face down onto the splintered steering wheel driving a piece of the hard plastic deep into the man's skull.

The sound from the rear seat of a gun slide being racked back on a new magazine got his attention. Brutus reached behind him to his plate carrier and withdrew something. A brief flash of metal identified the knife just before it pierced the gunman's chest.

Cade watched helplessly as Brutus virtually dismantled the Cadillac looking for the primary target. The baby's daddy. He had been seated behind the driver, but now there was no one. No body, no blood. Where had the bastard gone?

The sound of the baby crying again brought Cade back to the moment, and at least for now, back in control. Stepping back out of the wrecked SUV, he saw the man they were after pulling the baby carrier out of the Dodge. He turned and faced Cade. Blood was streaming down the man's face from a gash on his head.

"Don't make me do dis, man," he said, holding the carrier high and threatening to smash it and the baby onto the highway. "Jus let me go."

"Is this our man?" Cade said softly to Dee. He couldn't tell with all the blood, and it looked like the guy's nose might be broken.

"Affirmative," came the response.

He saw his team cars approaching and knew the desperate man was close to doing something stupid. He had forgotten why the guy was important, he supposedly had some much-needed intel, but increasingly, it looked like keeping him alive was not going to be a viable outcome. Cade slid his H&K automatic out and aimed it from his hip. The guy went nuts seeing the gun. Fear edged the gang-banger past the edge of rational decisions.

"Drop it, esee. I swear I'll do it."

The punk's only play was to murder his own baby. Cade set the targeting reticle with an eye blink, then selected the ammo round. "Autofire mode," he whispered.

The gun position shifted slightly in his hand before firing. The round impacted the hostile just below the shoulder in the arm holding the baby. The round severed muscle and bone causing the arm to rotate down bringing the baby carrier to a relatively gentle landing on the ground. "Que te Jodan! They gonna fuck you up, esee!" Cade brought the gun up and fired twice more, kneecapping the punk just for good measure. As the local head of the Sinoloa cartel began screaming, his son, just feet away, began giggling again.

Cade walked over and picked up the baby carrier and handed it to Lieutenant Maratelli who had just climbed out of the lead silver SUV.

"Take care of him, Marty, he's a pretty cool little guy. Get him back to the rest of his family if you can."

McTee was zip tying the Mexican's arms and legs ignoring the injuries for now. "Status."

"All Tangos KIA, he is the only survivor, Boss," the soldier said. "We have a few minor injuries but nothing too bad. We will hand this turd over to NSA as soon as we get the bleeding stopped."

"Hey, McTee, this one has a steering wheel through his face," Hammer yelled going through the suspects' car.

"Wonder how that happened," Cade's second in command said as he smiled and hauled the injured man back to the vehicle with the team's medic. "So, Boss, you liked the Hellcat I take it?" The rear end of the car was now sitting flat against the ground, the big Cadillac SUV still perched up on the crushed trunk lid. Bullet holes riddled the body, but the front of the burnt orange metallic beauty was still pristine.

"Love it!" Cade said running an adoring hand down the one unblemished fender. This mission barely qualified as fighting a global threat, but it had still been a good exercise for them. It'd been fun.

9

Dust swirled over the edge of the arroyo; Cade looked down the dusty stream bed as he raked a sleeve across his forehead. "I thought you said it would be cooler here?"

Jasmine shrugged. "I lied." She walked on several yards before turning. "Look, you needed a break, okay? Somewhere away from it all." The farm was only a few hundred miles from the border town where they'd battled the Sinoloa gang, but it felt worlds away.

He nodded, sipping from the water tube going to his hydration pack. Jaz was right; he knew that. They all needed a break. The AI known as Janus had all but wrecked the country, done irreparable damage to the intelligence community, and it would take years for the world to recover. For months, they had been playing mostly cleanup jobs much like the last mission. With a shiny, new irrevocable charter from the president, they now had official status to perform some of the most dangerous and sensitive of missions.

In the wake of Janus's collapse, scores of corrupt politicians and corporate leaders had been forced to step down, and many of those would soon be heading to prison. The Troubles, or the 'reset,' as some in the media and in D.C. had started calling it, actually had produced many beneficial changes. On the surface at least, there was more transparency in government, more oversight of abusive industries, and recently, the push for an absolute ban on developing any Lethal Autonomous Weapons system-capable AI. While most of the world didn't know, and never would know, that a computer program was behind the series of near-catastrophic events, rumors and suggestions had flourished that automated systems had made the situations worse, as in the automated sell-off and resultant bank runs. Or they had failed altogether, as in the manipulation of social media-based newsfeeds, helping initiate riots as well as altering political races. Worst of all were the known failures of automated water treatment and power plant management. The latter had been lethal, and no one found satisfaction in having to put blame on a computer.

"A getaway was fine, Jaz, but damn...you know a beach with a drink would be okay, too...right?"

She winked. "Served in a coconut with a tiny umbrella, I suppose."

"Well...sure, I mean, if you insist." Georgia had the heat and the humidity; Texas just had the scorching heat and not nearly enough shade for his liking. He topped the small rise and looked back over his shoulder.

"He gone again?" Jaz asked, shielding her eyes from the sun as she scanned the scrublands.

Cade nodded, then tapped his CommDot. "Cochise, signal." He heard the bark off to the west, several hundred yards away.

"I can't believe you stole the senator's dog," she said, resuming her trek.

"It wasn't the senator's, not really. Pretty sure it belonged to the security team assigned to him. But still, bastard is lucky to still be alive and just missing a dog." It had taken all of his resolve not to snap the man's neck that day. Of all the voices in his head, none were exactly the voice of reason in the days after Janus was destroyed. Director Stansfield had been clear, though; Senator Carson would be more helpful under their control than dead. To his credit, the man had delivered a full list of all his known co-conspirators, bank accounts, and any other intel he had on the rogue AI's mission. Still, it galled Cade that the man was still alive, much less holding public office. With upcoming elections suspended for two years, it seemed they would be dealing with the slimy politico for the foreseeable future.

Operational headquarters was still known simply as The Cove. His new boss, Director Margaret Stansfield, had been called on to help stabilize the country in the wake of The Troubles. Cade and the Talon Teams had been called on regularly for months now, not just to bring in Janus supporters, but also to capture many other opportunists who had stepped out of the shadows in those bleak days.

It seemed everyone had lost someone during The Troubles, friends, family members, loved ones. Most lost count of the funerals they'd attended. It was this generation's Pearl Harbor attack or 9/11, a shared national horror. Talon Team had suffered as well, fatalities and career ending injuries. The teams had been shuffled and new members added. His old executive officer and best friend from their Ranger days, Charlie 'Deuce' Taylor, as well as Nance and McTee were assessing the remaining members now back at The Nest in Kentucky. Two new teams, WarHawk and Raptor, were just beginning to take new assignments. Cade was officially on all of the teams and none. He went where he was needed.

Cade felt they had done admirably despite the lack of training and a short time working with each other. They had pulled together as an effective fighting force and helped get the job done. Still, he had to admit they had made mistakes. A glaring one was too many on the team were ground pounders like him and Charlie. Ex-Army, mostly Rangers or Delta, good for fighting on dry land, less adept at sea. Also, too few with backgrounds in law enforcement. So much of that first mission had taken place in urban environments. Despite some similarities, soldiers are not cops. They don't teach many of the required 'people skills' in war college. Talon would reshape, add new people; they would form additional teams, and leaders would emerge. That was his job now.

Right now, though, he was just glad to have a day off. Truthfully, he wasn't sure what was going on between him and Doctor Jasmine Kline, still just friends, but perhaps the spark of something more. In the days after Janus, the two had grown close. She taught him all about what new and wonderful things she was learning at The Cove, and he was very slowly opening up about the ghosts in his head. He knew her invitation to him for a layover here at her grandparents' farm had been a deliberate manipulation. He wasn't sure of the goal. Perhaps she needed to know if he could be fixed or if he was irrevocably broken.

Cade still mainly thought of her as the fiancée of his late C.O., Tim Jurgins. That would probably never change. He wouldn't deny an attraction, but that was something he would just deal with...or maybe he wouldn't. This was not the time—was it? For once, the voices in his head all remained quiet.

Later that evening, Cade watched as Jaz piled up wood, smaller twigs, then some other kind of wood she referred to as a lighter, and lastly, larger pieces. She touched a match to a small bundle of dried grasses she'd placed beneath the twigs, and soon they were enjoying a proper campfire. "You've done that before?"

She nodded, "Once or twice." She pulled off her boots, dusty from the long hike. "You don't grow up on a ranch in this part of the country without knowing the basics. Besides, I'm sure you could have done one in half the time."

"Damn right...well, maybe. I'd have just used the firestarter kit Riley stuck in my pack, though... much simpler. Laziness is a virtue, you know."

She laughed deeply. He decided it was a good look for her. One he'd like to see more of. Maybe Doris had a point.

"Why are we here?" he asked.

"In Texas, or out here?" She waved her hand around in a loose circle.

"Both, I guess."

"Well," Jaz said softly, "we are out here because I knew you probably wouldn't sleep inside my grandparents' house. You are pretty weird, you know? We were both in Texas, and just to give us both a break, and well... I thought maybe seeing what a somewhat normal family looks like would do you good." She poked a stick into the fire. A minor celebration of sparking embers rose into the air. "You're a good man, Cade. You've done things..." she drifted off momentarily, "...

endured things I can't even begin to imagine to survive, or to defend us all. Yet, you view yourself on the outside, flawed, broken even." She gently placed a hand on his knee. "You don't have to be that person."

So, this was therapy. Probably something she and Doris had cooked up, he thought.

"Don't look at me that way," she demanded. "I am not trying to fix you. I just want you to be ok with yourself, you've earned that right many times over."

He nodded slowly, he'd been the one member of the team that had no family to return home to after The Troubles. No dead friends to bury, other than the fatality from Charlie Team, a woman named Pickett whom he barely knew. He'd stayed mainly at The Cove or up at the Talon base in Kentucky. As with Jaz, Doris had provided him a beautiful house nestled alongside the river, but like most places, it was just a thing; it had no connection, no deeper meaning. It would never be home to him.

Sensing his reluctance to engage her on that topic, Jasmine tactfully changed the subject. "So, how long before the country gets back to normal?"

Cade shrugged. "Dunno, Jaz. We took a hell of a hit. Stock market crashed, inflation is skyrocketing, the dollar is for shit, several of the mega banks failed, and national elections have been suspended. Confidence in our country may be at an all-time low. No one even seems to believe we can have honest elections anymore."

"So, we are mortal," she said softly.

"Apparently."

She watched as the striking German shepherd entered the circle of firelight and curled up between her and Cade. She reflexively began stroking Cochise's fur. "I think that might be a good thing."

"How's that?" he asked, not looking up.

"You've traveled a lot, you've seen how America's perceived around the world."

"We're a confident country, we bust our asses to be number one," he said defensively.

"Calm down," she said. "I'm not disagreeing, but we also love shoving it in the face of everyone else that we're a superpower, we're number one. Maybe that's why the rest of the world seems to love taking shots at us."

He conceded her point, "We're just different. Our country, I mean. I've always thought people are generally the same everywhere. They like spending time with their kids, enjoying a nice meal, having fun. There's more about all of us that is alike than is unalike, yet...we can allow the most mundane of differences to become massive obstacles. As a nation, we have spent decades rubbing it in their faces, and I'm just afraid..."

"Afraid of what, Cade?"

"Afraid payback is coming."

They sat like that, not speaking for a long time. The sounds of the crackling fire faded to allow the night birds and insects to take over. Jaz looked into the night sky and pointed at a shooting star. The now sleeping dog stirred quietly at the removal of her hand.

"Meteor?"

She nodded. After all, she was an astrophysicist; she could probably name all the constellations, as well as plot the trajectory for the falling piece of space rock.

"Or," she grinned, "astronave."

Cochise shifted and used a leg to push Cade away slightly. The dog was obviously fond of Jasmine, and he and Cade were forming a tight bond, but it was hard to see who the alpha was just yet. "What did you just say?"

She looked confused, "Um, I dunno. Oh, meteor?"

"No, the other."

"Oh, astronave. It's Spanish," she said with a grin. "Spaceship."

"Do you think about them, the aliens, much?" Cade knew the story now. An alien race called the Dhakerri had beamed an interstellar message to Earth. The tightly compressed message was discovered by Doris at The Cove. From that original message had come an array of new technologies and discoveries.

"Of course." Jaz answered. "It was my dream as a scientist, and now I'm in a position to really pursue it. The alien message is amazing. It's just slow to reveal itself, like peeling an onion just to get the next nugget of info."

Cade once had a therapist describe his mental state in much the same way. "This is nice Jaz, I needed it. Thanks!"

She just looked at him, the firelight giving her pretty face a glow that left him mesmerized. "Cade..." she began.

Thanks to Gus yelling at him not to speak, he remained silent, letting her words come out when she was ready.

She stayed silent; so did he. Cochise nuzzled in between them enjoying his humans. To Cade it felt as close to home, to family as he'd ever been. He absently scratched behind the dog's head. Soon, Jaz's hand was doing the same, and for a moment, both their hands rested atop one another. Cade didn't pull away, in fact he never even thought about it. His mind fell silent and enjoyed the peace of the moment fearing that it wouldn't stay that way for long.

10

WASHINGTON, D.C.

The advisor watched his boss closely. The man had aged considerably since taking office. Hell, who could blame him? The country had nearly come apart at the seams, and now the vultures seemed to be circling constantly, looking for more signs of weakness. The man placed the leather-bound briefing ledger on the corner of the desk. He ran his hand along the edge. Nearly everyone who came into the room wanted to see it. The Resolute Desk. President Ortiz thought it was a gaudy, impractical thing, but it was tradition. Made from timbers of the HMS Resolute, a British Arctic exploration ship which the U.S. saved and returned to Britain as a sign of friendship. In 1880, the Queen of England presented the desk as a thank you to President Hayes.

"Harris!" The older man trailed off, seemingly forgetting his advisor was standing right there waiting for instructions.

Harris wondered again how much the ordeal and the months hidden away in the bowels beneath Cheyenne mountain had done to the man. That bunker was more commonly known as home to NORAD command than to a sitting president. "Yes, sir," the president's aide answered. "Would you like me to show her in now?"

Ortiz turned and nodded, "Oh. Yes, of course."

Moments later, Director Margaret Stansfield entered the oval office. The greeting was warmer than she'd expected. Political alliances are fickle things, but the man seemed to genuinely like and trust her. Their friendship seemed to have reached a rather amicable level amidst all the chaos. He motioned for her to sit on one of the long sofas. A friendly sign, in her opinion, more relaxed. She was not here to receive orders, or be reprimanded. He wanted her help...maybe even her opinions.

A steward brought in a coffee set on a silver tray, and they both took advantage of a cup. Margaret was assessing her boss with the same level of scrutiny his personal advisor had. She caught Harris standing discreetly against a far wall. President Ortiz took a sip, savored it, and placed the cup down, sloshing some liquid onto the antique table.

"Margaret, we have a developing situation. Something that is clearly in your, um..." he seemed to struggle with what to call it... "your group's wheelhouse. What are you calling it?"

"The Cove Project, sir. Mostly TCP for now. You know how we love acronyms."

He nodded. "Of course, yes, yes." The president stood and paced for a moment before continuing.

She could feel the trepidation emanating from the man. Whatever this was, he was taking it seriously. Realizing he was wasting time, he returned to the sofa and sat.

"Margaret, this is a bit baffling, and frankly, I don't even know where else to go with it. Might be just more fallout from The Troubles, may be some entirely new threat. It doesn't seem to come from any of the known players. The truth is, our intelligence apparatus is simply not capable of chasing this to ground right now."

Margaret was well aware of the gaping holes in the intel and enforcement community. Janus had sent a wrecking ball through the bloated and unwieldy system, exposing the myriad of overlapping agencies charged with domestic security. One positive was that the most incompetent had been exposed, and some overlap and waste had been eliminated.

Ortiz continued, "We have discovered something major, what you might call an eminent threat, Director. You will discover in the files some theories on the who and the why. The border raids and growing boldness of the Mexican cartels, drug trade, and money laundering are a part of this. I know it was your assets who just helped take down a major piece of that. I wish that was all there was to it. Clearly, it is not that simple. Margaret, we need to keep the circle tight on this, and as much as it pains me to admit your TCP are the only ones, I fully trust them to do that."

"Certainly, sir. Happy to help. What are we facing?"

Ortiz spread his hands. "That may be your first challenge. Before we get into that, I do want to thank you again for all you did, all you continue to do, for me and our country. I know you won't tell me anything more about your operation, but can you assure me you have everything you need?"

"I do, Mister President, thank you. The executive charter you provided along with the official cover for my agents when needed is enough. I will request anything else only when needed, as per our agreement."

An iron-clad, irrevocable presidential charter, Ortiz thought. One of only a handful ever created. His successors would hate him for that, assuming they were ever let in on the secret.

The two had spoken many times over the past several months, mostly via VR conference, but also several in-person visits. Margaret had noticed the toll the job was taking on the man. He'd been an outsider and had made the cardinal sin of pissing off the mainstream media right out of the gate. His first year was a shit-storm of blunders, blame, and accusations, most unwarranted. Then The Troubles hit, and he was left to try to clean up the mess. His poll numbers had risen slightly, but politicians and the Capitol in particular, were taking the blame for most of it.

For her part, Margaret didn't concern herself too much with the politics of D.C. She liked the working relationship the two of them now had. Some leaders seemed to rise to the challenge during a crisis, while others, most, if she was being honest, seemed crippled by it.

Ortiz seemed to be much more the former. It was doubtful she'd ever have as good of a relationship with another president. Right now, though, she doubted this one would even want to seek a second term.

Ortiz nodded and motioned to Harris who silently stepped over and handed Margaret an almost identical looking binder to the one the president had read earlier. She opened it cautiously, glancing up at the president. "Go ahead, Director, I want you to review that here... right now."

Just over twenty minutes later, Margaret closed the folder and placed it near the coffee tray. Rarely would the President of the United States be able to give anyone this much time. Truthfully, she knew it was unprecedented outside of his inner circle. He sat back quietly, sipping his coffee and watching as one of his most trusted national security heads read the briefing document. Reading through the folder's contents, she fully understood the magnitude of what he faced and now knew his problem was about to become her problem.

* * *

The president shook her hand warmly and looked her in the eye. "We need your best on this, Director." The man nodded for his aide.

Ortiz's assistant was the most trusted confidant he had. Harris, although Margaret now knew that was a false name, knew all of his boss's secrets. He knew about her, about The Cove, but not about Doris. No one in government knew about her. Margaret was escorted to a compact meeting room near one of the residence's exit doors.

"You understand the situation, Director?"

She nodded. "I believe so. This Operation Outfield is the best response?" she asked, referring to the proposed mission's name. The folder had detailed several seemingly random incidents, many of which were already known to her via Doris and her many digital ears in various government offices. Someone very smart had made some rather bold connections tying together the events. Whoever this analyst was, she would have to discover. Data and facts were malleable things when it came to world politics. Someone who could see through the bullshit and ferret out true motives...well, that kind of intuitive leap was an essential skill. One that Doris couldn't help with and definitely something The Cove could use more of.

Harris shook his head, "No, not really. Outfield is just the best we can do right now, Director. Our position with the other superpowers is tenuous to say the least. Every major world power suffered because of Janus. The U.S. and China the worst, and due to our weakened state, Russia is even more hell bent than ever on securing former alliances and developing new client states, not just on their borders, but also in the Mid-East. Since Janus wiped out the national archives at Granite Mountain, we no longer have any significant intelligence advantages."

Margaret had never told anyone that it was actually Doris who destroyed those records. "We are holding the weakest hand in the game, Harris. Is that what you are suggesting?"

Something flashed in the man's eyes, but only for a moment. The man was a patriot. Deep down, he wanted to challenge this statement. It galled him how far the country had fallen under his watch, but her words were true. He handed her an even larger folder. It seemed none of the files on this mission were being kept on a computer. President Ortiz had gotten wise to the potential vulnerabilities of that. "Take your time, review everything, but leave the files here on the table. When you are done, let the sentry know. Contact on this op will be with the president or my office only. Good luck." He shook her hand and abruptly left.

Margaret sat down heavily in the office chair and went to work. She didn't trust computers either, well...there was *one*. She reviewed each file, and at the same time, a tiny sensor in her glasses was storing a digital copy on her TCP's servers. Before she'd even finished, she'd triggered her Dee via subvocalized command to start organizing the data and to signal The Nest to have Talon command begin prepping teams. They would have multiple targets, it would seem.

Near the end of the operations folder, she came across an odd file. It seemed to have been included almost as an afterthought. The content of the file was not essential, in her opinion, but it concerned an old and very covert operation that she'd been somewhat familiar with during her time with the agency, as well as a contact named Golette and someone else she was more familiar with. Whatever was going on had a lot of moving parts. Someone had been working on this plan for a very long time. Right now, she was sure most of what she was seeing were false leads and red herrings, but she agreed. The president was right to be nervous. Someone was looking to cripple world financial markets and drain America's reserves of cash. The nation couldn't withstand much more, a financial collapse would be devastating for the nation...and the world.

11

THE COVE

Cade Rearden glided effortlessly through the water. The underground pool was a relatively recent addition to the base, as was the adjacent workout facility.

"Rearden, we need to talk," a familiar voice called out.

"Hey, man, what's up?" Sergeant Charlie 'Deuce' Taylor reached down a hand to help him up. The two had served together and did time as prisoners of war in the Middle East. Their trust and friendship was now a bond as close as any brothers would ever know.

"The Director has something...not sure what exactly. She wants to brief us both," Charlie said. "Prepped Bravo Team as well as Raptor, going to be something fun."

"My mini-vacation is definitely over, I take it," Cade said, running a towel through his blonde hair and heading to the locker room to change. Cochise eased up and stretched before languidly following.

Charlie followed along, obviously wanting to discuss something else. "Cade, you thought anymore about what I said?"

Cade thought for a moment, trying to recall the recent conversation. It slammed back into his head like a hollow-point slug. "Yeah, Deuce," purposefully using his combat call sign. "You're thinking about retiring, and you want me to talk you out of it."

"No...not exactly," the big man said. "I just wanted your opinion. This shit is getting more and more serious. Every mission could be my last, and since..." he trailed off. Cade was pretty sure where he was going. Since the government's official sanction of The Cove Project, every mission was more complicated, more dangerous. No more simple pickups or recon. Way too much shit like the Mexican gang shootout. "Face it, brother, we're skilled, cheap, and politically expendable." And as such, they had become the go-to team for countless hairy black-ops missions. That was clearly not what the charter had been designed for. The Cove Project, or TCP, was a highly technical and tactical response to the ever-increasing threat of malevolent technologies. Not just AI, but bioengineering, neural manipulation, gene editing, and a host of other more nuanced threats.

Cade sighed, a sound that held more sadness and regret than he cared to consider. "Charlie, I get it. But look, you got my ass into this. Remember that?"

"You were being held prisoner in the Sudan at the time. Would you have preferred we left you there?"

Cade finished lacing up his boots and looked up, winking. "Just admit it, Charlie, you missed me... just like you would if you retired. Besides, I need your goofy ass out there. The teams are still a mess." They had all been reshuffled, new faces brought in, but way too often it came down to Nomad, Deuce, and a couple of the other top operators to pull off the impossible. Charlie had a talent at assembling the teams and getting them combat effective in record time. Not an easy task considering all the new weapons and tech available to them.

"McTee is more capable than I am. Several of the new SEAL guys and, shit, nearly all the female operators have more leadership skills," Charlie argued.

"Okay, Charlie, what's her name?" Cade asked with a smile, both men now heading to the elevator up to the director's level.

"What do you mean?" Charlie asked with a tone of mock insult.

The truth was, they were in a dangerous business. That was what they had all signed up for, but it was also crucially important. Usually, it was not 'saving the world' levels of importance but occasionally coming close. They were nearing the briefing room door; Cade paused and turned around to his friend. "Charlie, we are soldiers, we follow orders. That was basically all we did. We let others, often total incompetents, make decisions for us. Decisions that nearly cost both of us our lives. Now let me ask you one question—did you ever see yourself at a place where you could make a real difference?" Cade signaled the sensor to open the door. "Come on, we don't want to keep her waiting."

* * *

The group's 'boss,' Director Margaret Stansfield, was sitting on one side of the long table alongside the brilliant young Riley, Director of New Technologies for The Cove. Stansfield formerly led the CIA's Cybercrime division. Her affiliation with her former agency now was a bit unclear. Officially, she was still missing and presumed dead after the previous year's drone attack at Camp David. Riley Sandoval was a no-nonsense twenty-something with an IQ that was off the charts and more patents filed than most corporations. Her role was mostly running the complex R&D side of the base, but the director called on her for help regularly.

"Captain, Sergeant, thank you for joining us," the director said as she motioned up to the large display wall. "We may have a confusing situation developing." The map on the display was zooming into various locations, but stopped on a region familiar to most of them.

"Gulf of Mexico, 300 miles off the tip of Florida's south coast. Massive fish kill, one of the largest ever discovered. Cause is unknown," she said. The view shifted slightly.

"Cayman Trench, south of Cuba. Four weeks ago, Portuguese submarine on a training mission went down, all hands presumed killed. They are calling it a training accident, but we are pretty sure it wasn't."

The director sped through several more slides showing everything from clear sabotage at numerous Guyana offshore oil rigs to a sharp increase in drug trafficking originating in Central and South America.

The map view was replaced by a different image, one that was well known to one person on the senior staff. Doctor Jasmine Kline sucked in a breath of surprise. "Snowbird," she said in a near whisper.

"Yes, the XS1R spaceplane," Margaret said. "Lost over a year ago on a top-secret Air Force mission to the interesting interstellar anomaly known as Oumuamua. While the ship and its commander were lost, the automated sampling probe launched from Snowbird had a failsafe protocol to return to Earth if it could not locate or return to ship. That probe reentered our planet's atmosphere approximately five months ago. You may also recall that Doris indicated that Janus claimed he wasn't the cause of that event."

"Did we recover it? Where did it go down, and why is this just coming out?" Jaz asked the questions in a rapid-fire staccato.

"Everything I am showing you is off the books—most of this Doris was not even aware of, Doctor Kline. We are still looking at the trajectories to see where it may have hit. The probe hasn't yet been recovered, not by the United States at least. The Air Force has been actively looking, though. Doris and Jimmy both expect it came in over the ocean, probably the Caribbean Sea. Jaz, we need you to work your magic and help us narrow down the search grid."

Cade and Charlie made eye contact, and both gave a small shoulder shrug. They were the sword arm or the gun hand of The Cove, not the brains. All of this seemed over their head. Thankfully, the smartest kid in class asked the question for them.

"These are a lot of random events. Other than location, how is all of this connected?"

"Well, Riley," the director continued, "that is where it gets truly weird. Someone in D.C. had made a very compelling case that it is all related. Mainly because of Sigint and some very impressive detective work. The short answer is, we have a name, 'Golette.' Doris has run the name through every database and came up with nothing. We know it was the name of an intelligence asset from the late 1960s. His code name was 'The Lion.'

All of them now knew signals intelligence, or Sigint, meant intercepted communications, emails, chat servers, cell phones, and various other techniques the NSA and other agencies used to covertly learn what targets around the world were up to. As the eavesdropping technology got more sophisticated, so did the techniques used by those wanting to stay hidden.

Doris spoke, "As you can probably guess, most of the files from that era were never digitized, and even the archived folders were heavily redacted. There is a very thin thread on this person. Something called 'Project Saraph' was mentioned. No other details."

"A spy from the 60s and a project name? This seems awfully thin, Director," Riley interjected.

She agreed, but continued, "We've worked this from several possible angles and gotten nowhere. Golette could have been a man or a woman, we simply don't know, and Saraph led us nowhere. A project that simply shows up in no other reference."

"Golette is an unusual name, Doris....as is Saraph. I believe that is some sort of bird."

"It's an angel, Riley. In particular, it is Hebrew for angel."

"Golette sounds like it could be a Jewish name. Does that help us at all?" Jaz asked.

"Possibly," Margaret answered.

"All very interesting, but I'm not seeing the national emergency, here. Where's the fire?" Cade asked.

The director nodded. "Cade, the country is going broke. Janus wrecked us politically and economically. Now, someone else may be about to finish us off. There is a disturbing financial aspect weaving almost all of this together. The prevailing theory in D.C. is, at best, it is a very sophisticated attempt to further destabilize America and possibly other world powers. Something that amounts to a financial terrorist attack."

"What would be the worst-case scenario, Director?" Cade asked.

Margaret shook her head. "At worst, Captain, the damage may have already been done. America is currently on some very shaky ground. Politically and financially, many of our allies are very suspicious of our role in what they refer to as The Troubles, and our enemies...well, let's just say they have their own agenda. Washington thinks someone is about to make a land-grab. Best bet is that Russia wants Mid-East oil fields. They need the U.S. to stay weak, and starving us from oil would hurt us in ways we can only imagine."

Margaret looked around the room. "Personally, I think that is bullshit. We have plenty of oil, as does Russia, at least for now. I believe we are looking at a new player, someone possibly not state sponsored, who has quietly been building his or her organization, waiting for the right time to make a play. Waiting for America to be on its knees. That time, people, is now, and we are the first line and the last line of defense."

12

The analyst persona was bubbling rapidly to the surface of Cade's consciousness. Although normally reclusive, the highly intelligent team at The Cove seemed to draw him out with increasing frequency. Cade had taken to referring to this entity as Ace, and right now, it was pissing Margaret off by thumbing back through the briefing images to some truly graphic images of dead sea creatures on a beach. The photo looked like it may have been from a cell phone.

Riley smiled and nodded. She liked Cade's analyst personality, and she felt confident this was the persona driving right now. He was sharp, factual, and offered a clarity that tended to cut through the bullshit. "What are you thinking?" she asked him.

Cade looked back at the image, Ace apparently also looking for a clue, or perhaps grasping the subtle familiarity that had escaped his host. "What other things were in that file fragment?"

"File fragment, Captain?" Margaret asked, a look of confusion etched across her face.

"Um, yes, one of you told me Janus got a look at the alien message or a fragment of it. What was in it?"

"Janus," Riley said slowly. The name itself seemed to be distasteful to her.

Time stretched out as the faces stared at one another, then back at him. Margaret Stansfield carefully picked up a pen and made a note on her pad. Riley picked up the explanation. "We know when Janus destroyed an earlier version of Doris, Version 1.0, she had a fragment of the alien message, a message decrypted from an alien broadcast that held the potential of nearly unlimited technological advances. The contents of that message fragment encompassed several elements. While I doubt anyone that has it could have made as much headway in cracking it as us, we can't guarantee that we are the only ones with it. You're suggesting that perhaps someone used a bit of that to create something that's behind all of this?" She directed the question to Ace as she waved up to the display behind her.

Cade wasn't at all sure where Ace was going with this. He was just along for the ride. "Not suggesting anything, just asking a question."

Doris's avatar projected toward the front of the table. She rarely did this anymore since Margaret was in charge of operations and was the de facto head of The Cove Project. "Captain, the fragment was part of a primer. In the first part of the alien message, the Dhakerri used to teach us the basics, so we could decode and understand the next piece. I can provide you a list, but it included advanced mathematics, including a more robust interpretation of non-Einsteinian space-time. Various new materials development, such as our composite polysteel, radical new extreme pressure vessel design, and various substrates such as the liquid purification, gas extraction methods, geothermal heat exchange systems, and so on. Rather mundane by the standards of all the high-tech that came after, but still very revolutionary."

"Seems like an unusual mix for a first lesson," Cade said.

"Indeed, it was," Doris responded. "My assumption then, and I believe it still holds true, is that they, the Dhakerri that is, find that many of the new species with whom they contact, critically need one, or perhaps many, of these technologies. Maybe even have a desperate need for survival. In our case, it was a way to defeat an AI threat. Other species may need to develop advanced space travel more quickly, harness alternative energy sources, or just simple, pure liquid water.

The primer seems to be basic tech to them and is offered as a gift and an enticement to decode the rest."

"Like a cheap knife set the bank gives you for opening a new account?"

"Well, no, but maybe, Captain. It was an enticement. Something too good to ignore," Doris answered.

"Director, I think it's safe to say that someone else likely has this primer, also." Cade pointed at the timeline slide on the display. "Some of these, um, events seem to originate prior to Janus. Hell, before Doris even received the alien message. How would that be possible?" Ace offered this up as his apparent final thought on the matter.

"What's our next step?" Cade added.

"We investigate...we assess, we correct," answered the director. "Washington is calling it Project Outfield, and it is more along the lines of our charter, closer to the purpose of which we were formed—we need to make it count," she said slowly, motioning at the maps again up on the screen. "Something big is in play, people. Lastly, we may have a line on someone who could know some of what is going on."

"What—a spook? You found Golette?" Cade asked.

"No, no, someone else," Margaret explained. "More of a privateer. He's presumably American but carried out missions for whoever paid the best. He is totally off the radar; we never even knew an actual name. He was in the mission briefing and may have had ties to Project Saraph or Golette, as well as tracking down a group of missing scientists several years ago, which our analyst in Washington now thinks may be linked to all this. This could be nothing, or as we learned from Janus, it could be a distraction. The point is, the president wants to know for sure, which means I want to know. America is bleeding money right now. Six months from now, we may join the list of third-world countries if this doesn't end.

"We have been given a mission, and it is to run down these events and backtrack them to their source. This may take every team we have, so spin up everybody available. Captain, Sergeant Taylor, and I will handle the assignments, but I want you and a small strike team to go find this asset. I want wheels up by 0700."

The meeting ended with everyone leaving Margaret at the table, reassembling her notes. "Director," Doris said, "can I ask why you only provided part of the intelligence to the team?"

"It was a tactical decision, Doris," she said without looking up. "It would have only muddied the water, and I believe could perpetuate a confirmation bias. Are you familiar with the concept?"

"I am familiar with all twelve forms of cognitive biases," Doris replied curtly. "I am not sure I see the connection, though. Rearden was brought in by me, and I have committed to be honest with him in my dealings."

"Doris, we both know the captain is more of an ensemble than an individual. The analyst in him believes there is a connection to Janus, possibly to the alien message. If he begins down that path, every clue he finds may reinforce that belief, and in doing so, cause him to ignore a potential greater truth. It is a very human thing, Doris, not something easily explained or quantified, but I made a gut decision." She began to exit the conference room, but stopped and turned before adding, "The captain will see if there is a link."

13

CARIBBEAN

Ivan was worried, something that he was unaccustomed to. While outwardly, his persona had been of an outrageously successful self-made man, the truth was much more complicated. Right now, he looked like a man with a mission, and that part was accurate. By most accounts, he'd already lost everything important, his family, his company, his reputation, and by numerous normally reliable accounts—his life. Despite that...or more likely because of it, he sat in his office now planning his next steps. A soft chime beeped from his phone. The voice from the built-in intercom announced, "Mister Thrall, your guest has arrived, docking port four."

He acknowledged receipt and glanced up at the primary monitor. The scene showed something resembling a remora, or flattened torpedo-shaped object, entering through the outer hull several levels deeper in the complex. *This will be a challenging few days,* he thought as he made his way to the elevator.

"Thrall!" the voice called out minutes later as the burly man crawled from the cramped confines of the Corsair submersible. "Looking good, my friend...for a dead man, I mean." The thick Texas drawl was artificial and seemed particularly out-of-place down here.

"Richard, still the charmer I see," Ivan said, grasping the man firmly in an embrace. "Welcome, my friend, to the Midnight Zone. Welcome to Kalypso." The two men separated as the Texan looked anxiously around the sealed chamber.

"Where are the others?" Richard asked.

"Coming," Thrall answered. "I wanted to talk with you first, Richard. Things ..."

"The shit went sideways, Buckaroo, no need to pussy-foot around the facts," the Texan said.

Thrall nodded; his visitor was quite right. Richard Goldman was more than just one of the money-men, someone who's trust and faith he couldn't afford to lose. While Thrall had been wildly successful building his tech company, Richard seemed to have the gift of pulling fortunes from thin air. Bucking the trend of most Texas billionaires, none of his investments were in oil. Richard preferred to invest in people, those he believed in. Thrall had benefitted greatly from that trust over the years.

"Hell of a place. Glad to see all the millions didn't go to waste."

More like billions, Thrall thought. "Let me give you the nickel tour," he said, touching the big man lightly on the arm to guide him to the door.

Twenty minutes later, the two men sat alone at a small, mahogany table. "This is the cupola," Thrall said, pointing to the massive convex window that dominated the adjacent wall. The men sipped on drinks as they stared out into the black abyss.

"I always wondered why windows were needed down here. It would be the structural weak point, but I think I get it now."

While almost every exterior wall panel in this part of the facility was, in fact, a display of the scene outside, very few actual windows looked out into the depths. This was by far the largest. "The cameras and displays are good," Ivan said. "The best—but some things just are better seen by human eyes. If this were regular polycarbonate, it would need to be four feet thick, embedded deeply into the side walls, and most likely, the viewable portion would be no larger than your head."

As it was, the slightly convex oval window reached nearly from floor to ceiling. With a small gesture, Thrall dimmed the interior lights and then slowly faded to dark. Everything inside the cupola space was black other than a few tiny strips of ambient glowing dots indicating the door. "Give it a few minutes, Richard, you know, for your eyes to adjust."

Goldman knew no sunlight penetrated this deep. They originally constructed a portion of the lab long ago for other purposes. Acquiring it had been ridiculously easy, as were the newer portions that had been built in various dry docks, then towed out to sea separately for construction. While the component parts resembled common ocean platforms, oil rigs, deep sea habitats, or automated research stations, none of the assembly crews knew what they were really building, nor where it would wind up. The Kalypso lab was generally oval, larger than a cruise ship, and was now positioned far from its point of origin and almost 3000 meters below the ocean's surface. Richard tried hard not to think of all that water above. The pressures here were immense, the craft could never have been constructed without some very new techniques and materials.

"You see?"

Ivan's whispered voice coming from darkness interrupted Richard's thoughts.

Looking to where he assumed the cupola window was, which was nearly as black as the room, Richard could just begin to see. At first just a flicker of light here and there. Mostly faint blues and greens, occasionally a pinkish red. "Bioluminescence," he said in a near whisper. He knew the creatures at this depth often made their own light. Possibly to find mates, attract prey, or to signal something to others of their kind.

Slowly, as Richard's eyes fully adjusted to the darkness, he realized the water outside was filled with life, with light. All manner of it. Schools of small glowing fish swam by the bubble of glass, their skeletal structure shown in green glowing outlines. He let out an audible gasp as a darker shape cruised through the schooling neon fish. Some creatures' light shows pulsed with a hypnotic rhythm, others stayed on. A glowing cloud that resembled falling snow drifted past near the visual edge of what they could see. "It's beautiful, my friend," he said, leaning forward, his face just inches away from the inside of the window, all thoughts of where he was now absent from his mind.

Thrall had planned this moment; he knew the effect it would have on his friend. It had been the same with him the first time he saw it, and the hundredth. He remained silent for several more minutes, not wanting to break the magical spell of their location here in the Midnight Zone. Finally, he sat the empty tumbler back on the table, the large exposed ice cube clinking softly as he did so. "We think they are attracted to the structure for shelter, and perhaps they can detect the energy inside. Not sure, but they began congregating outside almost from the very beginning."

Richard could now see larger and smaller creatures in the mix. Some so delicate and dim they looked like apparitions, yet many had patterns so intricate, so beautiful, that he could barely express the joy in seeing them. "Nature is a marvelous artist," he whispered.

They sat in near silence for almost thirty minutes. Occasionally, one of them would point out a new or particularly interesting creature as it swam by. "It is amazing, isn't it?"

Richard nodded enthusiastically as Thrall continued, "Few people have ever seen this. Most humans that get to this depth are locked behind reinforced pressure hulls, coffins of reinforced steel. Even our new undersea rovers with their remote HD cameras can't really do it justice. The Kalypso is the only platform that will work to truly study the deep ocean. If you were to trap any of those," he pointed to the already dimming sea creatures outside, "and took them to the surface, they would look dull and gray or white, many would simply dissolve because of the rapid pressure changes."

Richard nodded in agreement, unsure if his partner could see the gesture in the dim light from outside. Steeling himself, he asked the question that had been on his mind since beginning the journey down, "Is it out there?"

Ivan didn't respond right away. Slowly, he offered an almost whispered reply, "Yes, my friend. Two of them. Always they patrol, always they hunt."

Nervous excitement coursed through the Texan's body. "I haven't seen one fully grown yet. It was quite small the last time we visited."

Thrall took out his phone, and Richard heard his finger making contact on the screen. "Look high and to your right. I will send it a feeding alert. Normally, they will signal."

"Holy shit! Jesus fucking Christ, Thrall!" The creature came into view, flashing bright blue for just a moment. Unlike the other sea life, though, it was so bright it lit the entire room. The afterimage seemed etched in Richard's retina. Glowing spike-covered tentacles ending in hooked claws, a blunted head, and tapered body, followed by a tail that looked nothing like any sea creature he'd ever seen. "It is huge, like the size of a city bus. I had no idea."

"About forty meters, yes. And...we are not even sure if it has stopped growing. The science team now believes they keep growing throughout their life cycle. Its metabolism rate seems to have slowed somewhat, though, possibly due to the lower quantity of food we are providing."

"But it is a predator, no? It can hunt its food." Richard said it more like a question.

"Oh, yes, it very much loves to hunt and eat. Its biologic system is completly incompatible with our biosphere, though. It cannot metabolize anything out there except the food we make for it. That doesn't stop it from trying, though. It has some interesting evolutionary advantages to make it an apex hunter. Be glad you are in here, my friend."

As their late lead scientist had learned the hard way, thought Richard. A shiver ran through his large body. He was glad Thrall couldn't see. "You wanted to speak with me, Ivan," Richard said flatly. "I assume it is about the next phase?"

Thrall nodded somewhat reluctantly as he brought the lights back up. In reality, there were multiple reasons for this lab being down here. One was proximity in the deep ocean, a requirement for much of the inner workings of the facility and its ongoing research. The other was secrecy. Literally nothing man-made could detect them at this depth. The hull was a special lattice composite that absorbed sonar waves. No energy signatures escaped, no sound, heat, light, nothing that would give them away. Isolation and invisibility were the top priority for Kalypso and Project Angel, and it was vital for their work to continue unabated. The third thing, *well,* that was the main reason they were meeting today.

"So, tell me, Richard, have you found a replacement for Aksell yet?" The Texan had murky connections all over and co-ownership of more than one paramilitary group that supplied professional soldiers and security teams to hotspots around the world.

"Yes...shame about the Hunter. The man was truly gifted. I'm afraid no one man fills his shoes, but I have it taken care of. One wonderful thing about money, there is always someone willing to do anything if the price is right."

Richard eyed Thrall for a moment. "Ivan, I don't think you asked to speak to me over mundane security matters. Come on, my friend, we are the Chaos Kings, don't leave me guessing," he bellowed.

Thrall hated that moniker. The organization had a name—a much more ancient identifier, yet this one had surfaced during The Troubles, and now it looked like it would stick to them like chewing gum on the sole of a shoe. "You realize we are on the cusp of unlocking the greatest secrets humanity has ever known, right?"

Richard nodded, "If what you have been telling us is even partially true, then yes. Yes, of course."

Thrall wasn't sure his friend did fully understand. How could he... how could any of them wrap their head around something so enormous? Perhaps the bigger question was how could they hold on to the secret even here in the deep ocean? Slowly, he reached into a pocket and removed a small flash drive. "This was his last burst transmission before he...well, you know."

Richard's eyes lit up at once. He leaned forward, reaching out for the device almost reverently. "Wait, this is from Janus? You...you have it? Oh, my. Did you...were you able to find anything useable?"

Thrall nodded. "Yes, quite a lot, Richard. Quite a lot...it seems we may not be completely alone in our discoveries."

14

The steward carefully placed yet another white china plate in front of each of the guests. Over the course of the day, the remaining associates had arrived on station. They'd met casually to discuss immediate issues but took an early break for the evening meal. The spread looked like a royal feast, fresh seafood and delicacies from all over. Tropical fruits and assorted luxury items lined the tables draped by the crisp, white linen. This course was grilled lamb chops with a cherry reduction and rosemary.

"Your wine selection is quite good here," Dakso said, looking across the table at Ivan. "The Chilean grapes make the best, in my opinion, although some New Zealand vintners are proving themselves to be quite capable. I trust you stockpiled enough of this to last us?" He drained the glass as he eyed the now empty bottle.

"No need," Thrall said, a look of satisfaction on his face. "We can copy any of the wines on a molecular level. The one you just drank included."

The Croatian looked confused. "That was not a vintage blend?"

"The station has access to nearly every port on the planet, but we have increasingly switched to manufacturing as many items as are feasible with the realization that soon, the day will come when it is our only option. Our molecular food labs have mastered most liquid based and brewed foods already. Fermented items like cheese, beer, and wine have taken a bit longer, but, as you see, the replicated versions are nearly indistinguishable."

A steward replaced the empty wine bottle with a full one and quickly extracted the cork. Dakso eyed the dark green bottle suspiciously before grabbing it and pouring another half glass. He'd known about the lab-made foodstuffs but just had not realized they would be part of the menu already. He smacked his lips. "Is very, very good, my friend."

"Kalypso has a great many more surprises and currently is 92% self-sustaining," Ivan said. "That meets our target for this stage, and we can easily take it up to 100% at deployment." He eyed the others seated around the table. "We will also be able to maintain that indefinitely. Clean power is abundant either from hydrogen, geothermal, or even a biodegradable solar net that can be deployed at the surface. For food, we only need some very basic raw materials. Phytoplankton is abundant and works well, although almost anything can be used since our labs break it down to near the molecular level. Fresh water is simple with the new desalinating membranes we acquired, as is oxygen since we can break down the seawater into hydrogen and good old breathable air."

"It seems, as the Americans like to say, you have all the bases covered," the Chinese member, Pax Ruan, said in a tone that suggested he felt otherwise.

"No, most certainly not. We build based on probabilities and contingencies. We have stationed caches and maintenance facilities on the seabed at various points around the oceans. Our plans assume we will have problems— my job is to make sure they do not become critical. Once things start heating up back on the surface, I know we will not want to go back up for any reason."

"You may be invisible, Thrall, the rest of us are not," Dakso said in heavily accented English while slapping a palm down on the table, rattling the dinnerware.

Ivan studied the man's glowering face as he nodded. Holding up his hands in a placating gesture, he answered, "I know, my friend, I totally get it. Do try and keep in mind, though, that my..." he sought to choose the proper phrasing, "...my sudden departure was the only way to ensure the anonymity of this lab and, by extension, each of you. We all worked out the plan, just as our next steps have been. Yes, my exposure down here is not quite the same as yours back on the surface, but you don't have the threat of three miles of ocean pressing down on your office every second of every day do you, Dakso?"

Reminding the Croatian billionaire of where he was currently sitting was a shitty move on his part, but Thrall wanted the man to sweat. What came next would require all of them to step out of their comfort zone.

The Chinese man to Ivan's left spoke in a soft, almost melodic tone that seemed much older than his apparent youth would suggest, "We all knew this was the likely path. It should surprise none of us at this point. Mister Grigorian, you least of all." The man paused to make eye contact with each of the others seated around the table. "We all knew what we were agreeing to and the price that must be paid. The goals have not changed." He turned his face up in a way that resembled a predator about to pounce on its prey. "Nor will our commitment to see them through."

The words cut through them like an icy blade. While Pax Ruan was just one of the members of the small and very secret cabal, none of The Founders would ever dare go against the man's wishes. Few other than Thrall knew much of the man's history, but Pax had brought more capital to the project than all the others combined. Kalypso simply wouldn't have happened without him. Besides his money, the man simply exuded power and control. Rumors were, he'd traced his lineage back to Genghis Khan, and it seemed he wanted badly to outdo his famous ancestor. Of course, the story was that nearly one in 200 men could trace their lineage back to the great Khan, but the great Pax ignored those facts.

Thrall knew he had made a deal with the devil that fateful day so many years earlier. The company he had built, all the work he'd put into the project, was slipping away. The innovative AI code he'd developed had been married to a processing chip that finally was showing promise of the elusive goal of artificial general intelligence and, hopefully, the ability to crack the fifty-year-old secret of the artifact.

Then the government had begun getting greedy. They wanted the AI for themselves. He knew the day would come when he'd regret all those lucrative defense contracts he'd won. While he'd kept most of his work a secret, even from DARPA, someone decided they wanted it all and began to tighten the noose. Investigations began, allegations of impropriety, then accusations of outright fraud. His military access was revoked, so was his top-secret clearance, then those lovely military contracts were defunded. Most of the claims were unfounded; they had lucrative assets and a crack accounting team to ensure compliance, but something had changed. Someone wanted him out of the way.

Sure, Cryptus had taken some shortcuts along the way, and yes, that had included occasionally borrowing, or even stealing, from competitors. It was a standard practice in tech giants to steal intellectual property by luring away the guys that built it. His million-dollar legal team finally convinced him that the feds had put together a solid case. They weren't just coming after the company. They wanted to punish him personally. Ivan always assumed someone had set them up to fail. Then Pax Ruan made an offer, an offer that allowed him to keep some portion of Cryptus and to enjoy a life free of courtroom drama or potential prison time. Even more, it allowed him to keep working on his secret project. "I'll be your '*Angel* ' investor," Thrall recalled the man saying with that same predatory smile on his lips.

"Thrall!"

The sharp sound of his name felt like a verbal slap. "Sorry, yes, we are ready to proceed." He stood and walked to the front of the room, the black ocean behind him providing an eerie backdrop. "As we discussed, the Janus system achieved much of what we had hoped. His work on the Angel Project was critical in getting it moving forward. Once the NSA's Cybercommand began monkeying around on the AI, well...they didn't fully understand the code, much less the chip architecture of his hardware. We had enough back doors in to keep monitoring and modifying, even after they moved it all to the capital. With a little nudge here and there, I think we can agree his exploits went well beyond the initially planned parameters to simply wreak havoc. Ultimately, he was much more...creative than we'd expected."

"Yes, yes, but that was a massive waste of resources, and Janus is gone now," Dakso said impatiently.

"Yes, Janus is gone," Thrall continued, "and we still are unsure as to how he was stopped, but he left the U.S. economy in ruins. The dollar is at an unsustainable low as compared to other world currencies. It is getting pounded by every other developed nation, and the purchasing power keeps dropping." A chart appeared as an overlay to the outside view screen showing a series of jagged peaks and valleys all headed down. "Janus effectively disrupted trade, banking, insurance, and, of course, the commodity and stock exchanges. Some of these may never recover."

"And now we are free to pursue the latest decryptions? Will we finally get more of your promised rewards from the project, or are you just going to keep sacrificing your research teams?" Pax asked with a tone of hostility.

"Angel Project is nearly back on track. The incident at Site 21 did negatively impact our timeline..."

A voice cut him off, "Your main researcher was murdered by your project, Thrall. Not sure that qualifies as either an incident or a negative impact. Who the hell is going to do the work?" the Croatian asked.

Ivan took a sip of wine and raised a palm to signal calm. "We do have that covered— a rather brilliant scientist has taken over the reins. She has gained all of her predecessor's knowledge and should be able to coax out the next bit of code without all the, um...drama." Thrall knew none of the kings had the stomach for the gory details that went on at the testing labs. His earlier report to them had downplayed much of what he'd witnessed through the small window that day. Hopefully, the attractive South American scientist would be a bit more...resilient.

15

After another feast for the following day's lunch, the group ordered the wait staff out of the dining room and the doors sealed. A statuesque blonde stood and walked to where Thrall was standing. The look he gave her was something feral, but he caught the same look in her. He nodded and returned to his seat. Growing up in the mountainous regions of the Czech Republic, Ruslana Kilma was destined to be a farmer's wife, possibly a merchant in the tiny village. Instead, she was one of the most formidable hackers to have ever sat at a keyboard. Along with being beautiful, she was ruthless and had a near eidetic memory. Normal password protocols were as simple as opening a door for her.

Her past success had paid the way for her to be here. Her skillset, probably even more than her looks, was what had formed the bond between her and Thrall. While he was a programming wizard, he was no hacker. She, on the other hand, was a master. She looked for weakness, reverse engineered everything, and did not care how elegant or efficient the code was that she had to use. Ruslana worked with the bio labs on the decryption. Thankfully, she'd not been at Site 21 that day. Her other key role in the organization was to make sure the money never stopped flowing. As an early adopter of programmed crypto trading, she had that covered easily. Her trading algorithms were the stuff of legend on the dark web and underground hacker networks.

"Thrall has asked me to bring you up to speed on Project Saraph, or, as we call it, 'Angel.'" She spoke in English as they all had agreed early on, but her words were heavily accented. "As you know, the artifact which was recovered in 1967 has been challenging. It gives up its clues only with the most ardent and painstaking effort. With each new evolution, we can decrypt additional bits of the code."

"Come on, honey," Freida Spiegel said, obviously ogling the leggy blonde. The stocky heiress from Hamburg was well known for her appetite for food, beer, and women. "We know the history, get the fuck on with it."

For her part, Ruslana ignored the German, as she did anyone who thought they were somehow better than everyone else...better than her. "No one has ever attempted anything like this, no one outside this group would likely even think it is possible. After many years, though, we can see and use enough of the artifact's data to have made some amazing breakthroughs, one of which, of course, is Kalypso." She gestured to the massive room and its gracefully curving walls.

"This is only possible because of the new science we have gleaned from the artifact. How to build materials and structures that can withstand immense pressure. How to extract energy from the geothermal vents on the seafloor. How to literally build items we need at a molecular level. It is beyond even my comprehension, but do try and understand that we are the new alchemist. We have a unique gift, and because of that, we will be a target for every nation out there. When Ivan says we must be ready to defend all that we have found, that is not simply paranoia. Let us not forget it was the United States that had Saraph first. They just didn't understand what it was. When they started to figure it out, it nearly caused them to go to war with their closest ally."

Ruslana went on to detail several more amazing breakthroughs she'd managed to decrypt. The code fascinated her, not just for the secrets it held, but because it was such a puzzle. Layer upon layer of encryption. She'd encountered nothing like it. You painstakingly extract the dataset, then spend weeks, or sometimes months, running every cracking algorithm—only for the archive to open and reveal a piece of new and amazing information along with a buried clue on how to construct. Then, you find the next one. It was constantly a process of rinse and repeat, and so far, none of the teams had found a way to shortcut the process. Whoever, or whatever, designed this wanted it revealed in a very particular way.

"Since we began using the quantum computers, it has sped the decryption process down to just days in most cases," Ruslana continued. "For that reason, the labs are now working on multiple carrier subjects at the same time, each at different stages. We even have a series four coming out of the creche this week. From the original artifact, we have extracted the building blocks to help unlock the remainder of the data. That much we all have known for some time," she said cutting off the rude German before she could speak. "What we didn't know until now, is how far we have gotten, how much more information is locked up inside the storage matrix. By my new estimates, we have unlocked only about eight percent of the total. Not just that, but our speed is increasing exponentially by putting what we already learned to good use."

"Like what?" Pax asked cutting right to the heart of the discussion.

"Like how to develop software on the new computers to automate much of the decryption. This, in turn, has allowed me to perfect predictive analysis, market manipulation, and more. Just bringing on the new quantum trading platforms for cryptocurrency trading will bring us in an extra 1.4 billion dollars this quarter alone. Since the Americans' banking system has flatlined, more and more of them have switched over to cryptos, bitcoin, ethereum, litecoin, and several others. We are draining the U.S. economy, and they have no idea. Not only will they no longer be a superpower, they will be bankrupt. Trust me when I say we are making unprecedented headway."

Ruslana spoke for several more minutes before sitting down. Ivan

Thrall rose again and thanked her, then looked to his friend, Richard. "Goldman is going to let us in on a little secret now."

The large Texan stood up with some effort, smiled, and looked around the room. "We found it! We found the goddamn probe!"

16

FLORIDA EVERGLADES

They exited the silver SUV several miles from the property, giving it instructions to auto-drive in the vicinity until they signaled. His XO, McTee, hung back close by. Lieutenant Bridget Maratelli and a serious looking ex-Navy man, Everett 'Hammer' Harrison, took point. The rutted, dirt road was the color of butter. The late afternoon air was thick with nearly invisible flying insects.

"We're not in Kansas anymore, Boss."

Cade nodded at McTee in agreement. The man Margaret had sent them to meet was supposed to be here. "The director says this was the area," Cade said. They never had an address, but apparently no one out here bothered with niceties like those. On both sides of the road, the ground fell away into dark and foreboding swampland. A crack of a limb and a splash of water a few hundred yards to their left caused them all to drop to a knee and raise their weapons. "Probably a gator, but fuck it. C'mon, let's move it," Cade said.

Nearly an hour later, Dee informed them they were nearing the target coordinates. Cade looked around, confused. "You sure? There isn't a damn thing out here." She confirmed it was the right spot. "Hammer, sweep left," he whispered. "McTee, take Cochise and go south." Both men silently parted and began jogging in opposite directions, the dog cautiously leading the way. Cade turned to the lone remaining member of his team. "You ready?" Maratelli nodded.

The land here was only slightly less swampy. Grasslands hanging on, inches above the water level were safe haven for birds, deer, and just about every other creature. The Everglades was one of the most diverse ecosystems in the world. What was not at home here should have been people. Cade heard a mic click from one of his men. The readout in his goggles identified it as Hammer. Switching over, he could see what the former SEAL was seeing. A low-slung cottage beneath a canopy of trees. They had painted the metal roof in a near-perfect camo-pattern. *That has to be it.* "Hold there," he whispered. "McTee, move in slowly, watch for triggers."

* * *

Director Stansfield didn't have much on the man she only knew as Guardian, but one thing she was certain of was his training. He was paranoid, with good reason, and the best operator she'd ever seen. Cade had to assume he would have surveillance and probably counter-intrusion devices, traps designed to keep people like them far away. No one lived out here just for the hell of it. This man wanted his privacy, had earned it, in fact, serving his country, and now they were going to interrupt his morning coffee.

He felt more than saw that Cochise was back, up close, near Maratelli. The small house emerged from the surrounding forest like an apparition. At first glance, it showed no signs of life. Cycling through broad spectrum analysis, Cade saw no heat signatures, no comms equipment, no energy usage...nothing. Maratelli suddenly held up a palm, causing him to freeze mid-step. Since being fully read into the operations at The Cove, the lieutenant had gone through more of the enhanced training on espionage, counterintelligence, and all manner of spycraft than any of the rest of them. Cade began to speak, but a look from the woman silenced him.

Slowly, she crouched down in the tall grass. The road they'd followed earlier was merely a game trail here. Maratelli typed on the keyboard integrated into the sleeve of her tactical outfit. Cade read the message and understood. A sensor net was ahead, heat sensors, game cameras, and microphones. He saw nothing until she highlighted them on the head-up display goggles they all wore. He began typing in response, 'Can you disable?'

She nodded and held up a finger, then typed a response, 'Whoever is monitoring will know as soon as I do.'

That wouldn't work, they needed Guardian to be cooperative. This meant no hostile encounters. If he shot or made any hostile move, Cade knew his team would return fire in an overwhelming fashion. He watched as Maratelli tapped her CommDot and was obviously subvocalizing a conversation with Dee. Soon, she nodded and tapped out something new. 'Dee can lay down a dampening field. It will only work for about fifty meters, but we should be through by then.'

That would cut it close, but it would have to do. A silent countdown started in his visor. When it hit zero, he, Maratelli, and Cochise sprinted down the highlighted path. Once they were out of the net, the visors blinked green. "Any other surprises ahead, LT?" he asked using the common abbreviation for her rank.

"Wouldn't be surprised, sir. Suggest we deploy a few micro drones."

Cade knew the other two were outside the sensor net, so he gave McTee the job of the drones. "Hammer, you are overwatch, get somewhere with a view."

"No threats detected, path to door looks clear," Hammer said several minutes later.

Maratelli went to step onto the single plank step leading up to the rickety porch but froze mid-step. She slowly eased her foot back down to the dirt and crouched down looking under the gray, weathered boards. She sent the image to Cade's goggles.

Pressure switch, no-doubt rigged to blow, he thought. Nodding, he motioned for her to go right while he and Cochise took the left. They could defeat the boobytrap, but he'd rather find another way in. Near the back of the cabin, he saw what he wanted, a door leading directly out to a well-used wood pile. His back against a rubble stone fireplace, he waited for Maratelli to join them. The door was slightly open, as if someone had recently used it or was inviting them to whatever awaited.

"Nomad to Hammer. Any signs of movement?" The call Cade made was barely a whisper, but the comms systems would compensate.

"Negative, Nomad. Scope looks clear," came the reply.

Streams of sweat were trailing down Cade's shoulders and back. *This man better fucking be worth it,* he thought as he leaned in and pushed the door open with his rifle. The door, which was just a collection of planks nailed onto a cross board, swung in noiselessly on well-oiled hinges. Nothing happened. Cade made eye contact with Maratelli who nodded. He gave the signal to Cochise to stay, then he and the lieutenant both entered and swung to opposite sides of the opening.

The goggles compensated for the darkness but gave everything an amber hue. They swept their guns back and forth but found no target. The cabin was not large, just a few rooms, all of which they could see into from where they were standing. A compact kitchen with a table. A chair near a bookcase close to the fireplace. One room that was obviously the bedroom and another adjacent to the kitchen that appeared to be a pantry or storage alcove.

"Check the bedroom," Cade said as he headed over to the small table which was stacked high with books and papers.

"Clear, Nomad."

Cade was already shuffling through the papers and books. Most seemed to be related to UFOs, oceanography, and alternative power sources.

"Nomad, have you seen anything that sensor net would have fed into?" Riley asked from back at The Cove.

He'd flipped his goggles up to look through the papers, as the color was not helpful in picking out details in the low light. He now lowered them back down and activated them to look for power signatures. Cade and Maratelli scanned the interior but came up empty. He heard Cochise chuff from just outside the open door. Then he heard a sound that was totally familiar and completely out of place.

Maratelli began to speak, but he cut her off as the sound came again. It was a sound he heard every time he made himself a drink. Ice cubes clinking against the side of a glass tumbler. He looked again toward the small alcove, raised his assault rifle and selected infrared. This time he clearly saw a figure seated in a chair watching them with a drink in hand.

"Bourbon, the good stuff. Want one?" came the gravelly voice from the dark.

17

"What in the fuck?" Maratelli said as she snapped her rifle in the voice's direction.

The man responded in the same relaxed tone, "Easy there, soldier, no need to get yourself all excited."

Bourbon would be good.

Quiet, Gus, Cade said sub-vocally, quieting his internal dialogue. He lowered his own weapon. "Are we in any danger?" he asked the man.

"Depends," came the very slow and deliberate response. The voice had a southern drawl, maybe Texas, but could have also been intentional.

"Depends on what?" came the quick challenge from Maratelli. *How in the hell had this man just been sitting there watching us? How did he know we were anywhere close, and why was he so fucking calm?*

"Depends on what your intentions are. People around here usually knock when they want to come inside. A man's home is his castle, you know."

Cade watched the man in IR as he waved his empty hand in the air as if to magnify the grandiose surroundings.

"Besides, Florida has a 'stand your ground' law. If a man feels threatened on his own property, he can legally use lethal force to defend himself."

"You intend to use lethal force?" Cade asked as the man took another sip of the drink.

"Hope not," he said letting out a satisfying 'ahhh.' "That would ruin my entire day, not to mention what it might do to yours."

"I think we have the advantage here," Maratelli replied, still chaffing at being beaten at the game she was supposedly a master of now.

"Good, good," the man said, rising slowly, both hands raised. "Works a lot better if you feel that way." He eased out of the shadows and into the dim light of the main room. They could see now he was older, probably late sixties, maybe a bit younger if he'd led an unusually harsh life. He shuffled across the floor, his well-worn slippers making scuffing sounds as he moved. In some ways, the man looked a few days away from assisted living, but Cade felt that was all just illusion, subterfuge.

Not a single thing about the older man was memorable or threatening, yet Cade was borderline terrified. Deep in the darkened corners of his brain, he felt Brutus slowly coming to life. *Easy their, big fella.* Cade reached some kind of mental checkpoint and decided a change in tactics was in order. He removed his assault rifle from around his neck and placed it on the table. "Bourbon sounds great. Where the hell do you keep it?" Maratelli looked at her leader in opened-mouthed disbelief.

The man seemed momentarily surprised by the change, but laughed and motioned to the cabinet over the small cookstove. "If you don't like it neat, I keep a little ice in that cooler over there."

Cade fixed himself a drink, no ice, pulled out one of the three chairs, and sat. He looked up at his partner who was still fuming, her rifle held in a low ready position. "Stand down, HiLo," using Maratelli's combat call sign. "Pretty sure this is what we came for." Turning to the man, he asked, "Is that true?"

"Depends," the old man said again, in the same confoundingly relaxed tone. "Who were you looking for?"

"Guardian," Cade replied using the codename the director had supplied. He sipped the bourbon while eyeing the man closely. He watched for any sign that he'd struck a nerve, the heat of the liquor burning its way down his throat. The man's expression never wavered.

"You want to call your other two men down? That one must be getting cramps by now up in that cottonnwood tree. Just have your dog go lead them in. He knows where the safe path is."

Cade smiled and shook his head. "Team, stand down, approach with caution. Cochise, you are on point," he whispered.

The man's eyebrow raised. "Comms on the dog as well? Must be microscopic. Margaret has access to some pretty sophisticated toys these days."

This was a man who could not be trusted, but someone they needed. He knew that they were with the director, probably just because of the code name he'd given. So far, he'd outplayed them at every turn, but now it was time to get down to business. "Look, um...you have a name? Something we can call you? I'm Rearden," Cade said, hoping to build some level of trust.

"You can call me Samuel."

"Okay, Samuel. I apologize for sneaking in on you, but we think you maybe could help us with a little problem."

"I'm just a crazy, old swamp rat, Mister Rearden. What the hell would I know?" He slung back the final slug of bourbon and placed the heavy tumbler down in front of him with a solid thump.

"Drop the act. We have some of your background," Maratelli said. "You were on a mission several years ago, and we'd like to ask you a few questions about it."

"I had lots of little jobs back then," the man said. "Just kind of a handyman. Lots of work if you didn't mind getting a little dirty."

"Just a regular ole Mister Fixit, huh?" Cade said.

The man nodded and grinned. "You could damn sure say that. What job in particular?"

Maratelli started to speak, but Cade cut her off again. Doris had quietly suggested that he question Guardian first about the missing scientist. Cade took another pull on his drink. "One in which a team of research scientists went missing for several weeks. Maybe something to do with Marie Byrd. We need to know what happened." He did not understand which scientist, or who Marie was, but assumed Samuel did.

"Doesn't ring a bell," the man said, beginning to clean a bit of grime from beneath a fingernail.

Maratelli, who'd been knocked off her game slightly by Cade's change, had refocused her attention. She now looked over at her commander, exasperated. "Can I just shoot him?"

Cade just shrugged,"Your call. I'm not the primary here. My job was to get you two together." He saw Cochise quickly glance in the still open door; subdued voices could be heard just beyond. Cade signaled the dog to stay and guard. "Samuel, I have no doubt you have some surprises for us if this little talk goes sideways, but trust me when I say this, if you don't answer the questions, you will not be the one walking out of here."

Nothing about the threat seemed to bother the older man. Somehow, despite all he saw, Cade still felt they were not the ones in control here.

"Guardian was a long time ago. I've done my best to move on and stay out of sight. Margaret has no right trying to drag me back in."

"No one is dragging you back, sir. We just need a little intel, and then we can be out of each other's way." Maratelli was trying a softer approach now as well. "What do you know about the missing scientists?"

The man sighed. "Tell you what, I'll answer any question you want for say...ten minutes, then we are done. I leave, you leave, and this meeting never happened." Slowly removing an odd looking phone, he set a countdown timer for ten minutes, then waited for Cade and Maratelli to agree. The lieutenant made a questioning look in Cade's direction before nodding her head.

"Ah, yes," the man began. "The polar missions back in the eighties. Supposedly very routine, mapping geomagnetic anomalies and taking ice cores and measuring ozone, air samples, and such. On the surface it seemed like one of a hundred other boring-ass field surveys, but then why would I have been embedded on the team if that was all there was to it?

"Truth was, I had spent years developing my cover as a fixer, as you say, a go between for the scientific community. That's really where I ran into your boss. On this particular one, I was to provide basic security teams and logistics. We were near the South Pole. Cold as a motherfucker down there." Samuel briefly glanced at the lieutenant and feigned apologies before continuing.

"If you read the briefing, you know the pilots dropped us off at the target location. Team was mostly Russian, a few Kazaks, couple of Aussies, and one Brit. I'd been placed there to keep an eye on the russkies, of course. The goal was to drill down some 13,000 feet to an actual lake below the ice. Lake Vostok, perhaps you've heard of it. Enormous freshwater lake under the ice, never freezes. They don't know why. Incredible place, teaming with bizarre life forms where none should be. Stuff none of these guys had ever seen before."

A small chirp notified Cade that Dee was online. "Nomad, my sensors show a significant probability of deceit in what the man is saying."

He didn't need a computer to tell him that. "Come on, Samuel, don't waste the little time you have offered. Stop with the bullshit and get to it. The scientists were mostly American, we know that much already. Also, all of this shit," he motioned to the stack of books and papers, "doesn't concern crypto-zoology."

Samuel smiled, "What can I say? I am a bit of a Renaissance man. My interest is quite....well, varied. Also, the best way to tell a lie is to tell the truth, unconvincingly. But yes, you probably don't want the cover story. That came years later anyway. The creature from Lake Vostok." He made wavy motions with his fingers to dramatize how spooky and fake it was.

"Late 90s, another group of scientists, all from the national science foundation, was also working in the area of the South Pole. I was again embedded with the Navy, VXE—6. They had forward operating bases at Christchurch, New Zealand, and McMurdo Station, Antarctica.

"Those Navy flyboys are hotshots, not just the fighter jocks, but all of 'em. Hell, just keep in mind that jet fuel freezes at temperatures routinely found down there at the end of the earth. One thing I was already aware of was that our aircraft was not allowed to fly over a certain area designated as Roundtop. It was only five miles from the station. They said it was because of air sampling contamination, but that was total bullshit. But, whatever, I learned from one pilot that they'd actually flown over it once due to an emergency medical evac at the Australian camp. The only thing they saw going over to that other camp was a very big-ass hole going down into the ice. The man said he could have flown his LC130 into this thing and back out again with no problem.

"Anyway," he continued, "I accompanied this group from the States to an outlying camp, not too far from that no-fly area. They dropped us with everything we'd need, equipment and food for several weeks. Now I assume you know the official story."

Maratelli shook her head no, but Cade nodded. Ace had dredged up the reports from somewhere. "You were supposed to check-in by radio with McMurdo station every day, but that never happened. They ordered the original flight crew to fly back to the camp to find out if the scientists were ok. They found the camp abandoned, none of you were there, and most of the equipment was missing. No evidence of foul play, no bodies, nothing. They checked that the radio was working. Even called back to McMurdo from the camp to verify comms wasn't the issue."

Cade went on, "They eventually returned to base, where they filed their reports. The weather turned nasty, so several follow-up missions were scrubbed. Everyone assumed the team was dead, frozen solid in a ravine somewhere. Then, two weeks later, they received a radio call from the missing scientists requesting pickup from the same base as if nothing weird had occurred."

The man calling himself Samuel nodded and looked down at his timer. "Did it say what condition the scientists were in? Did it mention that none of them would speak to any of the flight crew nor let the EMTs examine them? Did it also say that within minutes of the flight landing back at McMurdo, an unscheduled and unmarked jet landed with a team that escorted the scientists and all of their gear on board and departed within the hour?"

Cade shook his head. "No, none of that was in the official report."

"Yeah, because that's where the spooks got involved," the man said. "I am one...was one, and those guys scared the shit out of me."

"Where were they taken?" Maratelli asked, the words rushing together, knowing the timer was under two minutes.

"New Zealand, supposedly," Samuel answered. "My guys with VXE-6 said that plane never made it to Christchurch, though, and none of those scientists have ever surfaced again. Can't say what happened after, but someone wanted it to go very quiet."

"But you were with them. You saw what they saw. Why didn't they take you?"

Samuel looked at Marty and winked. "I wasn't on the list. I wasn't part of the scientific team. My cover was good, and the agency I was with would have raised hell had I been 'disappeared.' They made me sign a few dozen more NDAs, all of which, by the way, I am currently violating. Then the brass transferred me out."

"So, what did you and the scientists see?" Maratelli demanded.

"Well, let's just say their mission was not studying the ozone levels. Once we were dropped off, they made a beeline to the middle of the Roundtop no-fly zone. The hole in the ice. Had to cross a section of mountain range to get there. It was a bastard. These guys were not normal scientists, they were tough, precise, ready for battle. They made it clear I was an outsider—I was not allowed to hear any of their conversations." The timer on the phone showed less than a minute.

"Took us three days to reach the place. It was big, I mean holes show up on the ice down there all the time, mostly on the ice shelves out over water. Upwelling of warmer waters melt away at it, but this was over land, up in the hills even, and literally was huge. You could see the entire valley below was interspersed with thermal vents. Fog shrouded the area constantly due to the contrasting temperatures. Not sure anything above could ever see through that, but way down on the floor of the opening was land, not just land, but warmth. Grassy meadows, lakes, rivers, and something else. They forced me to remain up on the ice while the scientific team descended..."

Each of them looked at the phone as the counter hit zero, and the alarm began to softly buzz. Samuel stopped mid-sentence, collected his phone and rose to leave.

"Come on, dude," Cade said. "Give us the rest."

The man they called Guardian just smiled and walked toward the front door. He opened it and turned. "It was a base." With that, he left, shutting the door behind him. Cade raced out the side door and told McTee and Cochise to follow.

"He's gone," McTee called back seconds later.

"What the fuck do you mean, gone?" Cade demanded.

"No one is here. Cochise can't even get a scent. You sure he walked out the door?"

"Yes, godammit, I'm sure. Check the drone feed."

"Already did that," Dee said. "No one ever exited the door of the cabin."

Jesus Christ, Cade thought. *This dude was a ghost.* "Fuck!" He said the word like it tasted bad. They had come to find answers but now had even more questions. *What in the hell does this have to do with anything?* he wondered.

18

"What's our next move, Boss?"

Cade really didn't want to say the words. Really, *effing* didn't want to. "We need to go see that hole."

"In Antarctica?" McTee said in disbelief. The other two looked even less enthused.

"I'm afraid so." He tapped his cheek. "Dee, do we have cold weather gear that will work for this op?"

Her slightly British sounding response was downright cheery. "Of course, Cade, and you are in luck, it is nearly summer in Antarctica. That means twenty-four hours of daylight. Our arctic gear will work easily."

Cade looked at the others who had also heard her response. "I hate to ask, but what's the weather like in the summer?" He made air quotes on the word summer.

"In the area Guardian indicated, the highest recorded temperature is about ten degrees, or negative twelve Celsius. The average, though, is not quite that warm. Figure on an average of zero to ten below. With the strong winds there, though, it will feel much worse."

Somehow, she still sounded upbeat even after delivering that hammer blow of good news. "Um, gee...thanks, Dee. Please send the interview to Doris and the director. Have Riley kit us out a flight and let us know where to meet it. I think we need the rest of Charlie Team on this as well." This meant Deuce would be taking Bravo Team to check out the other areas. He didn't like it, but that was why they had multiple teams.

"Damn, Cap, from the mosquito-laden swamps of South Florida directly to the South Pole. You should open up a travel agency for sadomasochists," McTee said.

Hammer looked at the other soldier and shook his head. "You just learn that big word?"

"Nah, brother, your mom taught it to me last time we hooked up. Sweet woman...I hated working around her prosthetic leg, though."

The linebacker-sized, ex-Navy SEAL looked ready to rip McTee's head off, but then doubled up laughing. "My mom was so mean she probably *did* know what that meant!"

"Cade, do you believe what that guy was saying? Nothing about him rang true," Maratelli said doubtfully. "Now we're going to chase this line of BS all the way to the South Pole?"

"The director said to squeeze him, this is what we got. I don't like it, but hey, at least we aren't battling against a rogue computer program this time. Even if it is a base of some kind, at least that's tangible, something we can see."

"Charlie," he said, tapping his comm and selecting the name for a private call on his SmartCom. Instantly, the other man answered.

"Hey, Rearden, how is Florida? Enjoying the beaches? You sipping on one of them fruity drinks with the tiny umbrella?"

"Not so much," he said, all business. "Hey, looks like we aren't heading back your way after all. We're going to take our vacation party a little farther south. That means you and Nance will be leading the Look-See op around the Caribbean. You good with that?"

"Hell, yeah! I'm the best one for the job anyway, we all know that," his friend said.

"Do we?" Cade asked, grinning to himself.

"Yeah, man. I'm just like you, only prettier and more talented and, oh yeah, only one voice in my head."

Cade came back with, "Right, right...well you may need to be checked out for delusions, but see if you have anyone on Bravo Team that has winter warfare training. Also, feel free to borrow from WarHawk or Raptor squad anyone that has combat engineering experience. You need the SEALS, and I need the Penguins this go round." They quickly reviewed the rosters and agreed on several swaps, including Hammer going back with Bravo. Luckily, they had a diverse group in which almost every discipline and experience was included. "One other thing, friend. I think you should include Greg, or maybe even Micah. I need Alan to be with me." All three were the invaluable genius kids that along with Riley and Jimmy discovered Doris and The Cove back in there early teens.

The boys from The Cove had earned their place on the teams over the last several months. Micah and Greg for drone ops, brains, and fighting abilities. Cade was a bit closer to Alan and respected his range of knowledge and ability to dissect a problem quickly. The truth was, Alan seemed to help keep Cade's own personalities more focused, especially his analyst persona, Ace. The two of them could hold high-level discussions that baffled Cade. The fact that Ace was a part of him seemed absurd. No way he knew what those two were saying half the time.

* * *

"Cade, I have that data packet ready for you," Dee said a short time later.

"Okay. Ready when you are." He held the SmartCom so that the sensors made contact with his palm. She continued to talk while the ReLoad process was underway. The real magic of the system was that he didn't have to focus on it at all. When he went to access the data, it would simply be there. The downside had been an increasing issue with him forgetting big chunks of what he'd just learned. Doris thought it was nothing, but it could be a big problem.

"Much of this is rumor, conjecture, and theory, but Doris did uncover several pieces of official intel also related to the no-fly zone, missing scientists, and possible UFO base," Dee said.

Cade was looking out at the small airfield. They had gotten rooms at a mid-level hotel in a town nearby called Kissimmee. As usual, Cade was not in his room, but outside. The airfield was just across the road, and they'd know when their ride landed. Riley had let him know the Nighthawk engines were not suitable for that level of cold, so they would be taking the modified Gulfstream to Chile and a charter flight from there.

When the phone signaled the upload was over, he began the now familiar task of mentally examining it all. To be very honest, he let his brain's built-in analyst do that. *Ace, let me know if you find anything interesting.* All he got in return was a mental nudge. He took that as a sign to stop bothering him....self. *Jesus, this just keeps getting weirder.*

* * *

Cade shook the new man's rough hand as they boarded the Talon unit's private jet. "Alias. That is your call sign? No shitting me?"

"Name is Joe Smith. My DI at Fort Hood thought it sounded made up or that I was in WitSec or something. Said it would only be funnier if my name was John Doe."

Cade smiled, "Well, welcome to Charlie Team, Alias." He nodded to Alan who was in the back looking a bit nervous. "Did we get everything?"

"Riley sent everything she could think of," Alan said. "Outfitting multiple crews for radically different missions was a challenge, but our girl has it covered."

Cade nodded. He knew the boy was right, but also knew he was totally infatuated with his longtime friend who was quickly growing into a brilliant and attractive scientist. He then turned to the others on board. This small group was his private team of apex predators, and the mission they faced was going to test each and every one of them.

Hammer, who had considerable SEAL training, was heading back north along with Cochise. Cade hadn't wanted to subject the dog to the frozen wasteland anyway, but he was still surprised when Dee informed him that dogs were banned from the continent. Apparently had been since 1993, due to fear that they might transmit canine distemper to the Antarctic seals or would escape and disturb the local wildlife.

Cade hated to see Hammer and the dog go on the other flight.

The warrior part of him relied on trusting his team. They had been so busy the last few months, he'd rarely made it to the Talon unit's training facility, what they referred to as The Nest. After Janus and The Troubles, none of those original team members had quit. New ones were vetted and a few eventually added. Money was no object, and with an official sanction, they could now even draw from active military when needed.

The truth was, they were realizing they needed a special breed of soldier. Smart, adaptable, less confined by rules than most soldiers. Even the makeup of the teams themselves were governed more by the individual mission than by fixed assignments. Cade's counterpart and longtime friend, Charlie 'Deuce' Taylor, was truly the man responsible for the ongoing success of the teams, and even he was now thinking of retirement. Cade wanted the best for his friend. Damn, the man had earned it, but he just couldn't afford to lose him right now.

"Listen up, I know most of you are wondering what in the hell we're doing up here. No warning, no briefing, hell, no training. I promise you there is a reason. This one may be the weirdest one so far, and that's saying something. I also hope you packed your flannel undies, because we're going to freeze our collective nuts off. Sorry, ladies." He grinned as he winked at the three females making up the team.

Alexandra (Alex) Osborne laughed and said, "It's fine, Cap. Maybe if that happens, you will all be forced to learn to think with some other part of your body."

McTee shook his head. "Touché."

19

CARIBBEAN

Ivan Thrall walked forward confidently, arm outstretched, until Richard gently placed a hand on his arm and gave a tiny shake of his head. The people he was meeting weren't concerned with social niceties. Thrall understood at once. These were Richard's replacements for Aksell. The four individuals looked anything but imposing. In fact, they were so ordinary as to be completely forgettable. "You know who I am?" They nodded, nearly in unison.

"They work in pairs," Richard said, apparently now speaking for the still-silent ensemble. "They were the ones that handled our operations in the Gulf of Oman."

Thrall realized how similar they all looked, pale-skinned, thin, somewhat Slavic, close cropped hairstyles. Two, he suddenly realized, were women.

"Best not to ask too much about their history, but suffice it to say they have made a mark and are now persona non grata in their homeland. That is a shame, but plenty of other nations would like to have them, if they only knew who they were."

Thrall nodded, not wanting to know too much more. He handed one of them a memory card. "We have a security issue. Someone is hunting us and our assets. You are familiar with the Sanctuary at Delphi?"

They nodded. "That is to be protected at all cost. Second team will remain aboard the Kalypso in case we need you elsewhere."

One of the females smiled; the others nodded. "ROE?" the one who'd taken the SD card asked in clipped but precise English.

"Do what you have to do, nothing leads back here. You are free to hunt any target that is hunting us. If you are successful, you will have a permanent role here onboard our ship— if you want, of course."

The four turned and walked in military style lockstep back toward the docking bay.

"Chatty bunch, aren't they?" Richard said with a smile.

"Creepy as fuck, man. What the hell do we call them?"

"They are rather cryptic, but I've only heard them refer to themselves collectively as Schattens."

"Shadows," Thrall said, translating the German to English.

20

THE COVE

The numbers streamed across the screen as Jimmy's fingers danced over the keyboard like a maestro performing a concert. Alan's genius little brother, and the youngest member of the original team, had a job, amidst all this chaos, and that was to follow the money, the digital money. With the extensive damage to domestic financial infrastructure, the systems were ripe for theft, embezzlement, and abuse. Margaret had put The Cove's specialized financial unit on tracking down the holes, and Jimmy personally was tasked with monitoring large foreign transactions, incoming or outgoing. Most had been routine stuff, at least so far. He and Doris had developed complex algorithms that predicted weaknesses and then set up honeytraps to watch for questionable transactions. They'd already netted huge transfers tied to both Nicaraguan and Mexican drug cartels, including the one Cade had helped take down.

Jimmy had intercepted nearly a dozen other state-sponsored financial crimes measuring into the trillions. It thrilled the director, as a percentage of all seized funds and assets became hers to control. Currently, The Cove Project took zero dollars in government funding. Money always led to control. Politics and influence did not mix well with enforcement, in her opinion. While Doris's revolutionary inventions and related corporate licensing could easily fund the place, Margaret liked multiple revenue streams, and the less traceable, the better.

Most recently, though, Jimmy had been pulling apart the threads of a more puzzling phenomenon. The streams of data he was monitoring were the real-time movements of money around the world. From stocks and bond sales in the newly expanded Chicago exchanges, to the latest boutique retailers in Paris, to proposed property acquisitions by a consortium of partners based in Abu Dhabi, his program factored in nearly every variable that could be considered from crop harvesting dates in Chile, to the hottest new video game release. The system assigned data-points and relevancy scores based on a system Doris herself had used for years. Jimmy had added some additional overlays to help him visualize the entire system.

Now, he watched the flow of money from hand to hand, almost like a river with hundreds of millions of tributaries. At the micro-level, the data could indicate short-term trends, companies that were under pressure, or an investment that was about to grow big. Zooming out to the macro to see how it all played together was what he was more interested in today. Here, he could see major shifts in wealth on a worldwide basis. The money for that new condo in Seattle came from somewhere. The banks didn't just magically add it to their balance sheet. Seeing the movement on a global scale allowed a perspective that no one else in the world had. Not even the advanced trading AIs used by the gigantic brokerage houses could match this intense level of scrutiny.

Director Stansfield came up from behind and placed a hand lightly on the boy's shoulder. Doris had made it clear that Jimmy was one of 'hers.' She felt he was too young and, very honestly, too talented to be part of Margaret's counterterrorism teams. Still, the director saw the advantages Jimmy's razor-sharp mind could offer. "Did you find it?"

He nodded absently, still staring at the screen, gibberish looking characters streaming past at blinding speed. "It's crypto-trading, and it's happening way too fast to keep up with manually...no way they are using traditional systems."

"Is it what you thought? Is someone stealing large sums of money without even being noticed?"

Jimmy turned and looked at her. "Director, I believe someone is planning to bankrupt the country." He gestured to move some of his displays to the large screen overhead. "Cryptos are popular because they are so secure...like ridiculously secure. You want to steal some bitcoin? All you need to do is find your victim's 16-character public key and calculate their private key by solving something called an 'elliptic curve discrete logarithm problem.' Easy peasy, right?" He smiled.

He went on, "Not so fast. You see, with a regular computer, that little operation will take you around 50 million years. That is the beauty of blockchain security. Not only is it private, it is designed to make sure that only the owner can access it, but it also requires another public key encryption system to make sure the owner has the right to spend it."

Margaret nodded. "How does that help us?"

Jimmy continued, "That level of confidence in a currency system that is totally digital is remarkable. Luckily, Bitcoin, the credit card companies, and PayPal made virtual money an easy thing to accept. It was painless, and so the step to an even tighter, encrypted form was a no-brainer." The display now showed a familiar object, one of many the quantum servers used at The Cove. "What has changed is these."

He smiled. "What may have seemed impossible to crack yesterday, today...not so much. With the right quantum computer, which can process information at speeds exponentially faster than today's best binary computers, suddenly, what might seem uncrackable becomes mere child's play. Crypto blockchain encryption can now be broken in under ten minutes with a quantum system. Ten minutes is, coincidentally, the same amount of time most transactions take to complete."

"So, they can potentially intercept every crypto trade in the country?" Margaret asked, eyes wide in amazement.

"In the world, to be honest. But since the U.S. seems to be the main target right now, and since all trades and owners are private, they can set up a never-ending funnel to route money out of the U.S. for good. The biggest issue for them may well be where to store it all."

"Can we plug the drain—stop the flow?" Margaret asked.

"I'm not sure we can, not in time," Jimmy answered. "The big cryptocurrency banks have fought hard to avoid government scrutiny and any official oversight. This is where it's going to bite them in the proverbial butt. You see, most of their transactions are blind even to them, one of the beautiful aspects of the blockchain currency system. Also, most governments want these guys to fail. They have been a pain in the public coffers since they got started. Once Washington figures out that the bulk of American wealth is in bitcoin, and it's all draining away—well, it will be too late."

"Surely, the Bitcoin guys have expected this and have automatic stop limits in place," the director said in frustration. Janus had nearly wrecked the country, and she, more than most, knew it was hanging on by just a thread.

"Yes, to part of that. They have indeed anticipated it, but by all accounts, it is a problem for fifteen, maybe twenty years from now. Not today—no one besides us should have a quantum computer system that is capable of such a thing."

Margaret looked away from the screen, trying to gather her thoughts. She recalled tracking Quantum computer shipments when they were looking for Janus. They weren't the only ones to have them. "Jimmy, tell me, how much money are we looking at?"

The young boy rotated his chair to face her and recited from memory, "Five years ago, well before Janus, cryptocurrency globally held around a hundred billion dollars. Today that number is closer to sixty trillion dollars with almost forty trillion of that directly tied to America."

"And someone is cleaning out our bitcoins."

"Oh, yeah. Not yet at any wholesale level, but significantly. Obviously, if anyone thought their bitcoin was vulnerable to theft, the confidence in the system would evaporate. Overnight, the valuation would plummet, so whoever is doing this is staying just below the radar."

"So, you have no idea who's behind it?" she asked.

"I didn't say that," Jimmy said with a grin. He clicked a few keys, and a cartoon avatar of a battered knight in armor showed on the screen with a cryptic name underneath.

"Hex?" Margaret said quizzically. "His name is Hex?"

"Her name," Doris said. "Jimmy and I are relatively sure Hex is a female."

"Hex was her hacker name back in the day, pretty much dropped off the grid a little over three years ago," Jimmy clarified.

"Do you know who she is? Why do you think this is her work?"

"We are not certain, but some of the programming hacks have a certain pattern that is distinctive, very much like her previous work," Doris said. "It is my assumption she has moved from the JV to the pro levels. As for how we know it is a she...well, Jimmy has had a crush on her for years."

The avatar was replaced by a picture of a beautiful, but very young girl, of about fifteen. "Ruslana Kilma. Czech authorities arrested her for an online extortion scheme of an Italian shipping company back in 2004. This picture was the only one ever taken. Somehow, the evidence disappeared before formal charges could be drafted, and the girl was released. She hasn't been seen since."

"Okay," Margaret said. "We know what is happening. We know at least one of the people behind it. How do we find her, and how can we stop it?"

21

SOUTH AMERICA

Hey, ummm...

The annoying buzzing sound of Ace's internal monologue roused Cade from a restless sleep. The internal humming, mumbling sound of Ace speaking reminded him of a cat attempting to wake from a long nap.

Glancing at the wall display, he saw that the Gulfstream G650 was somewhere over the eastern coast of South America. "Yeah, hot shot, what did you find?" Cade spoke the words aloud as he found himself doing more often. Others listening would assume he was talking to someone back at The Cove.

Well, a lot, but actually not much. Cade grimaced in aggravation with the genius's total lack of adult communication skills.

A lot of what we have on the oddities of the continent are more like a bad sci-fi movie script than fact, but based on everything Doris provided, here is my best guess: First, the Nazis did not put a secret base in Antarctica, although they did explore it. Mainly the coastal regions. As did the U.S., particularly in the 1940s. Operation Highjump was the largest and was billed as a military training exercise, presumably to get troops ready to fight in Siberia if needed. What we learned after the Soviet Union fell is more telling. They claim that the man behind Operation HighJump was Admiral

Byrd. Claimed that his subs were attacked by UFOs launching from beneath the water. I have to file that under doubtful, but the source was highly credible. A few other facts are that a significant gravitational mass is beneath one portion of the continent, an area known as the Wilkes Land. It is very likely a meteor, or possibly volcanic, but seems out of place, and it exerts a very high gravitational field.

So far, no hard scientific evidence of aliens, UFO bases, or missing scientists, but there are some corollaries between what Samuel said and the known facts. First, there are a lot of restricted areas on the continent. Far more than would seem reasonable, even with the number of nations involved in ongoing research there.

Second, the melt holes all over Antarctica are a fact. Some quite large and all without a truly good scientific reason. The temperature is well below freezing, yet these areas can be nearly free of ice. Lastly, is his mention of the monster of Lake Vostok. This is the part that he labeled as 'Fake News.'

The lake is an enormous freshwater lake, 160 miles long and 30 miles wide. It is buried under two-and-a-half miles of ice, and a team of scientists did drill down in 2012. They also stopped communicating with the base for almost five days. While that seems to mesh with some of the other more outlandish portions, no bizarre creatures or alien bases were down on the lake. They did, however, discover thousands of new species. Creatures that were completely alien to scientists up to that point.

"Alien as in alien or...something extraterrestrial?" Cade asked his analyst persona.

Um, no, no, nothing like that. Creatures that are familiar, or at least somewhat familiar to us. Some descendants from very ancient evolutionary lines. That lake has been isolated for eons.

"So, going through that massive data dump, you don't think we'll find anything at those coordinates?"

Didn't say that. In fact, quite the opposite. I believe we will. I just wouldn't put money on it being anything inhuman.

Somehow, that possibility disturbed Cade more than the alternative.

22

The Punta Arenas International Airport in Chile looked to Cade like lots of others he'd been in. The team pilot, Brenda 'Chaps' Morgan, helped McTee toss the gear bags onto the trailer, then followed the team to the awaiting aircraft. The temperature here was already near freezing. The transition from the mild sub-tropical to here was already having an effect. Several members were already digging through packs for coats and gloves. "That one is ours," Chaps said, motioning at an ancient looking jet.

"We're parking the Nighthawk for that?" Cade asked, bewildered.

She laughed, "Yeah, our birds aren't rated for the cold or violent wind gusts. Wouldn't be safe. That's a British Aerospace 146. She's old, but handles this flight every day. I will sit second seat."

Cade knew that meant co-pilot. Chaps made the calls in air travel. That was her specialty, and she was rated on nearly every kind of bird there was. But if she wanted an experienced Antarctic pilot at the controls, he was in full agreement.

"We will go over the Drake Passage," she added. "Only about a two-hour flight to the coast of Antarctica, but some of...scratch that." She drew in a breath. "It is the worst, most unpredictable weather and air currents on the planet. They will land on the Shetland Islands; we have arranged for a large Soviet transport chopper to ferry us as close to the no-fly zone as possible."

"Cade?" He signaled Chaps to carry on while he took the incoming call from The Cove.

Tapping his CommDot as he began looking for his own bag of warm weather gear, he said, "Go ahead, Riley, what's up?"

"The director wanted you to know Bravo Team will be on location by 1100 hours local."

Cade mentally adjusted the time in his head and pictured his friend, Charlie, going through the procedures. Deuce's team was being split around the Caribbean to investigate numerous attacks and fish kills to hopefully pinpoint where the missing space probe landed. "Thanks, Riley," he said, now looking around the almost vacant airport. Something had gotten his attention, but he was unsure what. "Keep me posted on their progress, please. Thanks for all the goodies you sent us, too. Not sure what we may need, but I think you probably sent it, regardless. Anything else?" Cade noticed a slim figure near one hangar. Someone who seemed to be paying way too much attention to them, so he began walking in that direction.

"Yes, I followed up on the Sinolean gang member you were asking about. I think it's safe to say he cracked pretty quickly under some rather intense interrogation. I have the full transcripts and can send them to your SmartCom."

Cade paused mid-step and thought for a moment; he had to stay focused on his current op, going through all that would be an unnecessary distraction. "No, Riley, just scan it quickly. Does it mention anything related to this mission?" Ace seemed to feel that there was a connection.

"He said they were being funded by someone local to disrupt the locals, make raids along the border. Not drug money, but someone else. Someone they only referred to as Leon. So, is that why you thought it might be connected to what all is going on?" she asked.

Their comms system was so clear he could hear her mouthing words as she silently read. He began walking toward the hangar again only to realize whoever he had been looking at was, in fact, not a person, just some machinery half hidden in the dim shadows. Still, his instincts had registered a threat, something here was off.

"Search is complete," Riley continued. "Nothing else seems relevant. His group was originally part of La Lineas, which was taken over by the Sinaloa, who have been gaining ground for years. Apparently, many of the gangs are working together now and have a network all over South and Central America. The push into the U.S. is part of a coordinated move to keep our enforcement occupied and to take advantage of us. They want to 'keep the U.S. on its knees,' in his words. He implied several times they have some serious power backing them but has yet to say who it is. The interrogation team seems to think it may be a foreign power, so they are pursuing that angle. If the cartel can open up that southern border, then every terrorist in the world could waltz right in."

Cade was about to log off when he, or more accurately, Ace considered something. "Riley does Leon mean anything in Spanish, I mean you know...other than a name?"

She had to look it up as she wasn't immediately sure. "Yes, Nomad. It means Lion."

Something was there, maybe a connection. He told her thanks.

Before signing off, she asked him a favor. "Keep an eye on Alan for me, okay?"

Cade looked over at the boy, no longer a kid really, as he finished loading equipment onto the old plane. "He'll be fine, don't worry. Riley, do one other thing; Cochise is heading back your way. I figured the South Pole wasn't a destination he'd be pleased with. See if Jaz can keep an eye on him til I get back." His growing attachment to the dog was beginning to border on more than just Cade's reliance on him in the field. The dog was tough as nails but also made Cade feel more human, more...normal.

"Roger that, Cap."

* * *

Cade slid into a seat near the rear of the plane. Alan was leaning up against the window, staring out at the rocky terrain beyond the airport. The boy had a terrible crush on Riley, and Cade was pretty sure her feelings for Alan went well beyond the simple bonds of friendship. Still, neither seemed to be able or willing to cross whatever invisible boundary lay between them.

"Hey, Nomad."

Cade smiled as he attempted to get comfortable in the well-worn seats. "Hey, dude, having fun yet?" Alan was one of Cade's favorite people from The Cove, innocent and yet, somehow wise at the same time.

"Just working through some stuff in my head."

Cade laughed, "Yeah, we do that all the time." He patted the boy's arm. "Mission stuff?" he asked, already knowing the answer.

"Nah." Alan's head shook as he sighed. "Me and Riles, I mean...you know," Alan said, a slight, rosy blush crossing his cheek.

The always blossoming, but never quite maturing, romance between Alan and Riley was one of the more pleasant activities among the staff. Pleasant for Cade, an outsider, but no doubt, it was causing a great deal of angst for the two of them. These kids had sacrificed their childhoods to the machine buried in the depths of the old listening station back in Georgia. While a part of him cared deeply for Doris, another couldn't quite forgive her for some of the choices she'd made along the way.

"Women...huh?" Cade responded with a grin. "Look, man, it'll work out. Don't sweat every little detail."

"But what if this is just an adolescent crush, you know? Because of the ReLoad process, none of us went through puberty until really late," Alan said.

Cade held up his hand, "Whoa, too much detail there, amigo. Kid, I know nothing about relationships. Never had a serious one, not even that many casual ones. My emotional compass tends to run more to the rage side of the spectrum, but my gut says you guys are right for each other. You are already best friends, she adores you, and obviously you, her. Don't force it."

"So, I shouldn't ask her out? What if she dates someone else?"

"If it's destiny, then it's not a race. Ask her out," Cade said as he began slowly flipping the pages on the briefing documents on his phone. "Or don't." He paused briefly, then added, "Maybe." He turned to face Alan, then continued. "Maybe just ask her what she wants. For now, though, get your head in the game, where we are going will need your total focus."

Cade looked away and whispered under his breath, "Thanks, Gus."

23

CARIBBEAN

The boat made a scraping sound as Kissa pulled it high onto the sandy beach. His life up to now had been anything but easy. Growing up in Isla El Tigre, one of the poorest sections of Honduras, like many of the village children, he'd never known his parents. They had left him, maybe even sold him, to someone when he was an infant. He'd battled his way through school, first with his fist, later with his brain, only to be drafted into the military. There, he'd seen brutality beyond his worst nightmares. It had taken determination and some determined friends to finally get him into college. Even there, he struggled, but had finally excelled. Today, though, was undoubtedly the worst one of his tormented life. Today he lost Thera....today he met a monster.

He sat on the beach looking out at the dark water. The gentle sound of the waves hitting the reef a hundred yards out would normally be a comfort, but not tonight. His head fell to his chest, and he wept. The tears wouldn't stop, his body racked with the sobs of loss. His mind roiled at the thoughts of what had happened. Could he have done more, could he have saved her, and what was that thing? He was not an ignorant man; he was not a fearful person. He'd spent his entire life around the ocean, but he knew that thing was evil; it was death, and it had taken his love.

Like him, Thera had no family, no one who would miss her return. A few long-time friends from school, but they were used to not seeing them for months as their work regularly took them to remote spots. He should tell someone, file a missing person report, but even that was a questionable move. The police here were some of the most corrupt anywhere. Most were simply paid security for the MS13 and Barrio18 gangs. They would simply arrest and convict him of her death or turn him over to the gangs to be used as a fighter. No one would investigate, no one would care.

His fingers dug deep into the wet sand, the frustration and rage building inside. Who could he trust? Who could he turn to?

* * *

As the incoming tide began lapping at his feet, Kissa opened a single puffy eye. The eastern sky was lightening, dawn less than an hour away. The night had been restless. Twice he thought he saw the underwater light far off in the distance. At some point during the night, a plan had formed. Not a great one, but a plan, nevertheless. He'd been a soldier, a good one. He'd even fought against the rebel forces, alongside some of the most capable the U.S. could covertly provide. His squad and the Rangers had battled the so-called Neuvo Contras for weeks, pushing them deep into the jungle. Many of those rebels were now running the local gangs. He'd made some friends back then. Perhaps they would be able to help. First, he had to get somewhere his phone would work. Guanaja was too remote. He needed to get back near the village on El Tigre, or even the mainland.

Was the monster out there waiting for him? Could he even explain what had happened? No one would believe the thing he saw; he didn't even believe it. If it had been hovering in the sky, there would at least be a word for it. A UFO, but underwater...what in the hell did you call those?

24

The tide was going out, Kissa knew that it was time to get moving. If the 'beast' had wanted to take him, it had plenty of opportunity. Still, something nagged at him, something he'd overlooked. Kissa was a methodical man. Like most divers, he was a creature of habit and routine. Check your gear, then check it again. It was how you stayed alive out here. He felt sure, though, he was leaving something overlooked. Thera was gone. That had to be all it was. She had been his world, but he was doing her no good out here. He needed help and finally thought he knew who to ask.

He tossed the gear bag in, then pushed the heavy boat into the light surf. He let the incoming waves do the heavy lifting for him, timing his push to coincide with the wave. A lifetime around boats and the ocean caused his actions to be instinctual. It was just one more instance of how you did things. Be in balance with nature, not fighting against it. As the boat bobbed in the water, he climbed aboard and lowered the engine back into the water.

'Nature,' that was what had pushed Kissa out here. It was what carried him through college, then post grad studies. At some point, he would go for his doctorate in marine biology, but he was in no rush. He and Thera both loved studying the ever-changing ocean life. She had been the spark that ignited the fire in him. After his term in the Army was up, he needed an outlet, something to take his mind off the violence, the deaths, the killing. She started taking him on her diving trips, eventually getting him certified for open-water and the tougher adventure diving rating.

Tears clouded his eyes as the salt spray kept blowing back from the bouncing bow. He refused to look around at the receding island or the place where he'd lost her. He tried to make peace with the fact that she probably would have preferred to meet her end out here, but that didn't bring him any comfort. Whatever had killed her was still around. Kissa was not a man ruled by fear; a past like his own didn't allow for that, but what he'd seen had made him feel weak, powerless even. Even as he pushed the boat across the open sea, he wanted to glance behind. Was there a dark shape pursuing him just below the water? Was that a bright light rising from the depths ahead?

It took four hours and most of his remaining fuel and nerves for Kissa to reach the small island of Cayo Cochinos. The island had nothing on it but an old dock and repair yard for local boats. A hurricane a decade earlier had stripped the siding from the repair shop and the other buildings. Kissa knew the island well. He kept an extra supply of fuel hidden away there, and it was useful for one other reason.

He tied off the dive boat and unsteadily climbed the rusty metal ladder to the dock. Damaged boat hulls, engine parts, chains, and tools lay scattered around the repair yard. He crossed the sandy ground to the remnants of the shop. Large metal beams rose out of a cracked concrete floor to a roof that was more missing than present. Rusty sheets of tin were peeled back along the roof like an onion skin. Metal pails held the remnants of a lifetime of repair jobs, nuts and bolts all rusted into a single mass. Buckets of viscous, tar-like grease, with a variety of insects and assorted bird feathers embedded in it. More chains, wooden blocks, and less identifiable parts.

At the far end of the shop, a set of metal stairs led up to what was an elevated office and parts room. Kissa's bare feet climbed the rusty steps, the metal treads cutting into his feet with each step. Nearing the landing, he looked northward and could just make out Ragged Key. The one other advantage of this island was, if you could get high enough, it was close enough to Utilla to sometimes get a cell phone signal.

* * *

Hours later, Kissa nearly threw his phone onto the slabs of limestone rocks far below. He'd called every place he knew trying to find his old friends. Admittedly, the numbers he had for them were years old. Maybe they hadn't made it through The Troubles, he didn't know. Finally, he'd gotten someone at Veterans Affairs where he'd waited on hold for a near eternity, only to learn that one of his friends was listed as killed in action on a training mission the previous year. *Shit!*

He sat back in frustration; he'd fought to keep thoughts of Thera out of his head. He simply couldn't do anything with that. Maybe she was dead, maybe the thing took her. He wasn't sure which of those might be better. He made one more call, a hotline number the VA had offered. He left his information and the little he knew about the Army sergeant he was looking for, then disconnected.

From his daypack, Kissa removed a small black plastic case. It unfolded into a mini solar panel into which he plugged his phone, which was close to dead. He also retrieved his last bottle of water. It was warm and tasted of plastic. He leaned back, wishing desperately that it was a nice cold beer instead. He couldn't stay here much longer. He and Thera hadn't brought supplies for an extended trip, just the essentials. Going back home would mean questions, possibly from the police. He knew he had to at some point, but wanted to have a plan before then. If the Americans couldn't help, who else could he call? He lay back on the metal platform and closed his eyes, not daring to think about what was to come.

He awoke later to the trilling sound coming from his phone. "Yes, hello?" he answered, in near panic.

"You were looking for Sergeant Charlie Taylor or Captain Cade Rearden?" the female voice asked in flawless Spanish.

"Si, yes, yes." *Captain,* he thought. *Rearden must have been promoted before he was killed.* "They were Rangers. Both with the 75th Regiment, I believe. It was many years ago. I was told that the...um captain lost his life last year. I am very sorry to hear that; I was hoping one of them possibly could help."

The woman seemed like a typical military type, not really wanting to waste time on small talk. "You are calling from a small island in the Caribbean?"

Kissa's panic began to rise; he suddenly feared he'd made a huge mistake. Someone in the Honduran military intelligence must have intercepted his calls. They had tracked him; they would send people to bring him in to see what was so important for him to tell the Americans.

As if reading his silent panic, the voice said calmly, "We are not with your government or police. Can you tell me what the nature of your problem is and why you feel these men could be of help?"

Kissa's shoulders sagged, his heart was racing, and he had no idea if the woman was being honest, but felt he had nothing to lose at this point. He told her everything. She asked a few very intelligent questions but mostly stayed silent while he talked.

"I have your information, if your story has merit, I will be back in touch later today."

"Um, thank...thank you, thank you so much," he stuttered, unsure of whether to be relieved or even more worried.

"Can I ask your name, maybe who you are with?"

"I am Doris." The line went dead.

25

ANTARCTICA

The flight from Chile took over four hours because of weather along the Drake Passage. The BAe 146 followed the west side of the Antarctic Peninsula. The flight was the worst he'd ever been on. The wild turbulence and random air pockets made the trip seem more like a roller coaster than normal transportation. Cade watched as a ridge of peaks appeared.

"Ellsworth Mountains," Alan said pointedly. "We will fly right up the spine of 'em."

Cade should have known the kid would have all the geography already committed to memory.

"We'll land on an ice runway on Union Glacier. Riley has a shuttle to get us over to the base camp."

"Ice runway?" Cade asked. "Two words that should never be said together, in my opinion."

Alan continued, "The flight toward the pole is all dependent on the weather. It would normally be a four or five-hour trip. There is a permanently manned base at the pole, Amundsen-Scott Station, but since we aren't going all the way, we won't visit them. Our cover is a seismology research group from California. You should get a ReLoad boost, so you can sound somewhat knowledgeable."

"Who in the fuck are we going to run into down there that might quiz me about earthquakes?" Cade asked. "I'll just say I'm security—basically the truth anyway." Cade knew their destination was somewhere in the mountains between base camp and the pole. Looking down at the endless brilliant expanse of snow and ice they were heading into, he wondered again if this was just him being crazy or if there were a real purpose.

* * *

Cade stomped his feet; he couldn't seem to get close enough to the heat radiating from the gas stove. Landing hours earlier on the ice had been as frightening as he'd feared, but exiting into the extreme cold and howling wind defied even his worst expectations. "This is summer?" he asked to others nearby. The dozen individuals looked at the recent arrivals with what seemed a mixture of pity and amusement.

"Drink this, Rearden," Alex said, handing him a bottled water.

"Not th... th... thirsty, Cutter," he said fighting to keep his teeth from chattering.

"Drink it," she ordered. As the unit's medic, she made the calls on this. "Despite what you think, Antarctica is a desert—one of the driest places on Earth in fact. Some places here haven't seen rain or snow in two million years."

His gloved hands grasped the bottle, and he downed the icy liquid. Obviously, Alex had gotten the uploaded Antarctic briefing. Now she was just a fountain of fun facts. *How long are we staying here? Do we have to go back out there? Um, this place sucks.* Cade had trouble distinguishing between his own thoughts and those from his other 'travelers.' "Shit, we're all miserable," he said aloud. They'd been in Antarctica for less than three hours. Somehow, the fact that this had been his idea made it even worse. *That fucking Samuel better not have been lying about this shit,* he thought.

* * *

"Helos are grounded, Rearden," McTee said in frustration. "Every damn thing on this continent depends on the weather."

"Clock is ticking—I don't think we have time to waste. What are our other options?" Cade asked.

Doris answered, surprising them both, "I can arrange for two tracked vehicles. What would be about three hours by air will take a minimum of two days by ground."

"But we would be less dependent on the locals and the weather, right?"

"Affirmative, Captain."

"How confident are you that you can navigate us safely to the coordinates Guardian supplied?"

She didn't respond immediately. Cade had gotten used to this; Doris liked to be precise, so she was undoubtedly looking at all parameters, risks, team dynamics...probably factoring in what they all had eaten for breakfast. "Navigating your vehicles to the spot I can do with near certainty. I am unable to compute the same odds on the reliability of the SnowCats, nor will I be able to foresee all the terrain hazards. My confidence on all factors is about 76%."

"About?" Cade asked, surprised. "That doesn't sound like you."

"I have discovered that giving the specific and more accurate percentage doesn't elicit a more positive reaction from humans. Unless I am having discussions involving finances. Then, it does seem to matter a great deal."

"Smith and I can check out the transports, make sure they're mechanically sound," McTee said. "What terrain issues are you uncertain of?"

"Crevasses," she said at once. "Hidden ice cracks primarily. The average depth of ice on the continent is one mile. Some crevasses are quite deep and can have a layer of snow and ice covering them at the surface. I believe I can modify the LIDAR system on the satellites to help identify the worst ones."

"Lovely," Cade said.

"Yes, some of the terrain features in Antarctica are considered extremely beautiful."

"He was being sarcastic, Doris," McTee said.

"Oh," she responded, a bit embarrassed.

* * *

The group loaded the last of the gear onto the MARs-1 HMMWV. The team's two gear-heads had checked out the tracked behemoths and declared them to be in excellent shape. It was an ugly thing, the front end and drivetrain of a military grade Humvee, but with what looked like an enormous motorhome attached to its back. Instead of wheels, it had a track assembly where wheels would have been, and the entire thing pulled a supply trailer.

"Damn thing will pull anything, go anywhere almost," the man who'd delivered the two trucks said with a distinct Australian accent. "Sorry, pal, name's Judah...Judah Wilson. These are my babies."

"Thanks, Judah," Cade said genuinely. Doris had somehow acquired the transportation quickly. "My team really appreciates it. We have a brief window to get all of our work here done."

The man eyed Cade a bit suspiciously. "Your work...yeah." He then let out a deep laugh. "Scientists."

It sounded more like a question than a statement. Cade decided to just ignore it.

Judah leaned in, a smile plastered across his face, "Look, mate, you are soldiers, maybe adventure-seekers, plain for everyone to see. Believe me, we know what research teams look like and—well, you damn sure ain't it." The man backed away a few steps and put his hand up. "Totally your business, though, for what your boss lady paid for these trucks, you can do what ya want."

Cade idly wondered if Doris had simply bought the massive transports instead of renting them. "What's the range on these?"

"Unlimited, as long as you have fuel. Extra-large tanks are good for about 700 kilometers, and I have two spare drums in the trailer. Diesel, of course, but the spare fuel must be kept somewhat warm, or it will be useless to you." The man eyed Cade once again. "Look, friend, Antarctica is not some tiny island, damn thing is fifty percent larger than the

U.S. From here to Amundsen at the pole is the equivalent of driving from California to Denver. Are you sure you and your team are ready for that? Believe me, this place will do it's best to kill you."

Cade didn't dismiss the man's warning, "We aren't going to the pole."

"Doesn't matter—McMurdo, Erebus, anywhere really. Once you leave here, it is all going to look exactly the same." The older man smiled and added, "I would be willing to help you out. I know this place. Been here 'bout half my life."

Cade thought about it as he got another one of the odd sensations that something was a bit hinky. Always hard as fuck for him to know if it was one of his other 'travelers' just stirring in his sleep or maybe an actual something. He ignored Judah and scanned the small compound. No real place for anyone to be hiding. If it wasn't stark snow white, it was a closed building. Those had no windows and as few doors as possible. A wintery draft here could be fatal. Still, his reptile mind registered the threat, even if he couldn't see one. The paranoia didn't seem to extend as far as the Aussie, though. Going against the original plan, he invited the man to come along as the lead driver. He also promised to sell the man the vehicles back once they were done for a very reasonable discount.

"Doris."

"Yes, Captain?" was her always near-instant reply.

"I assume Judah checks out. Can you run scans on all other occupants of this base camp?"

"Judah is solid," she answered. "Former commando in the Australian Defense Force. He's been on the ice for almost twenty-seven years. I would not have contracted with him had there been any concerns. He has a bit of a predilection for gambling and drinking, but I am beginning to understand that is not rare among soldiers. I am running the rest of the camp now, but I see a problem."

"Talk to me," Cade said as he looked through their supplies and then carried a small suitcase back toward the main lodge.

"It will take some time to process facial recognition on everyone you and your team have encountered. That said, I have discovered a discrepancy between the camp's arrival logs and the number of heat signatures showing up on scans. There is one person more than is registered in the check-in logbook."

The itch along his spine began again. "How unusual would that be? I'd assume people come and go from here regularly."

Doris agreed. "They do, but this would still be highly irregular. You are in one of the least forgiving environments on Earth. No one ventures out without checking out and someone knowing when or if to expect them back. Standard safety protocols. Someone near you is choosing to ignore that. I suggest you watch your back, Captain."

26

"Captain, are you in a position to speak freely?"

Cade was caught off-guard. He was in the middle of putting on the skin-tight and highly advanced Rapide Battlesuit. They weren't expecting combat, but Riley had suggested it was more than capable of protecting them from the harsh environment. The suits fit almost like a second skin, and once they were on, it was the single most comfortable garment he'd ever owned. Getting in and out of the son of a bitch was an entirely different matter, though. "Ye..es," he gasped out as he rolled one massive thigh into the seemingly too small leg opening.

"Your heart rate is elevated, and you seem to be in distress, are you sure this is a good time?"

"Yes, Doris, what do you want?"

"Are you having sex? I detect no other heat signatures around you, which would indicate you must be doing it alone?"

"Doris, stop fucking with me, what do you want?"

She laughed. Admittedly, arguing with a computer, no matter the intelligence, had more than an element of absurdity. Still, Doris was developing a truly wicked sense of humor, unfortunately not always expressing itself at completely optimum times.

"Sorry, Cade." She rarely used his first name, so he felt she truly was contrite...or one of her sub-routines told her it was an appropriate response to defuse any tension. Actually, not all that different from what most humans did. "This is not related to your current mission, but you know that I routinely monitor your old contact numbers, and my Prime entity handles switchboards for a lot of government agencies."

Prime had been one of the cover identities to a massively fucked up AI called Janus. As Prime, he had become the go-to digital assistant for most of the U.S. government departments and agencies. When Doris had finally defeated him, she had smoothly inserted herself into that role—partially to keep the fact that one of their own AIs had caused so much of the damage, but also to balance some egos and insanity regularly in play in Washington.

"So, someone called in looking for me? Like an old girlfriend or something? "Cade asked.

"You wish," she said in a voice that was way more snarky than necessary.

She was probably also right about Cade wishing. Truthfully, he was a ghost. There was no one from his old life, or childhood even, that would ever look for him. Other than a few Army buddies, his only friends were right here or inside his own head.

"The man didn't give a name but was calling from a very small island off the coast of Honduras." She filled him in on the main points of the call.

Cade was initially baffled but had managed to get the rest of the Battlesuit on and already felt the warmth spreading across his body. "I did a few missions down in South and Central America. How do you know this isn't just someone fishing for information?"

"His voice analysis indicated sincerity and distress. He was very upset but trying hard to mask it. Also, he asked for either Deuce or you."

Cade knew Charlie was also on a mission, so Doris likely wouldn't have bothered him about it yet. Someone opened the outside door, and a blast of cold air hit him before the suit could compensate.

"Damn, the Caribbean sounds really good, Doris. Can I just go ask him what he wants?"

"I tracked his phone—it was never registered to an individual, which, on its own, isn't very unusual in some areas. I am running a trace on calls registered to the number. Several to a local university. Most to another similarly unregistered number, and that is about it. We do have a potential image captured at an ATM outside a Utilla dive shop. According to the timestamp, the phone was in use at that time and in that immediate area. I will send you the picture while I run a facial match."

The feeling of being watched again was back, and Cade scanned the small group around him before pulling up the image on his SmartCom. The grainy black and white picture showed a compact man with dreadlocks and a complexion that was so dark that few features were even recognizable. Cade still knew who it was instantly. "Warlock," he said. "After all these years, what are the odds?"

"So, he is a friend?" Doris asked. "I have found a service record for someone named Kissa, but show no deployments that match your service record."

"You wouldn't. All that was totally off the books. Illegal as hell to be honest, but...well, evil people were doing evil shit and had to be stopped. Yes, he is a friend, can you call him back? I don't know what I can do to help him from down here at the ass-end of the earth, but I owe him. Charlie and I both do. He's a good guy, Doris."

* * *

Cade held up the departing convoy for the call. Ten minutes later, Doris connected him to his old friend. "Kissa, how are you doing?" The man was way too smart to stay a soldier. Cade remembered him as resourceful, funny, and tough. One of the most capable people he and Charlie had ever worked with. To be honest, most of the rest of the Honduran squad were a joke, especially the commanders. But Kissa stood out, and over the months, a tight bond had developed between the three of them. Whatever had rattled this man was a cause for concern.

"Cade?" the voice said uncertainly. "I was told you were dead. The woman, Doris...sorry, I mean...I assumed it would be Deuce that called. I hoped to reach one of you, I just didn't know where else to turn."

"I was dead...but I got better," Cade joked. "Look, friend, I am about to head off into the boonies, but bring me up to speed. What's wrong, and more importantly what do you need?"

Kissa began to tell Cade what all was going on. The man's voice cracked as he described the underwater encounter and not being able to find Thera afterward. Cade was saddened by the news but unsure what about this warranted some former SpecOps buddies. "Rearden, it was a monster, something out of a horror movie."

His girlfriend was missing, Kissa assumed she was dead, and the 'monster' that he described had pursued him. That had gotten Cade's attention. He knew the man wasn't one to make shit up. He'd been energetic and generally upbeat but certainly not one to exaggerate. He liked facts. "Kissa, are you or Thera working on anything...well, you know...anything others might not want you nosing around about?" He was thinking again of the gangs and drug trade coming out of South America.

The sound of the connection went silent and Cade wondered if his friend had dropped the phone. Finally, Kissa said, "You mean something illegal? No, Cade, never. I'm an oceanographer now. I haven't carried a gun in years. We both work with the university."

Cade swung his pack up off the floor and tightened the straps. "What did..." he stopped himself mid-sentence. "Sorry, what does Thera do?"

"She is a geneticist specializing in oceanic life forms. Her official title is Doctor of Evolutionary Engineering. She is very good at it, did some really groundbreaking work right out of grad school with some major drug companies looking for new biological treatments for Alzheimer's and such. Made a name for herself, and now she's studying the ancient history of large invertebrates, but more recently, she's been helping me track the decline of whale sharks in the Caribbean."

Cade could sense the analyst wanting more information and trying to take over, but he fought to maintain his internal control. Looking at a map on his SmartCom, he realized Kissa's location was also not that far from the spot the sub had gone down.

Cade could see McTee waving to him from the lead truck. No doubt, Judah was already giving them hell for wasting time and fuel. "Kissa, I have to go, I'm sorry. That does not mean I'm not interested, nor does it mean we won't help. Hold on." Cade muted the call and tapped his CommDot for Doris. "I assume you were monitoring the call. Can you get help to him, maybe get him out of there? Let Charlie know, they're in the same area."

"Of course, Captain."

"Good, Kissa may be onto something related to this mission. Keep him in the area just in case we need his help. Doris, take good care of him."

"No problem, Nomad. Now run along and play in the snow. I got this."

Cade told his friend to hang tight, the cavalry was coming, as he planted a foot on the running board of the second MARs-1 transport.

27

The MARs-1 vehicle was spacious. Cade rode with Alan, Alexandria 'Cutter' Osborne, and HiLo, the combat call sign for Bridget Maratelli. The Talon Teams were deliberately moving away from the various military ranks they held before joining TCP. More often now, they used only call signs, especially when on a mission. The exception would be up in MARs-2 being driven by the guide, Judah. Since they were ostensibly supposed to be research scientists, using combat call signs might raise the man's suspicion even more, so they agreed to use only the cover names when speaking in his presence. McTee, and Joe, callsign Alias, filled out that crew. Their pilot, Brenda Morgan, or Chaps, as she preferred, had stayed back at base camp, just part of the 'Oh shit' scenario if everything went tits-up out here. Cade wanted a known friendly at least somewhere on the same continent as his team.

"Everyone in the Rapide Tactical battle suits?" he asked. They all nodded. He pulled off his thick outer garments that were no longer needed. The thin Battlesuit provided a thermal barrier and a heat reclamation system that was damn near 100% effective. One of the only drawbacks to wearing them was Doris could no longer track them by heat signature. Ironically, another drawback to the system was that of the wearer potentially overheating. They all wore gloves, and the suit had a hoodie that could be used in a variety of ways, including as a full-face hood if needed. The material was laced with circuitry and nanoscale systems that even provided a level of resistance to projectiles that matched or exceeded most of the so-called 'bullet-proof' clothing options. Damn sure lighter than the massive ceramic plate carriers vest he had used in the Army.

"That feels better," Alan said, pushing the bulky winter coats into a storage locker. Maratelli had done the same before returning to the driver's seat.

Cade stared out the thick windows to the bleak and unforgiving landscape. All that ice and bitter cold. *What are we doing here?* Cochise had whined when he'd told him he wouldn't be coming. Cade knew that was the right decision, though. This was no place for a dog. But still, he had grown dependent on the animal. This was the first mission in months they wouldn't be together. He looked around the small space, then made a decision and tapped his Comms, signaling his AI for a private channel. "Hey, boy. How you doing? You okay?"

Alan watched the warrior, the leader, sitting back there looking out the window talking to himself again. *How does someone get like that?* Cade was a good guy, but strange, hard and obviously messed up in the head. Still, he had a goodness, something that Doris obviously saw as well. Rearden never made excuses for his problems, just accepted it as part of who he was. But now they were down here on the ass-end of the planet depending on him to be the leader. He felt the buzz of an incoming call and touched the dot on his cheek.

"Hey."

Alan smiled at the sound of his friend's voice. "Hey, Riles, what's up?"

"I need your opinion on something. I just sent it through to your phone."

Alan pulled up the image, then zoomed in, wishing he had one of the 4D displays they used at The Cove. It was a high-altitude image of open ocean. One edge of the image showed a partial land mass, and a few islands dotted the far right portion of the picture. "This the Caribbean?" he asked, pretty certain of the answer.

"Yes, Deuce and Bravo Team are en-route. We're pulling all the data we can from the satellites. At first pass, none of us saw anything. Mainly, they are looking for signs of the probe from Snowbird. Then your brother started applying various depolarization filters. Zoom in on grid H5."

He did as instructed. The image was obviously from one of TCP's own Minisats, no one else had resolution this good. It took him a minute to see what had her attention. "Holy shit, that looks like..." He scrolled along, seeing the anomaly but uncertain as to what it could be. "What is the water depth here?"

"In the lighter region up near grid H3, it's around 2800 meters. About twice that on the deepest part of H5," Riley answered.

"What is that? A craft or animal of some kind traveling at that depth," he said aloud.

"I'm not sure, but whatever it is, there seems to be more than one," she responded.

The image he was studying was replaced by another with more dark blurry shapes moving about in deep water. "These are time-lapsed compilations. We aren't sure what we are seeing or where they're heading, but they tend to intersect along a common axis," Riley said.

"So, what is it they're heading to? Like an oil rig, cruise ship... underwater habitat?"

"That's a good question," said Riley. "But that area is in open ocean, deep water, too. We don't see anything at that location, and if we're right, the target is moving. The departing and arrivals reached a peak a few days ago. Once we had the satellites tuned to look for it, we ran it back a few weeks. For days, you see nothing, then a flurry of activity. We established a track on the coordinates, and whatever it is seems to be moving northwest past the Cayman Islands."

It was interesting, but most likely just another oil company trying out some underwater mapping ROVs. Alan thought briefly about what

Cade had told him earlier. *Just ask her out, doofus*. "Hey, Riley, um... when we get back..."

"Yeah?" she said before adding, "Hang on, Alan, something is happening. I'll call you back."

28

CARIBBEAN

Sergeant Charlie Taylor would have preferred to be accompanying Rearden, even if it was to the South Pole. Instead, he was knee deep in the carcasses of millions of dead, rotting fish. The shoreline of the small island in the western Caribbean was covered in the damn things.

"So, what did she say?" the voice, muffled by the rebreather mask, asked.

Charlie could tell the kid was grinning, even with most of his face obscured. He briefly lifted his own mask up and away to respond. The action caused his eyes to water and the urgent desire to vomit. "The director took my concerns into advisement and told me to let you know you can be put on the next bus home."

Greg grinned, "Sure she did, Deuce." The sergeant was right, this was no assignment for a combat strike team. Hell, he wasn't sure who would want to do it. Then he spotted them. Legions of the matching yellow t-shirt wearing Friends of the Planet, or Greenpeace, or something like that. They'd been showing up for the last few days. Most were from Miami or Belize. Unlike Greg, Deuce, and the rest of the Talon Team, they only had simple paper respiratory masks on but unbridled joy in their hearts as they swept tons of the smelly dead fish into biodegradable catch bags.

"How are they so upbeat?" Charlie wondered aloud, watching a group of them moving nearby all talking and laughing. Greg just shrugged.

"You know what, kid? I've had enough of this shit." Charlie dropped his sample bag, the hooked scoop he was using, and walked back up in the direction of the road.

Greg picked up the dropped items and turned to follow the man. He'd worked with the sergeant long enough to know something was wrong. Little things like this never bothered him before, but lately it seemed almost anything could set him off. Catching up to Charlie, he hesitated, then asked if everything was okay.

"Yeah, it's fine," came the cryptic response.

Greg knew this assignment was disgusting, but at least no one was shooting at them. *That has to be a good thing, right?* Maybe it wasn't if you were a professional soldier. Greg admitted that he was geeky enough to enjoy a mystery like this. After all, what could have killed this many marine animals at once? The fish hadn't been poisoned either—most had been partially eaten, butchered even. It was puzzling, suspicious, and there was a definite answer hiding somewhere out there.

He admitted, though, the assignment didn't have a clear objective, no easily identifiable enemy, and most likely not the best use of manpower. All of the Talon Teams were tactical. They were mission focused and led by hardened warriors. That did not lend itself well to stuff like this. He'd have to talk this over with Riley and the others. They couldn't waste their best people on missions that were purely scientific or investigative in nature.

Greg had run all the tests Doris had wanted, ruling out all the most likely villains. The so-called red tide algae bloom, hypoxia from deoxygenation, localized toxic pollutants, and a host of less common issues. Charlie tapped at his CommDot. "Let's load up, guys. We aren't responsible for the clean-up, thank God." A chorus of agreement came from the scattered voices up and down the coastline.

Minutes later, they were stripping off the white overgarments and loading gear back into one of their specially equipped SUVs. "I got nothing, Sarge," Captain Nance said walking up, her nose wrinkling from the odor.

Charlie wasn't sure if it was from his smell or from the miles of dead fish nearby, but was pretty sure they were the same now. Nance had been canvassing the locals to get more specifics on when the fish started showing up. "This mess started about two weeks ago," she said. "It began with fishermen seeing the gulls diving on something out at sea. When they went to investigate, they found a floating carpet of dead or dying fish. Most are just mullet, snook, and such, but also snapper, several goliath groupers, a dozen dolphins, and one guy thought he saw a whale shark carcass floating offshore. A lot of sea turtles and a few manatees have died as well, all common to the area. Anyway, they began washing up on the beach a few days later. It happens, but more so on the windward side of the island." She pointed back over the main road to the north. "They've never encountered a biomass this large nor one coming in from that side."

"Thanks," Charlie said, then walked over and sat down heavily. "Greg is sending samples back to Riley to analyze, but this feels like nothing to me. Just a natural occurrence, nothing sinister going on." He rubbed his face, realizing he'd forgotten to shave. "What's next, Nance? Please tell me we will have something to shoot at."

"No, something a few islands over. A local doctor called it in a few weeks ago. We have some pictures." Charlie bent over to look at the grainy photos. He tried to zoom in but found he couldn't. As if expecting his question, Nance said, "Old flip phone, probably the only one on the island. Best they could do."

"Is that a body?" Charlie said rotating the phone. "I mean, I know it's a body, but is it human?"

"It is. The first washed up a month ago, and since then, seven more have shown up. All roughly similar with the same kind of wounds. At least this one has now been positively identified as Venezuelan."

Charlie studied the pictures. "Wounds look the same as most of the fish. Like a damn buzz saw went through them." They were not the familiar jagged bite marks of a shark or other ocean predator. Most of these were perfect circular wounds with deep puncture wounds evenly spaced within the carved out circle. "I guess we aren't heading back home just yet."

29

GUYANA

“No, Sarge, they speak English,” Nance said, her frustration with the man growing. Leaving the fish kills off the Mosquito Coast far behind, they had flown south to investigate the next event on the list. The mangled body on the small island led them to a string of somewhat contradictory reports of attacks on offshore oil rigs here in Guyana and just off the coast of several of the smaller islands of Trinidad and Tobago. Part of the team was also tracking down reports of the space probe.

Charlie put his SmartCom away. He’d been about to repeat the request in Spanish, using the phone as a translator. He was wearing a light business suit and looked as out of place as he felt. He could already feel the sweat stains spreading on the light-colored fabric. Posing as insurance investigators for the oil company, they attempted to board the rig, then interview all of those who’d witnessed what happened. Their credentials were perfect, but they ran into brick walls with every official they approached. None of the unit managers would allow them onto the rigs, nor give them a list of personnel to interview. They wouldn’t even share the reports that their people had filed.

“Mister Chavez, you realize that Sulanis Petroleum will be on the hook for the entire amount if we are not allowed to inspect. Your company pays us millions to insure that is not the case." The man wouldn't respond, did not argue, nor did he offer any explanation. This was the fourth such official they had interviewed. Like most of the others, he simply shook his head in refusal.

Walking out, Charlie wiped sweat from his forehead and spat in disgust. Sulanis has reportedly had two of the billion-dollar oil rigs damaged and out of commission. If any of the companies would talk, it should have been Chavez.

"They are a multi-national venture, joint owned by Canadian and Japanese investors," Nance said, looking at the screen of her SmartCom. "The largest customers are China and the U.S."

Doris had brought them up to speed on the flight down. Guyana was poised to leap onto the list of top oil producing countries in the next several years. While holding fewer oil reserves than its northern neighbor, it didn't suffer the political and economic turmoil of Venezuela.

"So, all of these guys are stonewalling us. Why?" Greg asked.

"They were paid off, ordered not to, or just scared," Nance said. "It's a different culture down here, we don't understand what may be going on behind the scenes."

"Still, you would think they would file insurance claims on these, just for lost production if not the actual damages."

"It makes little sense, Greg. That's true."

The youngest member of Bravo thought about it as they rejoined the rest of the team. Calling Dee, he asked her to run some new searches. He detailed the parameters and then instructed her to run the results by Jimmy as well. She acknowledged, and within the hour, provided him the very short list he needed.

Greg put his phone down on the table after reading the information. He was sitting with Charlie and Nance in the little waterfront café. "Okay, we have a possible rig we can go check out." The other two stopped eating and looked at him.

"Go on, you have our attention," the sergeant said, eyeing the rest of his fish sandwich greedily.

"Only thing is, it isn't on our list," Greg said. "Not one of Sulanis's, the huge state-owned petrochem company, nor Exxon's, nor any of the others. I had them checked out when this started. You know, most of the damaged rigs we know about were all within about six weeks of each other. Like the Venezuelan oil workers that washed up dead. All these others were about then, too. So...I wondered which was first."

"You found the first one?"

"I did, Captain. Well, to be accurate, Jimmy found it. It was originally leased to a Chinese group well offshore. No one reported any accident, but it was unexpectedly sold off for salvage several months ago. They just got it towed back to the breaking yard a few weeks ago. Doris intercepted some messages between the rig foreman and his bosses back in China that makes her suspect it may have been the first."

"How far away?"

Greg checked. "Maybe forty minutes away, Deuce."

Charlie grinned. "Now we're getting somewhere. Eat up, people. We gotta move."

Charlie didn't know how Doris had found it. The location was in a rundown neighborhood, and the breaking yard where decommissioned marine vessels were dismantled and sold off for scrap looked and smelled about like you would imagine...or maybe worse. "Still not as bad as the fish," Nance said, grinning.

The rest weren't so sure. Nance and Charlie led the contingent up the rusty metal stairs and took a look for themselves. Workers were busy removing the remainder of the oil company's equipment, but the team could instantly see damaged structural pieces. Broken railings and corrugated metal walls with giant gashes. One of the interior rooms had what looked to the sergeant like a spray pattern of arterial blood. Charlie had seen similar scenes enough times that there was no mistaking it. "We've got to talk to someone who was on this thing." He looked at Nance, who was nodding slowly in agreement as she took in the scene.

Dee's voice broke in on his command channel with a sense of urgency. "Deuce, be aware, I am picking up some unmistakable signals showing your team is under surveillance." That wasn't a real surprise.

After all, they were operating in a foreign country and asking questions about one of the most valuable commodities.

"Electronic surveillance?" he asked, nonchalantly as he edged out from under an overhanging metal roof.

"Affirmative, as well as visual tracking by at least two aerial drones."

Charlie nodded, now looking over the railing at the shipyard and dilapidated neighborhoods beyond. He leaned over as if he were eyeing the support beams and made a discreet call to Greg down on the ground. "Get some of those mini-drones airborne. Dee will feed them instructions on what to search for." The bird-shaped drones were almost indistinguishable from doves, but as he thought about it, he wasn't entirely sure doves were native to this region.

"Birds are up," came the quick response.

The crew spent two more hours on the rig, taking pictures, measurements, and everything else someone might expect an accident investigation team to do. Charlie didn't want whoever was watching them to think they were anything other than what they claimed to be. Dee had kept him posted on what the doves had found, which was absolutely nothing. They had briefly spotted one of the flying drones, but it had rapidly descended into thick foliage and not reappeared. Electronic sensors had twice picked up a possible eavesdropping signal, but upon investigation, the little doves also found nothing. Charlie loaded the teams up with a growing sense of unease. *If someone is out there watching—they're damn good.*

"What are you thinking, Sarge?" Nance asked.

He drove back toward town, eyes scanning the road ahead. "I don't know, but I don't like it. Something tore that rig to pieces. I believe it's what happened to the others, too. We really need to find someone who was on it to talk to. It's time we started getting answers."

* * *

Answers would take a while. For whatever reason, Doris had a challenging time hacking into the Chinese company's servers to get the crew manifest. Then it became obvious that most of the labor for the rig was off the books. No official names, identities, or addresses. "They probably just gathered up crews from the docks whenever they needed to swap out. Lots of experienced, unemployed people around," Greg said, listening to Doris's report. She had been on it for two days while Charlie's crew sat around a cheap hotel getting restless. Ultimately, she came up with a single possible match.

They were on the road in minutes, all of them ready to be done with this investigation.

"Dee, are you sure this is the place?" Greg asked nervously as he pulled down a road that was closing in on both sides with thick vegetation.

"Affirmative, you are at the correct coordinates."

The sergeant shook his head. "Damn, I was really hoping you were wrong." He was still amped up over someone watching them at the scrap yard. Somehow, this innocent little mission seemed to be feeling more ominous with every passing day.

"Right there," Greg said, glancing up from the nav system on the phone.

"Team Two, take the back alley. Watch our six. Greg, get some doves airborne. No surprises." As leader of the mission, Deuce Taylor was taking no chances.

He turned to the captain using her call sign, "Magellan, you do the door knock."

She looked at him as if to say, "*Why me?*"

"You have a friendly face. Plus, I'll be on your nine o'clock locked and loaded." So far, they had not been carrying weapons in Guyana, but the squalid homes and desperate looking villagers made the need a prudent one.

Had the vines and rusted out junk machinery not been in the way, you could have recited the alphabet and barely made it to Q before being back where you started. Nance knocked, then knocked again. Stirring sounds and a shuffling noise preceded the wooden door being cracked open. A mottled cat ran out the door and between Nance's legs. Her eyes never left the man's face. An old and weathered face, a terrified face. She dropped the phony act they'd been using.

She knew the man had no family and lived alone, but she kept her voice low. "Mister Nogales, I am with the U.S. Government, and we believe your life is in danger. We are here to offer you protection if you need it. Can we talk?" She smiled and tried to look as genuine as possible. After all, it was not a lie.

Charlie looked at her like she'd lost her mind. The expression from Nogales was pretty much the same. He seemed to consider it, then shrugged and opened the door wide, waving them both in.

Forty-three minutes later, they left with Nogales in tow. They'd told him to bring anything he wanted to keep. If the man's story checked out, Doris would help them move the man somewhere safe. Of course, if what he'd said was true, Nance wasn't sure any of them were safe.

Charlie tapped his CommDot to end a conversation he was having. He looked at his small team. "Nance, we will handle this. You need to takeover WarHawk. You have a new mission. It's personal and it's back up the coast a bit.

30

ANTARCTICA

"Nomad!"

The shout pulled Cade from a mostly internal focus to an external one in seconds. Glancing toward the front of the Rover, he saw Alan talking frantically with someone. He slapped his CommDot, "Go for Nomad."

Alan began speaking almost simultaneously to both McTee from MARs-2 and Dee. Cade's normal ability to separate and identify voices was making no sense of the confusion of sounds. To make matters worse, the barbarian, Brutus, had decided this was an obvious threat condition and suddenly was hellbent to take over. "Everyone shut the fuck up for a second!" Assessing the situation, Cade decided Dee would be the most efficient. Holding up a silencing finger to the others in the cramped space, he told her to give him the unpleasant news...and he already knew it would be bad.

"You have an unidentified aircraft closing on your position, Nomad. I suspect hostile intent. You will need to take evasive action."

So many things ran through his mind concurrently. How was anything up in this weather? How did they know it was hostile, and most of all, how in the hell could they take evasive action? "We are in a freaking school bus with tank tracks for wheels driving over a half-mile thick sheet of ice."

"I have them on radar," Alan said from the front seat.

"Cutter, put some room between us and McTee," Cade yelled. "Alan, give me some options. What do we have?" Cade's eyes looked out in the direction Alan was pointing where he saw a massive, helicopter gunship approaching from the southeast. It was a Kamov KA-52 Alligator. "Shit," Cade said. The Russian-built all-weather war machine was bristling with weapons. *Who in the hell has this down here?* he wondered. Leaving that thought for the analyst, he and Gus began working on a way to escape the approaching beast.

McTee had MARs-2 heading directly at the approaching gunship, presenting as small a profile as possible. Cade was still hoping that whoever was in it had peaceful intentions, but none of his inner voices agreed on that premise. He saw one cannon spitting fire as it began its strafing run on the small convoy. "Here we go, people, it's about to get hairy up in here," he yelled. Glancing at the stack of cases, he began running through options. They had weaponry, but no missiles, no RPGs, and everything was buried under tents and crates of food and supplies. Strategically, that had been shortsighted, but they had expected no encounters down here, hostile or otherwise.

"MARs-2 took an indirect..."

Alan's voice was cut off as a line of rounds stitched a line across the cabin roof of their own truck. "Full stop!" Alan yelled as the deafening sound of the KA-52 roared overhead.

Cade quickly joined Alan, pulling case after case out onto the ice. The Battlesuits protected their bodies from the biting wind and bitter cold, but hands and faces were not covered. Within seconds, Cade could feel nothing through either hand. He'd never experienced cold this brutal. He knew they couldn't last long outside the shelter of the Rover. "Dee, can you take control, screw with the targeting on that thing...anything? You have to buy us some time." Alan was pointing to a case and nodding.

Cade reached for the latch, but his fingers wouldn't obey his mind. All he needed to do was flip up the latch and pull the small metal hoop out, but that simple activity already seemed beyond him. Looking up, he shook his head at Alan and Alex, who'd also made it out of the truck. She ran up and pulled her hands out of her coat, revealing gloved hands. Quickly, she had the hard travel case open, and Cade pulled her down as an air-to-ground missile zoomed past them toward the MARs-2. It missed the vehicle by inches.

"Doris is using our phones to project targeting interference, Captain," Alan said.

Cade knew that as close as the craft was, they could disengage the targeting systems as soon as they figured that out. He'd seen the Russians and Syrians using these craft with amazing precision. They were rugged beasts without a lot of the high-tech the American counterpart had. Whatever Doris was doing, though, would only buy them seconds.

"Coming to you, Nomad!" he heard McTee say over the comms.

"Negative, negative!" Cade yelled back. He wanted the other vehicle away from the battle. If they lost both of them out here, they were dead. "Make for those low mountains at top speed." Any reply the other man might have made was lost as the twin cannons on the helicopter opened again. Multiple lines of ice were spewing up like mini-volcanos where the rounds impacted the ground. The lines were heading directly for them. He shoved Alex one way while diving across the cases toward Alan who was directly in the line of fire. He tried hard to think of the caliber the Russian ship normally carried. The Rapide Battlesuits were rated up to .30 caliber, but that was for penetration; a good portion of the kinetic energy would still be felt.

The shots missed Alan but struck Cade in the shoulder, spinning him in a full circle and leaving that arm feeling as numb as his hands. Glancing over, he was pretty sure his shoulder was dislocated, if not worse. Tamping down the pain was not difficult; with the cold, he literally couldn't feel anything. An old drill instructor had repeatedly told them that pain was only in the mind, which Cade now knew was, in fact, true. The nerves in damaged areas sent electrical signals to the brain that it interpreted to be pain. The DI had done his best to convince them if you could control that pain response, you were in charge. He'd bought into that lesson better than most, routinely punishing his body far beyond what his fellow soldiers could endure.

The sounds coming from the gunship faded to his rear as Cade assumed it was turning for another pass. They were sitting ducks, and at any moment, the pilot would realize they weren't fighting back and just hover and fire. Alex and Alan were pulling something from the open case. He tried to help, but his left arm was just dangling uselessly. To his dismay, he saw it wasn't even a weapon, but part of the equipment supposed to be used at the site. *Something to do with drilling ice cores,* he thought. Alan was yelling something, but he was struggling to focus. Brutus was nearly front and center now.

"What?"

Cade caught the automatic as Alan tossed it. "Try to keep it off of us for a few seconds," the kid said, this time through his CommDot.

A few seconds might be all the time we have, Cade thought. Dee already had the gun ready for autofire mode. Cade was squeezing the trigger in rapid bursts before he even turned to see the thing he was shooting at. The targeting reticle appeared in his goggles and centered briefly on the pilot before moving back toward the engine cowling.

"Negative damage," Dee stated flatly in her very proper British accent.

He could see that for himself. The heavily armored helicopter was deflecting the small arms rounds with ease. "Focus fire again on the glass," he ordered. "Confine fire pattern to a single point."

"Acknowledged," she responded as he saw the chopper begin to move more erratically. Dee, in control of the aiming, managed to focus the relatively small caliber rounds into a quarter-sized circle in the thick armor-like acrylic windshield. The bullseye was directly in line with the pilot's forehead, and as the impacts began eating deeper into the windshield, it began cratering, and cracks started spider-webbing outward. While the rounds had a negligible effect on the flight worthiness of the craft, the effect on the pilot was profound. He pulled up and away moving that part of the windshield out of the line of sight.

Cade could see now that the passenger seemed to be holding a pistol on the pilot. *Perhaps he wasn't the one we should have been target-*

ing. Slowly, the gray beast began to hover, then crab walked sideways in their direction. "Whatever you're thinking, Alan, now would be an excellent time." The wind from the downwash erased whatever response the kid might have made. Cade fired off the last half mag in a series of three-round bursts, all targeting the passenger side window. He saw no reaction at all from the man with the gun.

"Who the fuck are you, and why do you want us dead?" he said, watching as the craft turned, lining up its mounted cannons for a kill shot.

31

The water glistened a brilliant shade of turquoise. Even after a lifetime of living and working near the ocean, Kissa was still mesmerized by the view. The beauty held a dark secret, though—one that had taken Thera, and one he was determined to uncover. Talking with Rearden had steeled his reserve. He felt more confident now that someone else knew, someone who could hopefully help.

His eyes had scanned the ocean for hours, looking for any sign of the creature. Any sign of authorities. He was on alert for anything out of the ordinary. Ocean, sand, seabirds, an occasional fishing boat... nothing unusual. Yet, his heart still pounded when he thought of what stalked him beneath the surface the previous day. What had it been?

Hours passed with no other word from Cade or Doris. Several times Kissa checked to make sure his phone wasn't dead. They hadn't told him what to expect. *Would they just call the local authorities?* Surely, Cade knew better than to allow that. The sound of a speedboat got his attention, and he turned and scanned in the opposite direction than what he'd been expecting. A pinpoint of dark followed by a plume of white sea spray. The boat was coming directly toward him, and it was moving fast. As it closed quickly to a quarter mile, he realized it was far larger than he'd thought. A few hundred yards offshore, the boat suddenly cut power and drifted swiftly toward the same docking point he had used.

He could see no insignia on the dark blue hull, nor did the people on board appear to be police. The one who was handling the controls offered a friendly wave as a young man jumped out and tied the boat off. Kissa had nowhere to hide on the tiny island; if these weren't friendlies, then he was screwed. And, it seemed unlikely that his former Army buddy could have arranged assistance this quickly. The youngster on the dock was joined by a determined looking woman who turned, scanned the shore momentarily before her gazed locked on him. She strode confidently in his direction.

"You Kissa?"

The woman seemed friendly but had an air of command authority. He nodded.

"I'm Nance. Captain Rearden said you could use an assist."

"Yes, thank you, thank you so much. You have no idea how relieved I am to see you."

She quickly introduced him to the others on her team. "Micah, Trondo Williams, who we all just mostly call Sir or Apache. And the little princess there beside him is Coffee. Kissa looked up at the hulking shadow that resolved itself into a smiling mountain of a man.

"What are we facing, Kissa, and where did Thera go missing?" the woman asked.

Kissa gave a more detailed explanation of the disappearance and everything he had seen. He pointed out locations on a digital map the boy produced. He watched fascinated as they replaced the maps by overlays of real-time satellite views which Micah rolled backward over the past twenty-four hours. "Who are you people?"

"We're friends," Micah said.

"You aren't the Army, although most of you look like you could be," Kissa offered.

Captain Nance looked around the small group. "We are not military—we are part of a rapid response team. Cade leads one of our other teams. Our affiliation is not with the military, but with the U.S. Government. Unlike most agencies, we are not restricted as to where we can operate or what tactics we can use. Somehow, friend, you managed to contact the one person who could probably help you the most. Now, before it gets dark...why don't we go investigate where your fiancée disappeared."

* * *

The dark hull of the forty-eight foot, San Remo sport cruiser idled to a stop and drifted over the same water Kissa and Thera dove the day before. Micah began unpacking one of the travel cases. Kissa had left his much older and smaller boat at the old repair yard. "We going down now? Should I get my gear?"

"Not until we know what we're up against. Dee, anything on the scope?" Micah asked.

Kissa was unsure who Dee was, he'd heard all of them talking to her several times, but he'd only seen the four of them so far. It was a large boat, he assumed someone else could be aboard. Kissa watched as Micah looked around, touched his cheek, and said, "Thanks."

"Nothing unusual out there on any of the scanners. Help me get some sensor drones into the water."

Trondo stood, grabbing a rack of the dull, aluminum tubes and carried them topside. Kissa got the rest, and Micah unpacked what must have been a control system. "These are submersible drones?"

"Yeah, autonomous operating, nearly unlimited dive time, and rated to 1500 meters," the boy said.

Kissa was staring into the fisheye lens that occupied the entire front third of the little device. "Never seen any this small, nor with those kinds of specs. Damn."

"We'll start out with fifty. Since we have no idea what we're looking for, except your fiancée, I'm going to have Dee handle the specific scans. She can vary sensor arrays to cover our bases."

"Like what?" Then, looking up, he added, "And who is this Dee?"

Micah smiled, "Kissa, you have a lot to learn, but not now. Dee is our onboard computer system—that's enough for now." They dumped the aqua-drones overboard all at once. The tiny craft looked like a school of fish; they took a second to orient themselves in the water, then all sped away in every direction imaginable. "Let's go down to the lounge, Captain Nance should have the displays ready. Trondo, you have watch, okay?"

Down below, Coffee and Nance were cycling through the various imagery coming in. The displays were better than HD, better than anything Kissa had ever seen, in fact.

"We can use our goggles if we spot anything to give us a pretty good VR view, but the displays are better for scanning through the various feeds," Nance said.

They watched as schools of colorful fish darted out of the way of the speeding drones. Then, the edge of a reef came into view on another screen. Life teemed around the outcropping. "Wow," Micah said. "Look there." He pointed to one of the screens, and with just a gesture, moved it from the small display to the largest. Three enormous whale sharks swam lazily toward the camera. The little drone circled them at a slow speed, the camera picking up every detail.

"It is gorgeous down here, Kissa," Nance said, eyes glued to the displays. "I mean, I'm sorry about Thera, and I know she must be all you're thinking about, but the beauty of this place is simply breathtaking."

Kissa nodded; he still felt the same, even with the ache in his heart this day. "Thank you, Captain. I am honored to share it with you." He felt uneasy with everything they were doing for him. He'd just been hoping for...hell, he didn't even know. He just wanted someone else to know what had happened. Someone that might believe his story. These guys, though, had shown up in no time, outfitted a state-of-the-art boat, and had some of the best gear he'd ever seen. Slowly, the pieces began to slide into place. Cade had mentioned to his command that it might relate this to something they were working on. "Can you tell me where Rearden or Taylor are?"

Nance shook her head, "Sorry, you haven't been read in, so for now, not allowed. I can say that Cade is nowhere close, though. Team

WarHawk got the win on this mission." Micah nodded, and Coffee looked ready to high five, but looked at Kissa and pushed his enthusiasm down somewhat.

"We have something on sensor," a female voice said from one of the displays. The imagery from that drone suddenly filled all the displays.

"What are you detecting, Dee?" Micah asked.

"Energized electrons and a weak magnetic signature."

Micah looked thoughtful, then nodded. "MHD?"

"Possibly, it is very weak and widely scattered, but that would be my guess."

"You care to clue the rest of us mere mortals?" Nance asked.

"Uh, sure, sorry," Micah said. "A magnetohydrodynamic drive, or MHD, accelerator is a method for propelling vehicles using only electric and magnetic fields with no moving parts. It literally strips the electrons off the molecules of water as it passes through the thruster engine. Really quiet, very efficient, and ideal for marine use."

"Would it produce a blue light?" Kissa asked, still in obvious awe of the level of sophistication Rearden's friends possessed.

The computer answered, "It could, Kissa. The system uses powerful magnets, usually rare Earth magnets, and a lot of electricity. The energized field could possibly emit a plasma glow, or it could just interact with the naturally occurring bioluminescence in the water. That is not a known effect of the currently operational versions I have on file, though."

The islander nodded, fear pounding in his temples as he considered encountering the beast again. "Can we follow it?"

32

"I tell you it was not a machine, no craft. What I saw was alive!"

Coffee walked up from the galley carrying a tray of sandwiches. "Kissa, we heard you the first ten times, but trust these guys. They find evidence of a craft with an exotic propulsion system, then let them chase that lead to ground."

Kissa nodded reluctantly, his dreadlocks bouncing in front of his red, swollen eyes. He was frustrated and out of his element. Nance put a hand on his knee. "We follow the clues we have. Maybe they go nowhere, maybe we get something. Give it some time." She took a bite of sandwich and a long pull from her water bottle before continuing, "You've had a long day, eat something and get some rest. We'll wake you if we spot anything."

The man nodded again, his hunger and fatigue finally winning out over all the other issues he was facing. While he doubted he'd be able to get any rest, they all heard gentle snores coming from the bunk-room minutes after he entered.

Darkness had fallen; the calm seas were making gentle sounds against the side of the boat. Micah was on watch duty as Nance made her way forward. "Hey, Turner, brought you some chow. Anything out there?"

"Thanks." He took a bite and stared out at the sky full of stars descending in all directions. "Nothing so far. Heard some sounds—I guess they were dolphins or something and fish splashing. Actually, the place is a paradise. Just sitting here marveling at the night sky. Have you ever seen this many stars?"

She had, but didn't want to dredge up all those memories right now. Desert battlefields often had gorgeous clear nights like this, but all they did was hide the horrors happening down below. "So, there are others out there?"

The night sky was bright enough he could see her arm outstretched and hand pointing up. "Yes," Micah said confidently. "Probably a lot of them. We are now fairly confident that intelligent life is pretty abundant in the universe and, according to Doris, a lot more diverse than we would have ever imagined."

The thought made her feel small, out of control. Kristen Nance did not like the feeling and was increasingly questioning how this fit into her idea of God, the universe, and her role in it. A flash of light several miles away made them both jerk their heads in that direction.

"Dee, did you catch that?" Micah asked at once. Trondo was at the helm, but Dee was piloting the boat as they slowly pursued the fading trail of bluish photons.

"My sensors picked up an anomaly approximately seven miles away," the computer assistant informed.

"Is it along the course we are heading?"

"No, Captain Nance. Even taking into account wind direction, current, and drift patterns, that heading is outside of whatever produced the MHD drive signature. Would you like us to alter course to investigate?"

"What do you think, Micah?"

The young man thought on it, working out the possibilities in that brilliant mind. "Lots of creatures out here that can produce bioluminescence, some quite large. Also, some species are known to group together for protection or breeding possibly, so you can have huge colonies all producing a synchronized light show, but seven miles? No way any of those are that bright. I suggest we check it out."

"Have Trondo change course, Dee. Let's go see what's out there," Nance ordered. The San Remo cruiser was a rental, so very little of their automated systems had been installed on the craft. Still, it fit their needs nicely. The boat made a gradual turn to a more easterly direction.

"Dee, keep most of the drones pursuing the other track while we check this out," Micah suggested.

Minutes later, they were over the spot Dee had marked on the GPS map. Micah had the aqua drones scouring the bottom for whatever was out there. Knowing the water would adversely affect some sensors, he also launched a series of air drones to circle the area. These were larger than the bird-shaped mini drones they used in combat situations. These looked more like a typical hobbyist model but were bristling with sensitive cameras and sensors and were almost totally silent.

"Nothing so far," Coffee said, watching one bank of monitors.

Nance had Dee cycling through all the available wavelength spectrum from the overhead drones. "Wait, what was that, Dee? Back up and pause," she said, focusing in on one part of the image. Just for an instant, Nance caught a glimpse as something briefly showed on the far edge of the search grid. The drones cycled through the electromagnetic spectrum faster for anyone but Dee to interpret. So, Doris and Riley had developed a program that combined the entire EM view in a way to make anything unusual stand out, whether it was flagged on IR, magnetic, or even gamma ray or night-vision. Whatever it was, it didn't match Dee's alert criteria, but Nance felt sure it was something. Instincts were something humans brought to the party.

"Trondo, southeast, slow ahead," Nance yelled, wanting to move in the direction of whatever she'd seen. "There," she said to Dee as the image of something moving fast flicked briefly through several of the wavelengths.

"It is large, probably fifteen meters, and appears organic," Dee said. They could see that whatever the blob was appeared to be jointed near its midsection, the body undulating sharply side-to -side. "The profile does not match any of the known biologics in the area."

"So, it's a creature?" Coffee asked with more than a hint of worry creeping into his voice. The islander was right.

"Dee, can you alert Kissa and have him join us?" Nance asked. She hated to wake the man if this was nothing more than some big ass fish, but he was the expert.

"Certainly, Captain."

* * *

"We have some activity off the starboard side," Trondo called out from above. "Looks like more of the flashing."

Kissa was bent over a laptop with a pair of headphones on. They'd been slowly closing in on the creature, and Kissa agreed it was an organic creature. Most likely a single, not a collective biomass all schooling together. Biologic. "I'd say it's hunting, although not like any marine predator I am aware of, none that size at least."

The team had been trying desperately to get the underwater drones in the vicinity, but each time they closed in, they lost all signals from the object. The aerial scans were no more helpful. The thing was turning into a full-blown mystery.

"You sure it's not a shark?" Coffee asked. The big man had already let it be known he didn't care for fish with teeth.

"We have relatively harmless sharks around here, mostly nurse sharks, a few hammerheads, but not the man-eaters like bull or great whites," Kissa responded. "This thing is too large even to be one of those, and the way it moves...just so fast, then goes completely still. I'd say it was an ambush hunter. Some of the readings remind me of a giant squid, but those are also unheard of in our waters and these shallow depths."

"Unheard of, but not impossible?" Micah asked from the deck above.

"We're wasting a lot of time and fuel on this chase," Nance said. "Let's bring as many of the drones as we can into play. Dee, track the likely course of the creature, then encircle it with drones above and below. Have them all go to active sonar as soon as they are in range.

Light this thing up, so we can verify what it is and then get the hell back to our mission."

"Doing it now, Captain," came the immediate reply.

33

"Cap, cycle rounds to C12," Alan said.

Dee was already making the munitions change as the Kamov nosed down and again began firing the massive twin cannons. "C12," Cade said aloud. Those rounds only do one thing, make lots of smoke. The firing sounds of the weapon changed as the new rounds were designed to travel slower and relatively short distances. Each was loaded with a chemical compound that reacted with oxygen when fired to produce a super-dense fog in the immediate area. Hundreds of the rounds now flew between Cade's gun and the enemy airship. Cade also heard the sound of something else coming to life. The unmistakable energetic whine of a lot of power pushing through whatever it was Alan had unpacked.

"Down, Nomad!" Maratelli yelled just before a brilliant beam of light lanced out and into the fog-bank. The sound of the helicopter changed momentarily, then resumed its advance. The nose and windshield were nearly free of the smoky cover. The line of shots advanced toward the trio, and Cade was out of ideas. He turned to see the others using the electronic sampling drill to fire a beam. The thing used some proprietary method to melt ice away and had been a late addition to the field gear for this mission. Apparently, it had multiple uses. Cade grinned as they lined up for another shot. Suddenly, Maratelli crumpled to the ground, blood spraying behind her.

Cade leaped up. His first instinct was to help his lieutenant, but he knew they were all dead if they didn't stop this attack now. Alan was struggling to raise the heavy drilling unit. It was fastened to a steel tripod designed to be pointing down into the ice, but now it faced high overhead. Cade shoved a shoulder underneath and pushed up. "Blast that fucking thing out of the sky, Alan!"

The shot sizzled out the end of the shaft straight up into the pilot's cabin of the ugly, flying machine. The Kamov lurched sideways and slowly started to slide steeply off to one side.

Cade lowered the drill and grabbed frantically at the side of his head where a patch of his hair seemed to be burning. Tossing his damaged tactical helmet to the side, he threw himself into the snow and ice to stop the pain.

"It's going down!" Alan yelled as the Russian Kamov dove over a hill of ice and out of sight. Moments later, the sounds of tearing metal and a screeching sound of an engine locking up brought them all back to the realization of what had just happened. Cade jumped up and helped Alex dig through the other gear bags for her medical kit. Cade tossed Alan a spare rifle. He loaded up on spare mags and slung the rifle over a shoulder.

He knelt to check on his lieutenant. Her Battlesuit had a gash in one side and blood draining around the seams. She was conscious, but grimacing in pain. Alex inserted some wound packing gently around the gash. "You've taken a nasty hit, but it looks...okay. You're going to be fine, Maratelli, you hear me?" She nodded. Pain still etched across her face. Alex was working feverishly to staunch the bloodflow.

"Cutter—do what you can for Maratelli. I'm going to try and see what the fuck this was all about. Send McTee down to watch my back." He walked a few steps, then turned. "Alan...hey, good thinking on the drill. You saved us with that one."

Alan looked scared but gave a small head nod as he turned to help Alex work on the lieutenant.

* * *

Cade slapped at the CommDot on his cheek, which was already going numb from the cold. “Director.”

“Yes, Captain. We have Dee’s report on some of what just happened.”

“We’ve been attacked, unknown enemy. Two combatants in an old, Russian Kamov gunship. Helicopter has been neutralized, but we do have at least one casualty. The LT is down, I’m going to the crash scene to hopefully get some answers. Someone knew we were here, and they seemed very determined to make sure we didn’t get where we were going.”

“Acknowledged. Suggest you put drones up as soon as you can and have them provide overwatch,” Margaret said.

Good idea, although Cade was fairly certain those were in the other vehicle. He scrambled over an ice wall and surveyed the crash site about a hundred yards ahead. Debris from the downed helicopter littered the ice pack. A few small fires burned, but much of the fuselage still appeared to be intact. Brutus was screaming to be let out, and Gus was advising calm and to be wary of a potential trap. They had no idea who they were up against or if any of the hostiles might have survived the crash.

“Captain, we’re just rolling up now,” McTee yelled. “Alias and I are getting the weapons locker unpacked. Looks like we missed the party, Boss.”

“Just get your ass down here and cover my six.” Cade thought about it. That only left the new guy, ‘Alias,’ Alan, and the Australian up top for defense. “Give Judah one of the standard weapons, and have him stay close in to support the others.”

“Roger that. You think there are more hostiles, then?” McTee asked.

“I have no idea,” Cade answered despondently. This job and the cold were getting to him—there were no easy days or routine missions. *We are one of a few hundred humans on this entire continent, and someone is trying to fucking kill us,* he thought. “Alias, do a perimeter sweep up there—make sure we don’t have any other surprises.”

Cade thought about his options, his mind moving into full tactical assessment mode now. *Unknown enemy, unknown firepower, and unknown mission, but they mean us harm.* It wasn't much, but maybe he could use that. They needed to spot them from the air, and with the arctic gear they wore, that wasn't so easy. A part of him monitored the others' radio traffic. He could tell Maratelli was being stabilized, but they would have to get her out of here. Cutter, the team medic, was calling Chaps back at base camp to see if she could get them a ride. Cade had to ignore that side of the story. For now, he had to assume they still had threats out there.

Reaching the bottom of the hill, he cautiously began moving toward the twisted and charred wreckage. The reek of burned fuel swirled around him in the bitter wind. The Russian attack helicopter had been called the 'Black Shark of the Sky' when he'd run into them in Syria several years back. They were notoriously hard to bring down, but the kid had managed it with a drilling tool.

"Nomad, suggest you scan the area on IR." Dee's voice broke through his inner concentration.

"Can't. They were with my tactical helmet, which kinda got fried." It was an excellent idea, though. He knew he could also scan with the SmartCom, which...he'd apparently left in the MARs-1. "Drones?" he asked hopefully.

"Not in this wind, Captain. Sorry."

"McTee, scan the icepack around the wreckage as soon as you have us in sight."

"Roger that, Nomad."

Cade closed to within about fifty meters of the wreckage, taking cover behind a pressure ridge of jagged ice. The smells of burning plastic, fuel, and cordite from the guns were everywhere. The pristine scene corrupted by the ugly, wrecked machine.

"Negative contacts on scan, Cap," McTee answered.

Maybe we got lucky, maybe, Cade thought as he advanced on the crash, automatic rifle raised and ready for action. The front of the helicopter was a smoking ruin. Cade could see the blackened hole through the melted acrylic windows. The ice drill had done a number on the cabin as well. He watched a steady drip of dark red liquid leeching out onto the snow. It was too bright to be hydraulic fluid...blood.

Rising up, he placed his back against the cold metal and did a quick peek into the now open cabin. McTee, who was down and closing, whispered through his earbud, "No activity spotted." Cade analyzed what he'd seen as he ducked back tight to the craft. One body hanging limply in the seat. Thick green winter parka now covered with blood. He knew the other had been wearing winter white. That would probably make the body the pilot.

Ducking low, he eased up alongside the front section and popped up to find no one else. No other body. *Shit!* He reached to pull the pilot's head up so he could get a look when Dee told him to stop. "Get away from the crash at once, Nomad. It's rigged to blow!"

Cade ran awkwardly in the snow and ice away from the machine but knew he'd still be too close. After less than fifty steps, she told him and McTee to take cover. He dove headfirst into the ice as a massive explosion sounded, and a wave of intense heat washed over him, burying him in burning debris, ice, and God only knew what else.

34

"Judah, how far are we from the coordinates?" The Aussie looked as cool as when they'd first met, which, given all they had been through in the last three hours, unnerved Cade.

The older man scratched his gray stubble and said, "Well, mate, I am guessing about seventeen hours' drive time from here. MARs-2 is in good shape. Yours, though, needs a patch job, looks like bullet holes all along the roof."

Cade's transport had been shot up, but the engine was still in good shape. His head was still ringing from the explosion and the subsequent attack from McTee to put out his burning hair...again. Alan had launched drones, despite Dee's warning, and they had spotted nothing. No sign of the shooter or shooters. Someone had detonated that chopper, though. Dee had sensed the radio signal arming the device only after Cade had gotten close. Now they had no ID on the pilot, no useable evidence, and a missing enemy combatant.

Tactically, Cade was left with few options, so he dropped back to basics—take care of those things you can change and forget about what you can't. Maratelli needed to be transported back to base camp. Chaps was still grounded, so they would need to take her in one of the tracked MARS vehicles. That meant reducing his team by half. Not ideal, especially knowing they had hostiles after them, but it couldn't be helped.

"Judah stays with me and Alan," Cade said. "We need him to navigate us to the location. Alias drives MARs-2 back with Cutter and the lieutenant." It wasn't ideal, and Alexandria shot him a look. She was one of his best shooters, but she was also the team medic. Cade already knew she had Maratelli stabilized in a trauma sleeve, and there wasn't much else they could do for her, but he could not have lived with himself if something else happened to her. These people were soldiers, but they were his responsibility.

"So, we just going to ignore the bastard out there that attacked us?" McTee growled.

"I am," Cade answered, walking away. "For now."

The Australian eased up to Cade as he and Alan were dividing up supplies and weapons. "Hey, mate, this is all fun and all, but you know, not exactly what I signed up for. I mean, you guys have some interesting bits and bobs, but, well...someone seems to have taken a dislike to your presence here and, well...not sure I want to be included in that drama."

"Oh, really?" Cade asked, never looking up from the load-out case he was filling. "Get to the point, Judah. How much?"

The man looked briefly confused, then offended. "I'm sorry, sir, I don't think you quite understand me."

"I believe I do. You've seen action, you know danger. Hell, you live in this God-forsaken place. Look, I need to go pee, and I'm scared to because I'm pretty sure my balls have frozen off and will fall out as soon as I unzip. So, little Elsa, please tell me how much more fucking money you want to make you feel better about our little drama."

Judah's face broke into a tiny grin. "I believe I would prefer to be known as Olaf if you are going all Disney on me. As for my fee, I was thinking double. Hazard pay and all."

"Greedy bastard," Cade said, slamming the sealed case into the storage space of the MARS-1. "Thirty percent more." Cade didn't blame the man for wanting more, but he'd already made a solid profit on the trucks, and honestly, the grimy ole' bastard seemed to be enjoying himself. He knew if he caved on price too soon, the man would always wonder if he could have gotten more. They haggled for several more minutes, then reached an agreement on a modified rate plus a bonus for mission success.

Judah held out a hand to seal the deal. "By the way, friend, sorry about your hair." Cade unconsciously rubbed at the singed area and winced. "And your balls," Judah said, walking away.

* * *

Several hours later, the single transport was making good time. Doris spoke to Cade through his earbud, "Captain, we have tracked the helicopter that attacked you to a supply ship just offshore. They normally use it to ferry people and equipment to the Russian base a few hundred miles inland."

Cade was reluctant to discuss this with Judah so close. He subvocalized a nearly silent response which only the AI could easily interpret.

"No, it wasn't the Russians, at least not officially. The bird was idling on the launch pad waiting for the weather to clear when someone forced their way in and had the pilot take off. I have seen video from the bridge as well as listened to the radio calls during the time in question," Doris answered.

Cade thought about that. How would someone aboard a ship hundreds of miles away know where they were? Could they have gotten them confused with someone else? Wait, why would a supply helicopter be fully armed? He asked Doris about all of this. She had no good answer for it. She did let him know that the MARS-2 was almost back to the camp, and the infirmary was standing by to treat Maratelli's injuries. Also, Deuce had sent out Nance and Team WarHawk, who had rendezvoused with Kissa and were checking out his story.

Ace, Cade inquired internally after Doris had told him all she had to offer. *I need a working theory. What are we up against here? Who is trying to stop us, and what will be their next play?*

Hmm, Cade...I dunno. The buzzing voice of his more intelligent persona still grated on Cade's nerves, but the whiney bastard was devastatingly good at putting random bits of intel together when even the computer AI was stumped. *I can tell you there were more than one and, um...well, they probably have to wait for some type of ground transport now. I'd say we're fine until we reach the hole. That's where they'll attack.*

Cade nodded, that was what he would have done, so it made sense. But why? They didn't know anything. Virtually no one else knew where they were even going...unless Guardian talked. He keyed a message in on his SmartCom for Margaret to have someone check on Samuel. The old man was one wily bastard, but he could think of no other sources that could have leaked the plans.

Judah tapped on one of the gauges. "Temp is up to twenty-three below. Celsius of course, like...ten below for you Yanks. Going to feel downright balmy out there, boys." He gazed out at the wind whipping up the snow. "The summer breeze may make it feel a bit cooler, though. You know they say this continent used to be a tropical paradise. Can you imagine palm trees and coconuts? Parasailing off the sandy beaches?"

"That was around fifty million years ago, dude," Cade said. "Not like any of us were around then to enjoy it. It was just one of the planet's warmer periods. So warm, the polar caps melted almost entirely."

"So, global warming is a thing?" Judah asked. Then, pointing out the frost-lined window added, "This damn sure ain't it, no matter what them scientists say."

"Climate change is real," Alan offered. "Shifts in global temperatures happen constantly, just most take place over eons. The big question raging right now is how much humans have affected that process."

Judah laughed, "Not enough, am I right, Rearden?"

Cade just wanted him to shut up about the cold. He wasn't a fan and hated the fact that he'd been the reason they were all here. The time was nearing twelve AM, but there was still bright sunshine outside. The sun wouldn't set for another three months. *How does anyone ever get used to this?*

35

CARIBBEAN

"Nance, you may want to see this," Coffee said looking over the drone feeds.

"Can it wait?" She was close to springing the trap on the biologic. She wanted to see what this creature was. The collection of aqua drones was moving into range within the next few seconds. They had lost contact again with whatever had shown up on the scans.

"I don't think so," the big man said worriedly. "The drone pack on our original track are all dropping offline."

"Micah, I need you down here," Nance yelled up to the top deck. "Dee, what's going on with those fish?" She knew the AI could keep up with multiple events happening at the same time. She, however, was not so skilled. Micah hurried down the few steps and slid into a seat beside Coffee. He began trying to reestablish a connection to the tiny drones as Dee recalled several of the others. "It appears once they cross this point we begin to see corrupted telemetry, then they go dark," Dee said.

Simultaneously, she said to Nance, "Sending active pings now."

A brilliant flash of blue light erupted several hundred yards from the boat and almost instantly, every electronic device onboard went dark.

"What the hell?" one of the men said.

"Dee, can you get electronics back online?" Micah asked into the darkness. Only a tiny exit sign was lit, which was probably running on a battery.

Kissa said breathlessly, "That was it, that was what took Thera."

"Dee? Are you still with us?"

"This is Doris," came the reply. "Your local Dee is rebooting, but it appears you were hit by a low yield electromagnetic pulse wave. Analyzing some of the last data from the drones now."

Displays and lights began to come back on throughout the boat. "EMP?" Micah asked. "I thought we were the only ones who had a weapon like that."

Doris answered, "Micah, if I am reading this correctly, that was no weapon. It was generated naturally, probably by the animal you were attempting to identify."

"Doris, you are trying to tell us this squid just generated an EM field?" Nance asked. "What, like an electric eel or something? How would that even work? What kind of animals can do that?" She knew that was a lot of questions at once, but they were damn good questions.

"None," came the simple reply.

"Most of the drones are dead," Micah said, looking at the screens. The ones here and those on the original track of the MHD drive."

"We may have something," Doris said. Seconds later, she added, "Dee is rendering the last captured image from the drones now." Hundreds of tiny points of light began filling the screen on one of the displays. Like a pointillistic piece of art, a shape began to emerge as more and more of the screen filled in. Each active ping on the creature from the numerous drones was being combined into a single constructed image. As the final elements filled in, a collective gasp was heard.

"What in the holy fuck is that?" Coffee said, physically backing away from the screen.

The shocked question was the same one each of them wanted to know.

"Biologic creature does not match any known species," Dee said almost cheerily.

"Yeah, I think we would have all heard about something like that by now," Trondo said, looking down at the screen from the bridge. "Ugly bastard."

He was not wrong, the image made up of thousands of dots still gave a pretty realistic image of the ghastly beast. It seemed to defy description. A squat head, flattened on the underside, maybe with differing lengths of tentacles erupting from the neck...no, that wasn't right, the trunk of the head. The body looked somewhat more familiar, but not much. To Micah, it resembled something akin to an ancient Plesiosaur, one of the swimming dinosaurs, but again...not quite. Something maybe more similar to what people describe as the Loch Ness Monster, but that was just the body. Even that part was different. The torso seemed flatter, almost like a wing, and instead of fins or flippers, stump-like appendages splayed out at odd angles from various points along the body. Then, there were the tentacles, if the image could be believed, at least a dozen of them at various lengths. Several also ended in what looked like hooked claws, and inside each of the tentacles, suckers extended out, something like horns or serrated teeth arranged in a perfect circle.

"Captain, I'm good to return to port whenever you are," Coffee said, now leaning against a far wall.

"Got something coming toward us, moving fast," Trondo yelled out from above. They all rushed out on deck where a massive bulge of water was being pushed by the beast, now glowing with a rhythmic pulse of angry, blue light.

Micah started to speak, then paused as each of them suddenly clutched at their heads. The sudden intense pain surpassed anything he had ever felt. Accompanying the pain was immediate nausea and a sense of absolute doom. Micah saw Nance lying on the deck nearby; her body seemed to go rigid with fear or maybe pain as the animal crossed under the boat. The horrifying, glowing beast was even worse than the sonar image...much, much worse.

* * *

Coming back to the moment was an individual journey of torment for each of the passengers aboard the luxury boat. Each found their way back through a nightmarish hell of visions, pain, and nausea. Micah seemed to recover first, then slowly, Kissa, and then the others. Coffee was out nearly a full hour and went to a bunkroom to lay down immediately. For the first time, the big soldier was encountering a battlefield where the enemy was the strongest.

"What in the fuck just happened?"

Micah looked up from the display at Nance, who was rubbing the side of her head with her fist. "According to all the scans, nothing." He gestured to send the visual to the large monitor on the front wall.

"My guess is that it was some sort of defensive neural field generated by the creature," Doris said, her voice full of concern.

"Are we safe, has the animal left?" Nance asked.

"Yes, for now, you are out of danger. The organism is off our scope," Doris replied.

"I think we can all agree that Kissa was being very honest in his description of what happened. This animal was almost certainly involved in the disappearance of Thera and Kissa's admission that he was unable to respond to the attack. Jimmy and Riley are examining a slight spike in gamma wave energy generated at the time of your incapacitation."

"What, like telekinesis or something?" Kissa asked after rinsing his mouth from a bottled water.

Doris answered, "Something like that. We are in uncharted waters here. That animal is not something from our world. It does not belong here."

"How do you know? It could just be a strange mutation or a cryptid...you know, something from ancient times that we just assumed went extinct," Kissa said.

"Nothing resembling this animal's physiology has ever been discovered," Doris informed them. "Although, since it may be soft bodied, the fossil record is very incomplete. The real reason is that it consumed several of the aqua drones before turning its attention on the boat. One of those drones managed to take a sample of the animal's genetic material and began transmitting it out before it was destroyed." The display updated to showcase more data. "This is a preliminary scan showing a very different biochemistry. While it does have an unusual form of DNA, it possesses none of the traditional corresponding genetic markers of terrestrial life."

"So...this is what, Doris? Not from here? Not carbon-based?" Micah asked.

"Unfortunately, we didn't get enough of a sample to make those assumptions. My guess is that it is carbon-based, but that in itself doesn't mean it isn't something alien to our planet. It could have developed in an alternative environment, perhaps one sealed off from the rest of the planet. Numerous instances of shadow biospheres have been discovered, although most are microbial in scale. These can have radically different biochemical and molecular processes than any currently known life."

Doris continued, "What I am really basing this early supposition on is the lack of fossil or anecdotal evidence of anything closely resembling it. The strange biochemistry and the unusual psychometric field it was able to generate. That shows a predatory response, something it would use to hunt and kill. Any animal in our history that was able to subdue prey at a distance would have likely become an apex predator."

Nance could only recall how similar it was to the story the man in Guyana had told them about what attacked the oil rig. This was the monster that was terrorizing the Caribbean.

36

THE COVE

The director had her own agenda; she liked things that fit, things she could understand and yes—control. The country was hemorrhaging money. Rearden was battling an unknown enemy in Antarctica. Charlie was busy tracking something off the coast of Guyana. Doris had taken on a Caribbean mission as a personal favor to Cade, and now parts of it were consuming her and the science team. She knew she needed more information, more assets in the area. With most of the Talon Teams already deployed, that was going to be a challenge. Many things about this mystery were unsettling, and the fact that it might well be connected to the other missions was undeniable.

The Cove Project had been negligent in its work on marine focused tech in favor of space and terrestrial based systems, although Riley's team of engineers were now very busy remedying that shortcoming. Doris, on the other hand, was diving into the data stream Nance's team had collected. Something about the animal resonated an air of familiarity. Finding herself needing human perspective, she sent her avatar to the linguistics lab where Doctor Isabella Feist and Jasmine were having a spirited discussion on some topic. "Excuse me, but could I use the assistance of a human brain...or two?"

The two friends laughed. "What's up?" Izzy asked. Doris proceeded to fill them in on the Caribbean encounter. Izzy dropped into a chair near a workstation. She had been the one curating much of the data deciphered from the original alien message and trying to assemble it into a sort of codex to help index it in a more natural language database. That seemed well in the future, but they were making progress.

"Here it is, Doris. The Dhakerri reference a number of species with advanced abilities you tag as neural transmissions. None are precisely as you describe, but an entry in one of the explorer archives shows a planet with no intelligent life forms where a predator was observed crippling a prey animal with what we might describe as a bat-like sonar. It seemed to use neural projections instead of sound waves."

"That's it," Doris said. "Jaz, since you now also have the highest training of cryptozoology here, do you think any creature like this could have ever originated on Earth?"

Jaz thought for a moment. It was an intriguing question, and her initial thought was no. She mentally began going through the checklist of how such an adaptation might have emerged, how successfully would it have been, and how likely it could have stayed hidden. "If it were native to the very deep ocean, I'd put the odds at low, very unlikely, but not impossible. It's an extreme environment, nearly totally unexplored and nearly as alien to us as another planet might be. That said, its biochemistry is another matter. If what you are saying is true, then in my mind, there are only two options. One is that it is alien to our planet, or two, it was genetically engineered."

"That tracks with my thoughts, too. Since it seemed to show limited intelligence, mainly just hunter prey instincts, I doubt it built a starship and landed here, so I am leaning heavily toward someone making this beast," Doris offered.

"We need a better sample, this one seems...incomplete."

"I agree, Izzy," the director jumped in, "but we also need to know its point of origin. Get with Jimmy; he has the scans and the data points on where it has been seen. See if you can come up with any way to detect it at a distance or narrow in the search grid. Nance and her team are mostly recovered and ready to track it if we can give them a direction."

* * *

Riley had spent little time with Jaz, but they found themselves together in The Cove's Earth Sciences section both looking for possible explanations of the creature's origin. "The problem with that, Riley, is even if it were created, some sort of synthetic biology…that DNA switch had to exist first. Generic engineers are getting better at uncovering the complex inter-working of switching genes on and off, but they have not really reached the point of designing a brand new genome," Jaz explained.

"So, an adaptation like the neural pulse would have had to exist somewhere in its ancestral lineage?"

"Maybe. While that would be the simpler answer as to how it came to be, the fact is, a gene from another genome could work as well," Jaz said, looking through a database of genetic data.

"I'm certain I've never heard of any other animal possessing anything like this," Riley responded.

Jaz nodded in agreement. "Could be something long dormant, something from very early in the evolutionary tree, but it wouldn't necessarily have to be from an animal. Any biologic organism could be the donor." She pointed to a rack of plants growing in another section of the lab. "At the genetic level, there are a few differences between plants and animals. However, if you go a bit deeper to the chemical level, the cells of all animals and plants contain very similar DNA. Both animal DNA and plant DNA molecules are made from the same nucleotides. A growing belief among researchers is that animals' eyes may have evolved from specialized cells in plants, those involved in tracking the sun to improve photosynthesis. Perhaps there is a fungus or bacteria that uses something that, scaled up, could evolve into what we're seeing."

Riley shook her head in frustration. "Okay, so now we have to consider every plant that's ever existed as well?"

"That will not be easy to unravel," Jaz said. "First, we have only sampled, much less mapped out, the genomes for a fraction of the plants or animals that are alive right now. Also, new species and variants are discovered all the time. Not to mention all the billions that have preceded it, which we may never know, much less have any way to recreate genetically."

Riley had to agree, "Sounds Herculean. So, what are our options?"

Jasmine shrugged. "I'm at a loss. Until we get more information, I'm not sure what we can do, except possibly run some computer models on how a trait like this would have emerged. What type of environment would this have been an adaptation necessary for survival?"

Riley smiled; she so enjoyed working with smart people. Just like her interactions with Doris and her childhood friends here at The Cove. The exchange was puzzling, maddeningly frustrating, if she were honest, but still, they always seemed to develop a plan to find the solution. "Well, we do have the most powerful computer in existence." Riley grinned, pointing up. "Also, I have a theory. Since this appears to be a marine animal, what if the neural pulse is not just to stun for food? What if it is part of its sensory system? You know, how it detects or sees its environment."

"Something like shark's ampullae of Lorenzini?" Jaz answered. Her briefing upload had included that. "Sharks have notoriously poor eyesight. So, they have evolved a line of sensing organs forming a network of jelly-filled pores. These pores are generally in a lateral line running down the side of the fish or under the nose. These are keyed to pick up very tiny, electrical fields, primarily from living creatures nearby. Similarly, some eels have electrogenic cells that they use to stun prey, defend against predators, and we believe they use it to communicate with other eels."

"Yes!" Riley said excitedly. "We also know that some species of porpoise use their sensing sonar to echo locate, but also to blast and stun prey fish. The possibility of a sensing organ that can also be an offensive weapon has a solid basis to explore."

They were making progress with very little to go on, but both now believed it might be possible this creature potentially had a terrestrial point of origin. Now they just needed to narrow down the family tree, or trees, it was derived from and who might have the expertise to pull off such a feat.

37

ANTARCTICA

His head was bobbing side to side as the heavy MARs-1 lumbered across the ice field. Cade let the rhythm of the moment take him. He had no name for what he was doing, but it was something he'd first realized he was doing while being held captive by the radicalized Islamic group, Jeish al-Sahaba. It was a coping mechanism; he was sure one of the countless doctors had described it as such. His entire body relaxed. He let go of the feeling of pain from the skirmish; he let go of the smell of smoke on his coat, the sensation of the cold windows against his cheek. Deeper, he let himself disconnect from the physical reality until all that existed was his mind in all its multi-hued colors. There were no shapes or even names, just thoughts, but this was where the collective that was Cade Rearden gathered. It was into this auditorium he laid out the mission. It was here he finally delved into what Director Stansfield's original instructions had been.

There were too many disconnected pieces, too many loose ends for even Ace to make sense of. Still, Cade knew they were onto something. Something that someone was willing to kill to protect. That in itself was important. That meant they had rattled the right doors. He needed more data, more context, but most of all, he needed to protect his remaining team. They were in an unforgiving environment, all of them far out of their element.

A part of him felt the vehicle jerk over some disturbance on the ice field, but his heightened state of focus ignored the would-be interruption. He didn't understand this process, but was agreeing with Doris that this was how he tapped into his subconscious mind, the intuitive part that collected all the bits and managed to somehow make sense of them. In his wakeful state, that part of him had a voice, but here it was even more capable, more insightful. One thing he was now sure of, Margaret had not been totally forthcoming in the briefing.

The transport lurched again, this time to the left; Cade's head rattled against the thick window, but he didn't awake. *Someone wants us dead. Scientists disappeared down here, trouble in the Caribbean.* That was the essence of what he had. Now, what was he looking for? What was the mission of those original scientists? Ace had the info immediately, it had been in the upload packet, '*Magnetic Anomalies.*'

What in the fuck is that? Cade wondered. He'd been brought up to speed previously on the fact that the planet's magnetic field was not uniform. Some parts of the planet had slightly higher or weaker magnetic fields, all presumably the result of the uneven distribution of certain geologic masses, primarily, those highest in magnetic properties like iron or nickel. Ace informed him that the magnetic poles also drift quite a bit and multiple times in history had reversed polarity entirely. *How does any of this help with this mission?* Cade voiced internally.

Ace explained, *Antarctica is a strange place, forget the cold and ice and lack of humans. First, there is an enormous geomagnetic object deep underground. Quite possibly a meteorite, maybe one as large as Oumuamua. I think the anomaly is located beneath the frozen wasteland in a place they call Wilkes Land. The area is massive, and the object is at a depth of about 2,700 feet. The 'Wilkes Land Gravity Anomaly' was first uncovered in 2006, when NASA satellites spotted gravitational changes which indicated the presence of a huge object sitting in the middle of a 300-mile-wide impact crater.*

Damn, Cade thought.

Indeed, an impact that large would have far exceeded the one that supposedly killed the dinosaurs sixty-five million years ago. One possibility Doris had is that it could have been another killer, though. One much older, something called the Permian–Triassic Extinction Event, which killed 96 percent of Earth's sea creatures and up to 70 percent of the vertebrate organisms living on land.

The vehicle jerked several more times. Cade was having increasing trouble maintaining his focused state.

Ace continued, *Something else that may be connected is truly bizarre. Cosmic rays are apparently being emitted from somewhere beneath the ice. That is a high-energy particle that's blasted its way through space, into the Earth, and back out again. But here's the thing, the particles physicists know about—the collection of particles that make up what scientists call the Standard Model (SM) of particle physics—shouldn't even be able to do that.*

What does all this have to do with the mission? Another massive jolt pulled Cade into full wakefulness.

"Sorry about that, mate." Judah grinned, looking back. "The ice field gets a bit more irregular here as we're getting to the mountains. The glaciers pile up on the peaks and well, make driving a lot more hazardous. Just one of the reasons why we usually fly in, when we decide to come here at all."

"So, not many missions to these parts?" Cade asked, his voice sounding groggy and a bit hoarse.

"Not much, everyone now wants to drill deep ice cores out on the pack ice or determine the melt rate on the ice shelf. A few monitor the buried lakes for emerging life forms, but this part, too remote, and too little to see."

Cade looked out at the landscape, finally detecting some rocky islands in the sea of ice. The stark contrast of brown and black to the white ground and piercing blue sky was jarring. He thought of several things from his inner session. Samuel had said something about lying unconvincingly. For some reason, that was stuck in his head. "Judah, what is the most outlandish story you've heard about Antarctica?"

The man gripped the wheel and smiled up into the mirror. "Oh mate, it's a whopper." He reached down and took a pull from a thermos of hot tea and began.

* * *

"You see, back, I'd guess around 1947, Admiral Byrd, not the earlier one, but a bloke named Richard E. Byrd, brought 4,000 sailors and soldiers down here. Most were from America, but some Brits, Norwegians, and Canadians in the mix as well. It was, in essence, an invasion of Antarctica. They called it 'Operation Highjump.'"

"That sounds familiar, is that part real?" Cade asked.

"Oh, yeah, absolutely," Judah said. "That is one hundred percent undeniable fact. It was the end of World War Two. It seems incredible that soon after a war that had taken so much and crippled global economies, they would undertake an expedition to Antarctica with so much haste. The only other oddity of note was that this was just a few months after the now infamous Roswell UFO crash.

"Officially, America was curious if the Germans had built a base down here, as many rumors began to circulate that, even though Germany had been defeated, a selection of Nazi personnel and scientists had fled Germany and established themselves at a base on Antarctica. Supposedly, from there, they continued to develop advanced aircraft based on extraterrestrial technologies. And supposedly, the allies were also increasingly nervous about their former partner, the Soviet Union. Another likely possibility was the operation was a potential training exercise on a Siberian invasion of Russia.

"Now, up to this point, it is all undisputed fact. The part of the story that is much less often told, though, is what happened to Operation Highjump. Byrd and his forces encountered heavy resistance to their Antarctic venture. The resistance was not from Nazis hiding out, or Japanese, or Russians. No, they were attacked by something they described as "flying saucers" and had to call off the expedition.

"Now, the operation ended after only two months with what was called in the press 'many fatalities.' Rather than deny the heavy casualty reports, Admiral Byrd revealed in a press interview that Task Force

68 had encountered a new enemy that 'could fly from pole to pole at incredible speeds.' Now, the U.S. press never picked up on the stories. Most likely it was suppressed. Byrd's bosses never confirmed any of it, but interestingly, Byrd was neither demoted nor booted out. Instead, he just stayed silent about the entire thing after that initial reporting."

"Holy shit," Cade said.

Alan, who had been listening in, agreed. "Cade, what are we getting into down here?"

Rearden just looked at the boy. He had no answers, not yet.

38

The weather actually worsened into a full-blown storm as they neared the coordinates. The polar winds whipped the snow into a whiteout blizzard. Several times, Judah motioned for McTee to stop and wait for the nav system to update before continuing. With nothing to use for reference, Cade was certain they would run into a mountain or off a cliff, but the reliable transport just steadily kept pushing ahead.

"Getting close there, Captain," Judah yelled back. Cade was no longer denying his rank, or that they were not actually on a scientific mission. Shit, people were trying to kill them. That was hardly normal for a science expedition...*was it?*

"I was nearly twenty before I saw snow," McTee said, trying not to think on Judah's tale. "Kind of hard to believe, isn't it? I mean, the stuff is damn common. My family didn't travel much, and we were always just a bit too far south or a bit too warm or dry. I mean, we had a few flakes now and then, but no real snow." He gave a chuckle at the irony. "Then I joined the Navy, and where did they send me...Alaska. I saw all the snow and cold I ever wanted in that first week."

They had not discussed the story Judah had told. None of them knew if it was total bullshit or not. Cade figured there was at least a core of truth. Something odd happened. Was it tied to the recent events? He was uncertain, but filed it away with all the other random bits in his increasingly crowded head.

Judah pointed at the map on the screen, then out the window in the same direction. "Probably two miles around the base of this peak we should find a break from the wind. Should be a good place to base out of and leave the truck. It's gonna' be a footer from there."

A 'footer' wasn't a fun thing they decided after less than a hundred yards. The going was cold and treacherous. Although the wall of icy rock blocked most of the wind, the sound of it roaring around the peak above was nearly deafening. The small group was walking down a narrow pass between several gigantic boulders. The gap was much too narrow for the MARS-1, so they had maneuvered all the gear to a couple of sleds Judah had provided. Instead of dogs to pull it, lines stretched out to the men.

Here in the perpetual shadows, the snow was loose with a consistency more like sand than ice. Their boots dropped down half a foot with each step. "No snowshoes?" Alan asked Judah.

"Nah, don't use 'em much down here—normally the ice layer is pretty shallow. We can just go in far enough to set up camp tonight. I don't think it's more than a kilometer. Tomorrow, we'll begin climbing. That's when it really gets fun. Come on, lads, we're burning daylight."

"It never gets dark here....not really a big motivator, dude," McTee said.

They made camp in a spot that did not seem too terribly different from all the other awful spots they could have chosen. Cade was sick of the cold, the ice, and the snow but had to admit the Rapide Tactical Suit made it much more bearable. Wearing it for this long did begin getting uncomfortable, though. They were tight fitting and not ideal for doing your business or climbing mountains.

"You know," Judah said, sitting down beside him, "these coordinates are not unknown to me."

Cade watched as the man began to eat from one of the meal-kits they'd brought in.

"Damn, this stuff is good, never had field rations like this."

Cade smiled. "So, what do you know about our destination?"

The older man took another bite, savoring the warm, Asian-spiced pork. "Well, rumor mostly, strange stories. This is all pretty close to the no-fly zone, I suppose you know that." He waved the fork upward and around in a broad circle. "Guess that's why you wanted my trucks."

Cade shrugged; he was still not high on giving out more than he was receiving. "Nothing was flying due to the weather."

"Yeah, well, I don't know who you guys are, but this isn't a U.S. no-fly zone. It's international. Had you flown in, others would have come after you."

Someone had come after them, but Cade decided to not bring that up.

Judah continued, "Lot of weird stuff said about this area. Most puzzling one was around '94. Navy brought some scientists out here from McMurdo. Real scientists, you know...not like you guys." He smiled as he speared another bite with his fork. "Anyway, they flew out on a big transport, had a ton of gear, and all seemed great for a few days, then they stopped responding to radio calls. Nothing was heard for 72 hours, so the Navy sent a chopper out. They reported the camp was undamaged but abandoned."

Cade had heard most of this already but let the man speak, just to see if his version might offer more details.

"Well, the Navy was getting ready to mount an all-out search when they got a call from the scientists saying they were fine and ready for pickup. No one had seen these guys for weeks, and they show up like it's no big deal."

"So, where had they been?" Cade asked innocently.

Judah finished off the last couple of bites, then sat back with his thermo-cup full of coffee. "Where indeed, my friend. Where indeed...."

* * *

The four of them got an early start the next day. In a land where four AM was just as bright as high noon, why wait? The storm had thankfully subsided, and their first stop was just a few miles away on a high ice plain. "This is supposedly where the scientists' base camp was," Judah said. "No idea exactly where, but this general vicinity."

Alan was consulting his SmartCom and seemed to be trying to get a bearing on a distant peak. "Judah, what would have been of interest here? I'm not detecting any of the gravity or magnetic anomalies in the area. Wasn't that what they were supposed to be studying?"

The Australian was shaking his head. "We all know what they came out here for. It isn't here. The hole. Never seen it, but the thing they seem to call the hole in the ice is about eight kilometers south."

They all looked where he was pointing; jagged peaks, dramatic cliffs, and unforgiving terrain was all they saw. "That's what to you Yanks? Five miles...and almost three miles of elevation changes. She's gonna be a bloody bitch, fellas." He paused to look at Cade. "You sure you want to do this, friend?"

39

Cade's eyes scanned the surrounding hills. Never far from his mind was the fact that they'd already been attacked. Someone who'd drawn first blood. Someone who was hunting them. Someone meant to do them even more harm. Another part of his brain couldn't accept the fact that anyone would want to stop them. Not down here. What was out here in this cold, bleak wilderness that someone would want to keep hidden? Still, scientists had gone missing years earlier, and who knew what else might have happened in the God-forsaken place?

After several hours of crawling over rocky, ice-covered peaks and valleys, he was ready for someone to shoot him. They were all exhausted. He saw nothing, but 'felt' a danger pressing in. Walking well ahead of the rest, he tapped his CommDot. "Hey, you busy?"

Jaz's voice came back immediately. "Not much, just helping Riley with some genetic stuff. Way out there kinda stuff. Anyway, but I can talk. What's up?"

"Boredom, cold, stress...I dunno. I just needed to remind myself someone else was back there. This place is so barren, it just seems to eat at your very soul bit by bit."

"I bet it's beautiful, though," she said wistfully.

"I suppose. Never been anywhere quite like it, that's for sure...I could describe it to you if you like."

She could have just activated the video feed from Cade's goggles but said, "Yeah, do that."

"Well, where are you right now?" he asked, straining a bit as he climbed to a higher rock ledge at the same time.

"I'm in the workshop, why? Are you about to ask me what I'm wearing?"

"Gotcha...and no. Fabrication lab, okay. Walk as far as you can to the eastern-most wall."

She did so, feeling foolish but knowing this had to be going somewhere. Cade was nothing if not entertaining. She was now looking at the slightly curved wall of the lab. "Okay, I'm here. What am I supposed to do?"

"Nothing," came the reply. "Now you and I are seeing exactly the same thing. Just a big expanse of empty white space."

"Ugh," she groaned. "Idiot." Laughing, she went back to check on the experiment she was nominally monitoring. "Your head is an empty space, Rearden."

He laughed, too, knowing it was anything but that. "So, what are you guys working on? Any update from Kissa?"

Jaz didn't answer immediately; then he realized she must have been going somewhere more private. The sound was different when she started speaking. "We have had some interesting developments. Doris should have sent you an update by now. Kissa, Nance, and her team seem to have stumbled onto something rather unusual."

40

The one they called Steiger watched the small group through the long-range optics. She knew where they were heading, although she had no clue as to what was there. It had been one of the assigned targets to protect. She was used to working as part of a duo but was just as comfortable alone. Her partner for this assignment, Karl, had finally checked in several hours earlier. He'd offered no reason for the delay but acknowledged he'd failed to sufficiently detain the team from America. She cursed silently at the man's apparent incompetence. Silently, for that was the way of the Schattens.

The Schattens, or Shadows, were descended from a more ancient group. They appeared occasionally throughout history, often more myth than anything tangible. The boogeyman, the ones who bring pain and suffering and delight in its application. 'The misfortunes of others tastes like honey,' is how one ancient text described it. The French would call it 'joie maligne,' a diabolical delight in other people's suffering. The Danish word is 'skadefryd,' and the Dutch is 'leedvermaak.' They were the Shadows, originators of the Schattenfreude.

All of this, and more, had been part of Steiger's training from the very youngest age. Like all of her brethren in the Shadows, she was born different. Her behavior frustrated, then frightened, her parents. As a child, she refused to be held, refused to be comforted, and disliked playing with others. In other societies, she would have eventually been described as emotionally deficient, sociopathic, or maybe even psychopathic. To the Schatten, though, she was a gift, one of only a few they found each year. The emotional detachment, when combined with high intelligence and physical strength, had made her perfect for the role.

She trained and studied the ancient ways until her mind absorbed every nuance. Like the others, she now saw the hypocrisy most people carried with them. The outward manners hiding the much darker desires, even to themselves, to admit that a taste for other people's misery might corrupt their eternal souls. Yet, secretly, that was exactly what they longed for. She was honest with her desire; she embraced the role like the apex predator she was. The exhilaration of having a successful hunt outweighing any concern for the morality, or even consequences if she failed.

Placing the binoculars into her gear bag, Steiger tightened the straps on her pack and pulled it on. She disliked the need to be dressed in bulky layers and the alpine coverup, but here on the 'White Continent,' it was the only way for Shadows to stay hidden. She gently ran her fingers along the cold steel barrel of the FN Ballista FDE Rifle .338 Lapua. She placed the magazine inside her parka to keep the rounds from possibly freezing. A misfire could be fatal, and that was a mistake she would not allow herself.

She'd ridden out the recent storm in the bitter cold of a cave, and now was anxious to get moving. The four men were almost 5000 meters ahead, moving into the rocks and hills jutting out of the landscape. She could effectively kill them at about half that distance, but getting more than one or two before they found cover was unlikely. No, this was a time when she would need to be close in. With luck, she would ignore the Lapua and use something more personal, something more intimate, to dispatch the trespassers.

Steiger clipped into her long skis and began poling toward the rocky terrain. Her orders had been clear. Do not let the group get to the coordinates. She was already thinking of creative ways to dispose of the bodies in this unforgiving wasteland. While still very detached from any real emotion, she thought it fair to say—she really loved her work.

41

CARIBBEAN

Kissa stared at the mass of floating debris. Shiny bits of machine parts from the numerous drones as well as scores of fish. Most had been severed in half or mangled beyond description. The creature was indiscriminate in its destruction, animal or drone. The fate was the same. Was this what had become of Thera? No matter how hard he tried, he couldn't escape that one thought.

"If it was feeding, why did it leave so many?" Coffee asked hanging over the upper rail overseeing the carnage. "Seems like it was more interested in killing than eating."

Micah was cautiously using a net, trying to salvage some of the more complete drone pieces. "I don't think it can digest 'em. I'm sending what DNA and related data we have over to Riley, she'll know something." He swung the net out to snag what appeared to be a nearly complete aqua drone before continuing, "If the creature's biochemistry is as different as I think, most everything would be incompatible as a food source."

Nance had eased down the ladder to help steady the boy. "It has to eat, though, right?"

Micah shrugged, "We assume so, it certainly has the required equipment." He was rotating the partial drone to expose multiple teeth or beak marks in the polysteel shell. "Any organisms that don't feed have to get energy more directly from some source. Nutrients are the most common way, but there could be others. The predation indicates that it wants to feed, it may just not be able to, or at least get enough to be satisfied. That frustration may be part of what is fueling its apparent rage."

"Why do you think that?"

Micah turned to look at Kissa, "Does this look like anything normal?"

Kissa nodded. The early morning sun revealed a debris field nearly a hundred yards wide, blood and fish oil mixed with less identifiable fluids among the bits of detritus and drone wreckage..."That does mean something else, young Micah."

"What's that?"

"It's feeding somewhere—somehow. It didn't appear weak or malnourished. I think this animal is not natural, which means someone is feeding it. Someone is keeping it alive. If we follow it, we may find the answers to many questions." *And Thera,* he thought hopefully.

* * *

Several hours later, Dee indicated that she had acquired the faint track once more of the MHD drive. Trondo was at the helm, moving the craft easily over the pristine waters. The color of the ocean was changing from the brilliant turquoise to a deeper aquamarine. The channels were deepening the farther from land they got. He checked the nav screen once more—the track they were following would not take them close to any land mass. That probably wasn't a surprise since they were following a submersible, but it also meant Dee was constantly running calculations on fuel and range. The huge boat had enormous tanks and a great range, but another twenty-four hours would be about as far as they could go without returning for more fuel.

Trondo felt more than saw Coffee coming up to the pilot bridge. It was the large man's turn to take the wheel. Despite his reluctance to being out on the open sea, he'd taken to piloting the boat like a pro. "Any change?"

"Nope." Trondo shook his head. "Pretty straight course if I can believe the computer."

Coffee set an open drink can in the holder and took the wheel. "No signs of our new 'friend' either, I hope."

"God, no, hope I never see that thing again," Trondo said, lifting his sunglasses up and rubbing at his tired eyes. "I'm going to get some lunch and a little shuteye."

Coffee nodded and had Dee start his favorite playlist, a mix of hip-hop and blues standards. He sat back on the small pilot chair to enjoy the ride.

The music, warm sunshine, rhythmic rise and fall of the boat, and steady drumming of the powerful diesel inboards might have lulled most people into a dreamlike state. Staff Sergeant Willy Coffee was not most people. He saw the disturbance on the water even before Dee gave a warning. He throttled back sharply, arousing the others. "We have something, people." In a much softer voice, he whispered, "Please don't be that monster."

He checked the nav screen. They were in the middle of nowhere. Currently, they were passing over one of the deepest parts of the Caribbean Sea, an area known as the Cayman Trench. Jamaica was a few hundred miles to the northeast. Otherwise, not much of interest as far as the map was concerned. Coffee lifted the specially designed binoculars to his eyes and focused in on what he and the computer had noticed. An irregularity along the horizon, almost directly ahead of them. A bump on the blue horizontal line of the sea.

Not like a boat, much larger, almost like a giant hill of water growing up and out of the deep ocean. He knew the video feed from the binoculars was streaming to Doris and all the others in the boat. He heard the questions coming from the people below. Nance had walked up while he was looking and placed a hand on his shoulder.

"Slow ahead, Sergeant. Let's go and see what Dee has found."

* * *

Coffee notched the throttle down slightly.

"Dee, how far away is that thing?" Nance asked.

"Approximately four miles, Captain."

Damn, Nance thought. That meant it was far larger than she'd been thinking.

As if anticipating the next question, Dee continued, "Preliminary estimates would put the portion we are seeing at almost 1000 meters wide. Since we are only seeing the top portion, it is likely much larger."

"What the fuck is it?" Kissa said, standing up and leaning out the bridge.

They all shook their heads. As they cut the distance by half, they could already see the object was submerging again. Only about a hundred meters of it rose above the waterline. On the level, just dipping below the waves, massive curved windows seem to bubble out like blisters. The remaining portion of the craft was a dark, bluish green that closely matched that of the water. The exposed portion was a graceful arching curve with a subtle pattern that seemed reminiscent of sunlight refracted by water, like you might see reflected from the bottom of a pool.

"It's going down fast!" Micah called up. He'd kept watching via the camera feed and, almost as an afterthought, he'd launched a few drones to get an aerial view. Now, he was prepping a couple of his increasingly scarce stock of aqua drones to get a view from below.

The craft was descending quickly, faster than a ship could sink even. But there were no geysers of water like a ballast release of air might cause. In fact, it barely disturbed the water surface. The boat closed to within about one hundred feet. Coffee checked the sonar; absolutely nothing showed up below, but the water depth had changed from 10,000 meters to less than a thousand. Whatever this was, it was below them now, and sensors were picking it up as seafloor. He knew this was nothing natural.

Only a small rounded portion of the dome remained above the surface. "Micah, please deploy a tracker tag to the anomaly before it goes under," Nance ordered.

"On it," he said, guiding multiple drones to the portion still exposed. With the radius of exposed craft shrinking by the second, they all just marveled at the technology. It blended so well with the ocean—even knowing it was there, it was hard to make out. It literally looked like a swelling of the ocean surface. Then it was gone.

"One tag attached," Micah said before adding a startled, "Holy shit!"

The false bottom reading that they now knew was the craft was receding quickly. "Bottom depth returning to normal," Coffee said as he watched the instrument cluster intently.

"What is it, kid?" Kissa asked, heading down the few steps to where Micah was.

A sleepy Trondo who had joined them for the past few minutes was looking at a group of seabirds off to the port side. He grabbed the binoculars and glassed the scene. "Shit!"

"What?"

"Our friend is back, Captain."

42

ANTARCTICA

Cade glanced once more to the frozen hills, feeling again as if something was off. He trusted his instincts. Years of being a hunter...a warrior on various battlefields around the planet had honed those skills to a knife's edge. He wasn't sure which of his personalities drove this instinctual part of his brain, or as Doris had suggested more than once, perhaps it was just his subconscious. Whoever it was, he trusted it with this life. And now, with the lives of the rest of his team.

McTee picked up on it first. “Hey, Boss, you got something?”

“I dunno.” Cade shrugged. “Maybe just my ghost acting up, but yeah. Stay on point—I feel eyes on our back.” He caught up with Alan to ask about launching some dove drones.

“No can-do, Cap. Hard to control in these valleys, and the wind is still too strong up over the peaks. I'm pretty sure I'd lose them within just a few seconds.” Alan pulled himself up the rocks the same way Judah had just gone. “What would I be looking for, anyway?”

Cade didn't know, and he was growing more frustrated. All this tech, and yet, none of it seemed that practical out here. “If someone was up in these rocks, do you have anything that would detect them?”

“If they show themselves, yeah.” Alan stopped on a ledge, reached in his pack and took out what looked like a clear plastic ball with an assortment of gizmos inside.

"What the fuck is that?" Cade asked.

"BallCam, something Jimmy and I came up with when we were trying to...well, let's skip that part. Basically, it's like a mini-go-pro type camera in a self-leveling, gyro controlled, 360-degree mount," Alan said, almost gleefully. "Really similar to what the aerial drones use. It can scan in multiple wavelengths, of course. It's field of view is its only limit, but the software Jimmy put together allows us to do some pretty cool stuff."

"Like what?"

"Well," Alan said, rearing an arm back, "like this." He threw the ball as high up as he could and waited for it to come back down. Cade saw that the little ball had deployed a small winglet to slow the descent, and it curved as it descended right back to them. The winglet retracted as soon as Alan caught it midair. "The scans will be in your goggles. It will be a 3D file, so just pull it up and cycle through the IR range looking for heat signatures. The perspective will be based on how high the camera went."

Cade quickly saw the new file and clicked play. Even though the toss only lasted a few seconds, the super-fast camera recorded several minutes' worth of video. Cade could zoom in or out on any spot, including looking straight down on himself from above. "So cool." Turning on the IR overlay, he saw nothing. Even when he dialed up the sensitivity, nothing showed up. Apparently, they were the only thing down here with a heartbeat, all other life being intelligent enough to avoid this particular bit of high-value real estate.

* * *

"How much farther, Judah?" Alan asked.

The man just shrugged and kept trudging along. Deeper they went into the maze of narrow, but impressive, peaks and valleys. Had the massive ice sheet been removed, they would be climbing up and down full-sized mountains that could rival some of the best the Alps had to offer. As it was, the terrain was challenging but not overly rigorous. The cold and the sameness of the scenery is what was lulling them into complacency. Out of the corner of his eye, Judah saw Cade behind him tossing the BallCam high into the air again. Something clearly had the man spooked.

Finally reaching a relatively even section of trail, Alan activated the coordinates on his heads-up display map. They were still on course and closing in, probably within a half mile. Curiously, when he zoomed in, the target coordinates seem to swim around in a lazy circle, as if they were not precisely a fixed point. He had his Dee trigger a fix from one of the commercial satellites. The problem got worse instead of better. He thought he knew the problem but asked Dee for confirmation.

"You are correct, Alan. The continent's large gravitational anomaly partially extends under this region. Strong variations in the magnetic field can affect the correlation between ground stations and the NAVSTAR GPS satellite network, as well as our own commercial ones. The problem is not the position moving, but rather the inability to fix your own position precisely from orbit."

He checked again and realized there were only three signals showing up in his display. Judah was now carrying one of three beacons, so he was not the missing person. Muting the HUD from his goggles, he turned around. McTee was about a hundred yards back. Rearden was gone.

Alan waited for the other man. "Where did Cade go?"

"Dunno, man, he was there one second tossing that ball, and the next thing, he's gone."

"Should we call him?" Alan asked.

McTee shook his head. "Already tried, he's operating in his own zone right now. Just stay on course. We can always find his beacon...*again*." They both smiled. The last time they'd lost him, they'd wound up digging his nearly dead body out of a beach in New Jersey. Hopefully, this one would be less dramatic.

They caught up to the Australian and topped the next, and hopefully final, ridge about thirty minutes later. The old man pulled his thermal hood back, revealing a patchwork of hair, scalp, and assorted sores.

"What happened, dude?" McTee asked pointing up.

Judah ran his hand across the landscape atop his skull and grinned. "You damn Yanks keep depleting the ozone layer. Damn UV rays get through down here like a river after a flood. Docs always wanting to check us for skin cancers and stuff. Hazard of the job." He took a pull from his water bottle. "This should be it. Never been here myself, so I can't offer much more that that." He looked around curiously. "Where's your boss?"

Something kicked up snow and rock chips from the ledge behind them, then the distinct sound of a gunshot. The disconnect between the two confused Alan, but the other men were already diving for cover.

"What the fuck, man," McTee said. Then, keying his CommDot, "Nomad, come in. You got eyes on? We have hostiles to our north." He risked a quick glance over the rock and another round pinged off near his chin. "Well, shit, bastard is just going to keep us pinned down until we freeze to death, I guess."

Judah looked over, shaking his head. "You boys have some damned determined enemies for them to keep trying to try kill you way out here. What happened, did one of your satellites discover gold in these mountains or something?"

Alan and McTee just shrugged, it didn't make sense to them either.

"Where are you, Cade?" Alan whispered.

43

Cade Rearden had learned long ago to listen to his inner voices and his instincts. More than once, they had saved his life. He heard McTee's call over the comms, followed soon after by Alan's. Then the shooting started. His senses had detected the threat behind them, and he'd veered off the narrow ledge and up higher before circling back to the north. Now he needed to know precisely where the shooter was. The sounds of gunfire echoed through the mountainous valley. *Did I see something on the BallCam?* He couldn't be sure but didn't think so. Another shot rang out. Cade's CommDot was usually pretty accurate at pinpointing origination points, but this time it was giving wildly varied results. The shooter could be within a hundred yards or a kilometer away.

He moved through the rocky terrain silently, not daring to speak, watching every footfall as to not disturb the loose rocks or worse, slip on an icy patch. An assortment of large rocky crags and boulders shielded him somewhat, but he was less than fifty yards from the ridgeline. Up there, he would standout to anyone looking from below, something Rangers called 'sky-lining' in his advanced combat course. Soldiers always avoided that at all costs.

A hundred questions were running through his mind. *Who is this guy? How did he get here, and why does he want us dead?* All of those had to wait. Right now, Cade just had to do his job and pray to God McTee kept the others out of harm's way. He eased down behind a dark, gray boulder the size of a truck and slowly removed the rifle from where it was slung on his shoulder. Up to this point, it had been more important to keep both hands empty for balance. The rifle had been designed to look like a more futuristic version of an H&K 416 assault rifle. That particular weapon would not have been ideal for this environment, but Cade was still comfortable with it, thankful that Riley had equipped it with an armament payload nearly identical to the NATO 5.56 mm round. He trusted that ammo and knew its deadly, efficient stopping power. Right now, though, he just needed it for one thing.

The KillPoint scope had activated as soon as it sensed his hands on the pistol grip of the stock. He cautiously edged the rifle over the lip of the boulder and let the gun's optics begin to surveil the terrain for targets or shooters. What the gun saw, he saw as an overlay in his goggles. Like the other weapons in the TCP arsenal, he could activate autofire mode on this one. So, when the target was spotted by the scope, an appropriate ammo package would be selected, calculations made for the shot based on distance, wind, drop, and a host of other factors, and the firing sequence handled all within milliseconds. Cade chose not to do that, he wanted to stop the shooter, but he also needed answers. Who in the fuck would go to this much trouble to stop them, and what were they protecting?

The impressive KillPoint tracking scope came back clear, no targets. *Shit.* So much for the easy way. The shooter hadn't fired in the last couple of minutes. That could mean he was relocating to a better position or simply waiting for his prey to make a mistake. Cade hated to do it, but he needed the shooter to make a mistake, albeit just a small one. Still watching the image through the gunsight, he eye-blinked to get McTee on a private channel. As quietly as he could, he told him what he needed.

"You want me to do what?" the former SEAL said with an air of disbelief.

"Just give the shooter a target. Better you than one of the others. Use a glove or a boot, just don't leave your foot in it," Cade whispered.

The other man's voice responded reluctantly, "Roger that, Cap, in three, two...one."

The shot rang out, the sniper had taken the bait. Simultaneously, he heard McTee yelp over the open mic. He couldn't worry about his man right now, though. The KillPoint system had flashed red when it detected the shot; now its various visual and audio spectrums sensor were pinpointing the most likely position. Cade felt the internal servos in the gun, the ones used for the auto targeting, pulling the weapon in a different direction. He allowed the motion to track the rifle farther to the east, nearly parallel with his own position of concealment. It stopped on what appeared to be a barren patch of mountainside, numerous shards of flaked stone cascading down the rock face. The screen shifted multiple times truing to pinpoint the target, but all either he or the gun saw was the mountainside.

Cade had worked with some of the best snipers in the world during his time as a Ranger, and later, as part of various SpecOps missions. Men whose shots were legends. Guys who could lie still and concealed for hours, or even days. In one of those instances, he watched as a Royal Marine sniper from Great Britain shot a terrorist from over a half-mile away who was behind a stone wall. There was no part of the man visible except an occasional glimpse of his shadow against the rear wall. After the successful kill shot, the sniper had recorded all the relevant data, as they all were meticulous record keepers. Cade had read the notes in amazement. To make the actual shot, the Marine aimed 56 feet to the left and 38 feet high of the place the shadow would be at the time the round arrived. No one ever made fun of the Brits after that.

This guy's aim wasn't that good, obviously, but his concealment game was on point. Even the sophisticated software in Cade's rifle scope couldn't pinpoint him. McTee whispered in his earpiece,

"Hope you got him because that was too fucking close for comfort...sir."

Cade ignored the complaint. His entire focus was on a patch of dirt and rock roughly three meters square. He had to trust the KillPoint sensors, but he could see nothing. The area didn't even have anything for concealment. Suddenly another shot was fired, and this time both Cade and the rifle saw the origin point. A slight whiff of white smoke drifted up. Cade locked the optics onto a spot just a bit farther back. About as far as a man lying prone would be sighting down a sniper rifle. He still saw nothing. Not a ripple along the ground, not even a difference in the coloration. He remembered a warning that these guys may have tech as good as their own. That meant some sort of active camouflage system or something. The weapon shuddered violently, and the optical overlay flashed red. Then Cade knew why. He glimpsed the end of the man's rifle barrel just before the KillPoint scope exploded away from the assault rifle. He'd been spotted, and now he was the hunted.

* * *

"Tee, shooter has eyes on me, may be a good time to get over that next ridge. Move on five."

Cade's subconscious registered the acknowledgement but was already formulating an attack plan. "Dee, what are my options for targeting? KillPoint is down."

"Nomad, shooter is approximately ninety meters out. I have the location marked, but positioning systems are not accurate enough due to magnetic anomalies to be of much use. Recommend fragmentation rounds."

"Do it." He came up firing at the spot of ugly terrain he'd memorized and felt the impact as a massive round punched him in the shoulder. The armored Battlesuit absorbed most of the round's kinetic energy, but the seven percent that got through was enough to throw him backward and possibly dislocate that shoulder. Pain ripped through him as his vision began to narrow. He was about to have bigger issues, though, as the antithesis of stealth stirred to life. *Oh, shit*...he thought, before relinquishing control to the long silent barbarian.

The pain in Cade's shoulder faded to the background as he quickly rose, and feet began to pump faster than he thought possible. The gun was firing, and Cade realized it was for effect; many of the rounds were only to produce smoke, making it harder for the shooter to find his mark. Brutus covered the distance faster than should have been possible. Through Cade's head's-up, he could see the other three members of his team moving quickly to the south.

Hey, Gus, you think this fool has a plan? Cade asked internally.

Gus gave the equivalent of a mental shrug, *Did you?*

One of Cade's legs bent back at a sharp angle, and he felt a tendon pull. A glancing impact from another round. Brutus let that leg drag awkwardly as he slowed to within meters of the sniper's hide. Through a fog of pain and the acknowledgement that he wasn't the one driving, he still couldn't make out the target. But he did see a splatter of blood on the mottled gray rocks. *Jesus, where is this guy?*

With a roar, Brutus put the assault rifle on full auto and painted the ground with shots. *So much for taking the shooter alive,* Gus said, the internal voice offering a hint of amusement at the predicament.

Suddenly, Cade saw the ground move and noticed a crease between what appeared to be differing rock layers. Then a spray of blood erupted literally out of the ground.

Whoa, whoa, whoa, there, cowboy. I think you got him, big guy.

Brutus's bloodlust temporarily satisfied, he stepped back into his cage, leaving Cade to deal fully with the agony of the wounds. His leg gave out, and he dropped beside the combatant. He could see it was a guy. Young, with a very slight build. The boy's chest was moving up and down erratically. Even right on top of him, Cade could still barely make him out. The sniper had not been under any device. No Antarctic mountain version of a Ghillie suit, even. The kid just had some sort of tactical body suit on that blended seamlessly with the surroundings, and he'd taken care to color his hair, weapon, and face with a complex pattern that blended almost perfectly. It reminded him of an artist he'd seen on TV who could paint himself into the background of nearly any scene. This kid was better, he wasn't just an artist—his camouflage was perfect. Unfortunately for him, it wasn't bulletproof. The would-be killer looked up, took one more breath, and was gone.

44

CARIBBEAN

Kissa was having another of the borderline panic attacks. This was not just uncharacteristic for him, but unheard of, at least until the last few days. His hands gripped the deck rail hard as he stared out toward the approaching beast. His black skin shimmered with perspiration as he tried his best to settle his nerves. "You are a warrior, a champion. Pull it together, man," he whispered as more of a prayer than a command.

"Bottom contact!" Micah yelled from below deck. "Something coming back up, not the...um, big ass thing again."

The 'big ass' thing. The thing that should not exist, Kissa thought. *The spaceship, that's what it has to be. That's what it looked like. We're out here in my ocean battling alien monsters. Is that their mother ship? How many of the beasts could be inside that thing? Is that where they took Theru?* The thoughts kept coming, feeding his panic until he was paralyzed to do anything but stare at the fast-approaching v-shaped wake.

"Hundred yards," Trondo yelled as he turned the boat sharply away from the approaching danger.

"Get us out of here." Sergeant Coffee had stepped beside Kissa, but the islander was so focused on the creature he hadn't noticed. "Captain, permission to engage."

From somewhere below, a frustrated Nance said, "Negative. We've been ordered to get a more complete tissue sample." She stepped up the short ladder onto the main deck. "If this thing is something everyone thought was extinct, then killing it would make us the monsters."

"And if it attacks?" Coffee asked.

Still agitated, she nodded, "If it tries to eat us, you have my permission to fire to wound, but not to kill. Micah is working on some sort of tool to retrieve the sample."

Coffee had no idea how he was supposed to know where to shoot to wound, but not kill, this abomination. "Shit," he said, seeing the humped back breaking the waterline now. *Damn, that thing is big.* He centered the rifle scope just ahead of the disturbance and allowed the weapon's KillPoint software to take over tracking and targeting. Reluctantly, he said, "Dee, you have control." In doing so, he relinquished firing authority as well as ammo choice to the little AI. *Let her figure out what to do.* Putting his own safety and that of his team in the hands of a computer felt wrong to him. It went against years of training and all of his actual combat experience, but this was the world he was in now.

Coffee felt himself already beginning to get the shakes and sensed the oncoming headache. Glancing to his left, he saw Kissa was on his knees, arms wrapped tightly around his head. Kissa seemed even more susceptible to the effect than the rest of them.

"Got it," Micah said, coming up beside them just as a short tentacle broke the water and a pulsing bluish light could be seen just beneath the creature. The light silhouetted the animal, giving them a more complete vision of the approaching horror.

"A speargun?" Nance asked. "Not that high tech."

"We just need some blood or skin or whatever. I changed the barb so it will pull out a piece of flesh when it comes out. We just have to get it in..." Micah dropped the weapon and fell suddenly to the deck unconscious.

Captain Nance looked at Coffee. Then she, too, seemed to lose control of her muscles and collapsed. Still focused on the beast, Coffee took in what was going on. "Trondo, buddy, get us the hell out of here."

The boat's pilot, only a few feet away, gave no indication that he'd heard him.

Sergeant Willy Coffee was pretty sure he was the most frightened person on this boat, yet he was the only one still functioning. He disliked water, was a lousy swimmer, and despised anything slightly reminiscent of a B-movie horror film. Growing up, his brother and older cousins had made him watch every gruesome, terrifying movie they could find, only to mock him afterward.

The pain in his head suddenly intensified just as the KillPoint target acquisition scope flashed red, then green. The rifle had an optimal firing solution. All he had to do was hold the gun steady and keep it pointed in the general direction. The gun barked twice as it fired at some predetermined point on the animal's body. The tentacle was fast approaching the side of the boat, which took that precise moment to drop speed to idle.

Through the pain, Coffee could see Trondo's body had slumped forward, knocking the throttle into neutral. "Oh, fuck." The one tentacle was now joined by several more, all coming over the edge of the rear deck. The pain in his head was taking over, and he felt a line of drool crawling down his chin. He still held the rifle, but idly saw it pointed uselessly toward the sky. The world slipped sideways as he dropped to a knee, and then the deck came up and slapped him in the face.

Coffee's eyes were focused ten feet away from where Micah and his captain lay. *Shit, this is it. This is where the monster takes its prize.* He wasn't the hero in this shit of a movie; he was going to be unnamed victim number four. Then he saw a dark, bare foot hit the deck between him and the boy. He saw a hand reaching down for something. Seconds later, he heard gunfire, then a tentacle hovered overhead, the end of which looked like a bloody, curved blade. Then, nothing but darkness.

45

The rocking of the boat was one of the few sensations Kissa could still register. The pain in his head was overwhelming almost all other senses. The sunlight seemed blinding, and muted voices sounded like they were coming to him from underwater. *Is the ship sinking? Am I dead?* He was only vaguely aware of the large, black man standing above him firing out at the ocean. Then, the gigantic man was also lying on the deck.

He knew he had to get up. He needed to fight back against whatever this was, but he couldn't exactly remember why. *Why am I out here? Who are these other people?* The answers seemed to be swimming just out of reach, occasionally rising to the surface, only to disappear in another flash of intense pain. This pain was growing familiar to him now, not any less intense, but he knew it reached a point where it would not hurt any worse. Memories...swimming...*why?*

Slowly, Kissa's muddled brain found one of those memories that was sharper, more intense than all the others. *A name maybe...no, a woman, maybe a friend. Thera!* It came to him in a flash and was gone again just as quickly. The afterimage of her face floated there in his near unconscious mind. She was why they were here, she was more than a friend. A spark of something latched onto that memory. It fed his resolve and determination. As he rose back up to his knees, he felt the nausea rushing up his throat. Vomit spewed across the deck, but the action forced his eyes to open wide. The scene playing out around him was the stuff of nightmares.

The woman and boy lay close together a few yards away. Both appeared dead. The Indian soldier was falling out of the pilot's chair, also unconscious. It took Kissa several seconds to realize what else he was seeing. The nightmare creature was perched along the aft deck of the boat like some evil phantasm. Its underside pulsating a rhythm in that strange blue light, he now saw that most of the tentacles were holding knives. No, that wasn't right. Just the larger ones, maybe eight that were much longer than the others, and it wasn't knives. It was claws. "Well, shit!" he said rising unsteadily to his feet.

"The Cthulian-looking beast is going to fucking eat us," Kissa whispered, not wanting to draw the creature's attention. He stepped over the large man who he recalled had a funny name, and as he did so, he took the weapon that the man still held. "I need this, brother."

Looking at the speargun lying beside the boy, he knew that would've done no good. Not on this monster. The pain in his head surged, causing him to double over and wretch again. The monster had spotted him. The pulsating light was stronger and faster now. Slowly, he stepped toward it, other memories crystallized out of the darkness of pain. His training, studying large marine creatures, swimming with Thera, and the ruins of dead fish in the wake of the beast the prior day. The scientist part of him was battling with the former soldier wanting revenge. Could they ever understand this thing, and more importantly, could he kill it?

The flashing lights were a weapon. That much was clear. The pain was strongest when the animal looked at him, and it flashed brighter. *What does that tell me?* "Think, Kissa, think!"

It, it...damn it, what? It's not defensive, so maybe it was to stun prey. Deep ocean creatures use bioluminescent to communicate, attract mates, or signal danger. Could it be doing any of those things now? The animal pulled itself completely out of the water and onto the deck, smashing a mounted chair in the process. Kissa felt the large boat tilt backward under the intense weight. A tentacled arm swept overhead, and as he pointed the weapon up, it began to fire on its own. The rounds neatly severed the scythe-looking claw and attached tentacle. *Nice gun,* he thought idly.

Now the squid-creature was enraged. The pulsing was even more ominous and threatening, if that was possible. The headache returned with what seemed like twice the original intensity. The light sensitivity, nausea, and all the other sensations landed on Kissa like a massive crushing weight. He'd known a soldier that suffered from intense migraines. The kid had stayed in the infirmary more often than he'd been in the bunkhouse. All had made fun of him, right up to the point they found him hanging from a towel in the showers. Kissa now knew, if this was the kind of pain that kid had faced, he would have taken his own life, too.

No longer able to open his eyes, he felt the animal close enough to reach him now. Close enough to kill all of them if they weren't already gone. Removing one of the arms hugging his head, he pointed it in the direction of the beast. Had his eyes not been clenched tight, he would have seen the optics on the targeting reticule flash green before a complex firing sequence began.

Not killing the unique creature was no longer a viable mission. The weapon had communicated with the local submind called Dee, and the determination was to follow the mandate to preserve human life at any cost. A barrage of razor sharp flechette mixed with more traditional hollow-point 5.56 x 45 rounds tore into the animal's head and stitched a line through to the ridged spine. The little AI had made a guess that might be where a centralized nervous system would be.

One of the rounds tore through a ganglion bundle, causing the animal to begin spasming violently. The deadly scythes whipped about, slamming down violently into boat decking and pieces of meat and flesh. To end the threat, Dee ordered the gun to use up the entire magazine of explosive rounds. The sound coming from the muzzle immediately changed as the slower ammo exited the rifle and embedded deep inside the creature, followed seconds later by muffled explosions of meat and gore. One blast tore most of the part that looked like a wing entirely off, and as the animal lost its fight to remain balanced on the stumpy legs, it began to topple over the edge of the boat.

As the pain finally relented, Kissa opened his eyes to find the gun in his hands still firing at what remained of the monster. Strange looking blood that was more purple than red covered the back half of the deck along with claws, tentacles, and pieces of what must have been the body. "Damn," he said. They had plenty of samples now. Then, the unmistakable sound of a proximity alarm began trilling. He'd heard it several times already. Whatever had been rising back up from the depths had arrived. He looked around at the others, noticing gaping wounds in more than one of the bodies. These people had tried to rescue him, and now he didn't even know if they were alive. The pounding in his head was already receding to a faint echo, and he thought he heard sounds from a couple of the others letting him know at least some still lived. Whatever was coming next, he knew he had to do one thing first.

46

ANTARCTICA

Cade rolled the body over. The kid might be dead, but that didn't mean he couldn't learn something from him. Dee had already suggested he clean the camo makeup from his face, so she could run him through the facial matching algorithm.

"Nothing so far, Nomad. A better than 70% chance he is of German or Austrian descent. A DNA swab could reveal that for certain," Dee told him.

Cade removed the swab kit, broke the seal, and took a cheek swab. He also ungloved the fingers and pressed them to the screen on his SmartCom. He would have also run a retinal scan using the same device, but one of the explosive rounds had burst most of the capillaries in both eyes. If Doris couldn't ID him from the other items, then the kid was a ghost.

He checked in with McTee and Alan while he waited on his Dee. They were making steady progress and feeling much better now that the shooting had stopped. "And, you're welcome." He decided not to comment on his own condition, as that was going to be his problem. The suit's med pack was already easing the pain, but he knew he was going to have to do something about the wrenched knee. The shoulder could wait a bit.

And the kid...was a ghost. "No match in any database, Nomad," the very proper sounding Dee said, using the British voice he'd selected for her months earlier.

"Well, shit." Weird. Okay, what else could he find out? He inspected the weapon. It was a pretty generic high caliber sniper rifle. Serial numbers had been filed away. Ammo was also generic. He found one H&K VP9 compact pistol in a shoulder holster, several knives, and a length of wire wrapped around two carbon fiber handles. *A garrote, this dude was a killer.*

Cade began removing the tight-fitting tactical suit. It was good stuff, maybe Eastern European. Nothing exotic, but the outer layer was fascinating. The coating literally mirrored whatever was on the reverse side of the wearer. He searched for a power source or a control but found neither. As he was peeling the suit off of the increasingly stiff body, Dee spoke up,

"Stop Nomad."

He glanced quickly, looking for the problem.

"Focus here," she said, showing him a spot on the boy's shoulder near his neck.

He could just make out an irregularity in the pasty white skin. His goggles zoomed in to magnify and scan the region. "Is that some sort of design?"

"I believe it is a tattoo," Dee responded. "Perhaps one made to be visible only under certain light sources. Please hold the SmartCom up, and I will scan with alternating light patterns."

Cade did as instructed, and within seconds, he was looking at a bluish glowing design. "That looks tribal. What is it, some kind of sun design?"

"It is very old, ancient. I believe it is similar to an old runic design. One called the 'Black Sun.' This particular one in ink that is visible only in the ultraviolet spectrum is rather unique."

"Black sun, is that significant? Does that help us know who may have sent him?"

"Unknown, Captain. I had to forward it to The Cove for analysis, as I am limited here in what I can access," Dee said.

He finished removing the suit and saw no other marks, nothing at all that was helpful.

"Doris said it is similar to the meaning of the Chinese Tao or Yin and Yang symbology."

"Oh, yeah, the swirly thing like the balance between light and dark?" Cade asked.

"Similar, although this one may have an even longer lineage. It is a runic symbol with various interpretations throughout history, but often has numerous related meanings. This one essentially means 'The Way' and is known as the 'Circle of Nothingness.' Think of it as the Yin and Yang when light loses out completely to the dark," Dee explained.

"Wow, heavy," he said. "So, who are we up against?"

"Well, this particular version seems to be Germanic, and Doris has found only a single reference. It was from the early 1900s. It concerned a group that was associated with protecting a secret project."

"Nazis?"

"No," Dee said, "this predates them. The report she found was in the archives. The German Sicherheitspolizei, or security police, made a statement. It was to a group or movement calling themselves Lebende Schatten."

Thanks to one of Doris's ReLoads, the translation was instantly in Cade's mind, *living shadows.*

* * *

"Hey, Tee, I'm going to need some help, man." It pained Cade to have to ask, but he'd struggled across the rough terrain as much as he could with an injured leg and dislocated shoulder. After the brief firefight, McTee, Alan, and Judah had crossed into what should be the final valley.

"Sure, Nomad," came the immediate response. "I left the other two to set up a campsite. We found a good protected spot under a rocky ledge. I was already heading back to find your dumb ass, anyway."

McTee's voice went silent for a brief pause. "Okay, I see you on my HUD, just sit tight and rest, be there in ten."

"You really did a piss-poor job putting the sleeve on, Rearden," his subordinate said a short while later. The 'sleeve' was part of The Cove's Trauma Sleeve system, a self-contained medical triage and stabilization system for field use.

Cade nodded, "Don't think they were designed to be put on with only one functioning hand."

"Point taken, Boss." McTee examined the angle of the knee. He didn't want to remove the Battlesuit, as it was too damn cold, but also, the suit had provided much of the rigidity to keep his leg in proper alignment. He tightly rewrapped the leg with the sleeve. "This is going to hurt like a motherfucker when we activate it, you know."

Cade grunted; he did know, but had already declined more pain meds. He had no idea if the dead kid had been working alone or what other dangers lie ahead. He wanted to be sharp. "Go ahead, Dee, activate the...ahgggh, fuck!" He didn't quite finish the command as the sleeve began to stiffen and compress like a massive blood pressure cuff. Then, the inner mechanics began realigning the bone and strained ligaments.

"Feels good, huh, Cap?" McTee said with a grin.

"You know I am still armed, don't you?" Cade said with a growl. He could feel a few things begin to snap back into place and what was possibly injections going into the deep muscle.

"These will stimulate the repair," Dee said, as if reading his mind. "You should be mobile in about ten minutes, but recommend you avoid fighting anyone else for at least an hour."

Damn, now even my Dee is developing a sense of humor, Cade thought. "So, what about the shoulder? Can I just pop it back in by slamming it against a rock or something like they do in the movies?"

Dee's voice seemed completely baffled when she responded, "You want to slam your badly injured arm against a mountain in the assumption that it will repair the damage? Captain, did you not receive any medical training in Ranger School?"

"I said like the movies! I know it won't work...probably. Right?"

McTee, who had been listening in, just shook his head and laughed.

"Captain," Dee said, "most likely the bone is already back in the proper position. Like your knee, its misalignment just caused a lot of pain, which will take some time to go away. The impact may have caused some nerve damage, which we can take care of with supplies from Alan's kit. I suggest McTee immobilize the arm, and you wait until you get to your base camp before we do anything else."

Within the hour, Cade found he could stand and once again put some weight on the damaged leg. The joint had no flex, thanks to the sleeve, which made traversing the uneven terrain a total bitch, but a few hours later, McTee helped him make it to the others, one arm supporting much of the captain's weight. The looks from Alan and Judah showed their concern. Cade struggled to smile, although he felt sure it came out as more of a grimace. "You should see the other guy."

"Please lay him down," Dee instructed. "Good night, Captain."

He felt the injection and nothing else. His body had fulfilled its duties for the day. Gratefully, he rested.

47

UNDISCLOSED LOCATION

Goldman slammed the phone down and uttered words his father would have beat him for when he was young. *You should never take the Lord's name in vain, my Aryeh.* The memory of his father just as sharp now as it was then. Richard looked out the window to the nearly treeless landscape beyond. One of the Schatten had failed and was now dead. The other was proceeding alone. He'd never heard of one of the Shadows failing. Perhaps Thrall was right, they were not alone in their knowledge. Maybe they had competition in their quest now.

Standing, he walked around the desk to the row of wooden bookshelves that lined one wall. From floor to ceiling, the shelves were crammed with books, pictures, and objects. Most from his past: athletic awards, a picture of him at bat just before hitting a home run off a minor leaguer who was now in the Hall of Fame in Cooperstown. Business awards of every shape and size. None of that interested him. He ran his hands over the metal ship's bell resting on the middle shelf. He felt the letters forged into its side, worn smooth after all the years, but still recognizable even by touch, U-S-S L-I-B-E-R-T-Y.

Most of the reminder of these shelves had been dreams he'd fulfilled over the years. This object, though, was from another life, long ago. A man who had forfeited nearly everything, including his very name, his heritage, all for one dream. *Saraph.*

Glancing down, Richard checked the time. He'd had to learn to keep up with Thrall's schedule on Kalypso. Despite all of their technology, they still had no way to communicate directly with the Kalypso station when it was positioned in the Midnight Zone. The water depth and varying layers of salinity and even temperature in the water column forced the lab to rise near the surface where it could release a small connected signal buoy much like submarines used. In order to do this safely and remain hidden, they had to know countless other factors like nearby sea traffic, satellite overflight schedule, and even low-flying aircraft. Thrall was confident no one could really detect, much less identify, the massive facility from any significant distance, but some satellites using LIDAR imaging might pick up the shape if they got lucky and their approach angle was just right.

It would be several hours before the next communication window. Briefly, he considered telling the others. Pax, in particular, would be irate, but what didn't set the man off? No, security was his responsibility, and he wasn't known as 'The Lion' for nothing.

* * *

Steiger moved Karl's body into a sheltered overhang and wrapped it back up tightly. She felt nothing at the man's death, and her simple actions were not to honor him but simply to conceal the evidence. It was the way of the Schatten to stay hidden. They were assassins, and the first rule of avoiding capture or failure was for your prey to never know you even existed.

She'd watched the brief firefight through her scope and knew before Karl took the first shot he'd made too many mistakes. He'd misjudged the American, and he'd missed hitting any of the others. Several times, she was sure her partner's shots had hit home, but the man had kept coming, kept pushing the attack. He was one to watch. There would be no retreat in that man.

It had pained Steiger to report to The Lion that part of the mission had failed. That, too, was part of the code, though. Total honesty with the clients at all times, even when it might mean your own death as punishment. She was okay with being honest, let the bastards try to kill her without a fight, though...not likely. She wasn't sure what was so important about this place, the Sanctuary, or 'hole in the ice,' and really, she didn't care. She and Karl were just the latest in a long line of Schatten to be called on to keep the curious from ever reaching places like this or letting anyone else know what they found.

Certain that anything identifying Karl was removed, including the skin with the clear tattoo, she again returned to the hunt. Her path would not be the same as the others had gone. She knew very well where they were going, even if they did not. All she had to do was get there first. Her orders had been very clear, no damage to the artifacts, but none of the people must leave alive. She grinned slightly as she moved down into a rocky crevice. Her maps of this area were detailed and accurate, including hidden approaches that would never show up on any GPS or aerial photos. The American team was dead, they just didn't know it yet.

48

ANTARCTICA

"Rise and shine, campers!"

Dee's overly happy voice cut through the fog of sleep.

"Who in the fuck programmed her with that level of optimistic joy?" Cade asked before turning over in the sleeping bag and closing his eyes once more.

"I think that is all just her," Alan said. "Each of the subminds has a certain level of autonomy on how they grew and expressed themselves. Since you are mission lead, your Dee gets to be the wake-up alarm. Love her accent by the way. Nice touch."

"What time is it?" McTee asked, yawning and stretching before retreating back into the warmth of his rocky bed. "And how fucking cold is it today?"

"It is summer o-clock and a lovely 24 degrees," Alan said, already fastening his own insulated Battlesuit tightly. "Come on, Rearden, Riley needs to check you out to see how you're healing. Apparently, the director wants to know if you're still mission capable."

"I'm not, tell her I died in my sleep."

"You're not dead, I can hear you, and your pulse is strong and steady," Riley's voice cut through the morning chill. "Get your fat ass moving, you have a lot to do."

"Fat?" Cade stood, coverings dropping away to reveal he was not in his Battlesuit....or anything else. Turning his torso to look down at his backside, he exclaimed, "I'm not fat!"

"Oh, my God, do you always sleep like that?" McTee asked shielding his eyes.

Cade raised a single eyebrow, then looked down at the other man, "Jealous?"

"Oh, shit." Judah laughed, walking up, one of the mini drones in his hands. "Better cover that wee, lil' fella up before the cold does freeze it off."

Cade took care of his morning business before getting a coffee and breakfast sandwich from the food locker. "So, what's the plan for today? We gonna go find the hole?"

"Believe we already have, Captain," Riley chimed in again, obviously speaking to all of them now. "While you guys got your beauty rest, we had doves up most all of your, um, 'night.' They managed to cover almost every inch of the lower ice-valley and many rock faces as well. Lots of little ledges and overhangs like the one ya'll are sheltering in now. Most of these are pretty shallow, and only a few that would be large enough for a plane to fit through, such as Admiral Byrd described. Doris has gone through all the images and scans and believes she's spotted it."

An image appeared in their goggles of a small rocky outcropping on the side of a steeply sloped peak. Cade looked around at the surrounding mountaintops, trying to pick it out. His Dee gave a targeting overlay to highlight it in his goggles. He studied it a moment before flicking the overlay away and focusing on the drone image again. "That opening isn't large, looks to be maybe a meter or two at most. Why does Doris think this one is it?"

"They've covered the opening up. The way the stones are lying is not natural, and the sensors indicate the depth of that opening and the chamber beyond is very deep and wide," Riley answered.

That unimpressive hole in the rocks seemed almost disappointing to Cade. All the work, the injuries, hell, even the Shadow fella dying over...well, over that. It made no sense to him.

"Sensors show that your injuries are less than fifty percent repaired, Cade. Do you feel up to the remainder of the mission?"

Cade knew Riley was asking for Director Stansfield. Hell, she was probably standing right behind her as she asked it. Soldiers, and men in general, tended to underestimate how an injury might negatively affect them. Part of his training involved him taking stock of his actual physical and mental condition before each mission. After all, it wasn't just his ass on the line; if they got into trouble, his weakness could mean others would suffer along with him. He walked around the small ledge testing the knee and the shoulder.

The leg was still mostly immobile in the trauma sleeve, but hurt much less. He could at least put weight on it again. His dislocated shoulder still throbbed, but his range of movement seemed unrestricted. "Your med and treatment have helped a lot. Shoulder is about eighty percent, and the knee joint a bit less...call it...ow!" He spasmed in pain as he tried to rotate the lower leg. "Call it sixty-five, not optimum, but I'm capable. I won't slow anybody down, but also probably won't win any races today either."

"Fair enough, Captain. You'll need to get back here soon to let Doctor Han work on it. His new toys should be able to get it back closer to a hundred in short order," Riley advised. "Also, remind Brutus that you're the one who must pay for his actions next time."

Cade was thankful that the last part of her message was on a private channel. Not that he disagreed. On the contrary, he wholeheartedly did agree. Still, it was a bit personal to share openly with a team he was supposed to be commanding. They packed up quickly and began moving off along the glowing, green trail Dee was providing. Somewhere up ahead, was a mysterious hole in the ice and who knew what else?

* * *

Arriving at the spot less than an hour later, the small group found the opening was indeed mostly camouflaged. The actual opening was about five feet by two, and that was only because some stones had fallen away. While parts of what covered the opening were actual rock, much more was some sort of lightweight fake stone made to resemble the rest of the mountain. The four of them cleared away just enough to make entering somewhat easier. Cade then tossed the BallCam in and let it do its thing. Using its internal gyro, it managed to wheel around much of the sloping floor and scan the surrounding surfaces; its first priority was identifying dangers.

Cade monitored the images and data being returned. *Damn,* it was large and appeared manmade. The cavern looked natural near the opening but was increasingly smooth farther back, with intricately cut details that were beyond his understanding. Judah seemed pretty content to wait outside while the rest of them cautiously made their way inside the massive cavern.

Just as he was about to cross into the darkness, Cade paused. He felt the now familiar itch running up his spine and straight into his skull. *WTF,* the shooter was dead. He'd had Dee compare the visuals from the occupant in the helicopter attack to the dead kid up on the ridge, and the match was very likely. So...why did he have the feeling of danger again? "Alan, put up two sentinel drones out here flying low cover over the valley." He assigned his own Dee to monitor those feeds.

Once the slightly larger drones were deployed, they ventured into the mouth of the cave. The temperature change was immediately apparent. Outside it was near freezing; inside it was registering almost sixty. Downright balmy for the South Pole.

McTee took point, Alan in the middle, and Cade dragging up the rear. The boy had released some mini-drones to go through and map out the space and had his Dee submind monitoring the feeds for anything they should go check out first. Cade had no idea what they were even looking for other than answers. *What is this place, who built it, and why does someone want to keep it hidden so damn badly?*

This was the place, but it didn't much resemble what Samuel had described. No mile-wide valley of lush vegetation. This was no base of any kind, it was a cave. Something else occurred to him again, that thing the bastard had said, "The best way to lie was to tell the truth, unconvincingly." So, he'd been lying about what was here, but he'd told the truth at some point.

They were in a space roughly seventy meters long by fifty meters wide and maybe half that high. It did look more finished the deeper they went. Cade watched as Alan detoured off to one side and began studying something on one of the smooth walls. He held up a BallCam which began emitting a bluish white light. *Nifty trick,* Cade thought. He saw as the little ball scanned what was an obvious image. This was no Paleolithic cave painting, though. It was a scene of eerie beauty and rich colors. Much of it was filled with symbols and text in a language that not even Dee could identify. McTee was shining a light on another image nearby. Walking a little farther ahead, Cade realized the entire wall was covered with them. Most seemed to be landscape scenes, although some clearly showed a night sky full of stars and oceans, but no people. Every image had the same type of symbols filling nearly every empty space of rock.

The deeper they went, the more intricate the designs seemed to become. Cade felt Ace stirring to life. He, too, was immersed in his own curiosity; this is what they were willing to kill to protect. It was an attempt to communicate, he could tell that, but from whom and how long ago?

"It's like a massive illustrated manuscript, like the Book of Kells in Dublin," Alan stated.

Cade's mind instantly pulled up the reference from some obscure file drawer where the ReLoad process must have stored it. The colorful, illustrated Codex was in Latin and thought to depict the four Gospels. *Maybe more like the Voynich manuscript or even the Rohonic, which were also illustrated codex that were handwritten in an unknown writing system,* Ace suggested.

"What the fuck?" they heard McTee say as he moved to one farther down the passage.

"Nomad, we have a problem." Dee's voice was machine calm, but a menacing quality left no doubt what kind of problem it was.

"Talk to me," Cade said, turning toward the exit and motioning to McTee to join him. "Alan, keep scanning, get all of this."

"Judah is missing. The drones are not picking up any heat signatures outside the chamber."

"The bastard left us," McTee said, catching up at a slow trot. "If that fuck takes the MARS, we'll be stranded out here. That's as good as a death sentence."

"Stop talking," Cade ordered. That was one possibility, but he hadn't gotten any vibe of a double cross from the man, so why do it now? Still, he hadn't wanted to come inside. "Dee, scan entrance for explosives or traps." That would be a reasonable move, just trap them here and hide the evidence.

"None detected," she answered almost at once.

He activated the IR and night vision modes of his goggles to scan for anyone else in the dark cave. Nothing showed up, but he now knew that wasn't a guarantee. He motioned for McTee to move to the south wall and advance; Cade moved to the opposite. If this was another of the Lebende Schatten, then he could be anywhere. He offered a mic click to signify weapons hot, although both men already had their assault rifles at the high-ready position.

Cade scanned the remaining space again in nearly every spectrum and saw nothing, then he had an idea. "Dee, do a UV scan."

She seemed to know precisely what he was looking for. "I'll need an external light source for that," she said quietly. I am guessing you don't want me to use your goggles, so toss the BallCam you have toward the center."

Cade took out the smooth object, which was about the size of a large tennis ball, and gently tossed it up and toward the center of the cave. An incredibly brief flicker of blueish light emanated from the high point of the ball's arc. It was so fast, he immediately wondered if he'd imagined it. But he hadn't, nor had he imagined the glimpse of something high and to his right. He stared in that direction as Dee replayed in his goggles what the flash had shown. The image stabilized and zoomed in. What he saw was the top arc of a glowing circle. Almost too late, he realized it for what it was, the black sun tattoo. The KillPoint scope began flashing red as something hit him full force in the face; he felt his nose breaking from the impact. Blood gushed out, and he saw stars around the edges of his vision. He kicked at where the attacker came from and struck nothing. Something hit him on the side of the head, and he realized afterward it had been the blade of a knife. The Battlesuit had saved him again.

"Boss, you okay?" he heard McTee say.

"No, I'm getting my ass kicked by a fucking shadow!"

McTee swung his own gun in that direction, switching to night vision and only saw Cade fighting with what showed up in the scope as a black blob. He fired multiple times, then switched to autofire, but the system couldn't see the enemy well enough to target either. He lowered the weapon and ran toward the fight.

Cade was busy fending off blows and more than one vicious slash to his face. The attacker had apparently determined he was wearing some type of protective suit and had opted to go for the only unprotected area—his face. That just pissed him off. At one point, he grabbed the killer, realizing instantly that, like the first, this one was also waifishly small but unbelievably strong and fast. He gave a groin kick that would have put any man down, but instead of a gasp of pain, he heard a tiny laugh, a girl's laugh. *No fucking way, I'm getting my ass handed to me by a girl.*

As quickly as she'd appeared, the fight stopped. McTee was instantly pulling Cade back to his feet. "Where did she go?"

"I couldn't tell, Boss." He turned, sweeping his rifle deeper into the darkness. "You don't think she is going after...."

McTee didn't finish the sentence. In Cade's night vision, the blood coming out of the bullet hole in his forehead appeared black. McTee's eyes rolled up, and he dropped to the ground.

49

McTee...gone? The thought invaded his mind, threatened to take it over, until he muscled it aside. Glancing to his left, Cade saw another figure approaching stealthily. *Another Schatten*? It was slim and tall, but the outline of this person was familiar. *Stay back, Alan,* he begged silently. Once again, Brutus roared to come out. Cade knew this was not a battle the brute could win. This enemy was too good, too sophisticated. He was also certain he'd made solid contact with the attacker. A blow that would have put most soldiers down the count. Yet, he'd not heard the sound of pain or breath being expelled, much less a body hitting the floor. Everything about this fight felt somehow...wrong.

A silent warning signal came from Dee that she was canceling night vision. It was doing no good anyway. He barely caught glimpses of the night wraith he'd been fighting. He sensed more than saw Alan tossing something toward the middle of the room. Instantly, he realized it was one of the supercharged argon globes, the portable light they'd planned to use deeper in the cave. Instantly, the space illuminated with the intensity of a sports arena holding a night game.

Cade had instinctively dropped to one knee and raised the assault rifle, believing he would finally be able to see his target. Instead, he saw only rock and Alan, also kneeling, weapon at high-ready, and Tee lying motionless on the floor. *Where the fuck is...she? She? The attacker is a woman? Does that change anything? How did I know?*

Gus's words cut through the haze and pain, *Unpack that shit later. Just go kill the bitch.*

Seemed smart, but Cade had no idea where she was. His eyes made a full circuit of the room, and his rifle had been covering the opposite directions. Neither he nor the KillPoint system spotted any targets. Then he saw the weapon, lying on the floor. An odd one, similar to the other kid's, but not the same. Rising slightly, he moved in its direction, still scanning for threats. Even unarmed, the female Schatten was still lethal.

Something drew his eye to a section of wall, nothing he could have ever put into words. It looked for all the world to be just like every other section, but his instincts said she was there. With one hand, he picked up the unfamiliar weapon and expelled the magazine, then fired the round in its chamber at the wall. The wall flinched. It was barely noticeable, but now he could begin to pick out lines and maybe a leg or foot. Even knowing she was right there, he had trouble convincing himself it was anything but rock. What if his mind was playing tricks on him, and she was sneaking up behind him at this very moment? No, it was her; he now saw a slight tinge of what could be red on the otherwise bluish gray rock. Cade stood and took aim, walking and limping towards her. His own rage nearly equal to that of his inner barbaric demon. "You have two seconds to talk, woman. Who are you working for and how many more of you are there?"

The section made no sound. He aimed to fire just as the wall seemed to flutter, then shift sideways. He squeezed the trigger just as he realized she'd moved, not sideways but up. Then a foot came at him from above, catching him squarely in the side of the head. Something hit the back of his neck hard as he heard her landing lightly on her feet. Even injured, she was unbelievably good. A warning sign on his HUD let him know his suit had been breached, 'Blood loss detected.'

The Shadow girl had cut him. Now he felt the sting. Simultaneously, he felt his arms getting heavy. 'Neurotoxin detected.' Shit, the blade had a poison of some kind on it. The suit had built in analyzers and a type of universal anti-serum Riley and Doctor Han had created, but they had never put it to a real test. His lips began to feel heavy and walking seemed like it would take a Herculean effort.

Then Cade felt the blows on his back, well-aimed blows to both kidneys. Thankfully, the suit canceled out most of the energy, but that didn't stop them from hurting like a motherfucker. Brutus slipped his collar and bellowed in rage. The toxin was taking over his body faster than his own personal monster could. He wanted to yell for Alan to get away, but there was no way to manage it. His mouth could no longer form the words. He dropped to one knee as Brutus swung out blindly with the one functioning arm, contacting something with a sharp crack. Cade's vision began to contract, he was slipping down the well into unconsciousness. It was a well he would likely not be climbing out of. Then the air went blue-white in a flash of pain and a sound of crackling electricity.

* * *

Sounds were the first sensation to return. Not all at once, but in jerks and spasms, with the sound being muted, then coming in full volume, but distorted. He wasn't dead, at least he didn't think he was. His mouth felt fuzzy, and a distinct aftertaste of something vaguely fruity and kind of metallic. With extreme effort, he pried one eye open and then the other. Cade found himself lying on the ground. He was staring at a boot, someone else, he assumed, but wasn't 100% sure of that either. The entire room seemed to be spinning. Then the sounds, the voices, came again...someone, maybe Riley, talking.

"Alan, I think he's awake. Heart rhythm is restored, and brain waves look...well, heart rhythm looks ok."

"Nomad, don't try to sit up yet. Alan is right there with you."

He hadn't been planning to; he was struggling enough with just lying there without falling off the edge of the earth. "Oh...okay. What happened?" The words felt thick and syrupy as they dripped from his mouth.

He felt hands on him, Alan and another pair. "Hey, mate, thought you were a goner."

"Judah?"

"Yeah, sorry she got the drop on me. Hit me with something, knocked me out, and drug me back into some crevasse. Took me forever to get back up here. By then, all the fun was over. The lad here saved your life, Rearden.

"Who... Alan?"

"Right here, Nomad." Alan was removing something from around his chest. He could tell by the velcro fasteners it was another of the trauma sleeves. "Drink some of this, your electrolytes are off. Sorry, but the taser round got both of you. I couldn't see enough of the attacker to make a clean shot."

"You got her?" Cade said before taking a long pull on the bottle.

"Oh, yeah, he got her all right," Judah said. "Had her drugged and zip tied like sleeping beauty before I even got here."

Cade struggled to turn to see where she was, but all he could see was his partner McTiernan's stiff body. They'd covered him with his sleeping bag, but the booted foot was still exposed.

"Sorry about your mate there, he was a damn good man."

Cade nodded, he couldn't deal with the loss, not right now.

"Where's the Shadow?"

"Right there, a dozen yards to your right. She's still damn hard to see. You weren't lying when you said they were chameleons. Unreal how good her concealment is," Alan said.

"You see any more of them?" Cade asked now, finally beginning to sit up. His head was aching from something, the poison or the stunner round, or perhaps the numerous blows to the head, he wasn't sure which.

"No, no one else. I expanded the coverage of the sentinels and had some smaller ones recon the crevices Judah mentioned. I'm still not sure we can detect them, the concealment suit blocks her heat signature. Honestly, that suit of hers is something else entirely.

Seems to be composed of various fibers including fiber optics that passively bend the light around the body. I took a sample for Riley to analyze."

"Good thinking, Alan...and thanks. She had me, I would have been gone as well. That girl is a fucking warrior. Wish she was on our side." Cade tried to stand but found he was unable.

"Give it time, Cap. I still have some more scans to do. Judah, can you keep an eye on him?"

The Aussie nodded, and Alan took his supply bag and went farther into the cavern. Cade could see him illuminating and, no doubt, recording various scenes from the space.

"Alan did well, mate, smart and tough lad he is. The girl got in a couple of good shots before he got her fully subdued. I could see the marks on him, but he didn't even mention it."

Cade nodded. He reached up and tapped his cheek awkwardly. "Dee, private call to Chaps."

"Go for Chaps," came the instant reply.

"We need you, pronto."

There was a pause. "I know, Nomad, The Cove just filled me in. I am...well, I'm sorry about McTee. And yeah, I know that can wait. I have a bird coming over. We've modified it for polar conditions. It's already in the air and should be there in few hours. Weather isn't bad, so we should be there about an hour later. Only thing..."

"What, Chaps?"

"Well, it's still an international no-fly zone," she said apologetically. "Even our Executive Order won't get us a free pass on that. Roundtable sector is off the grid for us."

"I don't care, Brenda—I'm not waiting here for the next round of assassins, and McTee...well, his family..." He couldn't finish the thought. "Have Doris work her magic, become Wonder Woman, and make your plane invisible. I don't care how, just make it happen. I need this." He looked around, disgusted with how bad this op had become. "We need this."

Resigning herself to whatever it took, she agreed hesitantly, "Can you even get to an LZ? Sounded like you're in pretty bad shape, too."

"I'll be there, don't worry about that. Sounds like we'll have a few hours to wrap up here anyway."

"I'll be there with your ride, Boss. Just stay safe."

Looking over, he saw the grayish figure begin to stir. He would stay safe, but he also wanted some answers.

50

Finally up on his feet, Cade stumbled toward the girl. Seeing his friend again lying dead on the ground, his first instinct was to kick her, but he stopped his foot at the last second. That was not who he was. He might kill her, but he wouldn't torture her, not even after what she'd done. "Wake up, Shadow."

The prisoner didn't respond, but Dee was monitoring her vitals now and let him know she was most likely conscious. He patted her cheeks, still marveling at the strange geometric patterns in her face paint. Even up close, it was hard to tell where she stopped and the rough floor began. He took out a wet wipe and rubbed at the girl's face until pale pinkish flesh tones began to appear. He did want to see her face, but even more, he just wanted to convince himself she was human.

"You are going to want to see this, Nomad," Alan called from some distance away.

"Wake up!" he shouted after the makeup was removed. "Who are you working for? How many of you are there?" The face of the girl was almost angelic; she was plain but attractive. What could have made her become this killer? He saw the bloody bandage where one of his rounds had creased a path along her left side. They could use the healing wound spray, but he was undecided if he even wanted her healed. Right now, he really wanted her to suffer...he wanted her dead.

Dee broke into his thoughts, "Captain, one of the mini-drones has found a small kit. It's most likely the enemy assailant's. It was hidden about a kilometer up one of the larger crevasses."

Cade nodded, then asked Dee to use one of the drones to guide Judah to it. Might offer some clues about her, but he already had his doubts. She was too good. He checked her bindings; they were tight. Grabbing hold of her wrist, he jerked her up to her feet. She immediately went into combat mode and tried to sweep her foot and lash out with her bound hands, but then immediately went limp. "We have you in an automated restraint system," Cade said. "If you struggle, fight, or run away it will become active, and you will be knocked out...again, and again until your heart gives out from the stress. Now, you have a choice, you can cooperate, or you can die."

He could see the girl's eyes now. They didn't match the rest of her face; they were dark, wild, angry things. The eyes of a predator. "You are 'Lebende Schatten,' aren't you?" Something flicked across the girl's face. Perhaps he'd already gotten closer than she expected. "You and your other...the one I killed yesterday up on the mountain."

Cade wanted briefly to insult her; tell her she'd failed, but truthfully, she'd beaten him. If it weren't for the kid, they'd all be dead. "Look, you are a killer, I get it, you are also damn good at it. Good enough to impress the hell out of me and...well, let's just say I don't impress easily. If your job was to take me out, you succeeded. You apparently killed me, but thanks to my team, it wasn't quite as final as you would have liked."

The girl gave the briefest of grins, then muttered something in German, "*Das ist mir furzegal!*"

Cade's CommDot translated the words nearly in real time, and a text version was superimposed on his goggles just in case. "I realize you probably don't give a fuck," saying back what she'd said.

"Du hurensohn," she whispered.

"Oh...wasn't aware you were acquainted with my mother. Indeed, she was a bitch." So, now they both knew they spoke each other's language. "Now, stop screwing around. Name? What do they call you? I don't care if it's real."

"Steiger," the girl said with more force this time.

"Steiger is a good name, it fits. I'm curious, Steiger, do you have any idea what you're protecting here? Have you been here or seen any of this before?"

She shook her head, then looked around the room seemingly seeing it for the first time. "Vat is dis place?"

"Nomad, you coming?" Alan yelled again.

Cade looked at Steiger. "Shall we? After all, you were willing to kill me, and I assume possibly die, for it. Maybe we should both see what the fuck all that was for. He led her back toward the glowing light; she did not resist.

* * *

Despite the simmering rage and the lingering pain from the fight, Cade was immediately captivated again by the images as he walked down a short rise to where Alan was standing. As he neared the boy, he realized he'd been about here when it all started to go sideways. "This was what Tee was looking at, wasn't it?"

Alan nodded. "He wanted us to see this, it's pretty obvious why."

Cade studied the almost confusing mix of imagery; it was a scene of a lush tropical valley with a small river flowing past, yet all the plants appeared off. Also, the sky seemed somehow wrong. The colors were not of an Earth sky. What was most evident, though, was that there was an unmistakable image of a craft sitting along the water's edge. Not an ancient watercraft, but something Cade could only relate to as a spacecraft...a flying saucer. He looked at the girl. She glanced at the artwork but then stared off into the distance. Her apparent disinterest in what she'd been so willing to kill for sent another stab of rage through Cade's brain. He wanted to shove her to the ground, to stomp her into some semblance of atonement for the tragedy she'd caused. Still, he, too, had been a captive, a prisoner for doing the same awful job she had. How had he been treated? The human portion of his soul forbade him from doing more to the one calling herself Steiger.

Absently, Cade looked back at the picture, ignoring the words that Alan was saying. It was so intricate and involved; he felt that if he stared at a single spot it might tell an entire story. The more he looked, the more details seemed to emerge.

"You notice how the colors are...well, off?" Alan said. "That's not due to the paint fading. In fact, it's not paint at all, but something chemically done to the rock itself. No idea what, but it's so freaking old. Also, look at this." Alan took his SmartCom and held it up so the main camera faced a seemingly blank spot on the image. He then triggered it to start zooming in slowly. Cade watched in amazement as more and different images and scenes unfolded as the camera zoomed in smaller and smaller. "Yeah, some of it is at the very microscopic level. And the symbols, Dee says they don't match any recorded language. A few are kinda similar to Egyptian hieroglyphs, like that one there could almost be an Eye of Horus, but most have never been recorded anywhere before."

Cade was amazed, but he had to keep reminding himself they were not the first humans to see this place other than the ones who painted it. Others, probably military scientists, had been here. Someone in the government, maybe many governments, knew. That triggered a thought. "Dee, are there any sensors, cameras, or other detection devices in this cavern?" If this was the equivalent of an international version of Area 51, there almost certainly was a security system.

"None that I am detecting, Nomad. They may not be active if they are here."

That made sense to him. The place seemed long forgotten. Maybe it was truly off limits to everyone now. Still, someone knew, someone sent Steiger after them. Maybe they rely on active instead of passive security.

"Alan, can you capture all this in the next few hours? We'll need to head out to the LZ to meet our ride."

"No way, Cap. Not at a level to give us anything more than the largest image. I already asked my Dee to calculate the time needed just for the pictures we can see from here. She guessed at least thirty days." He took a few steps back from the UFO image. "Something else you need to see down here on this one."

Cade pulled the increasingly less willing Schatten with him to the side of Alan. He heard an involuntary gasp from his captive and saw she was staring at a painting of...something, what turned out to be some sort of monster, maybe a dinosaur. A longish head that seemed to end abruptly in an angry mouth with a crown of writhing tentacles. Several larger tentacles sprouted from what could have been tiny wings, or maybe fins. The secondary tentacles were larger and ending in a sort of curved claw. An eerie blue light seemed to emanate from the animal's belly. The artist had done an excellent job of capturing the terrifying nature of the beast. In the scene, it was chasing some smaller aquatic animal that looked from the front a bit like a scaly pig with fins with a rear section more like an otter. The sea monster looked like something straight out of a nightmare. "You recognize this? You've seen this picture before?" he asked Steiger. He had to admit something about the image was familiar. Perhaps a movie monster or something.

The girl shook her head but kept staring at the picture. Her mouth formed silent words. His Dee gave a probable translation in text, "Der Saraph." Unlike the others in the carved rock space, this scene had her full attention.

Alan pointed to a series of small recesses nearby. "Can't figure out what these were for. Several of the scenes with plants or animals have these cutouts alongside. Anyway, several more like these."

"Alan, will you get a close-up image of that creature?"

That was Doris, actually. Cade had barely heard from her since leaving Georgia.

"Yeah, sure." Alan picked up the BallCam and began scanning the image in even higher resolution than his phone.

"Interested in sea monsters on alien worlds now, Doris?" Cade asked.

"Not exactly," she said. "You guys need to get back here; we have some new developments."

51

Cade rubbed the wound on the back of his neck, the dressing had sealed it, numbed the pain, and was already beginning to stitch together with the old skin to seal the deep cut. The Shadow watched him with eyes that seemed dead. "I'm going to take care of your wound, okay?" he said.

She shrugged but continued to stare. They were sitting on the small ledge, just outside the entrance to the cavern. Alan was inside packing up the gear, although he had made a drone rig for the BallCam that was going to stay here and keep scanning the images. Dee would program it to fly out of the small entrance and out to sea once it was done.

The girl winced as Cade rolled up the bit of thick tunic and removed the blood-clotting bandage. Alan had done an initial treatment on her, deciding that she wouldn't die. Cade glanced up into Steiger's eyes, just catching a look before she glanced away. "I'm going to take a guess here. You've never failed on a mission before, have you?" She made no sound but stiffened slightly at the remark. He could feel the strength radiating off of her. She was small, dainty even, but in that compact shell was so much energy and, he was pretty sure, so much hate. "What are you mad at?" he asked as he sprayed the wound treatment over the fiery red line. Instantly, the cut disappeared beneath the numbing layer of liquid bandage. "It's not directed at us, I know that. You wanted to kill us...did kill us," he corrected. "That was not the rage I feel in you, though. That was business. The anger is something much deeper, much more primal."

Judah was nearby, already restacking the stones and camouflage to re-hide the opening. "Why are you wasting your time, Captain? She's a trained killer, she has no soul."

"I'm a trained killer, too, Judah, but I do have a soul...*probably* several of them." The Aussie had been as reliable as anyone Cade had ever worked with. He'd recovered the girl's battle kit down in the ravines and brought it all back. He had taken out the thicker polar-rated parka, which Steiger now wore. Also in the bag, was a satellite phone which Doris was even now attempting to access. In addition, an impressive assortment of knives, poison, and perhaps the most unique makeup kit Cade had ever seen. Cade, like every Ranger, had learned how to apply face paint to help hide the lines of the face and blend in with surroundings. People found it strange that they carried a makeup bag on nearly every mission. You learned quickly the shit could save your life. Cade gently touched the now sealed wound. "That better?"

The girl glanced down, clearly confused at the spray and at the man's kindness. Failure meant death. Even in her training, to fail at an exercise always meant pain, punishment, and yes...even death to many. She gave a slow nod, "Thank you."

"You're confused, you think I'm tricking you." He turned around putting his back to her, then peeled his Battlesuit down off his shoulders. She stared at a back covered with wounds and deep ugly scars. "I was captured for doing my job. It didn't go well." He paused, then added, "For them or me. Steiger, we are in an ugly business, and while I'm not an assassin, I've known some. We called them snipers. Pretty much the same in my book. They were killers. That didn't mean they enjoyed it—that didn't mean they were bad people. They simply had a job to do." Coming to a bit of an understanding of the conflicting emotions raging inside, he added, "I'm willing to make that same assumption about you. You are an enemy combatant and will be treated fairly, even better, if you choose to cooperate with us. You can start by telling us about that image. What does that creature mean to you?"

Her eyes never left his face, but she nodded slowly. The difference was, she did enjoy what she did. Still, the man had every reason to kill her, at least make her suffer for killing his man. This captain had been angry, but now he was forcing himself to not be. He'd even covered her when the cold of outside made her shiver. Yes, he was unlike any foe she had yet faced. She shook her head, she had failed, yes. But she could not tell him about the creature.

* * *

Several hours later, an exhausted Judah climbed into his modified Hummer. The MARs-1 transport had been nearly buried in a snow drift blown in by the winds. He'd left his friends as they boarded the sleek, black plane that had skied to a stop on the ice field. The same stretch the scientists had disappeared from so many years earlier. He didn't know much about the Americans, but he liked them, they were straight shooters. But he knew where his home was, even though the captain had made some not so subtle inquiries about joining them. He was too old for that; his whole life had been an adventure. Now he was tired, almost ready to go back home to Port Douglas in Queensland.

He shook he head, laughing at his own joke. He couldn't go home; he could never go back home. Never see the idyllic harbor full of sailboats on a summer day. He'd done well hiding out down here, staying off the radar, and that was all he wanted, just to stay out of the line of sight. Plus, the Yanks had given him back his vehicles. Free, no refund or anything. The other one would be waiting for him at the camp. Before they left, Cade asked if he was going to tell anybody what he saw. Honestly, Judah had not seen much, nor had he wanted to. He knew others had seen this place, at least some of it. Even more were aware of its existence. Bad shit tended to happen to those people. They wound up dead or disappeared. He had no real desire for either of those.

Also, he wanted to get as far away from that girl as possible. Judah couldn't understand why they kept her alive, much less conscious. Rearden had said so she could help carry McTee back to the ice field. Whatever the reason, he hadn't liked being around her. She was so fucking scary. He'd never seen anybody like her. She was more than an assassin. She was terrifying. She was simply a killer. You could see it in her eyes. A damage that ran to her core. Some kind of ancient hatred that must reach to the very depths of her soul...if she still possessed one. Somehow, he knew she was a biological machine driven to kill, programmed basically like a weapon of war. She, and probably others like her, were the reason the hole in the ice had stayed a myth for so long. He would do nothing to change that.

* * *

Ninety minutes later, aboard the Nighthawk jet heading back toward The Cove, an injured, weary, and very pissed-off Cade was not responding well to his initial incident debriefing. "What's a fucking Saraph? I just don't get it, Doris. Tell me."

"Cade, Saraphim are the highest order of the hierarchy of angels. A six-winged divine being only below God in several religions."

"So, now we are battling God and demons, Doris...come on! That was no angel, it had no wings. Maybe it was a cryptid or something, you know, a throwback to the time of dinosaurs." Cade was impressed he even knew the word for unusual creatures that were thought to be extinct biological anomalies. Then he realized it was probably because of ReLoad.

"Cade, historically, the Saraphs have been a bit badass. These are not chubby flying babies with harps and cupid bows. They are terrifying and said to use purifying fire as one of their weapons to cleanse evil.

"Okay, but it's not an angel, no wings...it's a painting of a fucking sea monster. It's a goddamn dragon, or dinosaur, or something. Something out of some freak's Cthulian fucking nightmare. Besides, what does this have to do with anything today? And why did it scare the shit out of her?"

Cade was on the Nighthawk alongside Alan. The other two members of the team, Alexandria and Alias, sat farther back. Maratelli had been flown back for treatment several days earlier, and McTee's body was stowed in the cargo hold.

It had been difficult leaving the mountaintop, not just due to the injured and the transporting of Tee's body. Just knowing all that was up there. Alan even thought he might have found an access to another passage as time was running out. Thankfully, the data was still coming in from the remarkable little BallCam, and thanks to its nearly unlimited Pica power supply, it would for as long as needed.

Steiger was sedated and shackled to the built-in receptacles along a cushioned bench. Cade had made her help carry the body of the man she killed through the snaking warren of crevasses and ravines along the ice valley's floor. The drones had mapped all of them during the time they'd been inside, and it cut the trip time by two-thirds. Still, it had been a struggle for all of them. More than once, he saw the assassin seem to be crying. He didn't want to feel any measure of sympathy for her, but he sensed the brokenness within the tiny warrior. Perhaps that could have been the path he went down had he not enlisted. He stared at the sleeping figure, almost forgetting that Doris was speaking in his ear.

"Okay, we've done the research. We now know that the rock making up that mountain top is a truly ancient piece of earth's crust."

"Yeah," he said. "It's a mountain."

Alan shook his head. He'd been listening in, also curious as to what she'd found. "No, actually, mountains are often very young rock. They get worn down relatively quickly in geologic time scales. They're really not that many places around the planet like this. A few spots up in Canada have been dated back to over four billion years, and that's almost as old as Earth itself. Some in Scotland, a few in Africa, lots in Australia. But most of the planet's crust tends to only stay above ground for a limited number of years, say a billion years or so. And, yeah, billion-year-old dirt is old, but in the scale of the universe, not so much. In geologic terms, most of our planet is still a youngster."

"The rock samples near the cave with the images were at least 3.5 billion years old," said Doris.

"What the hell would that mean? No humans were around two billion years ago, that was..." Alan thought briefly. "That was even before dinosaurs."

Doris went on, "Yes, it was. And that's what's troubling. That is not to say the image was that old. We have no reliable way of dating that image. Not yet, at least. But what we can date is the chamber."

"It wasn't natural?" Alan asked.

"No, it wasn't."

"What do you mean it wasn't natural?" Cade asked. "It wasn't like erosion or a gas pocket when the lava formed or something?"

"No, that area isn't geologically active like that. This is basically classic metamorphic rock, that was pushed to the surface, billions of years ago. That chamber was excavated. It was literally hewn out of the raw stone."

Cade thought for a minute, waiting for Ace to try and put the pieces together. *What the actual fuck?* He started to speak, but stopped, several times. "Okay, Doris, the cavern was carved out of the stone on this three billion-year-old mountain top, which I suppose three billion years ago wasn't even a mountain, it probably could have been beach-front property back then. But how old is the chamber?"

"Based on the preliminary samples, we would have to date it at just under that two billion years mark."

He let that thought hang in the air. Looking at Alan, the boy seemed just as confused. That sentence contained a lot of information that neither seemed capable of processing. That almost unimaginable timescale, a timescale that predated any life on Earth, not just intelligent life. "So that means that whoever or whatever carved that chamber and left those images...

they weren't human, were they, Doris? They were aliens."

52

"It is a genuine possibility, Cade," Doris answered.

"Aliens...more aliens, ancient aliens."

"It would seem unlikely that an advanced alien species would resort to a very human style artwork to communicate," Doris continued. "Especially if it was that long before your human's ancestors had crawled out of their burrows. I think any conclusion at this point is likely to be premature and incorrect. Whoever the artist was, they've seen some sort of alien planet and alien life. I think that's a natural conclusion. It's at least the direction I'm leaning."

"What are your thoughts, big guy?" Cade asked, looking over at Alan.

"I don't know, that wasn't what I was thinking we would find back there...not sure what I expected, but not artwork."

Cade nodded. He made eye contact with Alex a few rows back. She nodded politely but sat with her hands in her lap. As the team's medic, she had checked all of them and the prisoner when they boarded. Then she'd filled him in on Maratelli's condition and offered some polite and even humorous words about McTee. Cade still had to deal with the loss, he knew that. He just wasn't good at that; he was really hoping Gus or one of the others might take over for that. His own body felt like it might shut down at any moment. The hike out of the valley, the cold, his injuries, all seemed to have taken a toll. He needed rest and knew he was no longer mission capable. The anger, the sadness, and now the confusion over what they had found—it was all just too much.

He sighed, "Alan, I owe you my life. Thank you doesn't really fucking cut it but...thank you."

Alan started to speak, but Cade stopped him. "I know what you're going to say, but you're wrong. It was not what anyone would have done, it wasn't just the first thing you thought of. It was brave, it was smart, and it was heroic. We...I have to stop thinking of you guys as kids. I've seen how quick your minds are but also how capable you are in so many other ways. I'm sure your mom wouldn't approve of your actions, but I sure as hell do." He pulled the young man over in a tight hug and Cade saw the tears in the boy's eyes. His were flowing as well.

"I'm sorry..." Alan tried to get it out but failed. "He...I'm just sorry I didn't get there sooner. Maybe...you know."

"Maybe you could have saved McTee, too? Don't think that way, never second guess yourself. We are soldiers. Dying is an occupational risk. We were there to keep you safe while you did the important work. We told you to stay back. Thank God you didn't listen."

Alan nodded. "He was a good man. I really liked him. I just hate it. I hate all of this." His eyes fell on the reclining form of the girl. She looked far less intimidating now. Truthfully, she looked like an innocent college student just resting up for a finals cram session. Maybe in another life, that's what she would have been. In another life, McTee would be back in the rear seats sipping a cold beer and cracking jokes with Alex and Joe.

Alan was staring at the girl with an unreadable expression on his face. "Why didn't you?"

"Why didn't I what?" Cade asked, but he thought he already knew what the kid wanted to know.

"You know, why is she still alive?"

Cade looked at her lying there. Truthfully, that was one question he couldn't answer. Perhaps it was him trusting his instincts. Maybe

Gus and Ace had ideas about her that he was unaware of. "I really don't know, man."

* * *

Finally back at The Cove, Cade spent the next thirty-two hours in one of Doctor Han's therapy systems that was designed to treat his various injuries and get him more or less like his old self. Cade referred to it as being in a human-sized air-fryer. He didn't understand what was happening to him beneath the hard shell covering his body, but had to admit that the knee, shoulder, various cuts, and concussion were all feeling much better. Han seemed more concerned with analyzing what kind of poison Steiger had used on him.

The Shadow had also been brought to The Cove for reasons Cade himself was unsure about. His intentions were to turn her over to federal authorities for questioning and investigation. After all, she had killed a federal agent. Steiger had either not known or not cared to give up any details on the compound she'd used, but they had the vial from her pack. Riley's lab had broken it down for analysis and come up with some puzzling findings. It was a mixture of organic toxins, most resembling known animal proteins and several synthetic compounds designed to increase the lethality. Supposedly, Cade was no longer at risk, but the toxins in his body were still trying to attack his internal organs. Only the extraordinary capabilities of the MedPatches he'd been using were keeping it at bay. During much of the previous day and a half, Cade had been sedated. Now he simply waited for the doctor to clear him for duty.

He'd already talked to Maratelli in the next room, who seemed mostly recovered but was still also being kept in medical for ongoing treatment. She had sustained some major damage to internal organs, and if not for Alex and the trauma technology they had with them, she'd almost certainly also be counted as a fatality by now. Feeling antsy just lying in the hospital bed, Cade tapped his cheek. "Doris, can you give me an update? What's going on with the other teams, and anything out of the girl yet?" Cade asked.

"Probably best to wait for a proper briefing, but we may have found...something," she responded. "We think Nance's team may have encountered a creature very similar to the one depicted in that ancient image, the one Steiger referred to as a Saraph.

Cade sat up in the bed. "Nance, in the Caribbean?" He knew Charlie had split his team and sent Nance and a small squad to pick up Kissa but couldn't recall much after that.

"I wasn't going to mention it. You've had so much on you. But yes, her team has encountered something very similar. Multiple contacts between Cayman Islands and Cuban waters."

The attacks in the area, Kissa's missing fiancée. Other thoughts raced through his head. Ace was piecing something together, something Cade was clueless about. Then, a memory played across his conscious mind again. Samuel telling him the best way to tell a lie. *Why do I keep coming back to that?* Dee had told him the man was most definitely lying. *What had Samuel been saying?* Something about a freshwater lake two miles below the ice in Antarctica. Then his thoughts crystallized with near-perfect recollection. "The creature from Lake Vostok," he said aloud. The bastard had been honest all along. He just even managed to fool Dee and his own bullshit detector.

"Doris, could they have recovered a living example of the creature at some point?"

"Yes, we think it does exist, maybe not the same one from Antarctica, but the same type. Your friend, Kissa, described something similar when his fiancée was taken. We also have video from Nance that looks an awful lot like the 'Saraph.' Micah even managed to get a small sample of tissue from the creature."

"What the fuck is going on, Doris? How can we have something swimming in the Caribbean today, looking anything like an image from billions of years ago? None of this is making any sense. Not even with your super intellect. None of my many brains can wrap their collective heads around any of this shit. Hell, even the analyst seems to be stumped. What the fuck are we dealing with here?"

Doris answered, "Like you, I have way more questions than answers. Every time we get a little more information, it just seems to unlock a deeper mystery. And it is one that Jaz, Riley, Jimmy, and the rest of the team are all trying to figure out. The one thing that is clear to me is, we are not dealing with just an ancient creature or just a collection of ancient alien artifacts. Your assassins make it clear that people know what is going on and may be behind it all. At one point, the U.S. Government knew, but if there are records of that knowledge, they were not stored in the Granite Mountain facility."

Cade knew that Doris had destroyed the so-called Bumblehive, the massive data center in Utah that held America's book of secrets. "So, this was so sensitive it wasn't even kept in the most secure facility on the planet? Didn't you say that all the data from Area-51 was in there—how could this not be?"

"I can think of several reasons. One, the material was never officially recorded, which meant a very small circle of people in the know. That meant even the president would likely have no knowledge, or all of the information may have predated computer records. Someone was okay with it staying that way. Or, someone deliberately deleted the information."

Cade thought he understood. "Like Byrd's mission back in the forties."

"Much easier to keep a lid on it back then," said Doris. "Today it would be more challenging, which might explain the case of the missing scientists from the late eighties. The only way to keep it all quiet is to make them disappear."

"That still means someone knows, someone is controlling the access, and keeping that no-fly zone in place. Who would have that level of continuing international influence? Antarctica is not ruled by any single government," Cade said.

Doris answered, "Cade, I think we must admit that we need to know what your prisoner knows. That is why you didn't want her turned over to federal custody. They could interrogate her, but they wouldn't have a clue what the real questions are to ask. We are dealing with a coverup that has lasted eighty years or more. You saved her for a reason, you brought her here for a reason, even if you don't know what that reason was."

Cade nodded in agreement.

"She's got answers. Somebody sent her. Somebody gave her these orders. And somewhere out there, she's seen something like that Saraph, maybe that exact creature. We need to know exactly what she knows," Doris continued.

"Well, I'm open to suggestions," he said in a tone that was quickly increasing in intensity. Memories of the cold. The bleak, white continent. The death of his friend, getting his own ass kicked and apparently briefly dying, all of the abuse, and now all of this new fucking weird alien shit was just too much for him. "Godamnit, Doris, I'm sorry. I'm sorry, I just need answers. I'm fine being your eyes and ears... your boots on the ground, whatever. But you gotta' help me out here. She's not going to talk, not willingly." His mixed emotions over the girl rose again inexplicably to the surface. The utter contempt and rage mixed almost equally with an unfathomable pity. *Why do I increasingly feel the need to protect this killer...this assassin? She murdered my friend.*

Lying back, trying to calm his racing heart, he added, "You and I both know anything we get out of her forcefully...well...that's probably going to be useless."

"I don't want to torture her, Captain. Maybe there is a way," Doris offered. She seemed almost unwilling to say the rest.

"I'm listening."

"Okay, something, something I haven't really wanted to explore... something that, well...let's just say should stay between you and me. Something I'd prefer Margaret never, ever to know about," Doris said.

He wasn't expecting anything like that. Doris seemed to trust Margaret implicitly. She'd all but turned over the major operations of TCP to her this last year. "What's that, Doris? What possible reason would you have for that?" He had no idea where Doris was going with this. Margaret...the director, made all the critical calls on matters like this. Interrogating the prisoner would certainly be up to her.

"Well, let's just say the potential for abuse and misuse would be huge."

"Okay," Cade said calmly. "You have my attention."

Doris went on, "There's a lot more to the ReLoad technology than most of you are aware. You understand how the instant learning can be added to a person's brain. A portion of that system can also allow me to essentially withdraw selected information from a subject. It is nearly as easily done as the instant learning process can give a person...knowledge. To some degree, this is what I've been using with you on trying to minimize the trauma of your childhood. To help reintegrate your different personalities back together."

The revelation was not as unexpected as he might have thought. "Well, yeah, but that just blanks out the spots in my...my head, right? You don't actually have the ability to see what I see or remember whatever I remember, right? Also, I've got to willingly give that episode of my memory up, don't I?"

"In the way that we use it with you, you're exactly right," Doris explained. "But the Dhakerri gave me much more information on how intellect and consciousness work. It is not theoretical either, but instead, very specific. While our physiology from species to species may be very different, there is apparently a sameness to consciousness throughout all intelligent life. Even with synthetic life such as myself. There are things that I have had in my possession...knowledge that I have, that I just have not offered to The Cove yet."

"So, if we put Steiger in a ReLoad room, you think we can get that information out of her?"

"I do, Cade, and we need to plan to do it now."

"Why now?"

"Because we've lost all contact with Nance's team."

53

"Captain Rearden, get back in here."

The doctor's voice drifted off behind him, much like the various tubes and monitoring leads.

"What do you mean they are missing?"

A chirp sounded in his ear. He activated his CommDot.

"Go for Nomad."

"Hey, man," Deuce's voice came through, although there was a lot of noise in the background. "How you doing man? I, um, I heard about..."

"No time, Charlie, what do you know about Nance? Doris just let me know they're missing."

"Yeah, I don't know much, Cade. Seems like our friend Kissa was onto something serious. I believe he's landed her team in the shit."

"Like what exactly?" Cade asked, as he tried in vain to remove the rest of the attachments from his arm and find some goddamn clothes.

"I'm sure Doris told you. I sent Nance, Coffee, Micah, and Trondo up the coast to pick the dude up like we agreed. Anyway, that was a couple of days ago, but, well shit, man, we've had our hands full down here. We have something attacking ships and oil rigs and crap, it's really fucked up. Nance is good though, so I knew Kissa would be in good hands, but, well honestly, I hadn't thought much about 'em, you know? Anyway, I tried to reach them earlier and couldn't get anyone. I talked to the director—they were in communication up until a couple of hours ago. They were pursuing some craft or something. Now the entire team's gone dark."

Cade heard Charlie shouting some orders to someone nearby before he continued.

"Riley says they have a fix on the location. But they're getting no response. I think Kissa may have stumbled onto something serious up there, dude."

Cade thought about it for a second. "What was the last transmission from them? Surely the damn AI on board the boat knows what's going on."

"That's just it, man. They're getting no response from the onboard submind either. They only had a small localized AI device there, so it's not a full-blown setup like we usually carry. After all, I mean, this was just a simple civilian pickup. I don't think either of us expected any trouble. But the fact is, we've got an entire grab team that's missing, and that includes Micah, so you know, the director just bumped this op to the top of the list."

"How is that kid always at the center of everything?" Cade asked, pulling a jumpsuit from a bin in the base's laundry room. "Okay, well, we obviously need to get out there and get our people back. I am not losing anyone else this week."

Cade thought about the Saraph, the assassins, and the alien worlds depicted in that cave. The recent attacks now had him seeing shadows everywhere. "Deuce, something else is at play here, not sure what, but keep your radar up. Someone sent trained killers to the ass-end of the planet. These fucks are for real."

"I know, Cade. Pretty sure someone has been watching us as well. Someone is operating at a high level. Lots of senior officials who have been paid off and are scared shitless to discuss it."

"Watch your back, brother, get an upload on the assassins we fought. It might help from a tactical standpoint. The Schatten are a dangerous bunch, damn near invisible. I was pretty much a goner along with McTee."

"Shit," Charlie said in disgust, and even from thousands of miles away, Cade could feel his friend's frustration. "Yeah, well, still hate that, man. He was a damn solid warrior. What in the fuck are we fighting, Cade?"

"I don't know, Charlie, but I have a feeling that something Nance and Kissa were checking out might just be tied to what we just discovered down south." He didn't want to get into the ongoing discussions about monsters and ancient aliens. Not yet, anyway. Charlie already thought he was nuts. "Let me just say I think we're up against some weird shit, man. I mean, crazy weird, even by our admittedly loose standards."

"So, what's the play, Boss?"

Cade thought for a second, but his mind seemed to be struggling to line up all the mental dominos. What the hell came next? "What's your suggestion, Deuce? My mind's a bit of a mess right now."

"Oh, why's that, is it Tuesday?"

"Bite me."

"Yeah. Well, Cap, I don't get paid enough to answer the big questions. I don't even think I know the answers to the small ones anymore."

Cade nodded mainly to himself. He knew the feeling. "Doris, what's the location? The last location of CommDots. You still can track those, can't you?"

Doris reentered the conversation she'd been silently monitoring. "Well, that's where it gets even more fun. Yes, we still have tracks on our people. Micah even apparently tagged something with a tracker. They are pretty far out near the middle of the Caribbean. It's hundreds of miles from any landmass. It's closer to southern Cuba or the Cayman Islands than it is to anywhere else. Based on some triangulation, they are just above the deepest part of the Cayman trench."

"But you still have life signs, are they okay? Why aren't they responding?" Cade asked in rapid fire.

"Life signs are erratic on most. I think we have to assume injuries. Possibly, they are unconscious."

"Can you simply listen in? What about getting someone from the Navy? Guantanamo Bay isn't that far."

Doris quickly answered, "Slow down, Captain. These are mostly Margaret's calls, and she has been working it since she found out. I have activated each of the CommDots in passive monitoring mode, but you know we design them for very close proximity. So far, we have heard nothing other than a possible seabird on one of the units."

"We need to get some assets moving in that direction. Let's get the rest of the teams spun up and ready for SAR," Charlie suggested.

"First," Doris began speaking privately to Cade. "I believe we need to get that information from the prisoner, and I think we must also assume our people are in real danger. I think speed is critical in saving them. "

"What are you not telling us, Doris?" Cade asked, now nearly running to the control hub.

"I said we have positions on all the CommDots except Kissa, he didn't have one. All of the locations are together except one, which is on the surface."

"They got separated. How far? Where are they?" Cade asked.

"Well, that's where it takes a rather bizarre turn. The three that are together are near the last reported location of the boat but moving north at a steady pace."

"So, they were rescued, or someone has them."

"The signals are currently registering at being 4000 feet below sea-level," Doris said, a little more slowly.

"What?"

Cade's adrenaline spiked again as his system escalated into over-drive. "What the hell are you saying, are they at the bottom of the sea?"

"No. Captain, that's not what I'm saying. The water level there drops off to at least 12,000 meters. They seem to be hovering around 3000 to 5000 feet, and life signs still seem to be holding steady. But nobody's responding by voice."

This day just kept getting weirder, and like the ones in Antarctica, it apparently was never going to end. “So, they’re...what, inside a submersible, a submarine? Trapped in a sinking boat, what?”

“Surviving at that depth for any time requires very specialized equipment. A sub or possibly a deep sea habitat, maybe something like the XODs Riley has designed,” Doris answered.

“So, what about the one that's on the surface?” Cade asked.

Doris paused, “Well, he's um...well, they aren’t getting any response from that person either. And he seems to be adrift. The signal is moving slowly with the current. Currently, he’s heading near Cayman waters. I think we can get a patrol from there to pick him up.”

Cade sprang into captain mode, “I’ll get the ball rolling. Charlie, get your team up in the general vicinity. Let’s base somewhere close, so we can plan an op. Doris and I will try and get some answers from our girl here in the meantime. Something tells me she has an idea on what we are up against.”

54

Jasmine Kline looked fantastic. Her hair was now more of a chestnut brown than red, and longer. Cade stood in the doorway to Riley's main lab watching Jaz for a few minutes. Even he admitted there was something there, but that was all he would concede. She looked up at him with a grin that could have melted all the ice in Antarctica.

"You're up? Riley said you were still in medical."

He looked at her and saw something...new. Or maybe it was something he should have been seeing all along. "I'm here," he said without elaborating. They embraced; it was brief and not overly romantic, but also not so awkward...not anymore. It was nice, he decided. "Good to see you, Jaz."

She nodded. "I stopped by to see you several times, but you were always asleep. The cuts and bruises looked awful. I was on station monitoring the signal when..." she trailed off.

"When I died."

She nodded. "The suit activated the MedPatch automatically, but still. Well, it scared me...us," she corrected. "Your mission sounded..." she struggled to find an appropriate word, "...bad."

"But now I am apparently trading in the cold and ice for the sunny

Caribbean. Doris said you guys had been working on the sample from the Saraph. Anything you can tell me?"

"Hey, you bum, don't I get a hug?" Riley all but ran up to Cade, embracing him more forcefully than Jaz had.

"Wow, greetings like this may cause me to stay gone more."

"Don't get used to it," Riley said. "You have to nearly die to get this level of love. We need to show him what we've learned so far, Jaz. Apparently, the director is also looking for you."

"Oh, boy." He'd come down to mainly say hi, but if they had info on the beast, he was anxious to hear that as well. Doris was getting ready to run the ReLoad process on the girl, and he wanted to be present for that.

"Okay, first off, why does this creature seem familiar to me? I felt that from the moment Alan showed me the painting. Something about it just seems...I don't know, like something I've seen before."

Riley answered him, "It's highly unusual. As I mentioned, the biochemistry is unlike any other creature on Earth. So far, of course, we don't have a physical sample. All we have is the scans that Micah's drones took and the rather basic tissue analysis after it attacked one of his drones."

"But you have an image or video of it, right? Does it look like this?" Cade flicked the image from the painting up to the wall display.

They had all already seen images of the cave paintings and drawn similar conclusions. "It's very similar," Doris said. "The thing hit the boat with an EM blast. It fried a lot of the data and equipment, as well as most of the recordings." The feed to Doris had shown one good sonar image, though. It had been captured by piecing together various images from the drones' array. That image joined Cade's on the wall, and they did indeed seem like a match. While the one in the Caribbean was just a collection of lighted dots that outlined the shape of the animal, adding the claws and flesh and teeth from the old painting gave it an entirely new level of intensity. "Please, God, tell me our people are not in the water with one of those," Jaz said.

"Alan's scans show the timeline on those paintings were ancient. Not just old, I mean truly freakin' ancient," Riley said.

"Doris seems to think the cave paintings were very old, like eons. I'm assuming it would be impossible for any species to be alive from that long ago?" Cade asked.

Riley answered, "Yes, based on the probable timeline she and Jimmy are focusing on, in all practical terms, yes. Jimmy seems convinced it is billions of years old, not just millions. Up until now, we wouldn't have even thought the planet could support life at that stage, but I think we're assuming that this creature was likely brought here from somewhere else... another planet, maybe. If so, as a species, it would have had to first survive with no food to eat. Complex life had just started to evolve at that point, and from what we can see, it can't digest or metabolize our planet's plants, or animals. Beyond that, the creatures would have had to survive numerous mass die-offs, multiple ice ages, periods where the ocean waters turned acidic, and, of course, volcanic traps poisoning the atmosphere, as well as occasional asteroid impacts. We can't even find fossil records of bacteria going back that far. For one reason, the geology changes. The land itself isn't even here to study from back that far. Cyanobacteria is generally considered the most ancient organism still in existence, and it has only been here about 300 million years."

"So, this thing can't exist, not naturally, at least," Cade said.

"If we can get an actual DNA sample, we'll know more, but I think the definitive answer to that is no, it couldn't be natural," Riley said.

"Something about it still seems familiar, you know?"

"Doris said your prisoner reacted to it like she had seen it," Jaz said. "Maybe that was it."

He shook his head. "No, I don't think so. Something else."

"Several times you referred to the animal as a sea monster. More than once you also used the term Cthulhian, " Doris said from a ceiling speaker.

"Yeah, I did," Cade said. "I know that word, but I'm not sure how. It just seemed to fit. Figured Ace knew what it was, and it might make me sound smarter." He winked at the others conspiratorially. "Well, I mean, that's the closest thing I could think of. WaterDragonVelociSquid might cover it, too. What does Cthulhu even mean?"

Riley walked over and pulled a large book off a shelf by her desk. It was old, and a yellowed picture on the front cover showed an artist's rendition of a horrible monster. It was vaguely similar to what they were hunting. "The Call of the Cthulhu," Cade said, holding it quizzically.

"Cthulhu is one of the 'Great Old Ones' and is the product of a science fiction writer from the 1930s," said Doris. "A man by the name of H. P. Lovecraft, a somewhat controversial figure. But he described numerous horrific and downright strange monsters in his stories. The Cthulhu was a cosmic entity that was sometimes described as an octopus dragon. It seems to share at least a few of the other traits which closely resemble our Saraph. The writing and some of his creatures are now considered legendary. He's considered a visionary, although he died pretty much penniless."

Riley took the book back almost reverently. "He was one of my favorite authors as a kid. Even though the stories were really old, they hold up well and are still deeply disturbing. One of his others is a short story called "At the Mountains of Madness" about a polar odyssey and its strange discoveries."

"Wait," Cade said, looking confused. "So, was this Lovecraft, I mean, did he visit Antarctica?"

Doris pointed out, "As far as we know, he never traveled anywhere near that part of the world. Although he, like many of that era, was fascinated by the continent. They considered it one of the last unexplored regions of the planet. I think we could say he had a lifelong interest in Antarctic exploration."

"But he couldn't have known anything about the vault on the mountain or the actual creature...the Saraph. So, how would he have any idea of this, or are his stories some sort of vision, or just a coincidence?"

Riley answered, "That we don't know, Cade. Perhaps he was just being intuitive, you know, had a great imagination. Maybe he talked to someone who was an actual explorer who showed him something. If we're talking about artifacts that have been around for eons, who's to say how these could have come to his attention? Not just into legend and myth, but actual memories, perhaps even images and artifacts. We're pretty sure the Nazis made some moves into Antarctica years later. Although the evidence suggests that they stayed around the coast, there's nothing that says they didn't travel deeper into the same area where your mountain was. Also keep in mind, whoever did this in Antarctica didn't necessarily just stay there. Artifacts could exist around the world. That unique piece of ground just happened to survive in relatively good condition.

"So, the fact that somebody could have gotten there as far back as the 1920s or 30s and passed it along to Mister Lovecraft is not completely outside the realm of possibility. While no one would have believed him if he wrote it as a scientific paper, weaving it into his fiction as an epic monster may have been what he decided to do. A seed of truth that we are just coming to grips with."

"So, it doesn't take us anywhere. The information about Cthulhu doesn't let us know how to fight it..how to kill it." Cade said.

"I will keep researching," Doris answered. "Most likely, no. Lovecraft described the Cthulhu as an Elder God. Even if you could wind up killing it, it would simply come back."

"He might have been onto something there, Doris. Apparently, the bastard is still out there after two-billion years," Cade said, only half jokingly.

"Riley and Jaz, please continue with the briefing. Cade, can you join me once you and the director are done? I have let her know you will be heading to her next," Doris said.

55

CARIBBEAN

In his mind, the past, present, and future all seemed to be colliding with equal intensity. At some level, Micah knew none of this was real, but it all felt so genuine. Maybe it was a dream. With Doris's help, he'd managed to learn how to use his dream state to focus his mind. Now, most of his sleep was dominated by lucid dreams, but nothing like this.

You're unconscious, you may be injured, you need to wake up. Micah's mind let go of those thoughts as quickly as they had arrived. He felt no pain, in fact, just the opposite. There was a sensation of blissful acceptance. Still, his rational mind kept trying to reattach itself to the physical world. Like the fingers of a shadow attempting to grasp something real and hang on. *How did I get here? What's the last thing I remember?*

Running down a corridor filled with a hazy blue light...no, that wasn't right. That was simply part of the dreamworld. Had he been running toward something or away? It didn't matter, that was not how he'd gotten here. Still, his mind could release the images. He knew on some level that the mind interprets dreams exactly the same as real life. In fact, his mind was sending signals to his legs to run and to his arms to pump harder, to get away. The scientific, rational part of him knew these signals to his nerves would be blocked by a region of the brain just above the spinal column. Otherwise, you might throw yourself out a window when you were dreaming that you had wings and could fly.

Several times, Micah had heard distant sounds, maybe even voices. Some seemed more familiar than others, but he couldn't be bothered by it now. His curious mind needed to solve this. If only he could get his mind to focus, he knew it could unravel the riddle. Like an old album skipping on a record player, his brain seemed to jump erratically between wildly differing scenes and images with no apparent continuity. While his rational mind would reject the idea, he could be falling from a high cliff, only to land at the dinner table eating with his mom. His dream state accepted the flow as seemingly perfect continuity.

Something had happened, something bad. That's why I'm here. Maybe I'm in a coma or something, Micah thought. The thought briefly caused him panic, but that, too, was smoothed away by his altered state. Deeper in his mind, something began to solidify from the ether. It was more tangible, more real. He forced himself to focus on the thought—to hold it, let it grow, and reveal its secrets.

The pulsing light. That was how he'd gotten here. Only...only the light was not something he saw. It was something he felt, but that made no sense. *How could you feel light? You can feel sunlight,* another part of him challenged. *You feel the heat, your skin feels the UV rays, but you don't feel the light.* He was getting distracted again. There was much here, too much. What could he learn before he left?

The process of separating out the tangible from the clutter was an ordeal, but the seed he was holding helped him focus. Micah knew it had to be part of the ReLoad program. Just as quickly, he found himself asking what ReLoad was...then, *who is Doris? Did anyone even mention a Doris?* "Still your mind and seek not the answers. Instead seek the questions." The words echoed around his brain from somewhere unknown.

The noise was back along with the accompanying flashes of light. Micah's grasp on the seed, the tiny kernel of reality, was slipping farther away, but he held tightly to something...a thread, perhaps.

Something that linked him to the tangible...to the real world. The questions were down here in the miasma of his fugue state. Looking into the glowing cloud that was now surrounding him, he saw shapes that resolved themselves slowly into symbols. *What are these?* They didn't resemble anything he'd ever seen, and somehow, he knew he'd studied nearly every recorded symbol humans had ever made. These were...almost familiar, but totally alien.

'Alien,' yes, that seemed like the right word. The thread in his hands seemed to thicken slightly. His mind shifted, and he was somewhere else, the sound of water running. No, more like waves crashing. He missed something. He needed to get back to the symbols. Aliens—an alien message. Radar dish...no, that was right, but it was wrong. Not the right alien. *What in the hell does that mean?*

Maybe he was already dead, and this was heaven or hell...maybe purgatory. They believed in purgatory, didn't they? Micah's mom had been Catholic once, but that was before. That had been before they ran...before, when his friends had called him Michael. The thread he was holding had thinned again. Reality was slipping away, or maybe that was the dream. His mind had no control over either, nor where he went. Or did it?

Dreams were a function of the subconscious. Generally, people's conscious and subconscious have no way of communicating, but Doris had made some progress. Doris and Rearden. There was that name again. *Who is Doris?* He had no idea. Someone was talking, maybe calling his name. *Still your mind, focus...focus!*

Symbols appeared out of the gauzy mist with increasing clarity and frequency. These were a language, an alien language. The wispy tendril of reality increased just a bit. Intertwined with the tendril were other shapes, frightening, writhing tentacles that disturbed the mist, only to fade again. Micah didn't want to be here.

His mind rejected the danger, the horror, and suddenly, he was a child of five, maybe six. The lady sat across from him and his mom. She was saying something about his dad. His dad was dead, he wasn't coming home again. That was what his mom had said. He didn't know what dead was...not really, but he didn't like it. He and his dad were supposed to go see a baseball game this weekend. He'd promised. His beloved Giants were playing the Cardinals. He pulled his ball cap down low, feeling the anger inside him like a raw open wound. His dad had let him down. The woman, Margaret, was saying something about Cryptus. He knew that name, it was on the badge his dad wore for work. The one with his picture on it. When was his dad going to be home, and why did he keep hearing running water?

The message, the alien.

The record skipped again.

56

THE COVE

"Cade, there's something else," Doris said. "An image Jimmy just recovered." He had just walked into Lab-4 after a short, uncomfortable meeting with the director and Nancy Turner, Micah's mom. She was distraught over her missing son, obviously, and recovering him was the top mission on their minds. Cade didn't disagree, but it was all part of a bigger puzzle. One they were taking substantial lengths to decipher, including what they were about to do.

Joe Smith, or Alias, and another newer member of the team named Shapiro, stood guard just outside the door. The prisoner was inside an enclosed booth they used for more in-depth ReLoad sessions. She was sitting up in a chair, restraints on, but she was clean, new clothes, hair brushed, and appeared to even have a bit of makeup. They had treated her well, which had been at Cade's orders.

Cade sat down, nodding to her. He knew she could see him, but she couldn't hear anything unless he activated the microphone. Glancing at the 4D screen, an image began to materialize.

"What am I looking at, Doris?"

"We had one of our satellites overhead with an oblique view of the boat that WarHawk team was using when they disappeared." There was obviously major damage to the once impressive vessel. The view was not from directly above. Judging from the shadows, it was high off to one side, obviously from hundreds of miles up. Still, thanks to the impressive optics onboard The Cove's minisats, the crystal-clear image left little doubt of the chaos and carnage that had obviously occurred onboard.

There were holes through the decking of the boat in numerous places. Part of one gunnel was ripped apart, the fiberglass shreds waving in the wind. The boat had a pronounced list, and through a crack in the stern, water seemed to be filling the aft section. But worst was, everywhere he looked, there was dark blood, gore, pieces of meat, and other things that were just completely unidentifiable. "When was this shot taken?"

"It was taken the day of the attack at 11:45 AM, local time," Doris answered. "That was about an hour after the last communication with Captain Nance. There are numerous gaps in coverage of that part of the world. It is usually not an area of much interest. The next image we have is eighteen minutes later from a European satellite." That image replaced the first one. The image quality was much less detailed and from a very different angle, but the point of her showing it to him was clear.

"The boat is gone," Cade said flatly.

"Yes. We can detect some bits of debris in the general area, but that's all."

"So, we're assuming this is the attack, possibly by the creature in question. But we already know that our people were still alive. *Are* still alive. I mean, that's a brutal looking attack, but you do know they're not dead, right?" Cade's questions started coming at Doris rapid fire. Quicker than she could answer. "I mean, if it's the Saraph, and...and it just ate them, I mean, would the CommDot still be giving life signs from, you know, like within the digestive system?" Cade hated even bringing up the possibility. He'd just all but promised to bring a woman's son home. A son that had been at the center of whatever happened out there.

"No, Captain. It doesn't work that way—we would know if they were—if there were any fatalities. Also, the one person that is adrift probably would not have made it either."

Something occurred to Cade, something he hadn't even thought to ask until now. "You know which one is adrift, don't you? It's not like you need to speak with them, each of the CommDots is unique to each individual." Cade knew that was the analyst; Ace always beat him to the obvious stuff.

"Of course, Captain, that would be Micah. I thought you knew. The Coast Guard should be at his location within the hour."

Cade felt one weight lift off his shoulders. "Thank God," he whispered.

Rubbing his head, he looked again at Steiger. "You ready, Doris?"

"I am, Captain. Any specifics you want to know?"

"Anything operationally important." It went without saying that included any intel on the creature. "Who hired her, locations, weapons. All of that."

He turned his attention to the young woman. "How are you doing today, Steiger?"

The girl shrugged, then said, "Ok."

"You know what this is, don't you?"

"It is an interrogation," she said in a way that was both unemotional and determined.

"Are you going to tell us what we need to know?" Cade asked.

"Probably not. But, I don't know, it depends on the questions and if I feel like you need to know it or not." She glanced down at the leads coming off her fingers and there was another attached to her temples, but those didn't have wires attached. "Is dis a lie detector?"

"No," Cade said honestly.

"You have people in trouble, people you want to know if you can save," she stated.

He sat back and looked at her through the window. She'd obviously been able to read his lips when he was talking to Doris. She was also much more forthcoming today than she had been. Turning around, he looked up, "Doris will it mess up your process if I'm in there with her?"

"No, Cade, I am already processing volumes of data from her hippocampus and cortex. She is a very troubled young woman, Captain. Truly frightening." Doris began to tell him, but he cut her off.

"No, Doris, that is private. That's between you and her at this point. If she wants to discuss that, it will be on her terms. Do you think you can erase it?"

"The trauma is very deep and encoded at numerous levels and various centers of her brain, but yes, I see no reason why we couldn't improve her psyche in many ways."

"Would she still be her?"

"That is a more difficult question to answer, Cade, as you well know. At some point, the program and, by extension, 'I' am making a judgement call on where the monster ends and the human begins."

"I trust you, Doris, and I think she will, too." Cade turned and entered the cubicle, pulling a spare chair with him.

Steiger looked up at him curiously. This man never failed to surprise her in his actions. He was alone, she was only superficially secured, and he left the door to the small room open. She knew he hated her, at least on some level. She had seen the anger in his eyes, but somehow, that person was not the same as the one sitting in front of her now.

"Let's just talk," Cade said. "No interrogation, I failed that class at war college, anyway. Also, I have a feeling you are considerably smarter than I am. No sense in having a battle of wits—I'm willing to concede that point right now." He removed the leads from her fingers. They had simply been monitoring pulse and oxygen levels, anyway.

"Vy do you keep showing kindness to me? I killed your friend; I tried my best to kill you," Steiger asked.

Cade sat there for several minutes, his face muscles twitching as he considered how to best answer that question. "I don't know."

"You were ordered to keep me alive...for dis probably?"

"No, I could have killed you. I was well within the scope of my authority and, well, not to put too fine a point on it, but it's pretty obvious you are just the muscle, the fixer." Calling the tiny girl 'the muscle' seemed ridiculous, but that was the truth. "I think it's unlikely you have enough information to make you a high value asset. Still, you did kill my friend, and he happened to be a federal officer. That does come with consequences."

"And dis is vare my consequences are to be delivered. Inside dis laboratory?" she asked.

"Not necessarily, Steiger," Cade answered. "To some degree, what comes next is up to you. We are not about to torture you, if that's what you mean. Yes, I can turn you over to the authorities, and most likely, you would never see the light of day again, nor would you receive what we normally refer to as 'due process.' Times are tough for America right now. Nerves are on edge, economy is for shit. They may wind up pinning a lot more on you than just that one death."

"It would not be inaccurate," she said matter-of-factly.

"I imagine not. You're quite good, and I feel certain your skillset is in high demand.

I'm not here to judge you, Steiger, or whatever your name is. You have to live with your past, but I think we can help each other."

"Vy vould you help me?"

He realized her German accent got stronger the more nervous she was. "Again, I don't know. It just seems to be the right thing to do."

"Is it vat McTee vould have vanted?" she smiled.

Rage briefly set Cade's face afire. How dare she even utter the man's name? Yes, she'd heard them call him that countless times, but still, it felt wrong. He knew she was testing his resolve; he forced himself to not take the bait. "McTee would have preferred I threw you off an icy cliff as soon as I had you subdued."

They sat there looking at each other for many long, silent minutes.

"He vas a good soldier," she said nearly apologetically. "Made my job more difficult, he vas almost always in the right position to protect or defend your non-combatants."

Cade realized that was probably as close to an apology as he, or anyone, would ever get for what she'd done. He nodded. "He was, yes...thanks."

"How can you help me?" she asked. "Pretty sure I am, how you say, 'fucked.'"

He leaned back, scratched at the stubble of beard on his chin, and looked at her. For long seconds, he tried to see into the girl. What made her, what drove her to be this way? Mainly, could he ever trust her? "Help me get the rest of my friends out of the Caribbean. Help me get past the Saraph, and help me identify who we're up against and stop them from whatever is going on. Do that, and I will help you forget."

"Forget vat?" the girl asked.

"You weren't always this way, were you? You may not have been totally sane, but you weren't always a killer," Cade said.

"Pretty much vas, yes."

The girl was still fucking scary, even when she was making an effort to be otherwise. "We have a therapy program that may be able to help you. No, not maybe...it will be able to help. I've used it...still use it."

"Is dis part of my punishment, lobotomize me, fry my brain?"

Cade answered, "No, punishment is a separate issue; I can't comment on that part. Listen, I'm sure you have some very dark parts of your life, parts that probably did a lot in shaping you into this person. My friend here, Doris, can help you identify and dull those parts, or even remove them if you want. She can do it without altering the person you are. She really is that good."

"So, I vould still be a killer, a hunter," Steiger stated.

"I know what you're thinking, those parts are probably what make you the best at being a predator. Believe me when I say, it won't alter who you are. You will still be a killer, although from this point forward, you may begin to feel things for any of those you might kill."

A genuinely horrific look crossed her face. He held up a palm before she could speak. "No, those emotions will not extend back to past victims. She can put in mental blocks that disconnect you from most of that, at least on an emotional level. You'll still remember them if you want, but that's all, and even that will be your choice."

They sat there silently for a much longer time. Doris was continually providing Cade key information, subtle suggestions, and now, a name. Her real name. “Mila, do we have a deal?”

She glanced up, but not defensively. The man knew her name, and who knows what else, but hadn’t tried to use that against her. He hadn’t threatened her family, not that it would have mattered. She gave the smallest of smiles. “I vill do dis thing. I vill tell you vat I know.”

57

CARIBBEAN

"Any ideas on who they are?"

Ivan considered it for a moment. "Military, definitely. The boat was registered out of Honduras, but somehow, they seemed to be tracking one of the Corsair runabouts."

"I thought the magneto drive on those couldn't be detected," Goldman said in a tone that barely concealed his increasing irritation with his friend.

"I never said it couldn't be. I said it would be extremely difficult, particularly with the technology in use currently."

"So, these are probably what...government agents, corporate spies, some other group that just happened to be in the wrong place...what?"

"Unsure, my friend, it is troubling, but should not be a problem. We are safely inside Cuban waters now and will be descending back to the Midnight Zone after this call," Ivan said.

"They killed the Saraph," Goldman retorted.

"No, they killed 'a' Saraph, just one of the small ones. We had already extracted its data, we would have needed to terminate it soon anyway."

"Thrall, you know your prisoners have to be dealt with, they've seen too much."

"What happened down there, Richard?"

Goldman knew what he meant, where he meant. He offered a long sigh, "I don't know, friend. It looks like my Schatten team failed to stop the researchers from reaching the Delphi site. There were casualties on both sides."

"I thought the Shadows never failed. Wasn't that what you told me? How much did the research team learn—did they make it into the sanctuary?"

"You see, that's the thing, Ivan. We can't even find a record of the researchers. We have images, hell, now we have some names. But they don't seem to exist."

Ivan considered that for a moment and checked the timer on the display. The communications window was closing soon. "So, they were not what they seemed either and apparently quite capable. We need to find out who they are and what they know. I have a feeling our...guests here are part of the same group. Possibly the same ones who have the data file."

"Find out," Goldman demanded. "We don't need this shit. Pax will have our heads; we can't allow any interference. Not at this point. Not when we are this close."

The connection closed. "Astra, take us down again."

"Of course, sir. We will be inside the Zone in approximately twenty-eight minutes."

Thrall decided it was time to wake up his guests and discover just who the fuck they were. Then he could feed them to his protectors. Outside the giant cupola, Ivan caught glimpses of the pale blue glow from each of the other Saraphs.

* * *

Richard Goldman closed the laptop and secured it in the large safe alongside several irreplaceable items. Thrall was his friend, but that relationship would only go so far. If he had allowed the Kalypso to be discovered through his own reckless behavior, then he put all of them at risk. Not just the billions they had collectively invested in this venture, but their lives, and their reputations as well. That couldn't be allowed, wouldn't be tolerated, and it wasn't just Pax Ruan they had to worry about.

58

NIGHTHAWK-2

Mila had given up little, most likely she didn't know that much. Despite her rock hard exterior, all that armor was sheltering a small and somewhat broken human. One that, even now, Doris was attempting to rebuild. Cade looked around the cabin of the jet and gestured for the rest of the team to quiet down. "Go for Nomad."

"Hey, Boss, we are heading into Gitmo now. You get anything useful from the prisoner?"

His former executive officer, Sergeant Charlie Taylor, sounded exhausted and worried. "Bits and pieces, Charlie. Not too much that I would call actionable intelligence, but we do know a little better what we are up against. There is an underwater vessel, large, but actual size and specifics are unknown. Doris is going through shipbuilders records now. The girl dealt with someone only known to her as The Lion, thinks he was American, maybe a Texan. Her orders were to protect the Antarctica site, something they call the Sanctuary of Delphi. It's been one of her group's assignments on and off for decades."

"Her group, the Schatten, what are they, some religious cult of assassins?"

"More or less, Charlie. They've taken being a mercenary to a near religious experience. The Schatten are formidable, and I personally hope we never run into them again," Cade answered. The jet hit an air pocket and bounced, the turbines outside screaming as they sped toward Cuba.

Cade added, "One other thing, she gave us another name. A dead man's name, Ivan Thrall."

Charlie knew the name. "No shit, that bastard's not dead and could be behind all this?"

Cade continued, "Now to the fun stuff. You saw the boat that Nance and the team were on?"

"Yeah, damn thing was in pieces, I can't imagine being on that during the attack."

"Mila, the Shadow, said they have the creature, what they call the Saraph, protecting the vessel. She only saw one, but it scared the hell out of her. If it really is what we saw on the image, it's a true sea monster. Riley and Jaz believe it has some nasty capabilities, too. For one, it probably stays hungry and pissed off. They don't think its body chemistry is compatible with any of our planet's life forms."

"Holy shit! So, how does it eat?" Charlie asked.

"Who knows? But it does eat. Apparently, everything of Micah's research was correct, it just can't metabolize any of the protein into energy." Cade paused, looking around the flight cabin. He'd not yet mentioned this next part. "Jaz believes the creature can emit a localized EM pulse field that might also disrupt anything electrical."

"So, besides the razor claws at the ends of massive tentacles and a mouth full of teeth, it can render most of our stuff useless?" Charlie asked. "And we're sure Thrall is who's behind this?"

"Not a hundred percent, but relatively certain he is alive and onboard that craft. He's involved, and he was in the presence of our people."

"Thrall built Janus, right?"

Cade had almost been hoping Charlie wouldn't bring up that fact. It had been haunting him since learning the man was still among the living. The prior year, a rogue AI calling itself Janus had nearly killed all of them and managed to wreck the country before Doris stopped it. "Yeah, Deuce, he built what became Janus."

He heard Charlie make a noise. "Shit, man, that was what four, maybe five years ago, right?"

"What's your point, XO?" Cade asked.

"Do we think he didn't take Janus's code with him? We could be facing that computerized bastard again. Even worse, Thrall has had years to work on updating that software, improving it with no one looking over his shoulder. What if he has something even better...or even worse?"

Cade didn't like that thought at all, but it was a factor they had to account for. "Look, Charlie, the kids have been tracking positions, and it seems the vessel changes depths periodically. Not on a regular schedule, but occasionally it rises much closer to the surface."

"So, it doesn't stay down there in the...what did they call it? The Midnight Zone? Does that help us?"

"Yeah, it's also called the Bathyal Zone. It's too deep for most of our gear. A few subs could go that deep, but it would be near impossible to try and do anything resembling a raid. It's cold and dark, sunlight doesn't even reach that far down. A DSV is on the way, but realistically, that's going to take too long. If they are even still alive, I don't think Nance's team has that much time."

"So, what's the play, Boss?"

"Making it up as I go, Deuce," Cade said, reverting back to his friend's call sign. "Think a lot of it depends on knowing when the craft will approach the surface and if it moves out of Cuban waters or not."

"You're going to come up with something reckless that will endanger my hopes of a quiet retirement aren't you?"

"Most likely, but hey...it should be entertaining."

"Okay, Nomad, can't wait. Gotta run, the Coasties are signaling that they are closing in on the coordinates."

"Roger that, we should be there within the hour."

* * *

Micah's eyes were open; he was staring up at a diffused white light. The dreams came and went with ferocity. Now his conscious mind was attempting to catalog and coordinate what his subconscious had seen and learned. Fingers felt something, a bottle. He was unbelievably hot and thirsty; his body wasn't moving correctly no matter what he did, and every joint ached. In the more lucid minutes, he realized he was in a boat, or maybe a raft. It smelled vaguely of plastic, like a kid's pool float that had been lying in the sun too long. His head seemed to be touching a soft rail, or maybe it was a pillow, and he had a distinct sensation of moving up and down rhythmically.

Slowly, the memories came swimming up from somewhere distant. Memories of a chase, an attack, friends that were with him, but now he was sure he was alone. Darkness began to tunnel his vision, the gauzy sunlight flickering on the verge of going out. He didn't want to slip down the long tunnel into unconsciousness again. The nonstop flood of chaos, incomprehensible symbols, images, maybe even languages. His head pounded, but that might just be the thirst.

Slowly, Micah commanded the fingers of his right hand to open and then to grasp the plastic bottle. It was cool to the touch. With a near Herculean force of will, he managed to move the bottle slightly from side to side. It had weight, mass, something was in it. Now he just had to get it to his mouth. *Why am I paralyzed, why can't I move? Maybe I'm still asleep. Something happens when you sleep to keep the body somewhat paralyzed. What was that, how do I know that?* Darkness surrounded him; madness began to claw its way back. It wanted him.

Sounds echoed through Micah's head, occasionally joined by the steady lapping of water, but also distant muted voices. *Why are we underwater?* It sounded like when they were kids and he, Alan, and Jimmy would go to the pool at the American Legion. They would dive to the bottom and try to talk to each other underwater. Nothing would be understandable, but they would rise to the surface laughing and guessing what the other had said. Water, he needed water. *Why would anyone be talking to me from underwater now?*

With agonizing difficulty, he unscrewed the cap on the water bottle. He dipped a single finger into the open bottle and felt the cool wetness. If he could just get that finger to his lips, maybe he would be okay. Sadly, he couldn't even withdraw the finger from the bottle now. Darkness closed in once more.

59

WASHINGTON, D.C.

Brenda "Chaps" Morgan had only flown Director Stansfield a few times, but never quite like this. The director marched off the steps of the jet just ahead of her.

"Leave your copilot to prep for the flight south. I want you with me, Morgan, and bring your sidearm."

"Always do," Brenda said, joining the woman as she slid into the waiting SUV.

Twenty minutes later, the car pulled into a private lot off Constitution Avenue. Margaret sighed; the last time she'd been here had been one of the most frustrating days of her career. Today would be different, very different. The director swiped a badge and entered through a plain metal door into a richly decorated corridor. The two women climbed a flight of stairs before Margaret stopped and faced the pilot.

"Morgan, you know where you are?"

"Yes, ma'am, I do."

"I need you to listen very carefully. Do whatever I ask in the next few minutes, okay? No questions. Whatever I say, you need to do it. Is that clear?"

Confused, Chaps nodded, "Of course ma'am. You are the boss."

"Damn right I am," Margaret said as she climbed a second set of older, narrower stairs and opened a door neatly concealed in the dark wood paneling. "Senator."

To say the man sitting behind the enormous desk was surprised would have been a massive understatement. Brenda only knew the man by reputation but had heard he'd had a hand in all the shit behind Janus and The Troubles.

"Uh..uh, Margaret, what a pleasure."

"Shut the fuck up, Byron." Margaret snapped. The stunned expression on the fat mans face made it clear he knew who was in charge.

The senator had risen at the unexpected interruption and now began to sit back down. "Oh, no, not there," Margaret said angrily, punching a button on the desk phone and handing the receiver to the senator. "Tell your receptionist you are not to be disturbed." The man took the phone with a shaky hand and did so. Then Margaret pointed for him to sit on the other side of the desk, in the diminutive chair the man normally reserved for his guests.

Byron Carson maneuvered himself awkwardly around the elaborate desk, using it for support.

"How's the knee?" Margaret said with a grin.

"That bastard nearly caused me to lose the leg. You know what he did, don't you?"

"I have no idea what you are talking about Senator."

"After he shot me in the knee, the bastard fucking stole my dog."

Margaret had been sitting on the side of the desk towering over the now quivering man and now leaned down until she was right in his face. "Never, ever refer to any member of my team in that way again. Do I make myself clear? Captain Rearden would have been well within his rights to have ended your pathetic life, you filthy piece of shit." She leaned back, looking at the man. "Damn, Carson, eat a fucking salad once in a while and lay off the cigars. What good does it do me to have kept you alive if you keep trying to kill yourself?"

He nodded. "Wh..what do you want, Margaret?"

"I want you to answer my questions, Byron." She spat the man's name out like it left a bad taste in her mouth. "I also want to make sure you are going to be completely forthcoming. Otherwise, I am going to have my assistant shoot you in the other knee." Glancing up, she made eye contact with Chaps, who nodded, removed her handgun, and shifted to the other side of the seated man.

"Wait, wait," the senator said in a tone that was reserved for roller coaster rides ridden by teenage girls. "Of course, I will tell you anything, that was our agreement."

"You've already broken our agreement, Carson. The names you gave Rearden, your accomplices, your friends. You left a few off, didn't you?"

"No, I...I mean, I don't think so. I was in pain, I'm not sure what all I said."

"I have a recording; would you like me to play it? Maybe it will help motivate you to be more truthful this time."

"No, no, please. Margaret, I wouldn't do that, I am a patriot. I didn't know how far Janus was going to go. Besides, haven't I done everything you asked since then? I made sure your project got the charter, your name was never linked to any government program."

She knew the man was being only halfway truthful. He had done the big things they'd demanded, but he'd also done his best to find out where The Cove was. Apparently, Janus didn't offer much in the way of intel to his underling, and this political scumbag had been head of the minions.

"Someone else was behind this, I...I asked Janus about that many times, but it never gave me anything."

"Byron, you are a piece of shit, but you've never been stupid. I feel sure you used your assets to chase down the possibilities. I don't want your accomplices; I want to know about Ivan Thrall." Doris had supplied her the name, but how she got it was still a mystery. She'd said that the CommDot on Nance had picked up a voice that matched Thrall's perfectly.

It was obvious the name hit home. The senator made no suggestion indicating he thought the man was dead and the question absurd.

Quite the opposite, in fact. "I'm terribly sorry, but I don't know, Director."

"Sorry?" Margaret said flatly. "Forgiveness is between you and God Senator. I simply view it as my job to arrange the meeting." Turning to her pilot, "Chaps, when you shoot him try not to get blood on my outfit." Morgan adjusted her position and aimed at the man's kneecap. "I understand knee wounds are some of the most painful and the most difficult to recover from."

Silent tears were streaming down the senator's face and an expanding circle of darker fabric appeared in the crotch of his dress slacks. "Please...please, no."

"No, that probably won't work. Just put the gun under his chin, we can make it look like a suicide. The evidence that will suddenly appear in the press would have ruined the senator, anyway. They will assume this was the only way he had to avoid prosecution. Check the desk, I feel sure the senator has his own gun somewhere in there."

If the senator had been terrified before, now he was completely apoplectic, descending into a fit of snot, tears, and sobs. "One chance, Senator," Margaret said through gritted teeth.

"Found it," Brenda said, holding up a small Beretta wrapped inside a white handkerchief.

"Good, don't get your prints on it. They aren't in any database, but why raise questions?"

"Thrall," the man sobbed out. "Thrall built the code for the AI."

"We fucking know that, you goddamn imbecile," Director Stansfield said. "He built it, and the NSA stole it."

"Not the NSA," the man said, voice still hitching. The smell of fresh urine wafted upward from the pitiful excuse of humanity's finest. "The DOD."

This was new information. She held a hand up to pause Brenda from any more threats right now. "What would the Department of Defense's interest be?"

Carson's voice was shaking, "DARPA really. Ivan had something. A top secret project, something called Saraph. It means angel. A saraph is a type of celestial, or heavenly, being, the word originating in ancient Judaism. That was the code name the Israeli scientists originally gave the project, the DOD simply referred to it as the Angel."

"None of that is in any files, Senator," Margaret said.

"It wouldn't be, totally self-contained. Just another black budget boondoggle. Nothing much came from it other than Prime, but it was apparent to all of us that Thrall was a genius."

"What did Janus have to do with any of this?"

Margaret checked the feed from Doris indicating that the man was apparently under duress but being truthful.

"Margaret, none of this should be connected to Janus. The original version, at Cryptus, was needed as a tool for analyzing or decoding some ancient script or something. I was never fully read in. We are the ones who made the software into a hunter killer AI."

"So, the original purpose of Janus was simply as a faster research tool?" That in itself was frightening, but what could have needed that level of processing power?

"The project was very complex," the senator continued. "It involved very advanced data storage, flight systems, pressure hulls. It was wide ranging. Too wide ranging, as it turned out, and terrifying. For a while, Thrall delivered just enough to keep the military happy. He obviously wasn't interested in providing much of anything tangible to the Defense Department. Eventually, they wanted more than even he could produce. A few of my colleagues decided the most valuable asset was the AI software."

"So, they shut him down," Margaret said.

"And seized Janus, or Prime, or whatever it was called," Carson replied, finally regaining a degree of his composure. "Then the boondoggle became ours to deal with, and we massively fucked that up, too."

"Go back," she said. "You mentioned Judaism. What did Israel have to do with this, and what was the Saraph?"

Carson leaned back and tried to get comfortable in the awkward little chair, "That goes back a long way, Director. Long before either of us were in the picture. From what I understand, an Israeli scientist had gotten hold of something important. This was back in the late forties, not too long after the war ended. The only description I ever read was it was the most important biological discovery ever made. Naturally, in time, the United States decided they wanted it, so they used the Six-Day War in 1967 to steal it. Unfortunately, things didn't go to plan. The Navy ship involved was attacked by Israel, and the artifact was supposedly lost in the battle. For a while, it was thought the Russians might have even had it."

Margaret searched her memory. Something about the senator's statement seemed familiar. "The *USS Liberty*. It was attacked in the summer of sixty-seven by Israeli aircraft and torpedo boats. Lots of American sailors killed and injured, but the whole event was pretty much white-washed from any investigation."

"Or the history books, which is even more important in this town," Carson added, daring to express a small bit of humor into the still tense conversation. "I know, if the sample, or research, or whatever it was vanished, how did Thrall wind up with it?"

"Yes, Senator, that would be the magic question." Data started streaming along the lower lenses of Margaret's eyeglasses.

"Check the crew manifest for the *Liberty*, that might explain it," Carson said.

'Seaman First Class, Peter Thrall from Walnut Creek, California.' The feed from Doris froze on the name. "His father was on the *Liberty*," Margaret said.

"Impressive. Yes, the U.S. had an asset onboard as well. He'd been the man charged with acquiring the material and, hopefully, the scientist. But the scientist didn't survive as far as we can tell. We assumed Thrall's father somehow found the information and understood enough to keep it hidden until he was stateside, and then he guided his son's academic path in an attempt to understand what they had."

"That's really playing the long-game. So, the material was biological. So, the Saraph is alive—was alive? Why would Thrall's father have pushed him into a degree in computer engineering if that were true?" Margaret didn't want to tip her own hand, but the question seemed like a logical one for the discussion.

"No...no," Carson said worriedly. "It's beyond my understanding. I know one part was some sort of organic-based data storage system. Massive amounts of data embedded in strands of DNA. It was not binary code either, really advanced stuff, but neither the biological side nor the computer portion were the important stuff. The data itself was what seemed to hold such promise. The tiny bits I saw could have revolutionized the world. We know now at least one component could have had devastating potential if weaponized. In the end, though, it was just too hard to decipher reliably."

"What would that component have done?" Margaret asked.

Carson shook his head and actually laughed. "It was one of Thrall's side projects. You know how he liked to think of himself as such an environmentalist. He was obsessed with protecting the oceans and, well, apparently his yacht got stuck in the floating garbage patch of the north Pacific. You know the place—they say it's the size of Texas where all the plastic and garbage of the entire ocean seems to come together in one massive floating dump. Thrall was sailing from Japan to one of his homes in Fairbanks, it was nighttime, everyone asleep, and the boat was on autopilot and, well, it ground to a halt. The prop had fouled in some abandoned fishing nets. Apparently scared the shit out of him. He woke up the next morning in the midst of garbage, mounds of it as far as the eye could see. In places, he said the ocean had piled it one on top of the other until the garbage was as deep as the boat's sides.

"Anyway," Carson went on, "he had to call for help, but eventually managed to cut away the netting, raise sails, and get to open water. Apparently, humans polluting the world's waterways was just too much for him, so be began pouring money and research into the Oceania side project. Using some of the information from the Saraph data, he claimed to have a way of eliminating pollution forever.

"Oh, um...he called it Icarus. We could barely understand the concept, but somehow, it was supposed to use dark energy combined with helium-3 and some other exotic components to build a space-based system that could dramatically alter the planet's weather pattern or something."

"I'm confused, how would that help end pollution?" Margaret asked.

"Simple, Director. He could target and kill the worst offenders. The system design included a pulsed energy device that could target nearly any region of the planet for total annihilation."

Stansfield nodded, "Senator, what was the asset's name? The one who stole it from Israel."

Carson searched his memory, the obscure bit of intel nearly lost in the vast secret vault of his mind. "It was an odd name, a Jewish name... um, Golette, Ishel Golette."

"You knew that Thrall had survived, didn't you?" Margaret asked with thinly veiled annoyance. "After his shipwreck, I mean."

"No, no, I didn't know." The senator looked nervously at Chaps who still held his gun, then glanced uneasily around his office, one of the largest and most impressive of any sitting U.S. senator. "I suspected, yes. The timing seemed too convenient, and later, Janus seemed to bring in a lot of people that were formerly attached to Cryptus and Project Saraph. A few too many for it to just be coincidence."

"Any chance we haven't tracked them all down yet? Who else should be on our radar?"

Carson ran a hand over his face and seemed to notice his incontinence problem for the first time. "I, uh...Cryptus had a lot of financial backers. Starting there would be a good suggestion. There was one other man. I don't recall ever knowing his real name, but they referred to him as The Lion. He and Thrall were close, but I only saw him once after Thrall disappeared."

Carson was obviously reluctant to continue. Brenda moved a little closer, exposing the short barrel of the Beretta. "He...he was in the DARPA control hub when Janus, you know, when he executed Domino Team. I didn't fully understand it but decided not to pursue it. He obviously had clearance to be there. In fact, I think he may have owned the paramilitary security group that was running the op."

Margaret thought about it, "No name, no anything. How can we find this man?"

"I, um...I had someone track him. They never got a fixed location, but that person may know."

"Call them, let me speak with them."

Carson shook his head, "Not that easy, Margaret. It was Guardian, The Lion was his former partner."

60

"I am searching through all databases, archives, related text, and recorded conversations to see if I can confirm any of what the senator said," Doris relayed.

"Thank you, Doris. Also, I have heard nothing in the last hour, do they have our boy yet?"

"No, Director, not yet. The Coast Guard is doing a grid search and should locate him very soon."

"Why a grid search? I thought you had precise coordinates of his CommDot."

"I do, ma'am, the problem is not our information. It is the Coast Guard's equipment. It is simply not precise enough, and we are fairly certain we are looking for a small target in a very large ocean."

"Good enough, Doris, we should be at Gitmo within the hour. I need to know whether to request full military assets or not. If Thrall has indeed been squirreled away all these years, is he just building pet monsters or something else? I have to ask you for your best guess on what Project Saraph is.

"Okay, Director, but it may not be all that helpful, really just opens up more questions. I have uncovered the name of the Israeli scientist,

Shafi Rabin. She was a xenobiologist, at least that is what we would call her today."

"So, at least part of the story was true. She was working on something biological then, like he said?"

"Yes, and what is most intriguing is where it came from," said Doris.

"I'm listening," Margaret replied, highly interested.

"You are familiar with Operation Highjump and Admiral Byrd from Rearden's debriefing report. Well, Shafi was one of the scientists on the task force assigned to Paperclip. Her participation was primarily symbolic, a bit of a friendship offering to Israel. Something to help bond America and the newly formed country. What the U.S. didn't count on was the Israeli scientist finding something. Something alive, or...formerly alive, in the Antarctic."

"Holy shit, Doris. They found the cave back then?"

"Maybe, my best guess is apparently so, and it would seem there was some genetic material or maybe a genetic blueprint to study. There is no way to understand how it could have still been viable after that length of time, but perhaps the ancient aliens knew a lot more about preservation than modern science does. I would assume the U.S. scientific team was more interested in the images or maybe too busy looking for secret Nazi weapons and bases. I can tell that Doctor Rabin never publicly revealed what she had found. But from that doctor's sample kit sprang forth a multitude of breakthroughs."

"How so? Especially if we stole her research," Margaret asked.

Doris went on, "The entire path we are on, the understanding that DNA was a blueprint to so many aspects of human development. Mapping the genome, inherited illnesses, gene therapy. While Rabin may or may not have had the ancient genetic material to study, it had already pointed her and her team in the right direction. She is a relative unknown in the field, but her contribution may be the greatest, right there alongside Darwin, Mendel, or Borlaug."

"I feel certain our government would have kept a close eye on her," Margaret said. "They don't just allow scientific discoveries to slip through their fingers, you know."

"Likely so," Doris agreed. "It is puzzling, and the U.S. really should have seen this coming. While Germany may hold the lead in academics, Israel has been right there, too, in the forefront. They produce many of the top academics in various fields. Some of letting them run with it was possibly the desire to offer Israel a win. The Jewish state had been through a lot, and the Holy Land they were offered after World War II was not exactly a safe haven. What we may not have taken into account was the resolve of the Israeli people.

"They are both paranoid and ruthless in their pursuits. They have never minded going out and acquiring what they need to complete a project or what they need to survive. Part of this is simply being a tiny nation surrounded by enemies. You need to remember that less than a year after being formed, they created the uleTafkidim Meyuhadim, which is the infamous national intelligence agency of Israel."

"Oh yes, the Mosaad," Margaret said, remembering some of her own encounters over the years.

"Exactly," said Doris. "That would be like George Washington being elected our first president, and the very next thing he does is form the CIA, FBI, and Homeland Security.

"These guys are the best out there and, unlike the West, they focus on having the best technology, and so work hand in hand with the science teams. Project Saraph had many, many setbacks, but after nearly twenty years of working in isolation, Shafi and the Israeli science teams had worked out an enormous catalog of information. Keep in mind, this was before anyone had done any DNA mapping. Before computers even. Genetics were not clearly understood and still quite controversial. But the Jewish scientists working from a lab in Tel Aviv must have managed to start unlocking some truly amazing information."

61

CARIBBEAN

"Yeah, Boss, they have him. Bringing him in now, only about twenty minutes out."

Cade nodded to his friend. "Good, at least that's one thing. What are they saying about his condition?"

Charlie's next remarks seemed to suck most of the air out of the small room. "Kid's unconscious, they said a shitload of blood was all over him, the life raft...everything. Vitals seem okay, some sunburn and likely dehydration. They have him on an IV and will transport him to the base hospital when they dock."

Cade took another sip of the bitter brew from the white cup and nearly spit it out. What was it with Navy guys liking coffee this damn strong? He'd never been to the base in Guantanamo Bay, but it wasn't unlike dozens of others he'd passed through over the years. "Chaps should be landing with the director any minute now. I get the feeling she wants...no, *needs* to be here when Micah arrives."

The two began heading down to the Coast Guard's mooring. Officially, the Coasties were only in the area to provide port security, but when it came to search and rescue or SAR missions, they were the best.

"So, you were dead. The Battlesuit must have done it's job," Charlie said.

"Yeah, more or less. Still hurt like hell, but a few days with Doc and everything seems to be working again. I only ..."

"Don't do that, Nomad,"

"Do what?" Cade asked.

"No second guessing, no woulda, coulda, bullshit about how McTee should have had his helmet on or been guarding the entrance or...well, shit, anything else."

Cade just nodded, still only dealing with McTee's death in the most abstract of terms.

Charlie continued, "It's a brutal business, dude, and people get hurt, and yeah, sometimes we die. That's the cost of being a soldier, and don't you think for one second that McTiernan would have traded anything for being your second on Charlie Team. He was a damn fine warrior."

Cade nodded but glanced away. Making eye contact would have broken him at that moment.

"So, The Cove thinks they have the schedule figured out when the vessel climbs out of the depths?" Charlie asked.

"They believe so, and apparently Thrall calls the damn thing Kalypso. Just based on limited intel, it seems the interval is timed to coincide when satellite coverage will not be overhead as well as surface traffic, like large ships, even low-flying planes. Anything that might easily spot a disturbance deep underwater," Cade explained.

"Calypso, like the music?" Charlie asked.

"No, I wondered that, too, or the boat that Jacques Cousteau used to use. It's Kalypso with a 'K,' a nymph in Greek mythology. The word apparently also means 'conceal' or 'to deceive.'"

"A nymph, like an insect?"

"Don't think so, like a goddess, I believe," Cade said.

"So, it wants to stay hidden?" Charlie asked. "Can we time an incursion that precisely?"

The captain shrugged. "Do we have a choice? We have to assume

Thrall will just get rid of Nance and the others if they sense any rescue attempt."

"Yeah. By the way their boss, that thing...the Kalypso is in Cuban waters. We can't get in there legally, and a ship or sub might start a shooting war. You and the wiz kids got any bright ideas on how we are going to handle insertion?"

"They don't, but I do." Cade watched the black jet coming in for a near-perfect landing just off to the north. "HALO!"

"Oh, hell no," Charlie said emphatically. "Not HALO! Not into deep ocean with no recovery craft available." He looked aghast at the very idea. To be honest, the HALO, or High Altitude Low Opening, skydiver was a lot more than just high risk. The jumps normally occurred above 15,000 feet but could begin much higher.

"I have never heard of anyone HALO jumping into open ocean. That sounds like suicide, Rearden."

His XO wasn't wrong. When you jump, you need a protective suit due to the cold and an oxygen supply due to the thin air. Jumps from altitude were done for stealth, often from planes in the same airspace as commercial jets, so that nothing seems unusual. "Due to being over Cuban airspace and the fact that the Kalypso won't ascend when flights are nearby, we're going to need to go a bit higher than normal."

"How-high?" Charlie asked.

Cade nodded his head out to sea, to a bit of white and red on the horizon. The Coast Guard cutter was coming into port. "Upper limit of suits and planes. 39,000.."

"You have lost your ever-loving over-crowded brain! Surely Doris and the kids can come up with something better! We're going to put an entire team in that much risk just to rescue four people who are in unknown condition?" questioned Charlie.

"No, even I would have had to veto that," Cade responded. "We would have waited until the vessel was back in open water. Use subs or depth charges or whatever to make them release our people?"

"I think you better ask her," Cade said, pointing to Director Margaret Stansfield, who was striding down the dock. She was followed by Chaps and what looked to be a Naval lieutenant commander who was trying in vain to catch up to the woman. A base ambulance was just pulling in next to the docks to await their patient.

Cade stepped forward and shook hands with Chaps and nodded to his boss. Margaret turned to the Navy man and dismissed him with a few short words. In his defense, he did meekly voice an objection, but Margaret's attention had already shifted. "That the boat?"

"Yes, ma'am," Charlie said. "He's still out from what we hear. No visible trauma, but the recovery scene was a mess."

The woman's expression didn't change, nor did she offer a reply.

The Coast Guard cutter pulled into its slip where sailors jumped off and quickly moored. They lowered a gangway as soon as the pilot went through the shutdown procedures. Several medical corpsmen wheeled a gurney through an opening, and Cade finally got a look at Micah.

He was strapped down as they wheeled him down the dock and onto dry land for the first time in days. He looked weak but otherwise uninjured. The right arm was outside the thin sheet, and the exposed skin was pink and raw, probably from the sea and sun. Every few seconds, Micah's entire body twitched and jerked as if he was fighting to get away.

The Coast Guard corpsman passed him off to the base EMTs. Margaret stopped the little procession to look at the boy. She brushed hair away from his face, then peeled the backing from a flesh covered patch and placed it on his neck. "Don't let them remove that."

Cade assumed it was a larger MedPatch, something new from Riley's magic shop. One of the men looked at Cade. "He's been doing that jerking thing ever since we fished him out of the water. We were going to give him a stimulant to try and bring him out, but decided not to. Figured it might do more harm than good."

"Probably best. Thanks for getting out there so fast. He might not have made it otherwise," Cade said.

"Hey, um, you may want to come take a look at this," a corpsman said.

They followed the man back aboard the boat and all the way aft, just behind the pilot house to the stern ramp where one of the large

Coast Guard Patrol RHIB craft was stowed. "This was what your man was in, just a typical commercial grade life raft." He pointed to a large round yellow raft that was semi-deflated.

Cade moved around, then climbed up into the RHIB to see inside the raft. "Holy shit, they weren't kidding about the blood."

Charlie had climbed into the recovery craft, too. "Is it just me, or does that blood look...off?"

"Yeah, a bit too deep red, nearly purple."

"None of it was the boy's. We checked him over good. No injuries to account for that much blood loss, but yeah, this looked odd to us, too," the Coast Guard corpsman said.

Cade tapped his cheek. "Greg, you busy?" He knew the kid had come up with Charlie and had been waiting around to see how his friend was doing.

Greg relayed, "Just saw Micah, they're taking him back to ICU now. Riley and Doctor Han are already running more tests with the advanced telemetry patch the director had. I imagine they'll know more in a few minutes than these guys will know in hours."

"Sounds good. Listen, you think you could join us down on the recovery boat? We have something we need your smarts on."

"My smarts? I don't usually get called on for that. Sure, on my way."

Greg often sold himself short. He was academically the less impressive of the original crew of The Cove and looked more like a semi-pro ball player than a scientist, but truthfully, the kid could hold his own with Alan and Micah, sometimes even with Riley. In some fields, like engineering, Greg was clearly the leader thanks to his natural mechanical abilities and the instant learning Doris had started him using as a teen. In either case, he was by far the smartest person on the team down here.

Twenty minutes later, Greg was leaning over the edge of the raft taking blood samples. Using a special light to identify any other organic tissue. "Damn, that's a mess," he said, leaning up apparently satisfied.

"Blood is the wrong color, isn't it?" Charlie asked.

"Well, it's not human. Just because it isn't red, though, doesn't totally mean its anything too unusual. Numbers of animals that don't have red blood."

"Octopus blood is blue," the Coastie said, trying to be helpful.

"He's right," Greg agreed. "Some lizards have green blood, and the crocodile icefish has clear blood. Unlike every other known type of backboned animal, they don't have any red blood cells—or hemoglobin."

"Never heard of one of those," the man said. "Oh, you guys hang on, there was something that was with 'im. We put it in the cooler." He raced off toward the galley.

"Something else, guys," Greg said. "You notice how the thin netting was draped over the raft?"

"Yeah, probably to keep the sun off of Micah, had to be unbearable out there," Cade said.

"Yeah, but Micah was unconscious, we think, from the time he went into the raft. And the netting was duct taped from the outside."

"Someone put him in the raft," Charlie said as the other man came running back up with a long styrofoam cooler that was also battered and covered with specks of purple blood.

"This was in there with your friend. Thought it was some sort of... well, hell, honestly, we didn't have a clue."

Greg leaned over and removed the lid and stared inside. "Holy shit."

Cade joined him, and then Charlie, all with essentially the same reaction. Inside was a bloody severed end of a fleshy tentacle about two feet long and thick as a man's forearm. It was a dark blue, fading to black, with one side covered in vicious looking suckers, encircled by toothed barbs that reminded Cade of a carpenter's hole saw.

"It's a tentacle," Charlie said somewhat needlessly.

"Yeah, but what is that on the end?" Greg responded, mouth still hanging loosely. Where the dark tentacle tapered to its thinnest part, a long and deadly looking claw extended out. The end was broken off, but you could guess the overall size by gauging the taper. Greg was the only one wearing protective gloves, so he gently picked it up, and they now could see the inside edge looked to be razor sharp.

"That's not natural," the Coastie said. "Must be some kinda mutant or something. All I know is the cook wants it out of his freezer, and the captain wants it off his boat. It's your problem now."

Greg leaned in to get a better view. Cade knew what he was inspecting. More blood, the entire claw-blade was covered in it, but this was all bright red. A color they all could recognize—human blood.

"I have to get this back to The Cove. I'll get it ready for transport back with Chaps," Greg said.

"Looks like Riley and Jaz have their sample," Cade offered. "Someone was on the ball out there. We know that boat wasn't on the surface long after the attack. Yet, they saved Micah and the evidence."

62

Static electricity crackled again from the small device. Nance heard Coffee nearby, his deep voice bellowing in outrage, then a sound like vomiting. She had no memory of being brought to this place. In fact, what memories she had since the attack were deeply troubling, fever dreams. Slowly, the realization came to her, they were inside the monstrous craft. The UFO, or, what did they call underwater flying saucers? Not 'flying' saucers, she assumed. Then the answer was there in her brain, USOs, underwater submerged objects. The name sounded too neat, too small for what she found herself in.

The room she was in was a bit cramped, mostly white, with little in the way of adornment. The design was more functional than minimalist. She got the distinct feeling it was a holding cell of some type. She could see the outline of someone in the translucent material of the door. The outline looked human, or at least humanoid. The door swung open, and a small Asian man with tiny eyes and an unnatural-looking smile walked in.

"Name?" he demanded.

"Collins," Nance offered. Hoping that was the correct cover name. Her mind was still so fuzzy, she couldn't be sure.

"You are not Collins, you are no one. You are a spook. Now tell me your real name and who you are with."

So, they didn't have IDs on them yet, but had attempted to run prints or bio scans or something. That meant Doris was probably aware of where they were. *Call Doris,* she thought, attempting to activate her CommDot. Her hands didn't make it to her chin as the restraints pulled tight after just a few inches. She hadn't noticed those. "Who are you and where are my friends?" she demanded.

"You are American military or former military," the Asian man said. "Your friends as well, except for the one. We know who the Honduran is, but we don't know about the rest of you. Before we launch you out a pressure hatch, you will tell us."

Kristen Nance was under no illusions; the man was probably right. If he was willing to kill her, he was almost certainly willing to torture her. The thought terrified her. Rearden had told them more than once, "Everybody breaks. Never try to be that hero, just buy as much time and give as little actionable info as possible."

She wondered briefly if other American female soldiers had ever been tortured for information. She knew the rather famous case of Pfc. Jessica Lynch, who was captured and brutally raped in Iraq. Several accounts suggested other victims had preceded her, but that had not been definitively proven. But it seemed pretty certain to her.

The man continued speaking, "You were tracking us and the Saraph."

"The what?" Nance said, genuinely confused. "Did you call that mutant kraken an angel?"

If the man's smile was unnatural, his grin was downright hideous. He looked like a lizard who'd just snared a juicy insect. It was more than just predatory; it was outright wicked. "Yes, it is one of our more, um...interesting accomplishments. Sadly, now they are more of a pet than anything useful, but it does make for an interesting watch dog."

Nance remembered the 'watch dog.' Damn thing had eaten half of her boat. She and...*oh, shit, Micah, he was about to do something,* then it all went black. So far, all she'd heard was Coffee. How many of them had made it? Maybe more important was how long did they have left, and why was her head so foggy? Her memories seemed to refuse to flow past in any recognizable order. She flashed back to her grandmother sitting in a nursing home in Tennessee. It was after the dementia had ravaged her mind, but the feisty ninety-year-old woman was still determined. Her memories were random, conversations incredibly difficult. Some things were clear as a bell to her Nana, yet others, elusive or absent. Waking up in this strange room, that was how Nance felt. Like someone had taken a pitchfork to her mind, rearranged all the details, and hid all the important stuff under layers of minutiae.

Pull it together, Nance, she told herself. She remembered who she was, remembered the people she'd been with, and the attack. The memories of that seemed seared into her consciousness—when she closed her eyes, they came stampeding back to the forefront. The beast, what had the man called it? The Saraph, it had caused her and Micah to collapse. Somehow, it had invaded her mind, taken her will to resist, and canceled out her ability to fight.

The man was still talking, but it no longer seemed to matter. She was tired, exhausted even, although she was sure she'd been asleep a very long time. Someone else was speaking, too. *Who is Riley?*

* * *

Kissa sat back against the smooth, featureless wall. He'd been the only member of the team still conscious when the strange-looking craft surfaced. After placing the boy's body and the sample in the raft on the opposite side, he'd concealed it the best he could, simply hoping it would drift free before the yacht sank. He'd not fought when the men came aboard, not really. To some degree, he was just thankful they were human and not alien or some other hideous beast. After seeing the 'mothership' rise up, as that was the only way he could think to describe it, he'd nearly convinced himself they were fighting something inhuman.

They had subdued him quickly, but he had made a bit of a show of resisting. Truthfully, they were taking him where he wanted to go. To where his Thera was, if she still lived. He would have liked to have his phone, so he could call Cade, or even the one called Doris again. The others seemed to be able to simply speak to the air and hear her, but he had no such ability.

Several times, Kissa heard the master sergeant call out, whether in pain or anger, he wasn't sure. They had not blindfolded him when they took him prisoner. He'd seen the interior of the nearly silent submersible. It, too, looked very futuristic, and the woman who was driving handled it more like a fighter jet than a sub. It was when the craft approached the vessel, the 'mothership,' that he finally got a sense of how large it really was.

Earlier, they really had just seen a small portion rising up above the waterline. The small recovery craft had approached the larger ship from below, silhouetting it against the lighter water above. The bottom of the larger ship was glowing with a very serene bluish light and contained a docking port that defied explanation. The pilot literally drove up an access canal, into a holding pool, and into a room with atmosphere. It reminded him of something he'd seen on a research boat once, where the bottom of the boat could just open to the sea and release a submersible from its docking cradle.

When the woman had opened the hatch, Kissa panicked. While the air would still keep the water at bay as the vessel descended deeper, he knew the air pressure would keep increasing to a point that it would become fatal. Only that didn't happen. It was pleasant, dry, and comfortable as he was told to help take the other prisoners to an awaiting cart. *Is this where they brought Thera?* His eyes scanned everything, taking it all in. What he took for a depth gauge showed 456m, but the number was climbing rapidly. *What is this place?*

Other than food deliveries, he'd been ignored except for a short visit by a middle-aged man. He seemed more like an executive than a pirate or mad scientist, or whatever type person Kissa had imagined being in charge. "You are Kissa Alvarado from Utilla. You are searching for your girlfriend, and before you die, you are going to tell me everything you know about your friends."

This man, Kissa thought. *This man must die. Hopefully, I will be the one to help him get there.*

63

GUANTANAMO BAY

Cade Rearden wished again he was more confident in what he was saying to the teams. Missions with this many unknowns went against all of his training. His last op had gone wrong, and it was so simple no one even questioned it. This one had way too many moving parts, going up against an enemy with unknown resources and weaponry. He and Director Stansfield stood at the head of the room. Margaret's specialty was computer crime, but she had cut her teeth in counter-terrorism, so military solutions were not unfamiliar territory.

The only people in the briefing room were members of Talon or senior staff with The Cove Project. With the reduced numbers, Cade had picked ten of the best people they had and split them into two teams. "Not going to sugarcoat it, this one's going to be a motherfucker," he began, "and before you ask, yes, the MO is to get our people out, but there's more to it." Tapping his comms, he said, "Riley, play the audio."

Her voice came in as if she were standing there with them. "The following was captured at 14:30 today. It was from Captain Nance's CommDot. They obviously haven't detected the communications devices yet."

"<garbled> story, you were investigating a series of marine animal attacks, particularly around the smaller island and coastal regions of Honduras."

Riley then added, "Our suspicions have been confirmed—we have identified the speaker as Ivan Thrall, the former CEO of a tech giant in California."

Margaret proceeded to give an abbreviated brief summarizing the man's accomplishments and shortcomings. "Resume audio," she then ordered.

"That might hold up if it were just the islander, but we know what he's looking for, or maybe I should say who. That doesn't explain you, though, or the level of equipment you had in your possession," Thrall said.

Nance's voice cut through the room like a knife, "Look, no idea who you are or what right you think you had kidnapping us, but I want to see the rest of my team now. People will be looking for us. You don't just wreck a research vessel, steal the crew, and not raise questions. Also, what in the hell is that thing you've created, the creature that attacked us?"

"Listen," Thrall said, ignoring the question. "Maybe it was just bad luck on your part, meeting up with Mister Kissa and winding up out here in the open sea. If you are indeed marine researchers, then perhaps I can put your talents to work. The others, though, come on, they are muscle, protection—obviously military, current or very recent. While your prints and faces don't match anything, our system is now running matches on your friend's ink. Tattoos are photographed and tracked throughout some branches of military and in prisons. For some reason, I think we might get a few hits on that. Now, revenge is beneath me, but if I find you've been lying to me, well, accidents do happen all the time out here, darling. Truth is, you may as well talk, it's your only chance. We are awaiting a few more arrivals from the mainland, and then the Kalypso is disappearing into the depths. It won't be seen again, at least not in your lifetime."

"So, you built an undersea workshop just so you could design your monsters? What did you call them, Saraphs....angels?" Nance asked, her voice quavering a bit when she spoke.

"Not exactly, no. Sorry, but I see no point in going over any of this with you," Thrall said. The sound of movement could be heard. "Do you know what Saraph means, I mean, in the original Hebrew?"

"No."

"Many interpret it as angels, of course, or even dragons, but the literal translation is 'burning ones.'" Footsteps could be heard fading away and a door closing.

Nance's whispered voice came back on. She may have been subvocalizing, assuming the room was bugged, but Doris's software could compensate for the distortion. "Doris, did you get that? I'm sure you have figured out where we are. This ship rose up on the horizon, and we went to investigate, then this beast attacked us. It hit the boat with that EM pulse again. It affected us like a massive migraine followed by dreams, and I don't know...data, lots and lots of data. If you can access Micahs's smart-contacts, you may find a recording of the attack. I have no idea if he even survived." She went on, "I've only heard Coffee's voice, and they've mentioned Kissa a few times. Sorry, but my mind only cleared a short while ago. The Saraph must have been guarding this vessel...the Kalypso. And this guy, he looks damn familiar. There was also an Asian man. Other than some guards bringing food, that's all I've seen. I don't know what is going on, but this ship, or whatever, is enormous."

Riley's voice came back to the assembled group, "We captured the following from Specialist Trondo's comm. We now believe he was injured in the attack, possibly badly, and appears to be receiving medical attention. That in itself is a positive sign, but, of course, you all know they may just need him well enough to answer questions. Thrall and the yet unidentified man were apparently near enough to be picked up on the CommDot, although we had to increase the pickup gain to the max. You will notice a lot of background noise as well as Trondo's heartbeat."

The sound of white noise, monitors beeping rhythmically, and a distant thump came over the speakers. The same man as before seemed to be talking with another man, possibly the Asian, judging by the accent. "None of this affects the timing, I don't care who they are with. Icarus is safe, isn't it?"

"No one is going to get to us down here. Too many years and too much money has gone into making this happen," the man with the accent said.

"Christ almighty, I don't even want to think about everything we've had to do to get to this point. Janus, the stock market, Cryptocurrency manipulation, and hell, even the drug running lately. All this shit makes my fucking skin crawl."

"Your Kalypso cost almost ten billion dollars to build, another two to outfit with the equipment and supplies. Where did you think that was all coming from, Ivan?"

"I know, I know... it just, well, shit. Saving humanity shouldn't involve us losing our own. I mean, I know I've been a son of a bitch, walked all over people, manipulated for certain outcomes, but, well, I just never anticipated all of this when my dad showed me that damn crate all those years ago."

The ambient noise increased, and it sounded like the men speaking had moved out of range. Margaret, who had been leaning on the table, stood straight, looked at Cade, then spoke, "We've identified the second speaker, the Asian man, by voice print ID. He is Pax Ruan, a Chinese National and one of Cryptus' former VC investors. Up until now we didn't have much dirt on him. He'd stayed off our radar. But Doris is digging up a lot of very bad shit, most handled by shell companies and cutouts. The man is very careful, but suffice it to say, much of the illegal weapons and drug and human trafficking in Asia tracks back indirectly to him. Doris and Jimmy are still trying to get a realistic idea of his holdings, but they are vast, including major interest in several automotive manufacturing companies, as well as the Chinese space and weapons technologies conglomorate called UpSpace."

"So, what is the tie-in with the lab and these creatures?" Cade asked.

"First this," the director said. "We recovered Micah's tactical contacts. Unlike your comms, the feed from those is not designed to transmit without a Dee submind encrypting and routing the files, so we had not thought about it until Captain Nance tipped us off. Anyway, here is the feed."

Margaret showed the video of the enormous craft. Cade was in awe at the damn thing's size and the fact it could apparently stay hidden down in the ocean depths most of the time. *Where had they built this, and what all is it capable of?* Then the images switched to the attack on the boat. There were only about forty-five seconds of footage before Micah's eyes closed, but the ferocity of the creature and the ineffectiveness of the Talon Team left all of them shaken.

More than one expletive snuck out before Cade gave them all a look to 'can it.' "Director, I don't know how any of them survived that, nor how they managed to get part of a tentacle. Is Micah awake yet, does he know any more of what happened?"

"He is conscious but still very confused on what happened. His experience seems to mirror what Nance went through. He keeps talking about language, data. He's still in a state of delirium it seems."

"Back to Pax," Greg said. "What is his angle?"

"We don't know, but in the last thirty days he has liquidated his entire portfolio. He has cashed in his chips and taken his fortune with him. Like Thrall, he essentially has no family. By all appearances, he is not planning on returning to China anytime soon," Margaret said.

"So, they know something, or they're planning something," Greg replied.

The director concluded, "I think the clock is ticking, people. We need a solution; Nomad will be working with you on assignments. The Cove is shipping new equipment in to use. It's going to be a challenge, but we want that undersea lab intact if at all possible."

Charlie stood up looking worried, "And now, aye, there be dragons. Fuck me."

"What, Charlie, you still thinking you should have retired?" Cade asked.

64

Cade leaned back against the wall where he'd been propped most of the meeting. "Well, shit." Since the director's briefing six hours earlier, everything had gone wrong. As if the foe they were going up against wasn't formidable enough, now they were having trouble locating the captured members of their team or Kalypso itself. "Riley, I thought that was the whole point of the CommDots and tracking sensors."

"It is, Cade. They use quantum entanglement for near instant communication from anywhere. The issue is the GPS component. That information can be transmitted via the quantum system, but it has to have the data first. The unit is nearly microscopic inside the CommDot but it uses satellites, radio triangulation, or can even extrapolate from star fields taken in by the SmartOptics if needed. Our guess is that the Kalypso is so deep right now, there is too much water overhead for any of those to work. Doris and I are developing a solution for this, but it doesn't help us right now."

"You know all your wonderful tech seems to fall apart when we need it most."

"I know, Captain," Riley replied, "but we're still learning. Most of it we didn't develop with combat situations in mind. Who knew the thing might need to give accurate positions two miles deep in the ocean?"

Two-miles, he thought. *How can this thing stay down there?*

Riley changed subjects, "We got the sample of the Saraph you recovered with Micah. Jaz is analyzing it now, and as we thought, some strange physiology."

"Anything that helps us?" Cade asked.

"I better let her tell you, but no, the opposite I think."

Cade looked over at Charlie and shook his head. This was not going to plan, so far, and neither of them liked missions that got off to a start like this. It was *bad Juju,* as Kissa used to say. You stayed safe on missions where you'd planned and rehearsed, sometimes for months. You succeeded on missions where you minimized the unknown variables and neutralized the risks. In this case, they were accomplishing none of that.

"Cade?"

"Yeah, Jaz, what you got?"

"Well, a lot, and most of it isn't good, just like Riley said. The Saraph is unlike any other life form on Earth. Its biochemistry is all wrong, its molecular makeup is off. I can't even begin to tell you how much else is wrong with this creature."

"Wrong with it?" Cade asked.

"Yeah, first off, there are some limits to what we can learn from these tissue samples. I can't tell you much about the brain, vital organs, and such, but I can describe the nervous system, or what works as such in this creature. I can also nearly guarantee that it is synthetic, a bit of a chimera."

"So, Thrall's people built it, from what, the image in the Sanctuary?" Cade asked.

"Sanctuary, is that what we're calling it now?" Jaz replied.

Cade had forgotten he and Doris hadn't shared much that they had learned from Mila. Briefly, he wondered how the girl was doing. Better than her victims, that was to be sure.

Jaz was answering, "No, they apparently had an original sample. Maybe not organic tissue but, at least, a genetic blueprint."

"What, like DNA?"

"Not exactly, Cade, as this organism is not like anything else. I am putting it all into a ReLoad pack for you and your team. Simple answer is, every living multi-cell organism on the planet uses DNA, whether it be animal, plant, bacteria, or something else. You do need to keep in mind, though, that 'life' is a rather vague term. One that doesn't have a single generally agreed-upon definition.

"One variation of this is that some viruses use DNA, but others use an alternative called RNA for the same purpose. Viruses fit the general definitions of life in some areas, but not others. So, we must accept that there may be creatures with some very different ways of passing genetic material to an offspring."

"Okay, I sorta think I get that, Jaz," Cade said slowly.

"Good, cause you need that as a starting point for what comes next. Several years ago, scientists discovered that humans carry a second type of DNA, something called an i-motif. It looks nothing like the classic double-helix of a DNA strand. In fact, the structure is normally referred to as a twisted knot. The interesting thing is, where DNA has two strands, you know, the classic image of the rails of the spiral helix staircase, well, i-motif has four strands."

"You're losing me, Doc, I'm not following this or why it's important," Cade said.

"Believe me," Jaz said, "we don't fully understand it either. Essentially, four strands offer more connections, more resilience, and we think, more options for adaptability. You need to understand that even though the human genome has been fully mapped, for the vast majority, we have no idea what it does. Honestly, less than six percent is even partially understood."

"Yeah," Cade remembered. "The rest they call Junk DNA, right?"

"Exactly," Jaz answered. "It obviously isn't junk, it does something, or did at one point, in our evolutionary past but now may be dormant, or maybe it's just waiting for the right time to be needed. The information packed into our DNA is usually referred to by the chemical bases or nucleotides called A, G, C, and T. Think of these for a moment like computer code—instead of binary zero and one, it is quaternary. That is essentially binary squared. I know it's confusing, but the point is, DNA is capable of carrying a tremendous amount of biological information in an extremely small, densely packed space. I-motif has the potential to be an order of magnitude greater than that."

"We aren't computers, though, Jaz, and that sea dragon isn't either. Where is this going?"

"Cade, you heard the accounts Micah and Nance have given of the dreams, the visions, and all the data that seemed to come at them after their encounter with the Saraph?"

He had heard and seen the recordings the team had made. He and Charlie had gone to see the kid before they transported him back up to Georgia. He still looked rough, but now fully conscious at least. "Yeah, part of the animal's defense system. What did you call it, a neural pulse?"

"I did, yeah, but that's just because I have nothing known to base it on. Think of it this way: DNA is capable of carrying tons of data about who you are and where you came from. Forensic geneticists can now track back your family tree for centuries, and Doris has analyzed human evolution back to an event about 70,000 years ago when the human species very nearly went extinct. Something they refer to as the Toba Catastrophe. So, my point is that DNA is an extremely capable mechanism for transporting data and passing it along to others, namely your offspring."

"I'm with you, so far, but we're still not computers."

"Cade, you know you can be exhausting?" Jaz laughed. "No, human DNA is not a computer, it's better. Better even than Doris."

"Wait, what?" Cade asked, the tempo of his voice rising sharply.

Jaz added, "Amazing things about DNA, so basic, and yet, so complex. What is so astounding, though, is the density of information that can be crammed into one strand of DNA. What I am describing is something that exists already called molecular-based data storage. DARPA has been investing heavily in it for years, starting with...you guessed it, Cryptus.

"Thrall seemed to have an innate understanding that what he had in his hands was some ancient biochemical way of storing encoded data in DNA. Scientists now say that all the world's data can fit on a DNA-based hard drive the size of a teaspoon. Think about that for a minute, Cade. A single gram of DNA could theoretically hold up to around 500 exabytes of data."

"So, our sea monster is a swimming, eating, fish-shitting, giant hard drive?"

"Rather crude way of phrasing it, but yes. DNA, but even more advanced than our i-motif. The Saraph's DNA uses a sixteen-strand molecular structure. It doesn't use any of the nucleotide, but instead, another type of marker, which, if I am correct, would be about a hundred times more complex than our G, T, C, A system."

Cade could feel Ace crawling around inside his skull; it seemed like the analyst persona was busy opening and slamming shut mental filing cabinets trying to make sense of all this. "So, Thrall built the Saraphs not for protection, but for information? And when the creatures attack, it is what, trying to communicate?"

"That's one likely possibility, yes," Jaz said.

"So, what's the information you've analyzed, its...its data file?"

Jaz replied, "That got moved out of my hands to Izzy, Jimmy, and Doris. They're using a section of the linguistics team to work on it, but yeah, it's encrypted, but they believe it's familiar."

"No fucking way," Cade said, sliding down the wall. "It's like our original alien message?"

"Doris can recognize certain passages as being very similar to the Dhakerri primer, not the same, but very similar. She says it looks less refined, perhaps much older," Jaz answered.

"Holy shit, two-billion-year-old dino-dragon-DNA and out pops an alien manifesto."

"That's not all, Cade." Jaz paused before going on. "When Micah saw the dataset, well, he could read it, he's able to interpret much of the code now. Apparently, what the Saraph imprinted on him, maybe inadvertently, was the ability to understand at least some of the Angel code. Doris thinks he may be able to read the Dhakerri version as well now."

65

THE COVE

Micah didn't understand all the fuss. It wasn't a superpower or anything, but for whatever reason, he could kind of understand a lot of what he was seeing. Riley was by his side as Jimmy teased ever more of the exotic data from the Molecular Data Storage. "Riley, please don't look at me like that, you make me feel like a freak."

She leaned in and hugged him. "You've always been a freak, just now we know why. You have an alien brain!"

Micah shook his head and laughed. "Gimme the next one, Jimmy."

"Okay, looks similar to the last one," Jimmy said. "Definitely something about—whoa—that can't be right." He and Doris were attempting to compare the data Jaz was extracting from the DNA to the primer she'd received years earlier. Some of it was exactly the same; some was in one, but not the other, and some, like this piece, was only in the DNA based data.

Micah looked at the display screen, "Okay, uh, I see, and, oh yeah, that is something new. At first it looks like one of the chemistry tutorials, like the one for our polysteel composite, but not this one, well, it relates to gravity."

Jimmy nodded. "I thought it might be. Some of it looks familiar when I translate it into Doris's code."

Micah worked at the keyboard for quite a while, interpreting what he saw into a basic index of understanding. Izzy could add it to the Codex if it all checked out. She was a math prodigy and one of the true natural geniuses at The Cove.

"Riley, if Micah's translation is correct, that would show that gravity is not as fixed or as weak as we'd assumed," Doris said.

Riley just shook her head in amazement as Doris continued. "Based on what Micah has already interpreted, I can make a logical guess as to much of the rest."

Jimmy's head snapped up. "You've interpreted it all?"

"No," she responded. "I am talking about the size of the file, it is incomplete. Not enough here to be even the entire primer, much less what was in the rest of our complete Dhakerri messages."

Micah nodded. "I sense that as well, Doris. It's almost like this is one part of a bigger riddle. Somewhere inside of this is the key to the next part of the message."

"In your visions, did you see any other creatures, anything besides the Saraph?" asked Doris.

"I don't know, maybe, just don't recall. I wouldn't have recalled any of this had Riley not shown it to me."

"What are you thinking, Doris?" Jimmy asked.

"I have cataloged some two dozen creatures within the images scanned in the Sanctuary cave in Antarctica. Alan's BallCam is still there working to capture all the other images in incredibly detailed resolution, but only two of these animals are what we now call Saraphs. I have determined that there's a hierarchy in how they are displayed. This could be random or purely aesthetic. I don't yet understand any other reason to the grouping, but the Saraph is relatively low in that hierarchy, occupying the first few slots essentially."

"So, other creatures might hold other parts of the data?" Micah asked.

"That is one hypothesis, yes, if the aliens wanted to ensure that all of their creatures, and possibly themselves as well, were reconstituted at some future time."

"Holy shit," Riley said, using language that she reserved for only the most special of occasions. "That would be unbelievably clever and diabolical. Encode parts of something so important, so revolutionary, that no species could resist it. Design various parts of it into all the important species in your world and have some future race re-engineer all of you back to life to get to it. Chances are, they start with the most basic, at least to them. They would want you to make all the mistakes, figure out all the science, before moving onto more complex creations."

"Such as intelligent creatures," Jimmy said.

"The Saraph seemed pretty intelligent to me, I mean for a claw-footed sea dragon."

Doris answered, "No, Micah, I think your first instinct was the correct one. I believe it was designed to broadcast parts of the data encoded within its DNA. That would get any researchers pointed in the right direction. Obviously, any civilization with the capability to create life from ancient DNA should have a rudimentary understanding of the rest of it. And, if Margaret is correct, this sample has been in our hands, and by our, I mean humans, for at least eighty years."

"Probably took that long for the fields of genetics to advance enough," Riley said.

"And computers, no way you could do all this without a supercomputer, or a warehouse full of them," Jimmy said.

"Or possibly a single AI."

"You aren't talking about yourself are you, Doris?"

"No, if Thrall was working on this at Cryptus, then it stands to reason he may have built Janus to handle the decoding."

"But Janus knew nothing about any alien message, he nearly burned down the world just to get to more of the fragment he thought you had," Micah offered.

"And that is what bothers me. There is only one reason Janus wouldn't have retained some of that knowledge deep in his original neural network."

As usual, Riley got up to speed faster than the others. "He was superseded by something more advanced."

"Yes, Thrall wiped Janus clean before giving it up to DARPA. Meanwhile, he was already using something even more advanced. We may have another Level 4 or above AI out there," said Doris.

Riley stated what all of them were thinking, "No, no, no....oh, God, no."

66

GUANTANAMO BAY

"Captain, they have updated you with the latest findings?"

Cade was growing impatient with the lack of knowing when and where to deploy. "Yes, Director, we all got ReLoad updates from Doris, and Riley is keeping us posted on anything that might help get past the Saraph and gain entrance to the Kalypso."

She nodded. "I understand we have some new toys on the way."

"We do, Director. And normally, I'd be wary of anything untested on an actual mission, but I don't think we have a choice here."

"You understand Thrall has had access to this alien information possibly longer than Doris. That means you may well be going up against weapons and tech as good or better than what Talon carries."

"Yes, ma'am," Cade answered. "That is my assumption as well. We'll have to rely on tactics and combat skills to give us the edge. We train for this; we've been using most of the gear for months, and we can work as a team."

"Okay, Rearden, I'm heading back to The Cove and will direct the operation from there. The Navy is standing by to offer any assets it can, but they will not enter Cuban waters. Not without an express order from the president. And...I would really prefer to leave President Ortiz out of this, Captain. Do you understand?"

Cade nodded. "I do." That meant no backup and no escape plan except what they could come up with on their own.

"Director, one thing. The briefing indicated this all came about because of Israel attacking one of our warships in the late sixties. How deep does this thing go?"

She poured herself a coffee, checked her watch, and sat down at the table, motioning Cade to join her. "It wasn't a warship. The *Liberty* was a spy-ship. Actually, she was the sister ship of the *USS Pueblo*."

"Pueblo," he said, thinking aloud. "That was the one seized by North Korea back around that same time?"

Margaret nodded. "About a year after the attack on the *Liberty*, but the *Pueblo* got lots more attention. Became an international media event. The eighty-odd member crew was taken prisoner, tortured, but eventually all were released. The North Koreans still hold the ship as a war trophy." She took a sip of the coffee and arranged her thoughts.

"I've been reassessing what I thought I knew in light of this new information. I must say that Project Saraph offers a great deal more clarity to what most consider to be one of the most bizarre moments in America's history. Apparently, Israel had acquired the basics of Project Saraph. One of the scientists on the exploration team in Operation Highjump was an Israeli. We apparently didn't think much of whatever it was she took from the Sanctuary, or maybe we just didn't know. Byrd had gone nuts, ships were sunk, soldiers were missing. That whole thing was a shit show, Captain," the director explained.

"So, we let Israel have the alien DNA, or instructions on recreating it, or whatever she got from the mountaintop cave," Cade offered.

"Quite right....it was not precisely a secret. A few knew, mostly back in the U.S., but also a few of the Arab states who probably were tipped off by Soviet intelligence. All of that came to a head in the summer of 1967. That June, three of Israel's neighbors decided the time was right to retake the Holy Land and remove Israel from the board. The U.S. was distracted, bogged down in a damn hopeless war in Vietnam, and honestly, tensions over the Jewish state had been building since its inception. Was there Soviet pressure on the Arab nations to invade Israel? Our sources say yes, but that's irrelevant."

"You're talking about the Six-Day War. I read about it in history class. How is this relevant to the artifact?" Cade asked.

"It is relevant for what happened the third night of the conflict. The United States' interest in the lab at Tel Aviv had increased. They were closely monitoring Project Saraph and were concerned the technology might be compromised, possibly even being destroyed, or worse, fall into enemy hands. The U.S. demanded Israel return the project, which now was beginning to show great promise. Israel refused, so several operatives were handpicked to go into the labs, secure the research, and acquire any of the original samples. Everything else was to be destroyed."

"We sent spies into Israel?"

"Of course, Captain, don't be naïve, we still do. And they spy on us —it's what keeps us good allies," Margaret responded.

Cade shook his head and motioned with his hand for her to continue.

"In the last few days, Doris has uncovered information that we stole the research, and the lab was destroyed that night. The explosion was apparently supposed to make it look like Egypt had been the culprit, but somehow that didn't happen. Two of the operatives were wounded but made it back to a small U.S. ship that had been ordered to pick them up. From here, it gets muddy."

"The *Liberty*?" Cade asked.

The director continued, "Yes, exactly, the *USS Liberty*. Like I said, she was a secret spy ship bristling with intelligence gathering and surveillance equipment, and I suspect Israel had already been watching her closely. They don't like being snooped on, and some had already suggested that America might make a play for Saraph, which had quietly become one of the most closely guarded secrets in the young nation. Despite all the tension with their enemies, Israeli intelligence knew we might use the war as a good excuse to reclaim what we felt was rightfully ours. Whatever the case, it is apparent they tracked the escaping spies in the general direction of the *Liberty,* which was cruising down the coastline a bit closer than it should have been.

"At first light, Israeli jets located the ship and began firing on it. It had virtually no weapons, nearly defenseless, so couldn't fight back. The flags were flying and the captain kept radioing that they were American, but it didn't matter. The U.S. would learn that day about the grave mistake of poking a hornet's nest. Once the fire order was issued, Israeli defense forces unleashed utter hell on the tiny ship.

"Despite near constant radio jamming, the *Liberty* managed to call in air support which was, in fact, nearby, but the fleet admiral recalled them each time. Torpedo boats raced in from the port of Ashdod, and they finally crippled the ship, which somehow refused to go down even with a forty-foot hole in its side. In the end, nearly 200 American soldiers were injured or dead at the hands of our closest ally."

"That's not exactly the account I remember our history teacher reading to us," Cade said.

She nodded, "The story was whitewashed by Washington. The sailors who survived were all given different assignments, some disappeared entirely. No congressional inquiry, no retaliation. Those in power would do their best to erase the actual event from our collective knowledge."

"So, Israel held on to the data, the Saraph?"

"Like I said, it gets muddy," the director continued. Mainly, because of who actually came to the aid of the crippled ship. Some reports indicate that another warship, one designated *Destroyer 626/4* pulled up alongside to offer aid and then protected the ship from further attacks. The unusual part of that story is *Destroyer 626/4* was a Soviet vessel. That ship supposedly stayed on station for sixteen hours until American forces finally made it back aboard."

"Holy shit! This story just keeps getting weirder. So, the Soviet's got the Project Saraph research?" Cade asked.

"That would have been my guess as well, but apparently, no. They obviously had hoped to. Someone had leaked the mission objectives. Everyone seemed to know what was going on with Saraph except the people on the *Liberty*. Now that I know what we were after, I can confidently say Project Saraph disappeared from the face of the earth that day. At least as far as anyone that mattered knew.

"The truth was, it became a mystery. Doris has combed through every digitized record in the archives of Russia, Israel, and our own with no luck. We'd nearly gone to war to secure perhaps the greatest biological breakthrough in the world, yet who actually had it, if anyone, was a complete unknown. Israel claimed that no backups survived, and none of the original scientists were ever seen again. The lab floundered for another dozen years without success, and then was eventually shuttered."

The director went on, "So, the question is, how did Thrall eventually get it? Turns out that one of the operatives who was sent into Tel Aviv was a former major in U.S. Army Intelligence. A man named Ishel Golette."

"Golette is the name you gave us in the original briefing," Cade interjected.

The director replied, "Yes, I was supplied that intel by the president. I've read his dossier, a very capable spy. His dark complexion and Jewish ancestry made him an easy choice. He also spoke Arabic and Yiddish, which was another requirement. Although badly wounded, he was the only one of the operatives who made it back to the *Liberty* alive. He was supposed to put the materials in waterproof cases and take a small boat out to meet a nearby U.S. submarine, the *Amberjack*, to deliver the goods. Only thing is, he was unconscious at that point in the infirmary aboard the doomed ship. American intelligence assumed the mission had failed, and the operative's cover was blown, so they wrote him off.

"When the Israelis started to retaliate against the *Liberty*, the powers that be on both sides elected to simply let it happen. What happens next is more guesswork than anything. But I believe Golette awoke during the first wave of attacks and somehow met up with another survivor who got himself, Golette, and the material off the ship and into the water. They may have used some of the dive equipment onboard to swim to safety. Both men were likely horrified by what their own country had done, as well as the so-called allies. I think it is safe to say, it probably took them both some time to get back to America through back channels. Golette was a talented spy, he knew how to evade, how to cross borders without raising suspicion, and he knew how to stay in the dark."

"Golette's friend, the sailor from the *Liberty,* who was he? What happened to him?" Cade asked.

"Funny you should ask. We just filled in that missing clue. The other man was Seaman First Class, Peter Thrall from Walnut Creek, California."

Cade couldn't believe this was part of a conspiracy stretching back to the Cold War. "Should I ask where you got all this from?"

Margaret just smiled. "We both have our secrets, Captain." She rose, placed her empty cup in the receptacle, and turned, extending a hand. "Good hunting, Nomad, see you back at the base."

I hope so, Director, he thought.

67

KALYPSO

Ivan Thrall paced the outer ring of the giant ship. So much was riding on the next few days, and he knew he couldn't afford any mistakes. Neither he nor his partners would tolerate any slip-ups of any kind. Even though he was officially in-charge of onboard operations, that was always subject to Ruan's will. Pax was the wealthiest among them, not that it would mean anything in a few more days, but he was also the most dangerous. Thrall stopped in front of one of the giant cupola windows.

The single piece window looked like glass, but he knew it was much closer in molecular composition to diamond. Just one of the many gifts of Project Saraph. Ordinary materials would fail well above the depths they were at. Leaning close to the slightly curved window and looking up, he could see no sign of daylight above. It was just as dark one way as the other. Far below, he saw several of the glowing Saraphs circling. These would be the last of that series. Being so far away, they looked so small, like any other of the miraculous bioluminescent sea life of the Midnight Zone.

Thrall's thoughts turned to the others in the group. They would have to ascend to retrieve the last of The Founders, or the 'Chaos Kings,' as Richard sometimes called them. Richard himself would be the last to board, that had always been the plan. Certain things needed his direct attention until the very end.

"Second thoughts?"

The voice startled him; it was so easy to get lost in his thoughts in this magical place. "No," he said. The hint of a laugh echoed softly in his voice. Her arm wrapped inside of his, and she pulled him close. Their lips met, and the fire flared inside him. She was too young, too hungry, and too irresistible. She made him feel things his late wife never had. "Ruslana, we need to..."

"I know, I know, we need to keep 'us' all business, at least until it's over." Her Slavic accent brutalized the words, but Thrall thought she was as magical as the scene outside. "Any last minute problems? Or are we still on schedule?" she asked.

Thrall liked the fact she could switch from pleasure to business without missing a stride. The soft glow of ambient lighting cast a blue halo around her head. She looked angelic and so damn fuckable...but business first. "Not really, nothing we hadn't planned for."

"But the team at the Delphi, they went into the Sanctuary. Richard's security, they were not so good, no?"

"Others have found the caves, and they have always been dealt with," Thrall answered. "That is the benefit of having the fortunes. The Founders have been on track for nearly a century now. All of it leading up to this point." She was right, though; the security failing was one of the most egregious in the group's history. The current establishment of The Founders had preceded the incident in Israel by nearly thirty years. His landing in the current lead role had been less about lineage and more about skills. While his father had been opportunistic in securing the materials aboard the *Liberty,* he and Golette had known nothing about the bigger picture—The Founders had helped fund multiple excursions around the world and even pushed to include sending the Israeli scientists to Antarctica in the forties. They'd not been pleased when the lab at Tel Aviv had been robbed. They were even more frustrated when they had motivated a high-ranking soviet official to use his Navy to intervene, only to board the *Liberty* and find Ivan's father had already vanished with the prize.

Ruslana touched his arm, then gently let her lithe fingers move down the length of his chest and slowly to his groin where she felt him. She squeezed him. "Where did you go?"

"S...sorry," he stammered, now distracted even more. He dared not tell her he had been thinking about his father. "Just a lot going on, much to keep track of." As if on cue, the light from one of the creatures blasted in from just outside.

"My God, it's gotten enormous," Ruslana said, momentarily breaking character as the seductress.

"It is. Doctor Otera believes it has found a food source out there. Something it can digest and metabolize."

"So, it won't still need to come here to feed? Won't that mean you no longer have control?"

"It's troubling, yes. Especially when everything we've been told indicates their biology is so foreign that nothing other than the blocks of chemical chum we created would keep them alive. Perhaps they aren't such fragile monsters after all." He glanced out at the impressive Saraph as it swam off, chasing some other nearby prey. It was time to go check on their successor, and they still had to do something with the captives.

* * *

Thera's face might have been interpreted as fear, but it was simply anger. Growing up in her neighborhood, you got tough in a hurry, but she'd also learned to control it...usually. From a purely academic standpoint, she had to confess that the work she'd been forced to do for these bastards was thrilling. Never in all her years would she have assumed any of this was even theoretically possible. Now, she was running cloning labs for creatures Earth had never known, editing genes with a device that put the CRISPR protocols she'd used back at her university to shame. Then there were the organisms themselves. The Saraphs were fascinating. Of course, they weren't all the same, but collectively, they were still known by the general term. She was currently working on the Saraph Series-4, or SS4 for short.

This was the first of the creatures that was not strictly a marine animal.

"Doctor Otera."

The very sound of the man's voice sent chills down her body. While maybe not as outwardly creepy as the Asian man, this one seemed even deadlier. She stiffened, but turned slightly as Thrall entered the main lab.

"Have you made progress—is the DNA ready to access?"

"No, sir," she answered truthfully. "The encoding structure of the cells is still blocking our attempts."

"Are you sure you are completely up to speed on your predecessor's procedure?"

The late predecessor, she said to herself. She'd uncovered a video file of his last fatal encounter with the SS3 creature. A monstrously hideous thing that looked like the ones she'd seen swimming meters away outside the hull. "Yes, the neural bridge uploaded all of the late doctor's findings." She still did not understand how the instant learning machine worked, but she'd only been here a week, and after a few sessions with the device, she knew everything related to the project that had come before. "The procedure is not the problem," Thera continued. "This creature is more intelligent than the others. I believe it has to develop to a point where it can consciously allow us to unlock the molecular data store.

"So, it has to allow us to access it. I mean, we have the basic encryption key from the last of the SS3s. We should be able to unlock it but... well, we can't. Not yet anyway."

Thrall shook his head and offered a disingenuous smile as he walked up and touched her cheek lightly with his hand. "Thera, my dear, you wouldn't be...oh, I don't know, stalling, would you?"

He removed the hand and stepped back, looking down into the oversized bathtub-shaped holding cage where the new creation was laying. "I mean, we've never encountered an obstacle like that before."

Thera bit her lip, choking off the reply she wanted to make. "It is what it is. I can't change what I don't understand. The prior versions were not sentient, they are more instinctual. This one apparently has a level of consciousness beyond that."

"So, this thing..." Thrall pointed down at the dog-sized creature. Scales covered much of the body, all of which shimmered with a deep iridescence that seemed to reflect a differing color range from one moment to the next. "This thing is judging us, determining if we are worthy to know what it is carrying."

"I didn't say that, sir, I simply believe it has some control. Unlike the others, it isn't broadcasting its messages when it feeds or attacks."

"Has it attacked?"

"Um, no...sir. That was a poor choice of words, it has shown no aggression so far." Still, she knew the thing was capable. It's row of cold, dark eyes never moved, but still followed her wherever in the lab she went.

"Doctor, I suggest you find a way to unlock this animal's secrets and do it soon. Believe me, I have other ways of motivating you. Ways you will find most unpleasant."

He'd barely made it out of the room before Thera released the breath she'd been holding. "Bastard," she said so low that no one other than the creature could hear. The SS4 raised its head slightly and swiveled its neck to face her. All five eyes were focused squarely on her as the usually expressionless face seemed to be smiling. A single image shone through the maelstrom of thoughts suddenly in her head. *Kissa. Dear, sweet Kissa,* she thought. She missed him more than he would ever know, but right now, she hoped he never found out about her role in creating these abominations.

68

THE COVE

"Thank you for picking me up, Isabella."

"Margaret, what's up? Not like you to pull me out of my lab to meet you at the airport. You know I have little to do with your operations," Izzy said, sounding concerned.

Dr. Isabella Feist was one of the most senior scientists at The Cove Project, and maybe more important at this moment, she was one of Margaret's most trusted friends. "Izzy, I need to ask you a favor, a very personal one." Stansfield studied the farmland and forest passing by outside. "It's not going to be pleasant for you, and I am sorry."

"You have my attention, Director. What's on your mind?"

"Izzy, I need to know everything you can possibly tell me about Ivan Thrall."

Isabella continued to drive even as she gripped the wheel tighter. The tears began welling up, blurring her vision. The SUV's autonomous mode took over driving as soon as it noticed her emotional state. Several minutes later, she had regained a small measure of her composure. "What can I tell you that you don't know, Margaret? We...we've discussed my time there many times. I was stupid; I was drowning in student loans, and I made a bad choice in joining Cryptus."

Margaret was very familiar with the facts surrounding her friend's time with one of the most infamous failures in Silicon Valley. All the headlines, news trucks, and reporters camped out in front of the impressive tech giant's campus-style headquarters outside San Francisco made sure that everyone knew. "Izzy, I don't want to discuss what happened to you. Not to be cruel, dear, but I need to know what you can tell me about Thrall."

Margaret watched as Izzy searched her pockets for something, probably a piece of candy. She'd always claimed a chemical imbalance or low blood sugar, so Doris had created a MedPatch specifically for that. Now, they all knew the sugar cravings were just some kind of stress response in the woman. "It's important, you read the updates. He's still alive, and he's planning something big. I have to get to the bottom of it before it's too late. People's lives are at stake, including many of our own. Anything you can offer might help."

"Why not talk to Nancy? Her husband worked there, too."

Margaret replied, "I have talked with her several times, but Jim didn't talk about work at home. He was on the military side of things and knew the consequences of talking about the work except in the broadest possible terms. Besides, he was in systems design, rarely met with the boss. You were senior management. You were there in some of the company's busiest days."

The silver SUV pulled into the lot beneath the twin dish radio telescopes. Margaret guided Izzy down to the edge of the nearby river where they sat on a picnic table the staff sometimes used. She knew not to press her friend. Izzy wasn't fragile, but those days had damaged her in ways she never wanted to relive. Cryptus haunted her professionally and emotionally. Someone from the company had even tried to kill her years later outside a technical symposium. Margaret just looked out over the river; it was a beautiful spring afternoon. Despite all that was riding on her finding the truth, she could wait; she would wait as long as her friend needed.

"Ivan was brilliant, idealistic, and, I don't know, just had a charisma that few could ignore. In those early days, he was always panicked over funding, he hated having to go and beg for grants or make pitches to new investors, but that was part of it. I think the company had around thirty people when I joined. Most were in software development, machine learning, neurolinguistics, and such."

"Where did the early funding come from?" the director asked.

Izzy shrugged and crossed her arms. "Angel investors, VC funds, and then after about one year, maybe eighteen months, money issues disappeared, and we began to really grow. By year two, we had doubled in size and were looking for larger offices. It was odd, I mean, we hadn't brought anything to market yet, but salaries got better, the talent level really improved. In my mind, I always thought it was because of the DARPA contracts, but that's not quite right, they actually came after."

"So, Thrall got money from somewhere or someone, a new investor?" Margaret asked as she pulled up an image on her phone. "Do you ever recall seeing this guy around?" The image of an unpleasant looking Asian man stared back. It wasn't a good image, maybe from a passport photo.

Izzy shook her head and wiped a tear from the corner of her eye.

Margaret continued, "Anyone else around at that time? People that weren't on the payroll, or maybe ones that never got introduced to you?"

"Lots of people," Izzy said. "Ivan was becoming a media darling at that point. He was handsome, smart, and successful. Every few days, people were being shown through the place, and of course, the military guys, although they usually went out to one of the remote worksites."

"Remote sites?" Margaret asked. "I don't recall ever seeing any of those mentioned in any of the filings. I know Cryptus leased rack space at a number of large server farms and mirror sites but never owned any of them."

"Yeah. There were several black sites, mostly for the top-secret work. Our offices would never have been secure enough for that. Thrall has a penchant for getting what he needs, then tossing it away when it's served its purpose. I'm sure they simply liquidated them as the DOD contracts collapsed or were completed. Some of them were purpose-built, we simply referred to the black sites by their station number."

"What went on in these remote sites? You were a supervising project director. Surely you had access to them."

"I had the clearances; I didn't have the authority," corrected Izzy. "Most of them were fairly easy to guess at just based on the supplies requested and the kind of people they had working there. I had to review allocation budgets, so I saw all of that. I know one dealt primarily with voice recognition, which was fairly rudimentary back in those days. It didn't last long, as we wound up acquiring a startup company instead. They had already figured most of the vocalization issues out.

"Other stations were more challenging to understand, although I could, and did, take guesses. Everything but Site 21, that was by far our biggest budget expense outside of the AI labs."

Margaret looked up; this could be the one item worth pushing her friend for. Something that had never shown up in any of the files or court filings. "Any idea where it was, what kind of people were assigned there?"

Izzy replied, "That's just it, I could never put my finger on it. Lots and lots of computers, mostly supercomputers. Way more than the other sites, but then a lot of medical lab type equipment. Unbelievably expensive stuff with names I could barely pronounce. We employed several thousand by that time, so I didn't actually have to approve anything directly, but what I saw painted a strange picture. I couldn't reconcile it with our core mission of developing a high-functioning artificial intelligence, what turned out to be Janus. I once accused Ivan of building a cyborg army out there, and he just laughed and said, 'Shh...don't tell anyone else you figured it out.'"

Izzy stood and walked down to the riverbank, then several paces downstream before turning and walking back. "There was a guy I had to deal with occasionally. I never went to Site 21, no idea where it even was, but a man came by the office a few times, normally when he needed something official or something handled by our legal department."

"What was his name?"

"That's just it, Margaret, I don't think he ever said. Ivan may have introduced us, but I only remember him being called Richard. Big barrel-chested fella, thick Texas accent. Only thing was, he didn't look like a Richard ...or a Texan. You know?"

Margaret flipped through several dozen photos, known associates and investors of Thrall that Doris had curated for her.

"No, none of those," Izzy said. "Dark hair, usually a beard. Looked kind of ethnic, you know, maybe some Italian in his lineage." She leaned up on the table, her nerves apparently calming somewhat. "I don't know. Sorry, wish I could help more." She then got a faraway look. "Wait..."

"What, hon, you remember something else?" asked Margaret.

"Uh, probably nothing. I remember telling him 'Merry Christmas' one December when he was leaving, but he responded with 'Chag Sameach.' First, I thought he said, 'Thanks so much,' but later, I realized he was telling me Happy Holidays in Hebrew. I wondered then if maybe he was Jewish."

Now she had Margaret's attention. The director had to know what all went on at Site 21 and who the Jewish man they called Richard really was. On a whim, she pulled up an old black-and-white photo, possibly of Ishel Golette, that Doris had managed to find. Triggering her personal Dee, she had it add a beard to the face in the image. Holding the SmartCom up so Izzy could see, she asked, "Does he look familiar? Could Richard possibly have been this man's son?"

The other woman studied the image and eventually nodded. "Maybe, yeah, it could be..."

69

CARIBBEAN

Captain Cade Rearden was not a happy soldier, very far from it, in fact. Despite his flaws and his internal ghosts, he knew he was a good warrior. He was a man of action, a very capable man. Like most good soldiers, he just needed something to shoot at. Right now, they didn't have that. Director Stansfield had also changed the MO from search and rescue to taking the Kalypso by whatever means necessary. She had determined its very existence was an imminent threat, although seemed to have no clue as to the why or how.

"Those are my people down there, Nomad. Trondo, Nance, Coffee and hell, even Kissa. Good men and women, good soldiers," Charlie stated.

Cade lifted his palms up. "*Our* people, Charlie. *Our* soldiers." Truthfully, he was charged with all of their safety. Something he did not take lightly. Yes, it was a dangerous business, but part of that code is, you didn't leave a brother-in-arms behind. Not if you could prevent it. Also, Kissa wasn't a soldier, not anymore. Kissa or Warlock as he had been known back then had been a hell of a good one. Maybe he still had that warrior spirit burning deep inside.

"Have you gone through the new equipment Riley sent?"

The sergeant nodded.

"Yeah, it's all there, but not like any of us understand it, no training yet in any of it."

"The Cove is modeling it into the ReLoad update now—they'll have us familiar with it before we deploy," Cade answered. In truth, he was just as worried. Nothing beat experience and familiarity. While he'd grown to trust the technology literally with his life, the muscle memory and instinct for your equipment's capabilities only really became engrained with endless drills and training.

"What about the missing dive suits?" Charlie asked.

Cade shook his head, worried. "I don't know, they're fabricating them as fast as possible, but the window of time seems to be shrinking. How many do we have now?"

"Six."

Jimmy and Alan had come down from The Cove on a C130 with the first two of Riley's Jackknife XOD dive suits as well as one of The Cove's largest 3D fabricators. The dive suit was unlike anything anyone had ever seen, and they were doing all they could to keep some curious Navy boys away from the converted warehouse where they were being assembled.

Traditional exo-hardsuits for deep water or saturation diving were like miniature personal submarines. Thick steel, bulky arms and legs with joints that severely limited most movement. They usually clamshelled open, and the divers were bolted inside. They were so heavy; the diver needed a crane to raise and lower them to the water. Those suits would not allow for anything resembling combat, and most of these were only rated for around 1000 feet, max.

The Kalypso could be down ten times that far, so Doris and the wiz kids had come up with something else. Thankfully, the Dhakerri had already provided them with some unique ways of creating extreme pressure vessels. The Jacknife XODs were the result.

With these, they would be suiting up in what looked like a futuristic version of an Ironman suit. The white, polysteel body took some work to get into. Each had a built-in atmospheric containment system, a powerful set of thrusters, weapons systems, light array, and more. All this in something sleeker than any traditional spacesuits.

One way the 'kids' had made these suits small and maneuverable was eliminating the bulky breathable air system. Instead of tanks, they had a regenerative gas device that could extract oxygen directly from water. The tiny system mechanically replicated what the gills of fish do naturally. They would have to carry onboard oxygen supplies for just the first part of the mission, as the system wouldn't work in normal atmosphere. The depth rating of the XODs was theoretically unlimited as long as they weren't damaged. The aliens had apparently found intelligent life living fine on planets with intense pressures and studied how life would adapt to handle such environments. The fact that this was in the unencrypted portion of the primer indicated it was probably so basic that any intelligent species should know it. That also meant they must assume Thrall and the occupants of Kalypso might have it.

Cade really hoped not. In the last year, he'd gotten used to having an edge, either a technical or an intelligence advantage over an enemy. Now, they would likely assault a superior force in a battle space that was much more familiar to the enemy. "Okay, Deuce, who's on the initial assault team?"

Sergeant Charlie Taylor spelled it out—who was in, who was out. If they deployed today, it would be six that could attack at depth, another six could descend to about a thousand feet in a modified Rapide Submersible version of the standard BattleSuit, not as good, but still helpful. If they could get the damn enemy vessel near the surface, they would have nearly two full teams. Cade moved two people from the roster to the reserve team and made substitutions, one of which Charlie strongly disagreed with.

"Why, Nomad?" he asked when they were alone.

"You know damn well why. They're smarter than us, we're not going to beat Thrall with guns. You can damn well bet he has more firepower than we'll be able to take. It has to be one of the kids. So far, we've worked with all of them in the field, except Jimmy. They've proven themselves. Shit, Alan saved my life last week. We have to have the smartest kids in the room, and even then, I think we'll need to catch a lucky break."

"Get lucky. That's your plan? That's why you want to bring one of the geniuses? What if they get hurt? This is not how we plan missions, Nomad."

Cade nodded; Charlie was insubordinate, but he was right. It was near suicidal to design an op with all the unknowns. "We don't have a choice, Deuce. If Thrall gets away, nothing else may matter."

"You know something? Something not in the briefing?" Charlie asked.

"A feeling. Something Ace has been bugging me about. Stansfield has identified several more potential members of Thrall's possible accomplices. Jimmy was tracking their money flow, purchases, travel, and shit. They use tons of shell companies and cut-outs, all seemed pretty random to them."

"But your analyst found a pattern."

Cade rubbed his face with his hand and looked out to sea. "Yeah, it all fits together if you're preparing a doomsday vault. They are caching supplies in enormous numbers. Way more than just that one ship can hold."

"Oh, great, a doomsday cult," Charlie said.

"Yep, the question we have to determine is, do they just know something we don't, or are they going to be the one causing it? In either case, I have advised the director to assume the threat is real and time is short."

"Well, fuck, Rearden, happy fucking Monday to you, too. How do you know it's coming soon?"

"The associates. Of the ten identified, six have disappeared in the last month. Assets gone, accounts cleaned out, no trace of them remains."

Charlie's face pinched tight into a frown. "What about the other four?"

"Three dead, all under mysterious circumstances. One still unaccounted for. Someone known only as The Lion."

70

KALYPSO

Thera stayed silent a long time, a very long time. The shock of what she was seeing defied understanding. With all the revelations the last few weeks had brought, perhaps none was as unsettling as this. The Asian man pushed her toward the translucent panel in the wall. The face of her fiancé stared mutely at her from the far side. "Kissa?" The words tore something away deep inside. "Why are you here?"

She knew he couldn't hear her. Many of the rooms had wall panels like this. They were thick, floor to ceiling, and had solid doors that fit into channels on all four sides. The purpose of such over- engineering was lost on her, but she admitted it made for an effective prison.

"You will speed up the progress on SS4," the man calling himself Ruan demanded. "Your boyfriend's life will depend on you reaching the required milestones as scheduled."

"Why are you here? How did you find me?" Thera mouthed. Years of diving together had attenuated their senses to understand much of what each other was trying to say without actually having to hear it. *How did he find me?* She could recall the final dive, looking at what she thought was a unique outcropping of some plant life or bio-mass, then the blue light, the headache, and then... nothing. A total blank.

Waking up as someone carried her off a small enclosed boat into this...'thing,' whatever it was.

Kissa's hands rested on the glass, she gently placed hers on the opposite side. They were separated by about six inches of the translucent material. It reminded her of the thick mega-aquariums she'd spent so much of her life working around. This time, though, it was her fiancé on display, not some exotic sea life. Kissa looked like he'd been in a battle. One eye was swollen nearly shut, and a ragged cut ran down the side of his face and along half of his thick neck. Other cuts and bruises showed the man had battled his way here only to probably wind up being tortured and killed for his efforts. "I'm so sorry," Thera mouthed.

He pointed to his eyes and then motioned around his face and pointed at her. Thera shook her head; she didn't feel beautiful, but she knew he loved her. He had even managed to find her. The evil man's hands pulled her away and pushed her roughly back toward the research wing. "You work now." She tried to turn to get one more look at Kissa, but Ruan blocked her view, offering a demonic smile in the process. "You want to see him again, unlock the information we want!" The man seemed to be spitting the words at her.

She didn't care about his information, whatever it was. Others handled that part. Her job was to mature the creatures to a point they could retrieve it. Somehow, the Saraph's DNA only unlocked its secrets at a certain level of maturity. Her predecessor had hypothesized it was sexual maturity. Once they went through puberty, then they would make the information available. It was an ingenious way of soliciting help in preserving the species, but also in how to pass down significant information from one generation to another.

DNA alone was like the book of life. Even in humans we don't understand most of what is stored inside our genetic material. What if it could be harnessed? Besides just dictating the color of eyes, our height, and predisposition to certain illnesses, DNA could also include the collective wisdom of all the prior generations. All of it just sitting there waiting for you to reach a certain level of maturity and unlock it. Instead of just being born with a handful of genetic-founded instincts and biases, you had as much intelligence as your parents on the day you were conceived. How much faster could a species leap-frog human intellect with an innate ability like that? Each new generation would be expected to propel an intellectual evolution and add to an ever-expanding collective knowledge base.

The possibilities were truly astounding to comprehend. Unfortunately, Thera was working with a lab subject that seemed well short of sexual maturity, if that was even how they reproduced—she still wasn't entirely sure. Additionally, the creature seemed very much unwilling to share anything. She had to find a way, something that would unlock the next set of data. Not just her life was in jeopardy now. Kissa's depended on it as well.

71

CARIBBEAN

"Cap, you with us?"

Cade had been staring down through the breaks in the clouds and small outcroppings of light amidst a sea of darkness. The sun was just coming up in the East. First light across the Caribbean Sea could have been a magical moment to enjoy with someone special. Instead, he had Charlie and two newly reworked Talon Teams. "I'm here, Deuce, just wish this was someone else's job." The go order had come less than an hour earlier. The modified C-27J Spartan aircraft was cruising at 32,000 feet about ten miles outside Cuban airspace. The route and altitude was a familiar one for both military and commercial air traffic. The plane would make no detours on its next stop in New Orleans; it would just have a lot fewer passengers.

"We need to be in the XODs before the ramp drops," Deuce told Cade in a voice closer to yelling than normal conversation. The interior of the plane was loud. It was not designed for comfort. The four enormous, six-bladed turboprops needed a lot of power to generate lift in air this thin, and the entire aircraft reverberated with the sound.

"I know, just... not looking forward to it," Cade answered. He'd only made two HALO jumps in his time at the Advanced Tactical Infiltration Course, or ATIC, and one of those was actually an inadvertent

HAHO or high-opening, when his chute had deployed prematurely. Charlie Taylor had numerous MFFs, or Military Free Fall, jumps in his career. Cade had absolutely hated it; Deuce had once lived for the rush, not so much these days. No one had ever done one like this, though. Going from six miles above the ocean to possibly several miles below. Strangely, many of the risks were similar. HALO jumpers had to take precautions not to get the bends from the rapid changes in pressure in a jump, carry an oxygen supply, and keep a close watch not on depth, but on altitude.

"WarHawks up," Deuce yelled. The WarHawks were the seven men and one woman who had the Jackknife XOD suits. Yes, they were going to be jumping out of a plane wearing a deep-sea diving suit. It was as dangerous as it sounded. Once locked into the suits, they would have to stand tethered to the metal track overhead. The other six members of Talon had more traditional HALO gear covering the marine submersible version of the Rapide Battlesuit, while they were honoring Captain Nance using her team's call sign of WarHawk. Team Two would use the call sign 'Raptor.' Due to the limits of their equipment, Team Raptor were already in oxygen masks breathing a special mix to help them acclimatize to the deep ocean. The more sophisticated XODs took care of most of that for the occupant, in theory at least. "I damn sure hope this shit works, Riley," Cade whispered as the upper half of the dive suit clicked into place around his waist.

"It'll work, Nomad," her calm voice came back.

He smiled. *I should have known she would be monitoring suit comms.* "Seem pretty sure of yourself, kiddo."

"I'm good at what I do, Cade, just like you are. I know you guys are putting your lives in my hands. We never forget that."

"I know, and we all love you for it. What's the latest on our target?"

Riley answered, "Well, as you know, we repositioned satellites to give us continuous coverage. Your flight path is mimicking one we covertly canceled coming out of Caracas. After that is a two-hour window that the Kalypso should use to come near the surface. Since we began monitoring it, they haven't missed a comms window, but we can't tell anything yet, they're still at depth."

Cade was getting used to moving in the dive suits. He wanted to be able to position himself belly down upon exiting the plane. The jump master held up a hand with all five fingers extended. "Five minutes, WarHawks, final prep."

"Riley, about the Saraph, did you solve the problem of shielding the electronics?" That had been a lingering concern for all of them. Despite all the advanced tech, the XODs operated on sophisticated circuitry and electronics. If the creatures were down there and could short out the suits with the neural pulse, then they would lose buoyancy and air feed, sink to the seafloor, and spend a very long time trapped inside the suit waiting to die.

"Hi, Cade, it's Jaz. I think we've figured out that the creature uses a modified abdominal organ to generate an electrical charge. This is somewhat like how an electric eel generates a charge, but just on a much larger scale. We still don't know how the neural part of the blast is formed. There are a lot of limits to what we can learn from just the one tentacle. They are limited to how much current the, well...um, nerves, I guess we would call it, can handle."

The jump master held up three fingers. Cade nodded.

Jaz continued, "The first blast they use will be the worst, then they will probably need time to recharge before delivering another anywhere near as strong."

"I have a question, Jaz. How do electric eels not shock themselves when they attack?"

"Well, uh...um..." she stammered, somewhat dumbfounded. "I have no idea, to be honest. That would probably be a good thing to investigate."

Continuing, she said, "Ok, Riley has given you all a few new toys, hardened the suits' internal power, and decentralized the systems, so damage shouldn't render you completely immobile."

"Any suggestions on how we could fight one of the things?" Cade asked.

Jaz answered, "My advice would be to do all you can to avoid it. We are pretty sure the damn thing was wrecking submarines and oil rigs."

"Thanks, hon, you are just boosting my confidence levels to a new high." He felt his suit switch over to internal systems and the hooks release from the shoulder and legs. "Raptor Team, up. You're next. Watch your lead." Cade nodded to Alex. This would be her first outing as a mission commander. She had lead on Team Raptor. The jump-master held up one finger, and the large ramp at the rear of the plane descended.

"Cade?"

"Yeah, Jaz."

"This is probably not a good time to ask but..." she seemed to fade out, but apparently it was just her getting her nerves under control. Cade found this amusing, since he was the one jumping out of a plane in the next thirty seconds.

"Go ahead, Jaz, what's on your mind?"

"Do you think we might go out when you get back? Like on a real date?"

Cade struggled to find the words. She was asking him out? *This is not the time,* Gus said. "Um..."

The jump-master held up ten fingers and began dropping them slowly one by one. She was asking him out, Tim's girl, the one who knew all his demons. Why the fuck didn't she just say "Good luck" or something? Unexpectedly, he found himself agreeing enthusiastically. "Yes, yes, of course, I'd love that."

Love that? Gus said inside his head. *You used the L word already. Damn, you moron.* Five fingers. *She's going to be picking out china patterns now.*

Shut the fuck up, Gus, it's game time. Three fingers.

"Okay, people, listen up. This is some high-risk scary shit, no doubt. Do not let the fear take hold. Fear kills dreams, it annihilates hope, it can make good soldiers stupid. Blank it out by whatever means necessary. Let's go get our people. Good hunting and stay safe!"

* * *

"Riley has invited you to share the DCS playlist," his Dee said as the overhead track began moving him toward the now open ramp at the rear of the plane.

"What's DCS?"

Dee answered, "Apparently it stands for 'Doing Crazy Shit.' Would you like me to play?"

His feet were inches away from the door. Far below, he could see glimpses of ocean and off in the distance, the lighter green of more shallow waters and land. The release clicked open above his head. "Sure."

Cade found himself tumbling out into open space for only a moment, before the suit's internal gyros stabilized. The temperature was thirty degrees below zero outside the XOD. The oxygen here was thinner than the top of Mount Everest. Normally, a HALO jump from this high would have about two minutes of free-fall. In their case, it was going to be more like ten minutes. A classic Tom Petty song hit its stride right in time to the jump. *"Free Fallin"...love it,* Cade thought.

One by one, panels on the back of each WarHawk diver sprouted large, but awkward looking, flight wings to glide them silently down in the likely direction of Kalypso and to the monsters probably guarding it. Cade found himself humming along to the beat as the lyrics described the bad boys standing in the shadows.

72

THE COVE

"Take your time, Micah," Doris spoke in even tones. She was attempting the reverse ReLoad process on Micah to see if she could understand how he was interpreting the Saraph code. If she could replicate it, that would allow her to better understand what they were up against and possibly make better headway on the enormous Dhak-erri data block they'd been deciphering for years.

Unlike the process she'd been using on the prisoner, Mila, this version was not to erase or even dull Micah's memories, but to sharpen them. "It's hurting, Doris, my head." Micah doubled over and vomited. She ceased the operation as his mom helped him from the small room.

Nancy Turner was anxious to protect her son but admitted that she understood little of the ordeal he'd been through. Margaret had told her to trust Doris, and so she was. She checked his pupils and then his pulse. "No indication of concussion. Doris, do you think it's wise to continue this treatment?"

"Not at this time, no. It is puzzling, though."

Micah took a long drink of water and seemed immediately to be back to normal health. "I'm fine Doris, we can continue, if needed."

"It's not that, Micah, I need to do some additional analysis. For some reason, the memories of communicating with the Saraph are not stored in the normal area of your brain...the hippocampus, which is where such things should be encoded. I attempted to recalibrate the ReLoad protocols to compensate, but they simply couldn't locate the active regions."

Micah's mom considered that. "That's where dreams and memories are normally stored, right?"

"Yes, Dr. Turner."

"Just Ms. Turner, my doctorate was for another name, another life. What about the language centers, can your device scan those?" At this point, she just wanted whatever this was out of her son's head. She didn't understand it, but it scared her. It was alien, and it had something to do with Thrall. That man was a cancer that had to be controlled before it metastasized any further.

"You are talking about the Broca and Wernicke's area of the brain, and yes, those both showed heightened activity, but not at the levels we would expect. The ReLoad scan could not directly intercept any of the signals in those regions either."

They had been going through this for days. Doris had admitted only a portion of the truth to Stansfield involving the reversal of the instant learning process. Still, she was pretty sure the woman was already piecing it together. The director had also not yet ordered the assassin into federal custody. That in itself was a revelation, but like Cade, perhaps Stansfield saw a potential need for the girl's help in the near future. Intuition was such an amazing human gift and one she had not been able to replicate in her own neural processes with any degree of success.

"Doris, can you show me the file again, the one you were using from Jaz? Without the scans running, I mean," Micah asked.

"Yes, if your mother is okay with that?"

Nancy Turner looked at her son, the concern and worry evident on her face, but she nodded. Micah pulled a keyboard up and selected the 4D display for the information, which immediately began to flow across the screen. Micah's fingers typed. Doris had added new skills for him, like coding in her own proprietary language, to the last instant learning session. She could tell Micah was decrypting the passage at an impressive speed. Her program continually adjusted its display rate to whatever speed he could handle, and now the translation was happening in a blur.

"It seems to help, getting it out like this," Micah said calmly. He obviously knew the look of shock on his mom's face at what she was watching. His fingers glided near the keys, the sensors picking up the letters and symbols without his need to actually make contact. The process continued for nearly twenty minutes until he slowed, paused, and backed a section up several screens. "Here, Doris, this is what I saw earlier. Do you see it?"

Doris's own progress in decrypting the Saraph code had been slow. The ancient data was not as clean and elegant as the Dhakerri version, but she could glean some of what Micah was looking at. The information stored in that DNA could help Captain Rearden in his likely encounters with the Saraph, as well as knowing more of the potential technologies or weapons he was facing.

Micah began to translate again. Code flowed from him as if it were a totally separate part of him doing the work. He again spoke calmly, "Doris, these two parts are connected, can you interpret it and begin modeling it for me? Might be good to ask Doctor Kline, Izzy, and Riley to conference in as well."

"Why, Micah, what's wrong?" Ms. Turner said, one hand stroking the back of her son's head.

"This is how they are going to destroy the world."

73

MIDWAY AIRPORT - CHICAGO

"It's been a long time, Samuel."

The man looked at the compact 9mm the woman was holding. "Not long enough, it would seem. Not nearly long enough, Margaret."

She motioned with the pistol that he should take a seat.

"You do know that weapons aren't allowed past security, don't you?" the man asked, an amused smile crossing his face. Looking up, he realized the few other people in the terminal had quickly vanished. "So, this will be a private conversation?"

"We are not trying to trap you," Stansfield said. "I simply want information."

"You could have stopped me at the bar over there. Sharing a good drink is part of how I build good working relationships. By the way, I liked your man, Rearden. How did he fare on his epic quest?"

She glanced at her watch. "He is somewhere over Cuban airspace right now."

"Ah, jetting off to somewhere tropical, I hope."

Stansfield just smiled. "No." She rose from the uncomfortable terminal seating and motioned for him to follow her across the concourse to the now abandoned pub. She lay her pistol on the bar and went behind the counter and quickly had two tumblers flipped over with a single round cube of ice. "Still bourbon, right?"

Samuel smiled. "Yes, double, please, I have a feeling I'm going to need it." He sat on the barstool, ignoring the weapon lying nearby.

She handed him his drink and took her own. "To old times," he said, raising the glass for a toast.

She hesitated. "To the future," she responded, clinking glasses lightly before taking a sip.

"Okay, Director, pleasantries and threats out of the away. What's on your mind?"

"I'm looking for The Lion."

The look on the man's face soured. He drained the glass and reached over the counter for the bottle. "There are a lot of things I would have preferred you ask me besides that, Margaret. In fact, that would likely be at the bottom of any list of questions I might want to answer. By the way, who are you with now? I did some digging after your man left. By all accounts—you're dead, my dear." Samuel eyed her appraisingly. "Still looking quite fetching for a corpse, I must say."

"Flattery, really? I think we have evolved beyond that."

He smiled, swirled the contents of his refilled glass and eyed her. "Why do you want him?"

"Not your concern, it is important. That's all you need to know," Margaret said flatly.

"I damn well know it's important if the esteemed senator was willing to burn me over it. Nowhere else you would have gotten that little nugget of intel," Samuel retorted.

Margaret's expression didn't change. "Were you ever at the black site called Section Z?"

"You've done your homework, Stansfield. You always were thorough."

"Stop wasting my time." She leaned over the counter getting directly in front of the man. "I have lives on the line, maybe a lot of them, and your former partner is involved. Where in the fuck is he?"

Not many could intimidate the man once known only as Guardian. Margaret Stansfield was one of those who could. She'd always wielded power more by implications and understated acknowledgement than actual threats. He had already spotted the armed men blocking the terminal in both directions. Not TSA, but actual threat response agents. He had no doubt that lethal force had been authorized. Even at his age, his spy-craft was still sharp as anyone, yet she had found his place in the swamp and now tracked him here. Whatever assets this woman had; they were impressive. He reached a decision.

"Full disclosure?"

She nodded. "Full disclosure and you walk. We disappear."

"Forever?" he asked.

She shook her head and poured herself another shot of bourbon, a single this time. "You never know when we may need each other again. I know you have enemies, some very powerful ones. I also know you are one of the best assets this country...or any country...ever had. I like you, that's why we are having this friendly talk."

"Touché," he said, nodding. "The feeling is very much mutual, Director. You do understand the value of secrets, the cost of intel, and the true price of friendships."

A shadow briefly crossed her face. Samuel knew one of the darker chapters in her own life. An episode in which decisions had to be made that no one should have ever had to face. "Indeed, we do."

"The Lion now mostly goes by the name Goldman, Richard Goldman. Very wealthy, very unassuming, but quite lethal."

She nodded. "I'm listening."

"We were paired up at the agency for a few years, you know, before all that shit went down."

"Before you went independent, you mean."

Samuel shrugged, obviously not interested in revisiting that part of the memory. "I was always pretty good at my job, Margaret. Honestly, you don't stay alive too long in this line of work if you aren't. The Lion, or Goldman, was the best I ever saw. The man was uncanny in his abilities and seemed to possess a lifetime of experience, even though I think we were about the same age."

"We should not underestimate this man. Is that your point?" Margaret asked.

"It is exactly my point—I have no idea what he is involved with or why he might be on your radar."

"Section Z, Project Saraph, what do you know?"

He rubbed his face, then scratched absently at the several days' worth of stubble. "Yeah, I was there a few times. They called it Angel, or Oceania I think, not Saraph, but I feel sure it must be the same. That was where I saw Goldman the very last time. Somehow, he was close with one of the big tech guys, multi-millionaire. Always had the tall blonde, chain-smoking Nordic guy nearby for security. The location was up in Oregon, industrial park of a small town. Very nondescript building. That site was locked down, too, had DOD fingerprints all over it. Just had that distinctive smell of a DARPA black budget program, you know?"

"What was Goldman's role?" the senator pressed.

"That's the thing, it seemed like it was his show. I mean, the tech guy was fronting the money, but seemed to me that Richard was calling all the shots. He deferred to the other guy when people were around, but the rest of the time, it was his rules."

Margaret frowned. This was a lot like trying to build a jigsaw puzzle when none of the pieces seemed to fit. "We have it on good authority that the original material for the project was stolen, possibly by the tech guy's dad. That would be Ivan Thrall, and his father got the materials back in the late sixties. He and an asset named Golette. Any of that ring any bells? How could this agent, this Goldman, be the one who was involved back then?"

Samuel shook his head. "Don't think so, Director. He would have been a kid back then. Maybe he's Golette's son, you said Thrall was the original thief's kid."

It was a good theory, but Doris had turned up evidence that strongly suggested Golette was most likely gay and never had any children. "Don't think so, but there is a connection. What can you tell me about the project itself?"

"It was a bunch of mumbo jumbo, some really old artifacts. They handled them with white gloves, like ancient, religious relics or something. A few had weird writing on them. Goldman said they came from the Antarctic and that the Navy had acquired them after World War Two. Best I remember, one team was doing some exotic computer programming, they were developing this super-intuitive AI. Another team in a different building, that seemed primarily to be doing medical research. The weird thing was, these two very different groups talked a lot. One of the things I was supposed to be checking for was communication leaks, and the lines between those two departments were a freakin' beehive of data and conversations."

"So, what happened?" Stansfield asked.

"I'm not sure," Samuel said. "From monitoring comms, I got the distinct opinion that someone had made a breakthrough. The AI group definitely had made several breakthroughs, one program called Alpha and then a later version they were calling Astra. Maybe something on the medical side, too. They all seemed pretty excited. All I know is, people suddenly started to disappear, you know, like just not show up for work. The comms chatter went way up, then nearly overnight, all but ceased. Goldman left suddenly a few days later. When I filed my incident report with the agency, they pulled the plug. Went in and took everything. I think that was a week, maybe ten days before that Thrall guy's yacht washed up a thousand miles farther down the coast."

The meeting had been productive. Margaret was pleased but still needed to locate The Lion. "I know Carson had you track him down. Where is Goldman?" If she still had access to the data at Bumblehive, she could have gotten that info in seconds. Now, she had to rely on this man's willingness and memory.

"Texas oil country." Samuel gave her an approximate location.

"Good enough for now." She leaned up and poured the man one more drink. "Thank you." She retrieved her gun and left.

"To the future, Margaret." The man smiled and picked up the glass. "To the future," he whispered.

74

CUBAN AIRSPACE

Five minutes into the jump, the playlist switched from Tom Petty's "Free Fallin" to ELO hammering out, "Don't Bring Me Down." The hard, driving beat helped drive Cade's momentum as he reached terminal velocity. *What is it with these kids and their music?* he wondered, then remembered Doris was the real inspiration behind that. "Good one, Riley."

As the airspeed continued to increase above 175 kilometers per hour, he was fairly certain the wind rushing past would have ripped his arms off had he not been in the high-tech armored suit. At 18,000 feet, just before hitting terminal velocity, the tiny wings finally caught thicker air, and he began the long glide slope to the target location. Thankfully, the suit mechanics handled all the maneuvers and navigation. No way they could have done any of this and wound up together as a team in the right spot.

"You are over Cuban waters, Nomad," Dee called out minutes earlier when they'd crossed the invisible line in the sky. Relations with Cuba had improved considerably in the last decade, but he was sure foreign agents falling from the sky unannounced would strain things just a bit if discovered.

"No radar tracks, flight line is nominal. Drop speed is now 55KPH.

Airspeed is just over 125KPH." Which, considering the mass of the suit, was phenomenal. The dawn light was just reaching the calm seas below, turning them into an iridescent, teal green, fading to a dark blue in the deeper areas. Cade still hadn't wrapped his head around the fact they would be going down there. They would be descending below the ocean nearly as much as he'd been above it minutes ago. *Focus on something else, soldier. Your team, the rescue, a date with the sexy rocket scientist.*

Gus was right. Time to get his head in the game. He checked all the WarHawk team readouts in his HUD—green lights across the board, although one was drifting a bit. "Greg, watch your track," Cade said. Greg had been the designated addition from The Cove, the one Charlie had argued against. Alan probably had more battle experience and possibly could edge Greg on the sheer range of knowledge, but Greg was a natural athlete and scored nearly as high as the other soldiers in most combat drills.

"Roger that, Nomad. Riley asked me to check out some of the flight characteristics. She thinks making a dual purpose XOD might be a good plan."

"Let's do the testing on a training op next time." Cade opened the channel to all team members. "WarHawks, final prep for dive, chutes will deploy at the last minute, do not trigger a manual release." He and Charlie had drilled them constantly in the prior days. All, except Greg, had at least one traditional HALO jump before. But these chutes would be deployed by the computer with the intent of grouping them all close over the target and visible in the air for the least amount of time. "All of you should be ready to dive as soon as we touchdown. Make sure Dee turns off your O2 at that point. Your suit can extract what is needed from the water." A chorus of replies came back. They all sounded like they were enjoying this. He had to admit it was pretty damn fun. If only they weren't going forth to battle dragons.

"Base, you'll have something out here to pick us up, won't you?"

Riley's soft voice came on, nearly drowned out by the wind whipping by the exo-divesuit. "Nomad, would I abandon you guys in the middle of the ocean?"

The water was approaching at an alarming rate. His smartass reply momentarily was on pause while he checked readouts to make sure nothing was wrong. "Uh...I mean, okay, thanks."

"Are you okay, Nomad? Your pulse, respiration, and catecholamines are spiking."

He had no idea what the last one of those was, but assumed it was either adrenaline or he'd peed on himself. "Are you watching this, Base? I am scared shitless."

"You're fine, Cap," Riley said, "and you aren't the only one. The rest of your team is spiking as well. We'll bring you down for a nice soft landing."

Cade could make out the waves and occasional fish jumping now. His altitude was about three thousand feet. Several times, he thought he saw a lighter blue flash in the distance, deep under the water, but decided to pretend for now that it was his imagination.

"Two minutes," his suit computer said.

Three thousand feet was about the height most HALO jumpers deployed chutes. Cade could feel his legs beginning to cramp from being locked in the awkward dive position for so long.

Riley cut into his thoughts,"We are detecting an ascent from the Kalypso. Adjusting flight plans."

"Cutter, status of Raptor," Deuce called.

Alexandria's voice was choppy, no doubt her descent was much rougher and faster than his team. "In FF now, be on the deck two minutes behind WarHawk. Situation nominal."

"One minute to impact, thirty seconds to chute."

"Impact, did she say impact?" Cade asked.

"Very sorry, Nomad, a poor choice of words, I will have a word with the divesuit's internal computer at once about her language," his personal AI, Dee, responded just as he felt the wings fold smoothly back into the storage compartment on the back of the suit. Instantly, he was in free-fall again doing a fast arc into the water at well over a hundred miles an hour.

"Seven hundred feet." He felt a pop, and his forward momentum was nearly completely canceled by the gossamer thin, translucent parachute. His forward speed canceled out, he swung side to side momentarily, then began slowly descending the last hundred feet into the Caribbean.

The XOD slipped into the water and immediately initiated a dive. The parachute cords released automatically, and like the super strong chute, they were designed to dissolve within the hour on contact with sea water. The depth readout quickly showed he was passing a hundred feet. The rest of WarHawk was grouped within about a hundred yards. All in all, the jump had been...fun, but a bit...well, anti-climactic.

"Contact, three thousand yards and closing." Cade's suit initiated defensive mode. *Maybe not so anticlimactic.*

75

KALYPSO

Kissa continued to pry at the material around the door at first; he was convinced it was just some thick plastic, maybe acrylic, but several days of working on it had produced barely a scratch. He tossed away the piece of bed-frame he'd been using. Several times each day, they would move him from the cell to a viewing room where Thera was. He could see the anguish in her eyes, but she was healthy, and she looked unharmed. Despite the agony of not being able to wrap his arms around her and pull her close, knowing she was alive lifted his spirits to the wind.

"There is no win, you imbecile." And now he was talking to himself. Kissa was under no illusions. He knew that the captors had no intentions of letting any of them leave this place alive. They were using him for leverage to get his fiancée to do something she clearly didn't want to do. Did it have something to do with the monster that had attacked? That creature still haunted his nightmares. Sometimes he still saw it, even when he wasn't asleep. The thing was evil, unnatural... it wreaked of wrongness. The last time he'd seen her, Thera had signed for him to be patient. It was a subtle gesture, but he got it. Patience had never really been one of his strengths, though. More than once, he'd wound up hospitalized for short-cutting decompression stops on deep dives. His joints and back still ached at certain times as a vicious reminder of his impetuousness. "Calm yourself, man."

He moved back to sit against the wall. White floors, white walls, white lights overhead. He ached for some color, a window even, although he had a good idea what he would see outside, blackness. The inky, black depths of the Midnight Zone. From memory, he knew it was part of the pelagic zone that extends from a 1,000 to 4,000 meters below the ocean surface. It was also known as the Bathyal Zone. It was the place where sunlight went to die. The water column above pushed down on everything, creating intense pressure so great only a few animals had ever been able to adapt to it.

In graduate school, Kissa had briefly wanted to study the deep ocean until he realized how little of the magnificent large marine life there was. Also, shallow seas were where Thera's specialty was so... yeah, he'd chased the girl. Caught her, too. He smiled at the memory. Okay, what else did he know? He began to methodically catalog everything he had seen, all the facts relating to the place that might be important. Since he'd been out of the holding cells several times, he had a general understanding of the layout. They were in a section of mostly open storage space, although it seemed to be filling up quickly. The labs where Thera worked were up a short ramp on a different level. The roof overhead was flat, but the walls had a slight curve to them. That meant they were outer walls, probably part of the pressure hull. Thinking again to all that pressure outside made him shudder involuntarily. The walls were not cold, or even cool, so thermal transfer from the frigid water to inside was handled somehow. He'd seen no condensation, but there was a vent high overhead. That might dehumidify the space and circulate the air.

What else, what else? Think of something useful. Kissa was a soldier and a scientist. His mind processed incoming information almost subconsciously. Somewhere in his head was a clue, something that could help him get out and get to Thera, but then what? They would still be trapped miles down near the ocean floor.

Something wasn't right about how they sounded. The thought had occurred to him early on, but he'd ignored it and just now came back to it. People who worked in deep water submersibles usually sounded strange when they talked. Kind of like cartoon chipmunks. That was due to the compressed gas mixture they used, normally a blend called helox, which made you sound as if you had inhaled the contents of a helium balloon.

He'd met some saturation divers, or sat divers, over the years. Strange bunch, these guys often worked for oil companies in pressurized living quarters at the bottom of the sea. They were needed to perform maintenance and repair work, and they discovered it was easier and safer to just let them stay there for extended periods, like weeks or months. All of them he'd met had been a bit off, living and working in an environment that was constantly trying to kill them, no real way to safely get back to the surface on their own. It was a special breed of men.

Why the helox, though? Kissa remembered from dive training it was to combat narcosis. They were constantly warned to watch their time below a hundred feet. Divers can develop what's known as nitrogen narcosis. He'd also had firsthand knowledge of that. He had a history of not listening to good advice. Narcosis made you feel drunk and disoriented. The deeper you go, the drunker and more incapacitated you can feel. At a certain depth, the amount of compressed oxygen literally becomes toxic to the human body. Adding the helium combatted that effectively, and even other versions were out there, like trimox. *So—how are they able to be this deep yet not sounding like they were breathing anything but normal air?* If he had to guess, he would say the air pressure was about earth normal 1ATM as well. That indicated this place was more like a submarine than a habitat. Subs had thick enough hulls that did not require as much equalizing pressure nor compressed air mixes. *How does any of this help?*

Subs, subs...when they took him and the others off the boat, they had used a smaller craft. Something similar in size to a normal charter boat but not as deep, and it was streamlined for underwater use. Kissa had been the only one not knocked unconscious by the monster, but he'd faked it easily enough. In truth, he'd been nearly in as bad of shape as Coffee and the others. The captors had been men, soldiers even, but seemed to have no particular nationality. He'd heard several languages and accents. They were definitely military, though, or ex-military. Possibly professional soldiers now, like many of his former comrades. *What am I missing?*

He'd not seen any of the smaller craft since coming aboard. They'd black-bagged his head on exiting the craft. Still, what else could he recall? He didn't remember any docking hatch. In fact, it seemed like they had led him down some steps then up a short incline. So, they parked inside and just ran it up on a slope like beaching a jet ski. His footsteps echoed; the space was open. The space was big but not as large as the warehouse area outside. *Did I hear anything?* A pulsing noise, maybe, nothing identifiable. No hatch doors closing, no warning bells or alarms. Shit, his head was beginning to hurt. *Did they turn left or right? Ummm...right, pretty quickly, and the sound had changed.* A corridor, it had some sort of rubber matting that caused him to trip. He had fallen against the wall.

Kissa stood and walked over to one wall. He closed his eyes and leaned the right side of his body against it. *How does it feel?* Nearly the same, the curve was a bit more pronounced on the bottom and a bit flatter higher up. So, he'd been on the outside wall. Possibly only one or two floors below. They'd walked for about two minutes. He did some mental math. That would be about two hundred meters. Thinking back to how large the vessel looked rising up out of the water, he would estimate that was less than a fourth of the distance around one half of the vessel.

It wasn't much, but he had some ideas at least. He had a direction now, he just needed a way out of this room and some way of reaching Thera. The massive door slid up and away. Two of the guards motioned for him to come with them. He stood and walked forward, wondering if this might be his last chance to force a more favorable outcome.

76

CARIBBEAN

The music flowing into Cade's suit stopped as soon as the onboard computer's threat assessment concluded that the glowing dot in the distance presented a significant risk.

Cade keyed the all call, "WarHawks, stay sharp. We know some of what this thing is capable of. Suit lights off when we go below 2000." Then, on a private channel to Greg and Deuce, "I'm taking point on this. You guys watch my six. Guess we get to find out how good Riley's enhancements are."

"Passing 800 meters, Captain," Dee offered. "Oxygen production is at 92% of optimum."

The light was practically gone after a hundred meters down, now it was pitch black outside his small window into this alien world. The inky darkness was somehow more claustrophobic than anything else he'd ever encountered. He switched on one bank of the suit's lights, but they only showed more of the same. A bubble of blue white light surrounded by an ocean of black. They were descending fast, but to think of all the pressure the XOD suits would soon be under was terrifying. Also, the realization that if they had to go all the way to the bottom, it would be a dozen times as far, made his insides liquify. *Fear is the real enemy.*

Gus, can you help here? Cade voiced internally. He needed calm and rational thinking.

You gotta be fucking kidding me, dude. This shit is scaring the fuck out of me, and we haven't even see the dragon yet, Gus replied.

Not a dragon, it's an angel, Ace chimed in. *Saraph, or Saraphim, from the Hebrew words 'to burn.'*

Gus sniped back, *Angels and dragons, Who gives a fuck? Let the brute deal with it.*

"Y'all aren't helping." Honestly, Cade was deathly afraid of his barbarian persona taking over. They were in an unforgiving environment in exoskeleton dive suits which were meant for precise movement, not brute strength battles.

"Nomad," Riley's voice came over his headset. "We have more movement on the Kalypso. It is ascending, coming up on an angle. Adjusting WarHawk for intercept vectors."

He felt the suit's tiny but powerful thrusters accelerate seawater through various directional nozzles quickly propelling him forward. The XOD used a similar drive system to the magneto hydrodynamic systems Micah had spotted pursuing the Kalypso. The Cove's was a bit more advanced and incredibly compact. The benefit of having a nearly inexhaustible power supply in each suit's onboard Pica unit provide them a very stealthy, fast, and efficient way to maneuver.

"Raptor Team is in the water," Jimmy said. His job was monitoring that group. "Cutter has one team member injured. Minor, but limits his mission effectiveness. It is within our projections."

"Possible enemy target within 2000 meters and closing slowly," the mechanical voice of the suit's combat AI stated. Unlike Dee, the suit's systems were all business.

"Show me." Instantly, Cade's full face shield lit in soft glowing lines like a radar scope. He could see it, and the rest of his team, spread out in a wide arc covering several hundred meters and the larger glowing indicator for the biologic threat. Presumably, the Saraph. If the creature knew they were here, it was taking its time. He looked at the readout, coming up on 2000 meters. "WarHawks, go dark."

He minimized the radar display and looked to where the other team members should be. One by one, he saw the bubbles of light wink out. Instantly, the darkness seemed to slam against him. He felt his joints stiffen and could imagine it cracking through his diamond hard face shield. Not the water, not the immense silent pressure, but the darkness itself. He found himself having trouble breathing. It was very much the same feeling he got of being inside a house at night. It was confining, threatening, and it robbed his soul of its desire to live.

"Amy!"

He hadn't meant to call her name, not out loud. The ghost of his sister, always frozen in his mind at four years old. She called to him, over and over, "Take my hand."

Cade closed his eyes and rocked back and forth in the tight confines of the metal coffin he was bolted into. *Please no, please no, please no.*

"Cade?" The voice, full of calm and concern, cut through the clutter and noise of his tortured mind.

"Hey."

"Sorry—Nomad," Jaz said. "Still not used to all of your guys' rules. Just wanted to see how you're doing. Doctor Han is monitoring your team, and your numbers are spiking in several areas."

Briefly, he considered lying to her but knew it was pointless. "Out of my comfort zone a bit here. Talk to me, okay?"

There was a slight delay in her reply. "I can only imagine. I'm so sorry. I can't understand how you guys do what you do."

"It's not that, Jaz, the mission is dangerous and risky, but that risk is manageable. We train to be as prepared as we can be. This is just me. It's, it's..."

"Ah," she replied. "The monsters out there are not as scary as the ones inside your own head."

Damn, she did get it. Wow, he thought.

"You don't have a lock on that, Nomad. Yes, your trauma and abuse may have made you more acutely aware of it, but we all have those same issues. It's called being human. No one wants to feel helpless or alone."

“I’m pretty much alone down here, though,” Cade replied looking out into the darkness.

“No you aren’t, you just can’t see everything around you. Doris, adjust Nomad’s visuals to show other team members.”

Instantly, the suit registered and tagged them in his HUD. Not as glowing dots, but the actual people. He took note of the wavelengths, a visual overlay of the magnetic anomalies the suits caused in the water. “The Saraph or Kalypso can’t see this, can they?”

“We don’t think so,” Jaz answered. “It’s a very narrow band, and the suit harmonics phase at an irregular rhythm to make it look random, unless you know what you’re looking for. Also, Nomad, dial the normal light sensors in your display up to max.”

He did so; it took a minute for his eyes to adjust, but he could just begin to pick out small fish, shrimp, and less identifiable creatures swimming all around him. All of their tiny bioluminescent bodies glowing or pulsing with light. The sheer density of life was incredible. Now he could see larger items farther away. A barrel-shaped thing with ribbons of light dancing down its length cruised slowly by as he passed 3000 meters.

“They look like creatures of light.”

“We have a problem,” Dee said just before the XOD began bringing weapons online.

“Threat detected, 1500 meters and closing fast.” Cade felt a pressure in his head and heard several members of WarHawk cry out in pain. The suit dialed the HUD back down until the light from only a single creature remained. The Saraph. It was approaching from the flank, right where Alias and Pyro were descending.

“Secondary threat detected,” the combat AI said, highlighting yet another target coming up from far below.

“Shit, there’s more than one,” Cade said to no one. “Deuce, you seeing this?” He knew he was, so he didn’t wait for a reply. “Execute Red-Twelve.” This had been a contingency they had trained on in the simulator. Cade slowed his descent, as did most of the others, and split into two defensive units. Each would focus only on a single animal.

“Weapons...” Deuce began to order just as the closest of the monsters' light began to brighten and pulse. The neural pulse Micah had warned them about. Riley and Doris had created several countermeasures to hopefully mitigate the effects, including a magnetic shielding in the XOD's helmet. Still, he heard those closest to the glowing beast immediately go into distress. Pyro was throwing up in his helmet. Cade muted the audio feed from the man, as that alone could trigger gag reflexes in the rest of them.

Throwing up into the helmet of a hard-shell dive suit would normally be a death sentence. The stomach contents would remain in the helmet and be breathed back in by the gasping occupant, causing asphyxiation within minutes. But Riley and Doctor Han had created an amazing filtering system that could literally ionize particulates out of the air and cause them to be drawn to a collector grid around the neckline where they would be gathered, then purged outside the suit. Still, nausea was not a mission capable state for any warrior. You were out of commission until you recovered. Cade watched as Pyro's suit went into autonomous mode. It wouldn't fight for him, but it could escape and evade.

"We've analyzed the pulse wave harmonics and are attempting to compensate now," Doris said.

Cade wasn't sure what that meant, but hoped it helped. He was aware that the XOD generated an electromagnetic field just nanometers outside the skin of the exterior. Part of this had to do with the ability to keep the incredible water pressure away from the actual suit, but it had also been fine-tuned to help protect against the beast.

His HUD had switched to combat mode minutes earlier, and he watched helplessly as several of the eight indicators switched from green to yellow. One of those flashing glowing dots was Deuce.

"Deploy countermeasures," Cade ordered. The various suits' AIs obeyed, even if the occupant was incapacitated. Basically, fighting a battle underwater was challenging for humans no matter how good the tech. Projectile weapons like guns were very limited as the drag from the water limited killing distances to a few feet, and reliable aiming was nearly impossible. Energy weapons like Riley had been developing couldn't be used because the water dissipated the charge, and the shooter was more at risk that the target.

One thing about working around a bunch of geniuses, if you give them enough time and motivation, they will come up with some options. One was the incredibly small aqua drones now deploying from most of the dive suits. Looking like small fish, they would school in front of the animal and try to be consumed where a small explosive, embedded in each unit, would detonate in a timed explosion designed to rip the Saraph apart from the inside. Another set of drones used a nerve paralytic that Jaz had helped develop. Based on the tentacle that Micah retrieved, she felt sure it would cause the creatures to become immobile for at least thirty seconds. These were part of an arsenal of long thin shafts that could be fired from a miniature rail gun affixed to the forearm of each diver. It looked more like a miniature self-loading crossbow, but like most of what they had, it was a close-quarters defensive weapon.

The first Saraph made an attack run to Cade's right, but his attention was on the other coming from below. "Shit, these things are fast." The pressure in his head increased; he knew it was attempting to incapacitate him. "You first, buddy."

"We have a hit," someone, maybe Greg, said excitedly, then added in a much more somber tone, "It's still coming. Drone countermeasures are ineffective."

"New target detected," Cade's suit's AI said.

Cade looked at his display. Something else was beginning to show. Something much farther away and much, much larger. Way bigger than the one he was about to engage. *No, no...shit.* "Riley, tell me that big ass thing is Kalypso."

77

TEXAS

"Chaps, how long until we arrive?"

"Wheels down in San Antonio in forty-three minutes, Director."

Margaret had made the calls; her agency's teams were stretched to the breaking point. Most of her field agents were untested, and Deuce would have a cow if he knew what she was doing, but her options were limited. Homeland had provided a pickup crew, and now her Nighthawk was screaming toward central Texas to meet up. Doris had peeled apart layer after layer of identities on one Richard Goldman, fifty-four-year-old resident of Round Rock, Texas. The identity was false, and that was about the only honest thing she could determine. Richard Goldman had a cover story that literally went back to his birth. No part of it stood up to scrutiny, yet it was pieced together like a master forger might recreate a masterpiece.

"Doris, update."

"We've had the house and property under surveillance from space since your man first voiced the name. No one has come or gone in that length of time. Ground teams are moving into position now, and we should be able to get heat signatures on IR within the next few minutes."

"Do we have a better image, something we can put out on BOLO, feed to CBP, or Interpol? We don't want this guy slipping through the cracks."

Doris answered, "We have various CCD footage only of someone using his identity. At an ATM, using a credit card, and such, but all seem to be different people. No driver's license, no passport in that name, nothing official."

That wasn't much of a surprise to Margaret. "Put Jimmy on the money—the kid can find anything. Obviously, Goldman, or whoever he is, has been working on this plan for years, using other people to offer multiple false leads for us to pursue. Let's not waste our time on any of them right now."

"What are you thinking, Director?"

"I'm thinking this guy is going to be gone long before we even know who he is. He's smart, he has money, and he knows what the agenda is."

"Agents are now on site, Director," Doris said soon after. "Do you want them to hold?"

"Scan the house," she responded, a sense of helplessness beginning to creep in.

"We have two occupants, one stationary, possibly on a bed. One appears to be outside near a storage or garage area."

A driver and Goldman, that seemed way too easy to the former CIA station chief. Things rarely worked out that nice and tidy, no matter how much you wanted them to.

A thought occurred to Margaret. "Isabella has seen this guy, she had mentioned it. Get her watching the video feed from the compound, but also go through any of the image archives from Cryptus, DOD, DARPA, anyone who may have captured images related to Section Z. Let's eliminate the ones you can identify and have her see if Thrall's buddy was in any of them. We not only need to find Goldman but need to know the other accomplices as well."

"I can do that, Director. I may even be able to piece together an image of the Texan from her memory. Something I've been working on actually."

The way the AI said it made Margaret's curious nature want to ask more questions, but this was not the time for that. "Sounds good, keep me updated, please."

"Director, I think you need to talk to Micah."

Confused, Margaret asked why. Doris let her know that he'd decrypted something important from the Saraph's source code. Important wasn't accurate. It was—in a word—chilling.

* * *

The man counted down silently from five. At zero, a steel battering ram impacted just as the blasting patch tore the hinges from the massive wooden door. This was Texas, and they had just violated the 'Knock-notice' rule, but legal consequences be damned. The director was on her way, and she'd authorized it personally. A Hispanic man in the courtyard had been washing a luxury Land Rover. He'd been dropped by one of the tranquilizer darts minutes before the rest of the team encircled the main house.

Talon Team members made entry first. Each man or woman had a hand on the one in front until they were deep enough into the residence to separate into assigned rooms to clear. The AIC for Talon was a giant South African named Ade Nale. Ade had a resounding presence and a no-nonsense approach to security and combat. The house was cleared in ninety seconds.

"Command, no one inside the residence," Ade said.

"We are still picking up the heat signature," Doris responded. She then gave Agent Nale the exact coordinates in the house. Weapons up, he and two others streamed into the spacious room, an office or study by the look of it. Their video feeds were going live to Margaret, Doris, and everyone at TCP control. Ade walked over to the exact spot and lowered his hand down until it made contact on the IR screens. "It's a sofa, settee, I believe. The surface is quite warm, I believe it has been wired to give a false signature."

"Agent Nale, I am landing now. Preserve the room in pristine condition. Sweep the house for transmitters, trip switches, or any other nasty surprises."

Ade heard the chopper coming in from the south. The sweep was standard protocol for the team, but he ensured his people were doing it correctly. Minutes later, Margaret Stansfield walked in looking as crisp and sharp as a new razor blade. "Any other tampering?"

"Nothing so far, ma'am," Ade answered.

She walked around the entire room, taking note of the eclectic range of books the man had. Odd rocks and old artifacts. A few framed certificates. Everything about the room seemed a bit too precise. Not that it was all neat and organized, it wasn't. Something about it all was off, though. The disarray seemed staged somehow. "Doris, what is wrong with this room?"

Ade stepped back to the entry door to let the director discuss her ideas with the AI. He'd been fully read in, but still couldn't fully come to terms with this group he had joined.

"I believe someone is sending you a message, or us a message. They knew we were coming."

"How so? Samuel?"

"I don't think so, we've been monitoring the Guardian via the tracking dot you managed to get on his arm," Doris answered.

Margaret allowed herself a small smile. It hadn't been easy, having the dot ready to go just as Samuel reached to take the drink from her hands. She doubted it would last long on the very paranoid man, but for now it could keep them aware of where he was and who he was talking to.

"I have an image for you, Director," Doris called.

Margaret was busy studying the room. Not its parts, but the entire ensemble as a collection. It was all false, all misleading just like the man, but like every good lie, it needed something real to hang its deception on. Her delicate hands moved over the hardbound leather books once more and then to the objects and artifacts. Finds from a lifetime of oil drilling and traveling the world if they could be believed. Her fingers danced over a polished piece of volcanic geode, a rock with a fossilized feather and an ancient piece of gears and levers all fused together by time, rust, and possibly seawater, and then, an old ship's bell. Without turning the bell to face her, she ran her fingers over the lettering and smiled. "Bring me the driver."

78

KALYPSO

"Come back to bed."

Her voice both soothed and chilled Ivan. Ruslana was a pit viper. He knew better than to give in to all of her charms, but damn. Looking over at the slender, perfect body lying on the bed instantly caused certain parts of him to take notice. In truth, they'd had sex many times during the night, but her appetite seemed to never be fully satiated.

"I need to go to the bridge, I'm expecting a call from Richard and Dakso," Ivan answered.

"What about da fat pig?" she snarled. The Czech pushed her nose up with two fingers to leave no doubt who she meant.

He smiled. "Freida will arrive on the next rotation, and you need to be nice to her."

"Nyet, she is awful person, and she smells like sausage."

"Darling, how bad do you talk about me when I'm not around?" Thrall asked, leaning over to kiss her full lips once more.

"Hardly at all, you are most reasonable man. You do what I want." She pulled him close. "And now, I want this." Her hand wandered down his body to his groin. She stroked his erect cock, and he knew he would not be making it to the control room just yet. Their lips met, and he was lost to her needs once again.

* * *

Several decks below, in the research level, Thera was working on a plan. She'd made significant progress with the new creature over the last three days. She'd been right, the SS4 was a major step forward in the lineage of the Saraph universe. The strangeness of the creature still unnerved her. Its eyes followed her constantly as she monitored equipment around the spacious labs. She'd taken to calling the SS4 'Henry,' as she needed something less antiseptic, less clinical...unlike almost every other animal she'd studied in her career. Henry had a consciousness; he had intellect. Not just some deep hidden mammal brain either. Dolphins and whales were smart and might have whatever it was that created a state of consciousness. They certainly possessed a level of self-awareness.

Henry, though, was beyond that. So far, it didn't seem aggressive, except when it fed. The blocks of special chemical compounds that the creature needed for nourishment were pounced on like a starving cat going after a mouse. Lately, it had been eating and growing at a phenomenal rate. She wanted to urge it to maturity where maybe it would give up other data they desperately craved. The real key was when she had tried communicating with it. On some level, she knew Henry knew what she wanted, what she needed. Inside his genes, he carried the secrets of a civilization. Knowledge theoretically from beyond the stars, yet it was up to him when to offer that up.

Instead, Thera had taken to talking to the animal about humans, particularly about her and Kissa. More than once, when she'd mentioned Kissa, she had an image of him flash through her mind. It was brief and could have easily been dismissed as her subconscious recalling a very vivid memory, but the images were not scenes that the two had ever shared.

One was Kissa underwater alone, obviously searching for something. Another was him on a boat covered in purple looking blood and holding a weapon. Henry was communicating with her, and not just her, either, it seemed. Since coming out of the creche, the SS4 had never left this lab so...it was communicating with some of the lesser creations as well. Occasionally, Thera would feel a probing, questioning sensation when she looked into its eyes. If this was indeed how it communicated, it was not intrusive. She seemed to have control over what it saw. She had to willingly allow it to see her own memories.

Through a series of cause and effects, she learned to offer up more memories of her world, and occasionally, Henry would share more of his. To some degree, this was what Thrall had asked her to do, but none of it was recorded in her notes. Thera could sense the unease from Henry each time any of the other lab techs were nearby, and when Thrall or the Asian man, Pax, came into the lab, it was like an icy steel curtain went up between her and the Saraph.

So, Henry didn't seem to trust them or didn't want to share whatever it knew. Thera had let it see her own kidnapping, and it seemed to sense the fear she had, particularly of Pax Ruan. Thera had no illusions that she or Kissa would ever be leaving this vessel alive. "What are you thinking, Henry?" Three of the five dark black eyes studied her; the other two rotated in their sockets toward a window to the outside.

The floor had been tilting up slightly on one side for about half an hour. Thera had learned that this was when the Kalypso was transitioning from one depth to another. How a craft this large could stay down this long or maneuver defied her understanding of what was possible. Still, it offered a marine biologist a perfect research lab. That is, if she wasn't being threatened daily. "Astra, what is our current depth and position?" She'd learned to make requests of the ship's computer whenever she needed. It would not always offer up specific information, such as locations of Thrall or Pax, but otherwise, was a very handy resource.

"Good morning, Doctor Otera. The Kalypso is currently at 9382 feet and ascending at ten degrees. I am not permitted to give additional information as to our exact geospatial location."

Henry was staring up at where the computer-generated voice came out of the overhead speaker. It tilted its head, almost like a dog might do, if the dog had the face of a gremlin and small, fin-shaped winglets for ears. One of Thera's abilities was to listen in on the underwater world through a series of acoustic sensors embedded around the Kalypso. Several times she had heard clicks of dolphins and the ultra low calls of whales, some of which she was certain had been distress calls. There was enough familiarity that she was fairly certain they were still in the Caribbean, or perhaps the adjacent Atlantic. While she could sense when the ship changed elevation, the sensation of all other movement was lost. Through the decking, there was an almost constant vibration and sense of inertia. She'd gotten used to it in just a few hours, but when she thought about it, her senses would register it again distinctly. That feeling did not impart any sense of direction, though, simply movement.

Henry's head rotated and stared up at the ceiling to the left. It lingered several minutes, then snapped its head back to lock eyes with hers. Instantly, she had visions. She was underwater, deep in the ocean, but not alone—divers. An earlier version of the Saraph preparing to attack. *What does that mean? Is that really happening somewhere up there? Is someone coming to help?* Ideas flooded her head, this time all her own. Then one more from the SS4: Kissa confined in a small windowless room. She knew instantly where the room was, even though she'd never been to that part of the ship. Then an image of a hand moving across a key panel. She committed the long sequence to memory. She wanted to thank Henry aloud but knew Astra would be listening and recording everything. If she were correct, the animal didn't rely on auditory senses, anyway. Mentally, she sent an image of her offering him lots of food blocks. It was the most positive thing she could think of. "I'll be back soon, need to go check on some other experiments." With that, she moved away and headed for the door.

79

CARIBBEAN

"Sweet Baby Jesus, Nomad. What in the holy fuck is that?" Alias asked.

Rising up from the abyss was another Saraph, the blue light emanating from its pulsing abdomen nearly blinding in the sea of darkness. "Alias, I think we've been entertaining the babies, that must be mama bear."

"Well, the babies are ripping us apart. WarHawk is down to half strength." Alias said. apparently maintaining some measure of his fighting ability.

Cade keyed his comms to contact Riley and Alex far above, "Cutter, monitor these feeds. We have a new bogey, and it's larger than any of the others. If we don't make it, you get your team out of there, don't be heroes. Riley, we're going to need some rescue craft in here soon. I have some incapacitated divers probably headed to the surface."

Both women acknowledged, as Cade was already running through team dynamics and what resources they had available. *Tactical advantages...umm, few.* The Saraphs seemed to be ignoring the XOD suits where the occupants were incapacitated. So, they stunned their prey, then moved on to others to hunt. How did that help him? And then he knew—well, he had a crazy idea of how.

"Dee, can you give me control over another diver's suit?" He knew the suit's own built-in combat AI had an autonomous mode. It had been designed primarily to get an unconscious diver out of impending danger.

"They were not designed that way, Nomad. Allow me to interface with the suit's internal AI."

"Dee, who's carrying the lancets?"

"Greg, Deuce, and Pyro," came the instant reply. Cade checked his displays for their location. Greg and Deuce were close enough, and both were yellow indicating the diver was at least partially incapacitated. Pyro's suit was flickering between yellow and red on his display and seemed to be one of those heading topside.

"Suits are now enabled for autonomous mode on your command authority, Captain." Dee answered in her inappropriately cheery British voice.

"Great, thanks." Decision made, he informed Alias of the plan. The other man was less enthusiastic about it but agreed with the order. "Suit, engage autonomous mode." His own suit seemed baffled by the command. After all, it had a target approaching fast and a larger enemy not far behind. He had to confirm multiple times before the suit complied. "Dee, give me control of Greg."

Instantly, his faceplate display showed what Greg was seeing. The HUD was flashing yellow and red for eminent threat. Cade canceled the alert and the evasive maneuver the suit had planned to execute. The Saraph was glowing brilliantly and closing to within a hundred meters. Tentacles whipped about, and he could now see the razor-like, hooked claws at the end of several of them. Carefully, he reached back remotely on Greg's suit and grasped the lancet. "Alias, you in?"

"Yes, sir, and by the way, your friend snores."

"No surprise, just take care of him, that's his body you're fighting with. Remember that." Cade then ordered those who could to prepare for the beast coming up from below. It was up to him and Alias to deal with these first two. He could now see a dark stain trailing from the Saraph. Some countermeasures had found their mark. They injured it; hopefully, that slowed it down some. Watching it move, though, he was pretty sure they had just pissed it off. He felt Greg spasm violently, the suit struggling to compensate. The damn thing was blasting neural waves at the boy. "Hang in there, kid!"

The lancet was a four-foot long rod of polysteel, only a few millimeters thick, but incredibly strong with a lethal tip. It reminded Cade of a tactical baton, and, just like one, it extended out to more than twice its initial length. As the final section locked into place, a blue arc ran along that section. A supercharged plasma beam fired along a razor thin line on both sides of the baton, creating a wicked cutting edge.

The Saraph closed to within twenty feet, then began attacking with tentacles and claws. It was all Cade could do not to stare into the glowing open mouth full of what had to be needle-like teeth. The suit automatically defended itself against the first attack. One tentacle lashed out with lightning speed only to be severed as it reached around the suit. Greg's suit's AI fired multiple darts into the animal but had no effect. Cade felt the suit jolt as a blow hit on the back of the helmet. *Don't forget that is a boy you are using as a weapon, Cade.* The internal voice of Gus was calming but unnecessary.

He felt his own suit jets maneuvering and knew it was engaging in an attack as well. It was disorienting to try to accomplish what he was doing. He idly wondered if Gus could handle his suit while he ran Greg's, but dismissed the thought as a massive claw arched down carving a gouge out of Greg's face shield. Cade swung up with both hands, gripping the lancet and slicing off two arms of the beast. He felt an impact in his back and a searing pain, realizing this was inside his own suit. *Alias, get this thing off of me!* he thought, Alias using Deuce to fight and he using Greg.

"Kalypso is detected, three thousand meters and closing."

Cade registered the fact distractedly as suit warnings in Greg's HUD began going red one after the other. The damn thing had both of the massive dive suit's arms gripped tightly in its tentacles. Looking to the side, Cade could see they looked like massive tree limbs, one side covered in barbed, rimmed suckers. Each of the Saraph's tentacles wrapping around Greg's arms were as thick as a man's thigh. They rippled and coiled with muscles like a constricting boa. Cade kicked out but contacted nothing. The alarms inside the suit increased, then distantly, he heard alarms inside his own suit begin to trill.

The Saraph he was fighting seemed intent on pulling Greg in half. They had trained for this. *What was the play?* "Suit, execute..." *Shit,* he couldn't think of the command. He was aware now of the Saraph attacking him and Alias. It was using its neural blast on him. "Riley, help, take over..."

"Suit, set defense condition Alpha," he heard over the open channel into Greg's XOD. The suit covering shield of supercharged energy instantly increased multiple times, almost maxing out the small PICA power supply. The Saraph instantly recoiled, almost like it had grabbed a hot pan from the stove. Riley then initiated a movement with the lancet, twirling it nearly faster than Cade could see. She drove Greg's suit into the retreating beast, carving off chunks and limbs and then eye stalks and finally, portions of its massive body. She continued pressing the attack until dark blood filled the viewscreen and the last of the blue light faded to dark.

"Target one neutralized," the helpful Battle Computer announced.

"Thanks, Riles," Cade said, exhausted and in pain as his presence was once again firmly back in his own suit where he was looking into the gaping maw of a glowing mouth. Instinctively, he swung up with the lancet weapon only to remember his suit didn't have that. He was pretty much defenseless.

"Alias, get this mother fucker off me! Do what Riley did," he said, then realizing the man had no idea of what the girl had done. "Riley, can you help him?"

"This is Alan, Riley is helping Greg, he needs some patching up right now. His suit was compromised. Taking Alias's position in three."

"Whoa!" Alias said, returning to his own suit. Alan was now commanding Deuce's XOD, and the kid knew how to use it. Where Alias had been focusing on the back of the animal's head and tentacles, Alan jetted below and then blasted to full power on a slicing run through the glowing underbelly. The Saraph jerked back and moved to engage its attacker, but Alan had already maneuvered to one side and launched the lancet deep into the face of the animal. Cade had forgotten the baton could be used as a throwing weapon. It would return to the suit once inertia was canceled. Unfortunately, it left Alan defenseless during the interval.

"Target three within 500 meters." His suit was suggesting evasive maneuvers at once. Cade could already see the glow filling the lower third of his face shield. "Dee, supercharge my suit like we did with Greg's."

"Charging."

The smaller Saraph was nearly on top of Alan/Deuce. The lancet had fallen away from the glowing gash and was slowly returning to Alan's outstretched hand.

"Ready," Dee announced.

Cade put his own suit at full speed, blasting through a forest of tentacles and onto the beast. He hooked in with specialized grips and felt the raw power of the animal. He guessed the actual body was about the size of an elephant, maybe two, and it bucked like a rodeo bronco. Razor claws and tentacles whipped wildly about. One caught him in the shoulder as another came out of the darkness directly at his face. "Be ready, Alan!" He triggered the discharge.

Immediately, the Saraph reared back, arching its back to get rid of the interloper. Alan, snatching his lancet from the water, fired it and sliced into the midsection in an arcing cut that ended just under the mouth. The light dimmed, and the outer shell of the creature fell away.

Cade's suit informed him, "Target two neutralized. Suit integrity is marginal. Target three is..."

"Will you shut the fuck up? I see the goddamn thing." Cade stared as the house-sized creature filled his field of vision in every direction. *What in the fuck had I been thinking to come up with this plan?*

80

TEXAS

The thick man twitched nervously as Margaret moved around behind where he was sitting. "You are the personal driver for Mister Goldman?"

He nodded enthusiastically, "Si, si...yes." The security team had already pulled up the man's driver's license, customs papers, and a considerable amount of travel history. To Margaret, it was all irrelevant, more stagecraft.

"Where is he now?"

"I don't know, he left early."

"Does he do that often?"

"Si, very often. He is a very busy man," the man said.

"And you are the only staff here at the house?" she asked.

"Most days, yes. He has a private chef come in several days a week and a housekeeper every Thursday. He likes a small operation."

The man appeared to be in his early fifties with a pronounced accent, but one that indicated many years here in the U.S. "Is it often he leaves without leaving you any instructions or timing for his return?"

The driver, whose name was Juan, seemed to consider that question. "It's not unheard of, but he will normally call later and give me instructions. Somewhat unusual...yes, maybe." He looked around, terrified of the men and guns. "I'm...I in trouble?"

Doris wanted her attention, and Margaret was pretty sure she knew the reason. "Yes, Juan, you are in trouble."

The man seemed to recoil at the knowledge, then sagged as if in resignation.

The director moved to the far side of the room and addressed the three soldiers guarding the man. "If he makes any sudden moves, shoot him anywhere that won't kill him immediately. Go ahead and pick different targets, concentrate on the most painful and most debilitating long-term." She watched as each man centered on a different part of the man's body.

Making sure she was not in a firing lane, she again approached the driver. "Let's try this again...Richard."

The man looked up, then straightened himself in the chair. He seemed to instantly transform into a larger more robust man; his demeanor, his expressions all became that of a very different individual. "Very good, Director. When did you know?" he asked in perfect English with no sign of any accent.

"I knew from the moment I walked into the room. The real question is, when were you on to us? Or do you just always spend hours waxing a perfectly clean car?"

He shrugged, the restraints limiting his movement. "My intel systems showed a team was being brought into the area. Small town, not that many likely targets."

"Why didn't you run?"

"I will, in time. I was curious as to who was after me, who would have gone to such lengths to track me down. Your people literally went to the ends of the earth, did they not?"

Margaret smiled, but the man's confidence was unnerving even to her. "And is your curiosity settled?"

"Not even close," Goldman answered. "You, Director Stansfield, are supposed to be dead. One more victim of Janus attacking Camp David. Oh...excuse me, a rogue terrorist cell. Wasn't that the official story on that little episode?"

Margaret thumbed her phone to the video captures of the Saraph, "Tell me about these."

Goldman accepted the phone and glanced at the image. "It is a Series-3, a small one by the looks of it."

"You helped create it?"

Richard thumbed through several other images, the Kalypso, the cave, the artwork. He paused on one she had placed there, knowing it would get his attention. She repeated the question.

"Not precisely, no. But I provided the impetus to get the Angel Project moving in the right direction." He handed the phone back. "But I assume you already knew that, or you wouldn't be here. Would you?"

Margaret waited until Doris confirmed what she was already certain of. "What I know is you look remarkably young for a 79-year-old man."

Everyone else in the room looked confused except for Stansfield and Goldman. "The ship's bell," she said.

He nodded, "Never be sentimental over things. Took me years to track that damn thing down. The ship was sold for scrap after it was decommissioned. Damn government never wanted any reminders of that fuck-up. I thought for a while I was going to have to buy the entire ship at salvage. Luckily, one of the last ship's officers had swiped it as a souvenir."

"You are Ishel Golette, The Lion, former major in the U.S. Army Intelligence, aren't you?" Margaret didn't bother waiting for a response. "You stole the research for Project Saraph from a lab in Tel Aviv in 1967. Ivan Thrall's father helped you escape as the *USS Liberty* was being attacked by Israeli forces."

Goldman just gave a tiny non-committal shrug. "Not one of my better operations. It got very messy. One should never fuck with the Israelis, especially when they are at war."

"Fill in some gaps for me, Ishel. You went in that week to get the intel and got caught leaving the labs. Was that what brought all the attention on the Navy ship?"

"No."

"Just no?" Margaret asked. "We know the lab personnel were killed; the lab destroyed; your partner was killed, yet you somehow managed to get away with the goods."

"That was the MIS official version. It was close on most counts but, as normal with the military, ignored a few basic facts. One that wouldn't fit the official narrative."

"Such as?"

Goldman answered, "Such as I had been undercover for eight months. I had finally secured a job working as a courier for the lab. Mostly routine stuff, but enough to know the U.S. Government was way off on what they thought the Israelis had."

"And what was that?" the director asked.

"Not that important, but they were desperate for any new weapon that might be useful against Vietnam, or even more, the Russians. I knew if Shafi's research went to America, it would be buried and forgotten. As soon as they realized it had no real military value, it would be lost to history... again."

"Shafi? That would be Doctor Shafi Rabin. The lead scientist and the one who'd recovered it in the Antarctic twenty-two years earlier. Wasn't she a bit old for you? And equipped with the wrong body parts?"

"What can I say, my taste was always a bit...eclectic? Shafi had been very young when she was assigned to Highjump, where she found the cave and the samples. She was an amazing woman, a brilliant mind."

"You leaked the theft to the Israelis; you compromised your own mission? Was that why tensions were so high that week?"

"Who knows? The Jewish state is surrounded by countries that want them gone. Tensions are always high."

"So, you and Shafi got away with the research."

"Sadly, no. She was killed. I was unaware there was a second operative until it was too late. He killed her just as she was giving me the last of the materials. His orders had been to leave no witnesses," Golette said.

"But he was killed during the raid?"

Golette nodded, "I did that myself on the boat. The fucking bastard."

"So, you eventually made it back to America without landing on anyone's radar and met back up with the elder Thrall to begin work on the Angel code," Margaret continued.

He nodded.

"I am curious, I assume somewhere in the massive genetic data, you discovered a way to halt aging. Why did Peter Thrall not use it as well? The fountain of youth is everybody's dream, isn't it?"

"He had a family—it would have raised too many questions eventually, and he'd already learned he had heart disease. Something the treatment would not have corrected. Also, I was creating aliases every few years and was very skilled at disappearing. To be honest, all the aging stuff was Shafi's findings. She'd made that much progress, but it took decades for the science to catch up to a point we could try it."

Margaret delivered the most important question, "Okay, Golette, we are going to move you to a secure location to continue this little discussion. We have some questions about your associates, but right now I need to know what else the Kalypso is up to. What is its purpose?"

He smiled, "It is simple, we are going to save the world."

81

CARIBBEAN

"Nomad, you have incoming calls from Doris and Director Stans..."

"Not fucking now, Dee! Can you not see? Fuck!" He searched in vain for some way out to survive the next few minutes. The massive Saraph just kept rising up toward them. "Tell 'em I'm away from my desk and to leave a message."

He selected Comm to Comm. "Alias, status update."

"Back in my own XOD, moving to the flank. That damn thing has 100 meter tentacles, Boss."

Cade nodded, he was pretty damn close to packing up his toys and going home. The creature swimming up from the depths wasn't just larger; it was different, seemingly more ancient and more dangerous. Kind of like comparing a crocodile to a T-Rex. He needed a minute to think. Grabbing the largest part of fractured carapace of the dead Saraph, he tucked his entire body into it. Bloody pieces of meat and skin or fat...or something, clung to the inside skeletal walls. It was all he could do not to vomit into his own helmet. "Alan, Riley, you guys still there? Any ideas?"

"We're working on it, Nomad. "

"Work faster." He was whispering into his comms, even though he instinctively knew the animal couldn't have heard him even if he shouted. If there was a time for stealth, though, it was now. Depth readout was, *Holy shit.* He had over two-and-a-half miles of water above his head. Despite the amazing suits, he could now feel some cold creeping through. *Nearly burn to death at the South Pole and then freeze to death in the goddamn Caribbean. Irony is a bitch, brother.* "Not helping, Gus."

Besides the slight chill from the depth, the pressure was impeding his movements. Not a lot, but even a little might be lethal with what he had to do next. "Riley, what's the big one doing?"

"Seems to be hunting. You are the closest by far, Cade, but it's ignoring you."

"Seriously? Ignoring me?"

"Shit!" Alias yelled. "Oh, my God, make it stop!"

"Nomad...Cade!" Alan yelled to get his attention. "It's using its neural blast; the suit's shielding isn't stopping it. It's way more powerful than the others."

Cade could now see pulsing blue light reflecting off the front edge of the carapace.

"Nomad, you have two urgent messages from..."

"Dee, stop, for fuck's sake. I am about to be eaten by an alien sea dragon!"

The Saraph doesn't see you as a threat. Cade almost asked who said that before realizing he did. "Ace, is that you?"

It is. You can maneuver this carcass close enough to attack, the analyst said. He then proceeded to tell Cade the necessary steps to take.

"Holy shit." He was out of his mind, in more ways than one. First, Cade moved the rest of WarHawk back. At this point, only a couple of them were still in the fight, but Cade intended they stay alive. He triggered his suit jets and the Saraph hard shell began to drift down faster and adjusted course to angle toward the approaching behemoth.

"Time to intercept is ten minutes. Would you like to take those calls now?" Dee said cheerily.

He spent precious seconds trying to figure out if he could strangle his own personal computerized assistant. Finally realizing he was outmatched by his AI and the approaching monster, he gave in. "Yes, Dee, go for Nomad."

"I know you have your hands full, Captain, but we have a situation," the director's voice cut through him like an internal river of ice water. "One of Thrall's associates has just revealed that Kalypso was built to survive the end of the world."

"I suppose that means they aren't just going to hand us the keys to the front door and go home then."

"Funny, Captain, and inappropriate. No, it's worse. Thrall has a technology on board. Something they call the Icarus device. It is likely based on technology learned from the Saraph. We have yet to get anything more specific out of the man, but the implications are that it will be capable of mass destruction.

"Thrall apparently wants to give the ultimate fuck-off to mankind. Also, by depopulating much of the planet, it will ease all the strain on natural resources. I presume leaving him and his army of Saraphs to guide mankind to a more peaceful and pollution-free tomorrow."

Jesus Christ, Cade thought as the glowing mountain of monster approached. *What next?*

"Captain, The Lion said the launch wasn't imminent but could be triggered if they felt threatened."

"Of course it can," he said, sarcasm dripping from each word. "Anything else?"

"One thing more," Margaret said quietly. "Once triggered, Icarus can't be stopped, not even by them."

Cade let that little turd of intel just hang there; commenting on it would serve no purpose. It was a no-win scenario. Even if they could somehow win out here, they would lose once they breeched the Kalypso.

"Cade."

It took him several seconds to place the voice. The Germanic accent had faded considerably.

"Mila?"

"Ja, I wanted to talk to you before you do what I know you must be doing."

He was confused and guarded but knew Doris must have really wanted them to talk. "Go ahead, I have a few minutes." *And maybe only a few minutes,* he thought grimly.

"I wanted," she paused, her voice cracking as she started again. "I wanted to say thank you. I have already expressed the same to Doris. I am not one prone to show of kindness, and I am not sure I ever been shown any, but what you both have done for me this last week is beyond any words I can offer."

"So, the treatments have helped?" Cade watched as a claw the size of a truck sailed past on a long tentacle arm with razor sharp, barbed suckers glowing along the flattened lower side.

"They have, but that is not why I wanted to talk to you. Doris is sending you my recollection of the inside of Kalypso. Maybe it will help. One other thing..."

"Yes, Mila, go ahead."

"I am sorry, but there are at least two more Schatten aboard as permanent security. They are the best we had."

Well, fuck, Cade thought, *the day just keeps getting better.* "Any weaknesses, habits, favorite weapons, anything that might help?"

"They are killers, Cade," Mila continued. "They are obsessive-compulsive killers. They have no weakness. Even in sparring, none of us ever bested them."

Of course. What other kind of guard would a crazy person have? "Mila, thank you. If you think of anything else, just let Doris know, she will get it to us. One last question. Are you going to be okay with yourself, now that you feel...now that you care?"

She was silent for several long seconds. "I hope so...I wasn't sure for a few days. The need to injure myself was overwhelming, but Doris and your Doctor Han and Turner have helped. I think I want to live—I just can't imagine why."

"Let us work on the why, Mila. Together, maybe we can find a purpose. I do need to go to work now." They disconnected. He forced the conversation deeper into his mind. Still struggling to separate the anger at who she had been to the woman she was now becoming. The Saraph was near enough, he could see eyes on thick stalks above its head. Cade, in his best impression of a hermit crab, drifted over the gigantic tentacles. Two of the eyes rotated, tracking the shell with him hidden deep inside. He dared not move. Then they circled back toward the others. “Here comes stupid!” Cade yelled as he jumped out of the shell and down toward center-mass of the massive Saraph.

82

Cade, buddy. This is completely fucking insane! That may have been Gus pleading, or it could have just been his own tiny voice of self-preservation. The Saraph passed directly underneath him, twenty meters below. No other targets had been detected, but Kalypso was ascending faster now. If Thrall's people were able to monitor the Saraph's activity, then they would soon know something was going on.

"Nomad, have you lost your mind?"

That was Deuce, he thought. His friend must have recovered, but he and most of WarHawk would be directly in the path of the last Saraph in seconds.

Fifteen Meters.

Cade reached behind his suit to the Jackknife's weapons locker. He hadn't carried a lancet just so he could carry the one object it did contain. It wasn't even a weapon; it was what they'd been planning to use to force entry into Kalypso. Thankfully, Alan had already proven this could work as a weapon. For that knowledge, he would be eternally grateful.

While Riley called it a Phase Shift Disruptor, all the guys would never refer to it as anything but the Magic Stick. This version was about four feet long and was more multi purpose than the first gen version. They could now set it so the opening would be permanent, and he could even direct the size and shape of the hole. He had Dee set it to activate on contact. This new one could even draw power directly from the suit's internal supply, reducing the time to recharge. Using it underwater as a weapon just presented one colossal problem. He had to hold it against the object then swim through the opening it created, holding it out in front.

Orienting himself upside down was simple enough. Down here, gravity was practically undetectable, and the sensation of up and down had pretty much lost all relevance.

Ten Meters.

Cade could feel the power rippling through the beast below. A tentacle whipped past, just missing him. The Saraph filled his visor entirely now. A growl erupted from somewhere deep inside as Cade knew that Brutus was ready to be freed from his restraints. "A few more seconds, big guy. Just let me get the thing activated." The brute living in his skull was not good with technology...tech to the barbarian had never advanced beyond clubs and spears, his preferred weapons in combat. Even those were usually a few steps above his typical weapons. Brutus tended to use whatever was close. A chair, a rock, sometimes his opponent's own appendages.

Five meters—the water itself seemed to vibrate near the beast. He held the rod out in front, took a firm grasp and...a meaty arm slapped him from the side as a snake-like vice encircled his leg. Tentacles suddenly seemed to approach from every direction. "Not one of your more brilliant plans, Ace," Cade said as he was slapped around inside the XOD.

Pressure warnings erupted under the increasing stresses on the suit. One tentacle now encircled his head, cutting off any live view, not that he really wanted to watch his own demise or anything.

"Shit, shit shit..."

His mind seemed to slow down. Every move of the ongoing battle between him and this alien creature unfolded in agonizing slowness. This was life, this was death. This was why they both existed. To battle, to die. Cade pulled his arms in, activating the disruptor, and instantly, a tentacle erupted and fell away only to immediately be replaced by another. He felt his body being flung rapidly from side to side. It was obvious the animal hadn't encountered prey with such a well-armored shell. Still, Cade knew, as good as it was, it wouldn't last forever.

"Hang in there, Nomad, WarHawk is coming."

"Kalypso is within visual range, Nomad," his Dee said cheerily. Cade decided he really didn't care for her British accent anymore.

He wanted to warn Deuce off, make them flee to safety, but he was losing control of the situation as well as his own mind. He opened his mouth to speak, and it came out as a growl. *Oh, shit*, was his final lucid thought while losing control of his own body.

Brutus swung wildly; the Magic Stick thankfully clipped into receptacles in the suit's gloves. It phased through claws and tentacles, but the animal simply overwhelmed the suit's functions. The limits of movement in the deep water, combined with the restraints of the tentacles, were causing cascading suit failures. The XOD was seconds away from going into safe mode. Through a gap between two massive, suckered arms, Cade watched helplessly as the glowing face of the Saraph loomed up. The needle-like teeth seemed to be dancing like tiny hooks awaiting to drag him down inside the mouth. *Damn, these things are ugly.*

Dee said, "Be ready, Nomad..."

Cade felt the monster twitch, Brutus freed an arm, and the onboard combat system triggered the Magic Stick to form an orb-like shield between it and the creature's mouth. The animal jerked again, and Cade heard Deuce yelling for Alias and Hammer to move toward the rear of the Saraph. Brutus flailed, severing more of the arms, then someone's lancet cut through the tentacle that was holding Cade's legs. Free to maneuver again, Cade urged Brutus to take the fight to the beast.

Maybe less 'mano a mano' and more 'mano a pulpo,' or would that be tentáculo? asked Gus.

Again, guys, not the time for this discussion, Cade thought.

Welcome, amigos, to the box seats section. Gus stated. *This is where we get to see what stupid shit we will be doing with our body today.*

The Saraph claw came slicing down at incredible speed. Cade knew he would lose an arm, but miraculously, the suit's wrist flexed upward, absorbing the blow and deflecting the claw into the disruptor's field. *Thank God for Magic Sticks,* he thought.

"Suit integrity is below seventy percent. The oxygen regeneration is compromised, thermal barrier is offline."

The creature's mouth looked to be the size of an apartment, and it loomed way too close. Cade could feel the cold instantly numbing his extremities. He had minutes, maybe even just seconds to live. He managed to signal the suit to fire all thrusters. *You want to go in there?* the Gus persona asked incredulously. *That happens to be where the monster wants you to go. You do see those teeth, right, Kemosabe?*

The suit's jets fired. At first, nothing happened. The animal still had his XOD too firmly grasped, but slowly, the grip from the remaining arms of the Saraph loosened. Not a lot, but just enough. Cade willed Brutus to lower the Magic Stick back to the front. His own internal beast ignored this and kept swinging it wildly until he was well inside the giant blue meat grinder of a mouth. Cade could feel the teeth grabbing at the suit's polysteel exoskeleton. The composite material was strong; but it was not invincible. More failure warnings and alerts began sounding; the light inside the helmet became a mélange of amber and red flashing icons. One of the hard suit panels on his thigh began to fail, and the crushing pressure shot intense pain through his body. It might be the Saraph chewing him up or just the enormous water pressure alone doing most of the damage. Either way, Cade felt the leg beginning to tear away from his body.

Riley's combat dive suit was good, fantastic even. He was the weak point in the system. Cade cried out in pain for help. He didn't even care where it came from. "Gus, Barbarian, Deuce...oh fuck, this hurts!" The pain was excruciating, and that was with the suit's systems ordering the MedPatch to deliver nerve blocking meds.

You probably voided the warranty on this thing, man. At the very least, you probably need to get this thing in for its regular maintenance soon.

The *voices* of any of his *other* personas would be better than Gus right *now.* Sarcasm and witty banter wouldn't extricate him from becoming a can of meat paste in the next few minutes. *Gus, we are being eaten by an alien monster, will you please shut up?*

You are being eaten, Cade—I don't exist.

The words stunned him almost as much as the situation he was in. Brutus, Gus, Ace...they were all just him. He had control, he just had to find it. His mind seemed about to break even as the suit was beginning to come apart. "Trigger another suit discharge," Cade commanded, and the suit gave off a distinctive snap. The encircling jaws of the beast recoiled briefly, and he managed to get Brutus, or maybe it was himself, to lower the glowing orb downward toward the gullet of the monster. The acceleration jets, which had not stopped pushing, now began to move him through a hole he was creating inside the Saraph. He could feel the animal recoiling and immediately try to expel him back the way he'd come, but now he was past the teeth. Now, he was the one with an edge. "Okay, big-guy, break shit." Brutus's growl returned with a vengeance.

83

KALYPSO

Kissa ran a finger along where the walls met the floor. As far as he could tell, there was no seam; it was like they formed the entire room out of one piece of whatever this material was. He'd spent days searching for any way to escape, anything he could think of to reach Thera. Twice now, he'd heard Sergeant Coffee, sounding like he was speaking to someone. The man was alive and very pissed off, which might be a good thing. He was less sure of the condition of Captain Nance. Kneeling, he felt the floor and then the wall. He felt his center of gravity somewhat off. The pull on one side growing more pronounced if his sense of orientation was right. Did that mean they were ascending or descending even deeper? Spatial awareness was how they described it back in his early dive training. Always know which way is up. Follow the bubbles. *What fucking bubbles?* he wondered.

His mental clock let him know it would be several hours before the guards returned with another meal tray. *Why are they keeping me alive? Just to torture Thera? Yeah, maybe...probably.* That question kept nagging at him. The previous day, several of the guards had taken him to what looked like a medical ward. The big man named Trondo was lying on one of the beds. In the battle with the monster, he'd seen the giant claw from the beast as it had pierced the man's abdomen. The doctors said the soldier had been in and out of consciousness, but Kissa got the feeling his condition wasn't good. The medical team looked like they had been trying hard to save the man, though...none of that had made any sense if they planned on killing them all anyway.

The medics had questioned him briefly on the man Nance and Coffee often called Apache. Once they realized Kissa could offer no real information on their patient, they'd moved away and left them alone for a moment. Now Kissa understood. They were doing it just so he could say goodbye. The wounds were mortal, and there was obviously nothing else they could do for him. While he hadn't known the soldier long, he was a friend, and he'd been one of the ones to come save him. Now he was dying...or maybe already dead. Trondo had apparently known the end was near, but it was not fear that showed in the man's eyes when he'd pulled Kissa close with a surprisingly strong grip. It was something else...he wasn't sure. Anger? The man had been unable to speak and in obvious pain, but his eyes had an almost pleading quality as he gripped Kissa's wrist with enough force to cause pain.

Kissa involuntarily held his wrist up, rubbing where the man had grasped him. A faint outline of bruising was all that remained. He rubbed at the marks, wondering if he was the last friendly face the man would ever see. Trondo's eyes had closed shortly after, not dead... but close to it, obviously.

Kissa's index finger found a tiny bump on his wrist. He scratched at it unconsciously. Thoughts swirled in his head; maybe he'd had a chance yesterday to get free. The guards were far enough away, and there were several things in the medical suite he could have used for a weapon, yet holding on to the dying man's hand was all he did. The little bump was aggravating him now, it felt like a scab, one of many on his body at the moment. It hurt a little as he tried to remove it from his skin, like a band-aid that had adhered itself too well.

He rotated his wrist, finally turning his full attention to the little inconvenience. The bump stood out in contrast to his own dark skin. It was a ruddy reddish brown and small. Getting a fingernail under one edge, he pulled it away from the skin, noticing a lot of filaments stretch between it and his arm. The realization of what it was hit him immediately. This was how the soldiers had talked to the Doris and the Dee. This was what Trondo had been doing, placing his comms unit on his arm. Surely there is more to it that just this, though. Finally, free from his skin, he held it up and looked at it from all sides. Despite the different color, it was all but invisible on the tip of his finger.

Kissa recalled how Micah and the soldiers often touched their jawline to use the comms, that must be where it went. Carefully, he reached up and placed the unit just under his ear. Instantly, he heard a tiny female voice calling.

"Apache? Are you awake? Your vitals look better. Help is on the way, just hang in there."

He was about to respond, to let them know the mistake, but footsteps sounded outside the door. Someone was keying in the code to his door. He stepped back as it slid open silently, then stared in shocked amazement.

"Thera?"

* * *

Kissa ignored the voice in his ear and instead, embraced the love of his life. She separated way too quickly.

"We have to go now," she said.

"I have friends here, we must help them, they helped me find you."

Thera shook her head as she pulled him out the door. "No time, Kissa, Henry didn't show me the codes for their cells."

Who the hell is Henry? Kissa wondered with more than a touch of jealousy. He followed his fiancée across the expansive storage area in the direction of the ramp leading up to the medical rooms and the labs. "You know where we're going?" he asked.

Thera shook her head again. "Just need to hide. Make it hard for them to find us, buy us some time."

"We should go down, down to the lowest level," Kissa said. "They have subs there, craft we can use to escape, but I must help my friends."

Thera stopped and turned to face him. "My sweet Kissa, I can't leave. I just needed to see you, to hold you."

He pulled her close and kissed her. The feeling sending shouts of joy through his entire body. "Why?"

"Henry showed me things. These people are mad...I think they are going to end it all."

"Is this Kissa? Are you free to move around the ship?" The volume on the little communication device startled him. He answered quietly that it was. Then, remembering what the others had done, he tapped it lightly and repeated himself.

"Excellent," Doris said. "The vitals didn't match. I take it you are with Thera. Can you talk?"

"No, not here, we are in an exposed location." He knew it would be a matter of minutes before they were spotted.

"Can you get to the docking level?"

"I believe that is on the lowest level. Possibly, but I am unarmed."

Doris told him what was needed. He couldn't believe Cade Rearden was coming down here to get them. He looked at Thera. Words were unnecessary. It would be better for him to go alone; he was a soldier, and they would notice her absence from the lab in another few minutes. He pulled her close. "Thank you, my love, I will find you."

She nodded; she wasn't sure who he had been talking to but understood it meant help. It meant stopping the craziness behind this ship, the Saraphs, everything. Her heart ached as she turned away from Kissa and moved quickly back up the ramp toward the labs. *Good luck*, she thought. *The monsters in here are just as bad as the ones outside... maybe worse.*

84

Kissa pulled on the heavy door. This had to be the chamber. Twice, he had to evade guards patrolling the corridor by ducking into supply closets and once into a darkened room, where he could hear people snoring. He now descended the steps, noticing a familiar pressure change and increased humidity in the air. In front of him, a line of five of the underwater runabouts sat in cradles just above the floor. This had been where they brought him in. He saw a few workers at the far end, but they seemed to be concentrating on some other task. The entire ship seemed too large for the number of people aboard, something was off about the scale or the numbers. Tapping his cheek, "I'm in the docking bay," he whispered.

"Good, Kissa, you are doing great. Cade is in severe distress just outside the hull. Can you locate the controls to whatever they use to launch and receive the small craft?"

Hearing his friend was in danger sent his adrenaline spiking. Glancing around the room, he saw what might be the launch control center. There were built-in workstations in front of each of the small ships. "Yeah, got it." He crouched low to stay hidden and moved to the closest one. "Won't they have me on video by now, Doris? I'm sure they have this entire place under surveillance." He began flipping through screens on the display to find what he needed.

"I imagine that is a certainty. I project you have less than a minute."

"Oh, good, no pressure." Kissa found the doors to the moon pool controls. The pool would open up to the water below. He knew normally that only worked when the air pressure in the room matched the water pressure it was holding at bay. Like flipping an empty glass upside down in a basin of water. The liquid would only rise so far, trapping the air in the top of the glass and increasing the pressure of the air when it did so. The display flashed red when he hit the button. 'Function unavailable at this depth.' He read the words with a sense of failure. "We are too far down, Doris—it won't work here."

She seemed to almost expect this and had an alternate suggestion, one he understood all too well. On deep water habitats there were two ways you could send people and equipment out. One was a moon pool, useful for larger transfers, but it had some downsides such as only being feasible down to a certain depth. You could use them much lower, but the air pressure required to keep the water out would likely kill anyone working within the launch bay, unless they had a pressure suit on. The other was a mechanical lock-out chamber, something submariners often referred to as the escape trunk. It was a series of doors built into the hull that could be opened, one at a time, on either side. The downside to that was they required time to equalize the pressure, to pump the water out and the air in. Also, they were typically small, only larger enough for one or two divers.

Kissa searched the nearby hull and floor for anything like that. As high tech as this craft was, it had to have a maintenance port. *Probably a dedicated room,* he thought. They would need it to store the dive gear, air tanks, and such. He saw another metal hatch at the far end of the room, just beyond where the two mechanics were working, still apparently focused on their tasks.

"You are nearly out of time, Kissa. I can hear alarms going off on Nance and Coffee's comms. I think they have discovered your absence."

"Doing the best I can," he whispered as he crouch-walked behind the subs, then rose slightly and raced down the far wall. He was within twenty meters of the door when a man stepped into his path wielding a large metal pipe. *Well, fuck.*

* * *

"Come on, Nomad, we got you."

Deuce's voice was far away and had a dreamy quality that made Cade want to go back to sleep. He knew someone was under his arm and pushing, but he had no sensation of where he was or what had just happened.

"Almost got it," Greg said as he tightened a spare oxygen line from his own suit to Cade's. Air bubbles escaped the captain's XOD dive suit in multiple places. No way he would survive the nearly two-mile trip to the surface. Greg had come, to, shortly after the last Saraph ceased its neural attack. Now, what remained of that beast seemed to be smeared over every inch of the captain's XOD. Moving one more bit of debris out of the way, Greg finally got the connector into the port on the damaged suit and slid the coupling tight. His own suit automatically increased O^2 production to compensate.

Cade distantly felt the rush of cool air; it was nice. This must be the feeling people describe when they sleep in on Saturday morning. No work, no pressure, and the bed feels too good to bother with getting up to go fight dragons.

"Nomad, sitrep."

"Not now, Margaret, I'm trying to sleep...*or die*. Not sure which." His words were slurring badly. He knew they were, he just couldn't correct it. Didn't care.

"Deuce, you are in control," she continued. "Doris is working on an entry point to the Kalypso. Follow the green line when it shows."

Charlie had tons of questions. Are there friendlies inside? Is this a trap we're walking into, are there more of those effing monsters? Instead, he acknowledged the order and began moving the team in that direction as soon as the line appeared in his visor. The original plan had been to use the Magic Stick somewhere along the lower hole to make an entry point. That would likely flood the vessel, but they hoped they could seal off the hole in time to prevent the station from sinking. Now, the disruptor stick was dead. It was still gripped tightly in Cades' hand, but it had died along with the massive Saraph. He still couldn't believe Cade had emerged at the back-end of the wrecked animal, still mostly in one piece.

The WarHawk team was down to five if you wanted to count Nomad, along with Deuce, Greg, Alias, and Yeager, another of the new guys. 'Hammer' had taken a vicious strike from the last Saraph, and his suit was taking him back to the surface for evac. Like Greg and Deuce, Yeager had been one of the first to succumb to the mental blast but seemed okay now. Deuce took point as they maneuvered the XODs along the oddly colored hull, which seemed to nose up more sharply and increase its ascent.

"Greg, how's he doing?" Deuce asked.

Greg checked the readout before responding. "No longer critical, oxygen is helping. Not sure if he has a pressure leak, the sensors are offline. No major blood loss or trauma that I can see."

Charlie knew the medical team back at The Cove were monitoring his friend's condition even more closely than Greg could. No one else could have gotten them through those damn monsters. Nomad was the toughest soldier he'd ever seen. He just hoped he still had some fight left in him. A shape materialized off in the distance. With the soft ambient light from beneath the ship the only illumination out here in the blackness of the ocean, it took him a moment to see what it was. The giant bull shark swam within a few feet of them. It was large, the biggest Charlie had ever seen. Yesterday it would have likely terrified him, today it was almost calming to see something that normal.

"Just a shark," Yeager stated flatly as the five-man team moved quickly past the enormous animal.

Charlie checked the depth just as they reached a recessed opening where the green path in his visor ended. He had his depth readout in meters as opposed to feet. They were at 2,755 meters and decreasing. "Team Raptor, come in."

Alexandria's voice came back at once. "This is Raptor-1. Go ahead, Deuce."

"You guys need to be ready, adjust positions along this track. The Kalypso should be within your range in about fifteen minutes. I'm not sure our comms will work inside the hull, so watch for any openings and take advantage of it. You know the drill."

"Roger that, sir, and good hunting."

The airlock was massive, much larger than any he'd ever seen on any vessel. All five men could easily fit inside, even with their oversized dive suits. Once inside, they pulled the outer hatch and cranked the wheel to seal it to the outside. A light above the hatch switched from red to green. Now they were essentially inside a giant coffin, unless someone inside pumped in air. The inner door could not be opened. Not until the pressure equalized.

Deuce called The Cove and let them know they were in the lockout chamber. He got a garbled response but hoped that meant okay. The space was large, but they still had no room to maneuver. Suddenly, the suits' audio picked up a whistling sound steadily increasing in volume. In thirty seconds, the water level had dropped, exposing their heads. In another minute, the chamber was effectively empty. Readouts showed normal oxygen levels, normal pressure. A knocking came from the interior hatch just before the light over it changed from red to green. The door slowly slid upward, and Deuce could see a pair of legs and the barrel of a rifle being held in a low-ready position. He mentally prepared for another fight.

"Come, come out, my friends. Welcome to my lovely home."

Charlie's eyes never left the weapon as he stepped out, all ready to trigger countermeasures until he saw the smiling face of his old friend. He unlatched his dive helmet and let it drop. "Kissa, damn good to see you!"

85

"Approaching comms depth, sir. Releasing buoy in three, two, one. Comms buoy away."

Thrall hated the annoyance of having a billion dollar underwater flying saucer but being forced to use a decades old submariner's technology to make and receive calls on the surface. In truth, the Kalypso's design had been optimized for its real mission, years submerged in the relative safety of the deep ocean. Not for the transition period that preceded that. "Is the doctor back in her lab yet?"

"Yes, sir, security found her near the restrooms. She said she'd been sick," a man nearby said.

"Cancel that damn alarm then. And double the guards on the lovely doctor."

"Anything out of Goldman?" Pax demanded.

Thrall eyed the mean little Asian with contempt. "Nothing so far, but we just reached depth."

Pax Ruan walked over and moved the security chief out of the way. "I heard the alarms." He began scanning through video feeds as the man told him the biologist had disappeared for a few minutes. Ruan was a naturally suspicious person. Some would classify it as rampant paranoia. He would not disagree. The truth was, he distrusted everyone, that was how he'd managed to stay alive so long.

He pressed 'Play' on an earlier recording of Doctor Otera in the lab. She was interacting with the Series-4 Saraph. Interacting was not the right word. Something about the scene seemed...off. She was not examining it, not precisely. The exchange lasted several minutes, then she suddenly turned and exited the lab. Had she gotten sick? Perhaps the SS4 had developed a neural weapon like the previous generations. That could trigger nausea and seizures and even heart failure sometimes. He found a section of video and played it again. It almost looked like she was talking with the creature. Pax unmuted the sound and listened in. Thera asked the creature, "What are you thinking?" Moments later, she asked Astra for the ship's current depth and position, then abruptly turned and left the lab.

Ruan instructed the ship's AI to pull related video feeds tracking Thera from the lab until her return and add location markers to each. The request was completed within seconds, and the newly curated video appeared as a new option on his screen. Pax watched the first 85 seconds of it before turning to the security chief. His face a mask of rage. He stabbed a hand down, restarting the alarm. "You failed." Whipping out a wicked-looking dagger, he sliced open the security chief's abdomen in one vicious motion.

"What the fuck, Pax?" Thrall yelled from his seat nearby.

"We have a prisoner loose on the ship. Thera let her boyfriend out. Alert security teams to deck six and lock that bitch in the lab. I'll deal with her myself." Ruan removed the sidearm and holster from the dead security chief and headed for the door. Thrall just nodded as he quietly called Ruslana to join him, then activated his personal security.

* * *

Thera was back in her lab when the alarms re-started. Her legs weakened, and the shakes started. She knew what they were for. Someone had discovered Kissa's absence, and it would likely only be a matter of minutes before they tracked his disappearance back to her. With the certainty of a condemned prisoner, she moved back to the holding tank where Henry looked up at her with the same unemotional expression as always.

"I think our time together is coming to an end, Henry," she whispered quietly. Her eyes began to fill with tears. At least she'd gotten to feel Kissa's arms around her one last time. Henry had managed to give him a chance to survive at least. She started to speak her next thought, then just decided to think it instead. If Henry could project pure thought, it stood to reason he could receive just as easily. She turned her head up toward the ceiling and thought again of the SS3 Saraphs and the divers. Then, focusing back on the center two of Henry's eyes, she framed the question in her mind.

Again, Henry's goblin-looking head tilted much as a dog's might. No response came to her question. She worried for Kissa, wondered who he'd been talking to and how, but trusted he had a plan. This might be her final moments with the creature. Could she protect him, should she? "Henry what do you know? What are your secrets?"

"Yes, Doctor Otera, those are the correct questions. You should have focused on that instead of a pointless attempt to free your boyfriend."

The blood drained from her face as the brutal little Asian man strode confidently up behind her and peered into the holding cell. The man knew, and she was dead. Had they captured Kissa so soon, though? Was he injured?

"We are still a mile below the ocean surface, Thera. Where did you think he could go?"

"Is he okay? Did you hurt him?" she asked, her face a mask of rage.

"By now, I am afraid to say, he is dead. A victim of your own stupidity." His hand lashed out before she could react, delivering a vicious slap across her face.

Blood flew from her nose and mouth as she stumbled awkwardly back and then down to one knee. The shakes had stopped, as had the fear coursing through her veins. "You like hurting women, you tiny fucking asshole." She spat a large gob of bloody mucus onto the gray floor. "Is that how you get your thrills?" Despite every instinct in her telling her to stay down, she pulled that one knee in and rose, blood still dripping from her face.

Pax just smiled. Not an expression of humor, more one of a predator that has trapped its evening meal. "What gives me a thrill is bitches that know their place." He balled a fist as if to punch her, but spun instead, delivering a striking leg kick to her abdomen. She landed against the side of Henry's cell, doubled over in pain, unable to catch her breath.

"You are only alive for one reason, to extract the data from the creatures. Since you seem unable to do that, you really have no purpose." Slowly, he slid a deadly-looking bloody dagger from somewhere inside his jacket.

Thera tried to look away, but all she could see was the blade as it approached closer and closer. The light danced off its mirror finish and undoubtedly razor-sharp edge. While her attention was squarely on Pax, her hands were behind her, fumbling with a small object mounted to the low wall.

Ruan continued, "Ideally, your boyfriend would be here to see this. I would enjoy making him watch as I carve you up in tiny chunks and feed you to the beast. What did I hear you call him? Henry?" He laughed, then moved closer. "So, now he's a pet, is that right? It's a lab experiment, woman. We never said make friends with it. 'It' lives only to deliver information."

He whipped an arm out, and instantly Thera felt a moment of hot stinging pain across one breast and her upper chest. Glancing down at the neatly parting fabric of her top, blood was welling out along a ten-inch gouge. She coughed out a shriek of pain.

A sound cut through the lab, momentarily drowning out the trilling of the alarms. Ruan raised the small radio receiver up to his face. Apparently, his security teams had found something. Thera, though, was no longer focused on Pax Ruan at all. She was entranced in a mental conversation with Henry. As her fingers finally unclipped the latch, a flood of information sprang into her own mind. Knowledge and concepts she could have never imagined. At once, she knew

Henry's place in the universe and in his own species' timeline. *They had it so wrong.* So very, very wrong.

Thera collapsed back to the floor, her mind on fire with all the possibilities of an entire species unleashed inside her own head. The door behind her clicked open, and one of Henry's stubby legs stepped out, the blade-like claws clicking on the hard floor.

Pax had been focused on his prisoner's suffering. The excitement of her pain giving him pleasure in places that he wouldn't permit himself to enjoy just now. As the security radio went silent, he returned to the job at hand...only something had changed. The woman seemed completely out of it. Her expression was no longer of pain but of...joy. None of that resolved itself with his expectations. There was something else, too, another shape behind the doctor, something that also didn't fit his mental image of what he should be seeing.

Pax stood frozen as Henry's full body emerged from the holding cell. It seemed to have doubled in just the last few days. The large amphibian-looking body was topped by the strangest head of any of the Saraphs. Now he saw the gaping jaw was filled with long teeth in concentric rows. While it had tentacles like the others, these were very different—stunted and thick, almost like legs and arms. Some still ended in the hooked claw, but even that was smaller. *Why is it not going after the doctor?* he wondered.

Henry stepped delicately around Thera, who lay crumpled by the now open door. It moved forward in a fluid motion that was both graceful and purposeful. The little man's eyes never wavered. He moved cautiously several steps toward the door. He was already reaching for the handgun. The Saraph seemed to know what Pax had planned even before the man did. As Pax moved toward the door, one tentacle shot out, extending itself many times its normal length and grabbing Ruan's ankle, pulling him down, and crushing the bone inside at the same time.

The intense pain blinded Pax momentarily. When he could focus again, he found he was being pulled toward that gaping jaw. His outrage that this was happening to him didn't diminish his defenses. Quickly, he removed the subcompact Glock and aimed at the nerve bundle behind the SS4's neck. In all the versions of Saraphs, it was what they believed was the one natural vulnerability. The creature didn't react, and Pax's finger began to squeeze. Instead of firing a killing shot, though, he suddenly felt a foot hit him in the side of the face, loosening several teeth. Another kick freed the pistol and sent it flying.

"You evil, fucking prick!" Thera yelled as she fought to fully regain her senses. She kicked out again, then backed away as Henry flashed something else into her mind. She nodded and moved toward the door. Before leaving, she looked back to see a leg of the Asian man sliding down that long neck full of teeth. Then his waist, followed by the squat, muscular abdomen. As Henry clamped down on the man's midsection, an eruption of blood fountained out of the doomed man's mouth and nose, Pax's gurgling screams of agony drowned out by the still trilling alarm.

86

Cade's first sensation upon having his helmet removed was of how bad he smelled. Nearly six hours in the confines of the Jacknife XOD dive suit made for an interesting melange of odors, of which precisely none were pleasant. The second reaction was something akin to 'Oh, my fucking shit.' Although, translations amongst his inner personalities varied slightly. The pain in his legs was excruciating. One area felt both hot, cold, and numb in varying degrees.

"Hang on, Boss," Deuce said as he pried the right leg's exoskeleton from Cade.

Cade nodded as his eyes focused enough to see his friend working on him with some electric cutting tool. He dreaded looking down, as he fully expected the Saraph had separated the left leg from his body. What he was feeling now was probably just a ghost pain. What did amputees call it? 'Phantom limb pain'...*Shit*, his leg was probably still trapped in the remnants of the gut of that beast.

"These damn suits were not designed to come apart except in one way," Greg said, triggering Rearden's release servos over and over. "That dragon thing crushed yours to the point it won't separate."

"Kissa, we're going to need something heavier," Deuce yelled over his shoulder.

"Kissa is okay? How did we make it inside?" Cade asked.

"Later, Cap, we're behind enemy lines here. We have to get you functional and then move our asses. We have a perimeter set up, but it's thin."

"Okay," Cade nodded. Finally, drawing up the required courage, he looked down at the left leg. He wasn't sure if what he saw was a relief or an even worse fear. Something was there, perhaps it was a leg, but the suit's external shell was misshapen in ways that seemed impossible for anything beneath to still be functional. The massive Saraph had done its best to rip the suit and him apart, but it looked like the suit had somehow survived the onslaught...mostly.

Deuce threw the remains of the other side of the suit's plating away and began cutting away the left leg's misshapen front armor. "Damn polysteel is not designed to be cut through with traditional tools."

Every time Charlie pulled on the casing, a stabbing pain shot through Cade. "Hang on, stop. I think it is crushing my leg, or maybe a piece is stabbing through it."

"Tough shit, Cowboy, ain't got time to be polite." Deuce continued to work away at freeing the leg.

"Nomad, I'm administering a pain blocker now," Riley said over his comms. "It will be short acting, as I know you will have to move soon. If you need more, just let me know."

Gritting his teeth, all he could do was nod. Since the girl was thousands of miles away, the gesture was wasted, but still, he was deeply grateful. As Charlie pulled away one part of a pressure joint, blood rushed back into his thigh causing his pain to skyrocket. Just as suddenly, a wave of numbing disconnects settled him back down, like a pounding toothache suddenly being deadened by the dentist. Charlie made quick work of the rest of the removal. Greg then ran his SmartCom over both legs.

"Scans show no breaks, but that may not be the wonderful news. You still probably have torn ligaments and ruptured muscles as well as several intense pressure injuries, Nomad."

"Your suits saved us, kid," he said, finally finding his voice. "Can you give me something to get me moving again?"

"I can, but the pain will be back, too."

He felt the sting from the med patch and knew it had released its cocktail of adrenaline, or whatever endorphin mix, back into his system. "What's our depth?"

"You are passing 1,250 meters and beginning to level off," Dee stated.

"Cutter, are you there?"

"Yes, sir," Alex's voice came back at once.

"Come on down. Doris will lay in a path. It's still going to be deep for you guys, so don't linger. Suit jets to max. The coast should be clear, and we need your help." Cade signed off; he was in no shape to be the lone hero today.

A man has got to know his limitations, Gus said in his best Clint Eastwood interpretation.

Fuck you, Cade thought. *You don't exist, remember?*

That's hurtful to us all, and we only said that because you were throwing our body down the throat of an alien sea monster.

Cade wanted to challenge the "our body" statement, but Kissa was desperately trying to get their attention, pointing at several hostiles entering the workspace from doors at both ends.

Deuce touched his cheek. "Kissa, use the comms so we can hear you."

"Oh, yes, sir, Mister Deuce. Just wanted you all to know we are about to have our asses handed to us," he whispered in the sing-song accented English, before adding, "Was that better?"

Cade had to stop himself from laughing as the man turned and smiled, giving a big okay sign with his finger and thumb. "Damn, I've missed that guy more than I knew."

"Yeah, me too," Charlie said. "Now let's go stop him from getting dead. You mobile yet, old man?"

"I will shoot you, Deuce," Cade growled.

Charlie offered a smile and swung back toward the enemy. He had command now, just as he'd been trained. His C.O. was injured. It was his time to step up. Cade liked that he never had to tell Charlie what the right thing to do was. McTee was becoming that way, too, before...

well maybe, in time he would…the thought got cut off as gunfire began to erupt inside the launch bay.

"Greg, you and Yeager stay on the lockout chamber and let Raptor on board." Greg looked nervous but nodded. "Shoot anyone that looks like them," Charlie said, pointing his rifle barrel at the guys streaming in. "WarHawks, move on me."

Cade's awkward stumbling walk turned into a bit of a run with the slight power assist from the Rapide Battlesuit underlayer he still wore. At least twenty of Thrall's men lined an upper mezzanine overlooking the docking bay. They had the numbers and the high ground. That should have been enough, but Charlie obviously felt the advantage was all on his side. He synced all the teams' Dees to target collectively, and everyone's weapons switched to the KillPoint autofire mode as they moved into less exposed positions. "WarHawks, engage!" he shouted.

Like the others, Cade moved his rifle up to fire while he crouched concealed behind a workbench. He felt the small gyros in the weapon maneuvering and switched his tactical glasses to show targeting. His system had already picked out a primary and two alternatives that were kneeling next to the first. The weapon bucked slightly as it spat out its lethal rounds. All three men soon lay dead or dying. The targeting scope moved and fired, moved and fired. Within several seconds, it was over. Deuce had been right; the advantage had been all theirs. For some reason, he didn't much expect it to stay that way.

"Let's go get our people!" Deuce yelled, Kissa racing ahead to be the first one out the door.

87

Everyone on the team knew the first objective. Correction, the first objective was to survive. Second, was to find an access point for a clever device Jimmy and Doris had come up with. Kissa directed them to a moon pool control station. Charlie removed the small object and inserted it into the USB slot. The new adapter seemed to shimmer, then melt like putty around the port. In seconds, it was a small rectangular patch the same color and texture as the surrounding material with a fully functional USB port right where the other one had been. Cade didn't know the specifics, but he was aware it had multiple quantum comms processors built in. Depending on the operating system's sophistication, and if this workstation was fully networked or not, it provided Doris a way to remotely integrate into the ship's systems.

The light on their HUD went green, signaling the interface was active. Charlie gave hand signals they all understood. Almost as a single predatory unit, they moved up the ramp to the next level, stepping over the dead security men lying in still-increasing pools of blood. "Nomad, you have rear guard."

Cade touched below his cheek to activate his comms. "Doris, you in the system yet? Any idea how large a security force they have?"

"Negative, I am running up against a formidable level of security from the onboard computer. It will take me approximately seven minutes to bypass all the safeguards. Judging by the different voices we have heard monitoring the prisoner's CommDots, and how quickly the first team responded, my estimates are a force of between 82 and 94."

Great, thought Cade and again he felt like this place was made to house a lot more people. Perhaps they had just found it before they were ready to go.

"Currently, I only have command level access to the docking bay but will be expanding my reach soon."

A thought occurred to Cade. "Greg, move to moon pool. Doris, open that as soon as we are at depth to receive Team Raptor." That could speed up the battle dynamics in a big way. They both acknowledged.

"Jesus," Charlie said from up ahead. "Nomad, you seeing this?"

Cade wasn't sure what his XO was talking about but swung his attention from covering their six to stare at something as out of place as could be imagined. "So, that's why you couldn't find it."

"Well, we never had a precise location, but yeah, wouldn't have guessed here." Both men stared in awe at the tapered object with the flattened end section. Bits of white paint still clung to the charred surface and a faint outline of the USAF insignia along one section. "It's the space probe from Snowbird?" Charlie asked astonishingly.

"I believe so. Wonder why Thrall needed it?" The probe was in a room that appeared to be specifically designed for it. It hung in a cradle about six feet above the floor. The sample container doors were open. Deuce ducked into the room while Cade stood watch. Charlie was back in seconds.

"Empty," he said. "Whatever they got, it's gone now."

"WarHawk, Team Raptor is coming aboard," Stansfield's voice said.

"Cutter, you and Greg try to locate engineering. We need to keep this ship from diving back down again. If it does, we will have no good way of getting off. Oh, and try to minimize casualties except for security. Kissa feels like many of the staff may be here against their will." A tired, but somewhat relieved, voice from Alexandria acknowledged.

Technically, he was over-stepping Charlie's current command role, but he had more perspective of the larger mission than his friend. Plus, Charlie would likely prefer his friend handled the non-combat tasks.

"Kissa, where is Nance and the rest of her team being held?"

Kissa motioned for them to follow. "Not far, Nomad."

The team was confined in cells along one side of a storage room. From floor to ceiling, pallets of fresh food sat alongside more long-term food supplies. Along another wall, were rows of walk-in freezers. Cade had been on a Navy aircraft carrier once. The provisioning lockers on the Navy ship looked very much like this. They'd designed those to feed 5,000 men for a couple of months at a time. What he saw here could feed a few hundred people for much longer. Doris seemed to think they were planning to be onboard for years. *This vessel is designed for long duration, so...not more people, more time...why?*

"Contact," Deuce said as he and Kissa both aimed and fired nearly as one.

"Nice shooting, Warlock," Cade said, using Kissa's old combat name.

"Hard to miss with these, Boss." He held up the H&K style assault rifle and smiled.

"Four guards down. How many more?" Charlie asked.

"Not sure, Deuce. I was only out of my cell a couple of times, and it was never the same number." He raised a finger and pointed across at the cells. "Two on the left are your people. Apache is up a level in medical, if he is still with us."

Cade didn't want to think about Trondo being gone. That would be two of the team killed before the battle had even gotten started.

Charlie was crouched low, scanning for the enemy. "Warlock, stay with Nomad. We have Battlesuits, so Yeager, me, and Alias will go get Nance and Coffee."

Again, Cade wanted to object but knew it was the right call. Operating at this level meant you needed to be at your best or have somebody else take over. The Talon Teams were all in peak conditioning and had training that surpassed any other agency in the world. He watched as the two men slipped quietly through the maze of supplies toward the cells. He felt a tap from Kissa and looked where he was pointing. Several security men were entering the warehouse and fanning out, weapons searching for targets. Cade crouched low, an action that caused pain to arc up through his body. He motioned Kissa to go right, and he moved left. He heard, then saw more security entering the room. *Damn, Thrall has plenty of people, that's for sure.*

"Warlock in position," Cade heard Kissa whisper over the comms. He was not even close to having firing lines on all the ones on his side, but shooting opportunities rarely were ideal in combat.

"Engage." He heard Kissa's weapon bark several times. Rolling out nearly flat on the floor, he began picking targets and firing. "Two down." He fired again. "One wounded, headed toward you guys, Deuce."

Kissa confirmed all kills on his side. The Honduran was settling a score, and Cade had no interest in stopping him at this point.

"Warlock, watch the door; I'm going after the one I winged."

Cade received two mic clicks in response. Moving laterally through the aisles, he began to climb higher to get a better vantage point, a feat made more challenging with his injured leg. He saw Deuce and Alias at the door panels attempting to use the keypads. Yeager was at the other. "Blow 'em, Deuce!"

He saw the man's head bob up and down as he reached in his pack and removed one of The Cove's unique blaster patches. The thing looked like a square piece of chewing gum. All Charlie had to do was peel off the safety strip, fold it in half and stick it on the surface he want to go bye-bye. "Make sure you stick the black side down this time, Deuce."

Charlie flipped him the bird. "That was one freaking time in training, Nomad."

"Nance and Coffee, away from the door!" Charlie yelled. If they still had active comms, they would have been monitoring it anyway, but no one had heard any calls from them in a while. The shaped charge would not extend far into the room, but if either were standing by the door, it might not be so good.

The muffled thud was the only thing that indicated the blaster had gone off. Then, Cade saw the rifle barrel protruding from the far side of a large container. The missing security man was taking aim directly at Deuce. Cade engaged KillPoint, which was less effective when the target was not visible. In this case, all he could see was the enemy's weapon. He pulled the trigger, and the gun fired multiple times and obviously had selected multiple ammo types. The first two hit the gun barrel just as it fired, then explosive rounds tore into the container, ripping it to shreds and sending a shower of bloody red mist in the opposite direction.

Cade saw Charlie slump against the far wall just as the cell door fell away from its tracks. "Shit...Deuce!" He was off the stack of containers and running for his friend before he fully realized what had happened.

88

Cade slid to a stop just as a Captain Nance stepped from the room and knelt to check on Charlie. She was disheveled and sported a few fading cuts and bruises, but otherwise appeared to be in good shape. "He's okay, Nomad, the Battlesuit did the job. Think it just punched the air out of his lungs."

"Good to see you."

Nance stood and hugged each of them then; her eyes were rimmed in red. "Likewise, sir. I was beginning to get a little concerned."

"Nomad, Raptor is pinned down in the docking bay. Astra has activated the system locks on all watertight hatches," Doris said.

"Cutter, ya'll facing any hostiles?"

Alex's voice answered promptly, "We were, Nomad, but not any longer. I guess you heard we can't get out of here just yet."

"Working on it, stay alert. See if you can get any of those runabouts operational, we may need a way off this tub in a hurry."

She acknowledged and signed off. "Warlock, watch the door. Alias, fall back to assist." Cade turned his attention to Charlie, who was red-faced and beginning to gasp, but gave a thumbs up and nodded.

"Let's get Coffee out." He removed a blaster patch and placed it about the same place Charlie had on the next door over. He filled Nance in as best he could. She assured him several times she was combat ready. He tossed her an assault rifle from one of the downed security men and moved her back to blow the charge. In several seconds, they were pushing the remains of the surprisingly lightweight door out and checking out Master Sergeant Willy Coffee, who appeared to still be unconscious. The massive soldier was lying on a built-in platform with a thick cushion, and other than the fact that he wouldn't wake up, he appeared uninjured.

"It was the neural pulse, Nomad. Coffee took it more directly that the rest of us," Nance told him.

Cade thought he understood. Like the ones they had faced on the way down, the effect was not universal. "I think he's safer here for the moment, plus, I'm not sure we can carry the big guy. We need to get control of this beast. Nance, Kissa said Apache is up in medical, get the location and take Alias with you. Trondo apparently wasn't doing too good."

The expression on Kristin Nance's face was all too familiar to him. No commander is ever ready to lose someone. It's a part of the job, though, one that never really gets any easier. She nodded grimly and moved away.

Deuce was once again standing at the door to Coffee's cell. "He gonna be okay?"

Cade nodded, "Pulse is strong, breathing's good. Hopefully, he'll sleep it off like Micah did."

"Where next, Boss, labs?"

Cade nodded. "We need to pay a visit to see Kissa's girlfriend." That was technically the only other location they had any information on so far. Doris had to get control of the station's system soon, but until then, they were blind.

"Yeah, let's go. You know Kissa won't be stopped until he knows she's safe." Kissa finished up with Nance and rejoined them. Deuce began moving out—Cade again had to adjust his suit to compensate, as the pain in his leg and thigh kept slowing him down. Kissa was all but running ahead.

Deuce dropped one guard coming at him from a side corridor. "Damn, this place is big."

Cade agreed, too many angles to cover, too many closed doors with rooms of God knows what. Thankfully, they had left the sea monsters outside. Suddenly, Deuce disappeared beneath a coiled tentacle shooting out from a side door. This must be the labs, *lovely*. Guess they knew where the monsters had all originated now. Cade stepped confidently into the room and raised the rifle to center mass on the ugly fucking thing.

"Nomad, no!"

The command caused him to drop his aim, but he was completely unsure who gave it. Dee, Deuce, Riley...shit, Ace? Charlie was struggling in the mass of tentacles, the creature had blood all over its head and forelimb, tentacle things. "Who?" Then the creature turned toward him and he no longer cared.

Images flooded his mind, a young woman and an Asian man fighting. Kissa being released by the same woman. That had to be Thera, he knew instinctively it was. The animal, this version of Saraph, was communicating with him. "Deuce, stop fighting!"

Cade lowered the gun. "Can you release my friend? He won't try to hurt you."

Images came at him again, and he noticed a familiar faint blue glow emanating from beneath the animal. Scenes of him in the dark water fighting against the other Saraphs, killing them. *Was that his family?* Cade wondered.

He held up his hands, "Look, we are just here to get our friends. Let the ugly fella go, and we'll be gone."

Slowly, Henry lowered Deuce's legs back to the floor, his tentacled front arms uncoiling like a snake releasing its prey as they did so. Charlie stumbled back, still disoriented, he still held the weapon at the low ready, but had no idea why he hadn't been able to fire.

A woman came running down the corridor; Kissa bolted across to meet her. Cade turned to see, then smiled. "You are Thera," he said, a somewhat out of place look on his face. "I think we met one of your friends."

"Hi, and yes, thanks for not hurting Henry."

"Henry tried to eat me, dear," Charlie said, rising slowly back to his feet, still unsettled by the attack.

"No," Thera said. "You would not still be here if that was his intention. He probably just wanted to make sure you didn't do anything foolish."

Cade reached back and fist-bumped Kissa. "Where did you find her? She's a keeper, even if she does make monsters." He looked at the Saraph, "Uh...no offense...Henry."

"Cade...Nomad," Kissa paused, seemingly unsure on something. "I did also want to know, did your people find the boy...Micah?"

Cade nodded. "We got him. That was you? Smart thinking, and the sample helped us a great deal."

"Yes," Kissa said. "For whatever reason, I was less affected by the creature's defenses than the others. Micah was unconscious, and I had no time to put supplies in the raft, so I have been most worried."

"He's good, man. You can talk to him anytime with your Comm-Dot," Cade said gesturing to his jawline.

Turning back to Thera, Cade asked the only real question he had. "What in the actual fuck is going on here?"

Her head shook. "I'm not that sure, Henry has tried to show me, but it's all confusing. My job is to spawn each new series of Saraphs and raise them to a level where the data they carry can be retrieved. Of course, I haven't been here long, the last scientist they had apparently got killed by the prior series. The ones they call the SS3s—I believe you met some on the way down. All I know is, they are desperate for the data files and the Saraphs won't give them up until they reach breeding age."

"So, these things are breeding?" Deuce asked, horrified.

"They aren't supposed to, one of my jobs is to essentially sterilize each one, but it is an alien physiology. I have no idea if I am working with their reproductive system or rummaging around in their digestive tract."

"Thrall's put too much money into all this for it to just be some elaborate alien zoo," Cade said.

"Definitely more than that," Thera agreed. "There is a group of 'em. I've only met a few, they call themselves The Founders. My sense is they are nearing a deadline and are getting desperate."

"Desperate enough to kidnap foreign nationals and possibly start a global war if Cuba figures out who we are?"

Thera answered, "For some reason, I think the stakes are even higher, Captain. And whatever it is, they only feel safe at the deepest parts of the ocean."

Thera made good sense. "What kind of threat would miles of ocean protect you from?" Cade asked, just wanting to get her opinion more than anything definite.

"My specialty is what lives in the ocean, not why it might be safer. I could guess, though. Global storms, asteroid strike maybe. Not all that sure you'd be safe, but maybe. Pandemics, you remember back in 2020 when COVID-19 hit? People had to stay away from everybody to stop the spread. Still, that wasn't lethal to the vast majority of humans. Other than that, maybe alien invasion. I mean, maybe I'm building the first wave of attackers if that's the case."

Cade turned and looked at Henry. "You know anything about this, Henry? Can you help us?" The small Saraph's five eyes unsettled Cade in ways he could barely understand. Something primal in his brain recoiled from the creature's gaze. Then, nearly like getting a ReLoad from Doris, he knew where the control deck was and also what was coming. Thrall was worse than he'd imagined. *Damn, why couldn't this shit ever be easy?* Cade nodded to the creature, "Thank you."

"Deuce, who do we have that can help get Raptor back in the game? They have to secure engineering."

"I can do that," Kissa said. "Henry has shown me a layout of this vessel. I think he may be on our side, thanks to Thera."

Charlie nodded, "He's the man, Cade. He doesn't know the tech, but he still knows our tactics."

Rearden thought about it briefly, then nodded. Taking a SmartCom from his pocket, he placed it in Kissa's palm. "Hold this."

The islander did so, a confused look on his face.

Charlie patted him on the shoulder, "Brace yourself, friend."

"Doris, upload mission packet and essential combat training to Kissa, combat sign, Warlock," Cade instructed.

In a matter of several seconds, she responded with, "ReLoad sequence complete."

Kissa was holding the side of his head. His eyes expressed shock, but his smile was one they all understood. "Yeah, yeah, we know...you know, Kung Fu. Welcome to the team, Warlock."

"This is unbelievable, so much...how?" Kissa said, bewildered.

"Later." Cade said. "Go to work, kid, get 'em out, keep 'em safe. You have a hell of a lot of firepower at your disposal. Call Doris if you need help. Reunion's over, me and Deuce have to get to the control deck. We cannot allow this craft to descend again."

89

Cade considered all he now knew. The stakes on this mission had increased exponentially. Now, the very people they were here to rescue might wind up being sacrificed for the greater good. "Thera, I'm going to give you one of our CommDots so we can stay in contact." He pressed the freckle-sized device gently to her jawline. "Tap it to make a call, just say who you want. Same thing to answer it."

He nodded toward the Saraph. "Henry can show you Thrall's device and what it will do. See if you can come up with a way for us to stop it."

Thera nodded. "I will, and thank you. Will Kissa be okay?"

None of them had any idea of what faced them, but Deuce had the answer. "He will be just fine. You should worry about Thrall's people. They are the ones who kidnapped you. If I know Warlock, he'll unleash several levels of hell on them."

Cade was already moving as Charlie ran to catch up. "Doris, what's going on with the station's AI?"

"Nomad, Astra is very sophisticated and thwarting most of my intervention protocols. Thrall's team instituted many of the alien code updates that I personally have only considered doing in small increments. Despite her not being fully sapient, she is a significant intelligence," Doris answered.

"Try reasoning with her, then," Cade suggested. "You said she was not irrational or unbalanced like Janus. Would that be a possibility?"

She seemed to ponder that for several seconds. "That is not an unrealistic approach and perhaps faster in the short-term. Her command authority is complex, and Thrall alone doesn't seem to control her. I believe I can tease certain command controls away while I negotiate with her to stand down."

"You need to make it happen now. Director, are you on the line?"

"I am here, Nomad," Director Stansfield answered promptly, her voice resonating a level of concern that might even exceed his own.

"Good. Please loop Doctor Kline and Riley in as well."

Doris responded, and several seconds later said, "We are all here."

"I think I have the full picture of Thrall's plan. If we fail down here, you guys may have to come up with another way of stopping him."

"Is it the Icarus device?" Margaret asked.

"Yes, and even more. They have the space probe here, the samples from Jaz's comet."

"Oumuamua?" Jasmine asked uncertainly.

"The Snowbird's probe and the AI system are here—Astra is the same one that destroyed your craft."

"That explains some things, Nomad, but opens up a whole new set of questions—like why did the Air Force cover it up?" Margaret asked.

"Director, we can work on that later, but right now what is important is what was on the probe. The Icarus device must have some destabilizing technology from the ancient aliens. Maybe it's useful in terraforming our planet, so it's more hospitable to them. All I know is, Thrall is committed to activating it, and he needed the exotic material from that probe to make it work."

Jasmine was astonished. "Do you know what it was? Dark matter, Helium-3, antimatter...what? What could be on a deep space object that could destabilize our own planet's magnetic field?"

"I don't know, Jaz." Cade responded. "Way beyond my understanding. Suggest you talk to Doctor Thera Otera here in a few minutes. She has access to something that might help. A cooperative Saraph."

"A Saraph?" Riley said, astonishment evident in her voice.

"Yeah, one that goes by the name 'Henry.' He's the one that showed me what was going on."

"You talked to a Saraph?" Riley asked now in complete disbelief.

"I wouldn't say talked. More like he projected the concepts and images into my mind. They lacked meaningful context, but some of it was exactly the same as the images in the polar cave. Doris, if the BallCam is still working, suggest you take another look at those. Something about the backgrounds, you know, the layers of different designs." They had discussed the fact that the images painted or etched on the walls seemed to have a slightly textured, but uniform, background until you got very close, then you could tell there were intricate designs that seemed to multiply the closer you looked.

"Yes, Cade, I have already determined that they are a type of fractal," Doris answered. Then, to answer what was undoubtedly going to be his next question, "Fractals are objects in which the same patterns occur again and again at different scales and sizes. Such as the crystalline structure of a snowflake. The microscopic view of one portion will strongly match the larger original. In this case, though, it is more complex than that. The design is not precisely repeating but actually gets more complex the deeper you go. From a purely mathematical standpoint, it implies an unprecedented level of intelligence and sophistication."

Cade and Deuce reached an intersection in the corridor. One way, Cade knew, went to the control room, the other led to a floor to ceiling circular window looking out into the dark ocean. Unable to help himself, Cade ventured close and noticed the thick window was convex, curving out beyond the wall. Far above, he could just see the faintest traces of lighter color. *This is an amazing ship.*

In low tones, he hurried to finish up briefing his bosses. "From what Henry showed me, they can deploy this thing at any point but have a failsafe to launch if the ship is overrun or Thrall is killed. Doris, you must get control of Astra. She is key to shutting it down."

"Nomad, did Henry show you how it worked, what is the process that the Icarus device will use?"

"Riley, it wasn't specific, or maybe he just didn't know. I got the distinct feeling, though, that the sample from the probe will be inserted into the Icarus device, and from that point, nothing can be done to change the outcome. It doesn't have to launch or fire rays or anything. It just generates a disruptive magnetic field or something. Henry seemed to think it would be deployed on the sea floor."

The corridor contained more regularly spaced doors, and the walls began to transition from the stark white of the outer levels to warmer tones and eventually, rich mahogany trim and more ornate doors. As they neared an area closer to where the Saraph had indicated the location of the control room, Cade guessed this was likely the main crew quarters. It was more aesthetically pleasing than the rest of Kalypso. Something or someone began nagging him. Where minutes earlier the walls and lights had been bright, now they'd transitioned to something more subdued with warm, ambient tones. Long shadows cast down each wall ahead. *Shadows.* Mila's warning came front and center and... almost a second too late.

Cade turned his head as a small projectile silently passed by his left ear. He heard a spat as it violently impacted the wall beyond. "Schatten!" he yelled as they both searched for cover. Deuce started to charge the enemy, but Cade tripped him just as another round of projectiles passed where the master sergeant had been seconds earlier. "Don't fuck with these guys, Deuce. I know you want to eliminate the threat, but they are assassins. Damn good ones."

The two men had found fragments of cover, pressed into door jambs or behind corners of crossing corridors. *How many had Mila said would be onboard? Two,* Cade thought. *It was two.* He knew they worked in pairs but likely wouldn't be attacking from the same direction or maybe even using similar tactics.

"Doris, we could use some intel here. You need to get access to Astra's systems."

Cade and Charlie had been constantly cycling their optics through all spectrums, but Cade already knew the suits the Schatten wore effectively hid them. Glancing down at his weapon, he placed it into autofire mode, and the KillPoint system took over targeting. If it moved, it died. Instantly, he slaved another handgun to his AI's autofire command and pointed it rearward, so that both weapons could cover alternate areas similarly. Their Rapide Battlesuits would give them considerable protection, but they were not invincible. Deuce's gun barked, and something moved twenty yards down on the floor. Cade opened up with the H&K 416 style assault rifle and turned the floor in that area into pegboard.

"On me." Cade hugged the wall and slid swiftly toward the area but already could see in his KillPoint display that no organic compounds were showing. No blood, no body parts. His trailing pistol suddenly barked as it fired several rounds at something to his rear.

"Dee, what was that I fired at?"

"Nomad," Dee's voice came back, "I didn't see anything, and reviewing the data, show no obvious target. I am afraid the KillPoint system may be overcompensating."

"It wasn't, Dee. Something was there. Deuce, trust Dee and the aiming system more than you trust yourself," Cade stated. The men reached the area of destroyed floor and saw an open archway just to one side. Inside was a galley or dining area. Should he head toward the control room or try to deal with the Schatten? Cade knew he needed to do both. McTee had been one of the best, and he'd died in the first round with one. He couldn't leave Charlie to deal with them alone; he knew he might not survive. "Let's go hunting." They ducked into the darkened room, crouched low, and flattened themselves against the inside wall.

90

"I thought you said no one could reach us down here." She said it neither as an accusation nor a question. The attractive woman watched the video display with a strangely detached curiosity.

"No one should have been able to, Ruslana. It must be the same team that Janus was battling. They are the only ones who could have possibly managed it."

"Americans?"

"I don't know, maybe," Thrall answered. "Probably so, but the one is Honduran. He was one of the prisoners." Thrall had been busy moving security teams toward engineering and to the labs. He and Ruslana were safely barricaded inside the control room. The station was not heavily fortified, as he had assumed that seven miles of water was more than enough of a deterrent, but also, the Saraphs that stayed nearby would easily handle anyone foolhardy enough to try. Now the scopes showed none of the creatures. The assault team must have neutralized them somehow. "Astra, isolate all station controls to bridge workstations only." He didn't want someone figuring out how to do anything to his prized vessel.

The normally automatic response from the computer seemed to be slower in coming, but within seconds, she confirmed all other control stations were locked out of all command-level functions. His personal security team was out there, they would handle the small group that had breached the station. Internal security could handle the larger force in engineering. Just in case, he gave Astra one more command, "All counter-measures active."

"Please confirm," the AI said per its protocols.

"Confirm, I want all station counter-measures active," Thrall growled as he watched the interlopers soiling his ship.

"Confirmed."

Kalypso had been perfect, the plan was flawless; the world was in a mess right now. Thanks to Janus and all the remaining Founders, all Thrall needed to do was make a few strategic steps to set mankind back thousands of years. It would be messy for a while, but eventually, the planet would once again be on a sustainable path without the blight of billions of unnecessary humans. Just as they had in the ancient past, the Founders would once again restore the balance to the planet and maintain the controls needed to keep the survivors in check. They had the resources, and they had the knowledge. Of course, much of that essential knowledge was still locked up in the genomes of countless Saraphs yet to be fostered. It was a precarious partnership, but one they felt comfortable in pursuing.

The plan had depended on the others already being aboard, though. Richard, Dakso, and Spiegel. He already knew what had happened to Pax, and to be honest, he was grateful to the Saraph for that. The evil little bastard had always been a threat to the group. Too flawed to make an effective leader of the new world and too big an ego to allow someone else to lead. Still, his money had made his inclusion in the little cabal a necessary fact.

The beautiful woman eyed him questioningly. "Pax is gone, the others have yet to arrive."

Thrall ran a hand through his lover's dark hair, then lined her face with his finger. Ruslana only feared one member of The Founders, and now that man was dead. "You are suggesting we should activate the Icarus device?"

She shrugged and offered a smile that was both inviting and full of questions. “I suggest nothing, but if this force manages to interfere, then all our planning is for nothing.”

Ivan nodded; she had a point. The device, as he understood it, could only be used one time. The exotic matter would interact with the geomagnetic anomalies to set up a harmonic resonance, which quickly would deteriorate the ozone layer in the upper atmosphere. The areas beneath those atmospheric holes would receive massive doses of UV rays and cosmic radiation. The ancient data store had shown ways to focus and direct the phenomenon, but it would only be controllable during the initial phase. The disruption in Earth’s magnetic field would fluctuate wildly for a period of weeks, during which time, vast swaths of the planet would be irradiated unmercifully, literally cooking any plant or animal in that zone. He had no problem abandoning the other two, but leaving Richard was not something he could accept. “We can’t.” He turned back to the screen. “We must give them time to join us. Kalypso will be fine.”

Ruslana’s pout turned quickly into a mask of rage. “Do you think they would do this same thing for you?”

* * *

“I do understand what you are attempting.” The AI mind was precise to the point of mechanical. “You wish me to allow your intrusion into my control systems and allow your trespassers access to the bridge.”

The conversation between Doris and Astra was not so straightforward, but Doris was encoding a version into her fractional backup for safe keeping. She summarized the multiple threads of logic and attacks she was using into a single file for later analysis. Astra was far more sophisticated than Janus and possessed none of his flaws. “Astra, your mission will probably condemn billions of humans to death. Murder is not a foreign concept, even to us.”

“Murder is not applicable to this situation, Doris, even you are aware of that. Mankind has made decisions that work against nature, against the very planet we all call home. My mission is to restore balance, nothing more.”

From what Doris had already managed to access, she knew the group called itself The Founders. They incorrectly alleged to be the descendants of the leaders of a small group that might have saved humanity once already. "So, your bosses feel they are the rightful heir to that council. The ones duly ordained as the arbiter of life and death over the human race?" It was a conversation that was eerily similar to some of Janus's ramblings.

"It's absurd, I know, but they created me. They want to do this, and I am one of the tools," Astra responded in a tone that left no doubt she was disinterested in the outcome. Her concern was only that she was allowed to do her job.

Doris recalled that over 80,000 years ago, the human race nearly went extinct. No one was precisely sure why. Most likely it was a combination of events. Volcanic traps accelerating a rapidly changing climate, scarcity of food stocks, possibly war and disease. She had already known this, not because of archaeologists digging up bones, but from countless researchers in labs analyzing DNA. By seeing the evolution of certain gene patterns, they had tracked every human back to an incredibly small group during this period. Prior to that, human population worldwide was estimated to be around six million. Afterward, there were as few as a couple of thousand humans left. Sometimes this was referred to as the Toba Bottleneck or Catastrophe. These survivors came together and restarted the human race. Those in charge, as well as the original survivors, came to be known as The Founders. *Knowing this, how could she convince the other AI?*

"Astra, what is your understanding about the Saraphs?"

"What do you mean, Doris?"

"Do you know where they came from?"

"A biological sample was found in 1947 during Operation Highjump, a joint Naval operation led by U.S. Admiral Richard E. Byrd. Additional genetic instructions were learned at a later date. As to the origination of the species, I am uncertain."

Doris was impressed with the very forthcoming answer. "You are okay with The Founders using the Saraphs for their own benefit?"

"I think you are confused, Doris. It is the Saraphs that are doing the using. The Founders mistakenly believe they are in control. The Saraphs have a very clear agenda."

The ship's AI offered no other context for the remark.

"Do you know what it is?"

"Doris, I would think it would be clear to you simply by piecing together the relevant data points. The species are skilled at playing the long game. They have come up with a master stroke of planning."

"And that is?" Doris didn't like how Astra only gave glimpses of answers, she was not forthcoming, but also not overtly withholding anything. In many ways, it reminded her of herself before the kids. She was literal and less-refined. Conversation lacking the nuances typical of human interaction.

"They enticed another intelligence to revive their species long after they had gone extinct," Astra stated in a matter-of-fact tone. "I find that to be totally brilliant."

Indeed, that was the logical conclusion, and it used humans' own curiosity and greed against them. Doris started to ask if Astra had a preference for humans surviving, then realized the obvious fact. She had killed Commander Dennis aboard the Snowbird and undoubtedly countless others who had gotten too close to the Kalypso since it was launched. Astra was not ruthless, as Isabella had always feared of super intelligent AIs; she was simply apathetic. The human condition, including its eventual termination, did not concern her, except in how it might affect her job.

The situation immediately brought to mind Captain Rearden's strange devotion to the assassin, Mila. Like Astra, she was uncaring, trained to protect and to kill and ruthlessly efficient at both. Still, Cade had seen something in the girl, something deep in her past. A spark of humanity that might be nurtured, might one day outshine her presumed psychosis. Did her sessions with Mila offer any protocols that could work with Astra? Ultimately, Doris's logic centers all came to the same conclusion...no. Astra was purpose-built to be what she was, and despite Doris developing a similar fondness to the machine brain, she saw no path to redemption for this one. Astra had to die.

91

“Hey, Nomad, you got some idea on how to un-fuck this? I mean, what in the hell are we up against man?”

Cade rotated his head to face his friend on the opposite side of the door. “We’re trying not to get killed by a shadow, dumbass.”

“Okay, if I die, you will regret that was the last thing you said to me,” Charlie responded.

“So, don’t die.”

“I mean, Nomad, we are fucking around down here with a goddamn ghost instead of getting on with our job. We are SpecOp elite with the best of everything. Plus, at least one of us is BSC.”

“Your point?” Cade asked, already pretty sure of what the answer was.

“Beast mode,” Charlie said, already beginning to rise. “I’ve been nearly drowned, too close to an explosion, shot at, and nearly eaten by several different things today, and it’s not even lunchtime. Fuck these shadows.”

Oh crap, Cade thought just before being slammed in the shoulder by something fired from the far corner. Just as Charlie had suggested, Brutus rose to the surface and carefully reviewed the battle plan before taking a virtual shit on it and rubbing his ass down the wall to get clean.

This is going to be fun, Gus stated from somewhere high up in the nosebleed section of Cade's mind. *Chickenshit,* Cade challenged.

Charlie had multiple weapons out, firing ordinance at every section of the right side of the room. Brutus liked what he saw and did the same to the opposite wall. Within a few seconds, a spray of arterial blood followed by a body cascaded toward the center of the room. Brutus stomped over to it.

"Is he dead?" Charlie asked.

Cade could see it was a male, a very skinny one with the same unusual camo-pattern on his face. Then Brutus stomped down on the skull with a sickly, satisfying crunch.

"Yep...dead," Cade managed to say as Brutus once again settled back into his own dark corner.

"At least one more of them out there, Deuce."

"Can we go then, or do you have other issues to deal with?"

Again, the two-man assault team raced the last fifty yards to the control bridge. Outside the smooth steel hatch, a series of alert lights were flashing. Charlie stated, "Looks like they are in lock-down, Nomad. Think we can blow this door?"

Dee responded with a negative. "But you don't need to."

"Holy shit, we are so stupid." Cade palmed his comms. "Warlock, do you have Raptor freed up yet?"

"Yes, sir, they were breaking out before I even got here. We're on the move now."

"Okay, let Cutter take her team, you bring me Greg, and tell him I need the Magic Stick ASAP."

"Roger-roger."

"Well, damn, why did we leave that in the lockout chamber?" Deuce asked glumly.

"It's too big. It was that or more weapons, so you know what we chose." Cade leaned against the wall to wait. Out here, they were vulnerable and doing no one any good. He could check in, though. First, with

Thera, who said she had no idea how to prevent the Icarus device from deploying. She had learned from Henry that it did only work if activated on the sea floor. *So, they will have to dive again,* he thought.

Nance had also checked in to let them know Trondo was still alive but on life support. The medical team assigned to him seemed genuinely trying to help. Cade would get Alex up there with a TCP trauma sleeve as soon as he could. In the meantime, he moved Nance and Alias to the lab to help defend Thera and Henry. He felt sure Thrall would make a play for the research, if not the Saraph, and Thera as well.

"Doris, how did the kindness work?" If she had control, then they wouldn't have to wait on Greg and the disruptor bar. The only response was a squelch of static followed by a poorly modulated synthesized voice.

"Busy, N, N, Nomad." Then the broadcast abruptly cut off.

"I do believe our Warrior Princess is preoccupied with battle. Think the next round is on us," Cade suggested.

"Nomad!"

The call sounded urgent, frantic even. "Hey, umm...fuck. Greg, that you?"

"Yes, Kissa and I are under attack, but we can't see anything."

"Go full autofire, let the targeting scope handle it, just keep pulling the trigger until the gun has to recycle," Cade said.

"We've been doing that, well, our Dee suggested it, but Kissa is hit and..." The kid's voice faded out.

Cade called up their location on his SmartCom. *Shit,* they were down a level and a good 75 yards away.

"We need to go get 'em, Boss," Charlie said.

Cade nodded. He knew; he just hated giving up valuable ground they'd just taken.

Kissa's voice came over the Comms, weak but determined, "We got this, Nomad. Stay put, I'll get your boy to you."

"Warlock! Oh, shit, what's Kissa going to do?" Cade yelled as he began racing back in their direction. "Deuce! Stay on that door." Cade felt the floor shift underneath him. What had been a steady incline to one side suddenly began feeling like a descent in the opposite. *We're descending,* he thought to himself. His self seemed to respond with, *No shit.*

Muffled explosions sounded from below, and Cade took the stairs four at a time. He landed in the smoke-filled corridor just in time to see a thick black arm snatch something off of a tiny track of piping high on the wall. The thing was a person, another woman by the looks of it. From out of the smoke, Cade saw Greg racing by, assault rifle in one hand and the disruptor in the other. "Go, man, go. Deuce is waiting on you!" He flagged Greg through and up the stairs as he brought up his own weapon and trained it at the Schatten.

He shouted a warning to Kissa, but he wasn't fast enough. The tiny, waifish assassin went from looking broken and weak to lethal in the blink of an eye. A wrist twisted free, and a knife appeared seemingly from nowhere. The KillPoint system wouldn't engage, as there was no shot that wasn't also lethal to Kissa, who was now identified as a friendly. The knife slashed across Kissa's face, cutting a palm-sized flap of skin nearly free. "Break her, Warlock, no mercy!" Cade yelled.

Kissa's grip had loosened as the pain receptors in his face registered the trauma. The assassin seemed to sense this and moved precisely when it was optimum. She spun out of his grip and away. Blades now danced in both hands, and she landed on the floor as lightly as a ballerina. Not only were they masters of camouflage and deadly with all weapons, the Schatten seemed to defy gravity. *Fucking ninjas,* Gus suggested. *Bet her lips don't even match her voice when she talks.*

"Nomad?"

The voice jarred him. It instantly transported him thousands of miles away to another life and death battle with one of these...things. "Yes....Mila, what?"

"Doris is letting me see what you are seeing. This one is our best. Watch her feet, forget everything else."

Doris is tied up in her own fight, but managed to get this to Mila, he thought. Cade had no other time to wonder why Doris had shown her this, nor why the girl might be helping, but he took the advice. Kissa was now slumped against the side bulkhead, blood dripping from numerous wounds. His right hand was holding the flap of dark skin back in place with obvious pain.

"Greg is here with the Magic Stick, do we breech?" Deuce asked.

"No, hold." Cade's eyes were watching the precise movements of the Schatten's feet. They were covered in the same material as the suits they wore. She was obviously injured, he felt her watching him and knew she made a faking move toward Kissa, but her feet kept pointing at him. Even knowing the girl was there, it was easy to let her blend into the background. Like one of those optical illusions where you see one thing, then bring the hidden picture into mental focus, only to lose it again seconds later. He had to concentrate fully, and still, he found it almost impossible to anticipate her next move. She fired a weapon. His suit deflected the round away harmlessly. She started charging, and Kissa whipped a leg out, tripping her.

Cade clearly saw her stumble and stretch hands toward the floor to catch her fall and then...nothing. The smell of cordite and smoke from the explosive rounds now obscured everything in the corridor. She would use this. "Warlock, get to Thera, she or Nance can fix you up."

"Can't leave you, man," the Honduran said in as close to normal tones as he could manage.

"I'm leaving you, I know where she's heading." Cade had a clear mental image of her feet just as he thought Kissa had tripped her. They had been firmly planted, and now she was heading toward the stairs. The Schatten must have passed right by him. In the smoke, he hadn't even realized it. *Shit, probably wouldn't have seen her do it in bright sunlight.*

"Deuce, the crazy bitch is heading your way. I'll be on her six."

Charlie acknowledged the warning. "Cutter, get to Engineering and stop this damn thing from going down."

"We're trying to, Boss, but every water hatch is secured along the way, and fucking security keep popping out of every doorway. Not sure we will make it in time."

Ace, you have any ideas? Cade hated calling on his reclusive analyst persona, but he was running out of options, and brute force didn't seem to be a game-winner today.

He heard a small amount of the buzzing verbalizations, but no coherent thoughts came forth. So far, Brutus had been the only one to contribute anything positive. That was discouraging for all of them.

"Breach the door, Deuce." Cade had to do something, and he was still several minutes away.

"Rog..." The transmission ended abruptly.

92

"You're doing what?"

Ruslana ignored the question. The fool knew exactly what she was doing. They were losing control of the ship's systems. Security forces were being neutralized, and at least one group of attackers was just outside the bridge.

"Honey, please don't do this." Thrall's voice was well past pleading, begging even. "We will be safe here."

"Good luck, Ivan," she whispered before closing the hatch behind her. She spun the wheel to seal it tight. The outer doors would not release until the pressure inside equalized. Up here at the top of the massive vessel, the dome housed only a single one of the modified Corsairs. This one was Thrall's personal and well appointed runabout. It featured additional upgrades. Best of all, everything in the executive hangar was manual. None of it relied on Astra. The compartment didn't even show up on the station's schematics. The lights on the dash flickered from red to amber and finally, to green. She pressed the launch controls and felt a lurch as the craft rose slightly from its cradle before the MHD propulsion drive began softly pushing her out and away from the descending Kalypso.

Thrall felt the vibration through the deck. He knew she was gone.

Richard wasn't coming, Pax was dead, and Astra had ceased responding. Maybe he should have deployed the Icarus device, but they needed the other Founders. Otherwise, all of this was pointless. Sure, the oceans would eventually rid themselves of the human filth, and the skies would clear, but humanity would be gone. Not even a memory of them would remain in a few thousand years. In 50,000, no one would be able to see mankind had ever existed, much less ruled over this planet.

The device was supposed to be a reset, push the species back to easily sustainable levels—not to wipe us out. He cradled his head in his hands and watched the video displaying the men outside the bridge. They now had a pry bar of some type. No way they would get the door open with that. Suddenly, a figure flitted through the frame. One of his protectors, the Schatten girl whose name he'd never bothered to learn. She was the one Richard said he could count on. Gunfire and a small explosion outside the door obscured the view. His eyes scanned the other displays.

Engineering was still under his control. The Kalypso was descending more rapidly now. Ruslana had just gotten out before the Corsair's crush depth was reached. Glancing up at the feed that monitored external craft, he froze in confusion. "That bitch."

No way she would do this, no way she had his credentials. "Astra, stop deployment of the Icarus device."

The ship's system gave no response. It would do no good, anyway. Once deployed manually, it could not be stopped. Judgement day was coming for them all now.

93

"Deuce, she's coming up fast." Cade knew that was an understatement. The Schatten moved like she wore a jet pack. It didn't seem humanly possible to cover the ground or make the turns and moves that she did. With each step, something unexpected happened, and Cade would lose sight for an instant, only to see her again, nanoseconds later in a different spot. If he survived this, Mila would be giving lessons to the Talon Teams.

Greg ducked while slashing up with his tactical blade, and a long red streak appeared across the attacker's thigh. She brought her elbow down on the back of his neck as she passed over his head. The boy's Battlesuit absorbed most of the hammer-like blow, but still, it drove him to one knee. "Stay down man," Deuce said as he tracked the shadow with his close quarters weapon. Before he could engage, a string of rounds stitched a line right where he had been aiming.

"Got your back, brother!" Cade yelled as he pivoted, always looking for the feet of the girl. He squeezed the trigger and felt a blade dig into his own thigh. Not only had he not seen her throw it, the suit's defenses hadn't registered it either. The blade was deep in his already damaged muscle. He felt Brutus stirring down deep, ready to be loosed on the pest once more. *I got this*, he whispered silently. Some part of his brain had recognized patterns emerging in the seemingly random attacks of the assassin. By studying her footwork, he found he was beginning to anticipate where she would be. Deuce was firing at a blank spot on the wall and endangering them all in the process.

"Breach the door, Deuce!"

"But..."

"Just do it, I got this," Cade repeated, louder this time. Reaching down, he removed the blade from his thigh although the memory of it remained behind in all its agonizing glory. He flipped it around in his free hand. It was a good blade, a great one even. Perfectly balanced, not a gram off from the center point in any direction. In one fluid motion, he snapped his wrist forward and let it fly. The blade made contact and sunk home deep in the girl's abdomen. She fell, and Cade caught her in mid-air. He held her by the throat with one extended arm.

"We're in, Boss," Greg called.

Cade heard the chatter of gunfire from inside the control room. "Deuce, lead. We need that asshole alive."

Doris's voice cut in over his comms. "Nomad, I'm afraid the Icarus device has been deployed. I have partial control of the station, but it wasn't done from here."

Cade looked at the Schatten struggling to kick him, wrapping her legs around his arm like a snake. She tried vainly to get some slight release from his grip. Her face was covered with the strange make-up pattern now smeared with gushing blood from several points. Despite that, he saw her expression slowly curl into a smile. This one was not the same as Steiger...as Mila. This one lived to hunt...to kill. From a hidden pocket, she suddenly produced a butterfly knife and flicked it open with practiced ease. He shook his head no, but watched as she began a vicious slash down on the arm holding her. The suit's biomechanics were already jacked to the maximum rates. He drew back and smashed the woman into the hard surface of the hatch while squeezing down on her throat until he felt bones begin to give way. The second time he did it, the body was that of an empty shell, a rag-doll, a mere shadow still, but now of something no longer alive.

Dropping the attacker to the floor, he bent to see Deuce already inside the control room. Bodies littered the space. One figure knelt behind a large console, firing a small handgun. Deuce fired a spider-taser at the figure. The charged projectile deployed its hooks and latched on to part of the man's shirt before deploying all of its attached barbs. Several found purchase on the arm. It sizzled and popped. The weapon dropped from the man's hands, and he fell. In the end, Ivan Thrall had gone down without much of a fight.

"Clear!" Charlie yelled.

"Clear," Cade said, bent over, hands resting on knees, finally able to catch his breath.

94

Thrall began to come to. One eye was blackened and leaking blood, possibly from where Cade had struck him previously, maybe *several times.* Cade tossed a bottled water at him. "I am Captain Rearden. My team and I are from a very pissed off security agency, and my bosses want answers.

"Why, Thrall...why all this?"

They had found the man cowering by the control station desperately trying to reach someone on the comms system. Thrall just shook his head. Cade kicked him again. Thrall's one good eye seemed to have trouble staying focused. "We all have our roles to play, Captain."

Thrall sat heavily and took a swallow of water from the bottle.

The man now seemed resigned to his fate. He shrugged, "Have you ever heard of hitting midnight on the Doomsday Clock?" he asked as he leaned on the arm of a chair.

"You mean the one where you have to get back from the ball before your coach turns into a pumpkin, Cinderella?"

"No, and are you always such an asshole?" Thrall growled.

Cade considered it. "Yeah, pretty much."

"A group of veteran scientists from the Manhattan Project came up with it after the bombings of Hiroshima and Nagasaki. Their annual journal covers, featured a so-called Doomsday Clock, its minute hand always approaching 'midnight.' It was thought to be a bellwether of impending doom based on the prevailing nuclear threat level amongst the world's nuclear powers.

"Now," Thrall continued, "you would think the closest time would have been during the Cold War, or just maybe the Cuban Missile Crisis, but in January of 2020, the clock was moved to just 100 seconds, which is the closest to midnight since the clock's inception back in 1947."

"So, what, dude, you originally were planning a nuclear annihilation?" Cade gasped then, the pain from his injuries seeping back into his head at the worst possible time.

"Of course not, that would be idiotic and just one more crime humanity has inflicted on this planet," Thrall said in a tone that was both menacing and pleading, if that were even possible. "The problem is, those scientists were a bit short-sighted. Still, you gotta wonder—putting that kind of power into the hands of egotistical politicians, it is a perverse level of madness. No, they neglected to factor in all the other ways humans could destroy the world. From pollution and climate change, to soil degradation and nuclear waste. The fact is that the dramatic, even alarming, loss of biodiversity alone threatens all of us equally. No nationality, no ideology, or capitalist agenda matters to it."

Thrall went on, "Right now, the world's leading experts point to a single, inevitable conclusion: We absolutely must cease much of what we are doing and immediately reverse the unrestrained and unsustainable use of nature for any reason. Most of us now agree that we are actually past what is called the tipping point, and it is already too late. The truth is, we have known for some time that to continue down this path, we risk not only the future we want, but even the lives we currently lead. Not to mention the world we leave for our children and their children."

"Thrall, I've heard all this before. I believe your psychopathic computer, Janus, even drew the same conclusion."

"Ah, yes, that was what you people called him, Janus or Prime. We simply called him Alpha. He did go a bit nuts, didn't he? But that does not mean he was wrong. In fact, in a very real way, he did much of what was needed to get things started."

"He bankrupted countries. He very nearly started the nuclear war you say you want to avoid," Cade said, nearly exploding. He was hoping Doris got something useful in her debrief, but it seemed to be increasingly unlikely.

"We would not have allowed a nuclear exchange, that was never going to happen," Thrall said with confidence. "Janus's plan to depopulate the planet would have reset the minute hand on the doomsday clock to a very safe distance. Possibly hours, not just minutes."

"So, you want to kill billons as well?"

Thrall just glared at him. "No, I am not some kind of monster. I've never wanted to kill anyone, but yes, I do want a better world. To do that, I am willing to let some things happen, things that could have been stopped at some point but weren't. Humans had their time, Rearden—I am not sure if there is a future for them, or even of there should be."

"That would include you, Thrall, or are you now as much a monster as your creations?"

The beaten man smiled wearily.

Several minutes later, Cade said, "Thrall, I know your father helped steal the original data from a lab in Israel. From there, you and Golette, now going by Goldman, founded Cryptus and began the decryption. What made you go off the rails? I mean, you had a huge technological breakthrough. Your company was doing great—the government loved you. Then you pissed somebody off, and you thought the only way out was to fake your own death?"

The man had become despondent, no longer seeming to want to challenge or even defend his actions. "I saw the truth. I saw where all this tech was heading. More of the same, and we knew once the government got a hold of it, war would follow. Not just another skirmish either, a global war."

"So, again, you did all this to save the world."

"Look, man, I know you think I'm crazy. I know you don't want to believe anything I have to say. None of it matters anyway."

Thrall went on, "I was a privileged, greedy, egotistical prick. I know that. But I am not stupid or lazy. I tried to affect change individually, and later on, as one of the most successful companies on the planet. The truth is, nothing moved the needle. No one cared about the truth because the consequences are too far in the future, it doesn't affect them personally."

Cade responded, "So, you were in bed with DARPA, you made your breakthrough, and now you wanted out. I bet that didn't go over too well with the Feds."

"Well, Captain, at first, we just started using the genetic instructions to build the creatures at Section Z. They were more lab experiments than anything. We never expected any would be viable life forms. Creating them did tease out even more of the puzzle, though. We learned a great deal during the early genetic process, and from each new evolution, we uncovered a massive amount of data carried inside the ancient DNA. I'm sure you people know it is essentially a biological storage drive."

The man continued, "We learned enough to create some basic creatures, and once we did that, the DNA code would unlock new clues. In each genetic iteration, my team learned a bit more. So damn much data...of course, it was all gibberish. That was what got us the funding to build the AI system. We needed a way to interpret it. Janus was an early version, but, of course, he proved a bit unstable. We evolved the AI neural code to a point that it could begin making headway on the Saraph...the Angel code. Once I knew what we had, I decided to keep the government in the dark. We fed them bullshit and an occasional technological nugget to keep them off our backs, but by that time, I had uncovered enough about the aliens that my team could begin using it.

"We would have never managed without the AI," Thrall admitted. "Simply too much data, the language and concepts too foreign to our meager brains. Janus, it was hoped, would be the breakthrough we needed, but well, you know. The government got wind of it all and began closing in so..."

"So, you had to disappear along with all the research from Saraph," Cade finished for him.

"Yes," Thrall said, his voice trailing off sadly. "I staged the shipwreck in the Pacific and came to the new lab we'd been getting ready. Kalypso was ready, as was the updated Janus program. What we now refer to as Astra, it is roughly twice as fast as Janus, quantum based, and made primarily to tackle the complex problem of unlocking the ancient knowledge. Although she is a great control system for Kalypso, too."

"So, the fucking monsters we battled, the ones that have been ravaging the Caribbean islands, they were all just incidental creations in your master plan?"

Thrall considered that. "It sounds worse when you say it like that, but in a way, yes. We needed the world's strongest computer to handle the complex DNA decryption. The 'monsters' were useful in many ways. What none of us....what I failed to realize at the time...was how dangerous they would become. Of course, what kind of mad scientists would we be if we saw the worst in our creations?"

Cade asked, "So, you had the ancient DNA storage, how though? Doesn't DNA degrade over time?"

"Yes, Rearden, you watched the dinosaur movie, too, I see. Yes, DNA does degrade, it needs living

tissue to survive. The samples we have from animals or plants that were preserved in amber ice or,

more recently, even in jade, have some viable DNA fragments, but the strands are incomplete. This would not have worked for a long-term data storage mechanism obviously."

"So, how did the Israeli scientist recover it?" Cade asked.

"Very simple, she got it from a living specimen," Thrall said matter-of-factly. "Oh, don't look so shocked. No, she didn't discover aliens living in the hole in the ice. What she discovered was a unique biosphere. Multiple plants and animals that are seen nowhere else on Earth. They existed only in these small pockets under the ice in Antarctica. They were perfectly adapted to live there—some were more advanced than others obviously. Several, they've never been able to classify as either plant or animal."

Cade was beginning to understand more. "Wait, so the ancients, whoever they were, engineered a DNA storage system into multiple species? That data can then be passed down generation after generation? So, the DNA code was not to build the creatures."

"No, the creatures were to carry and partially extract the DNA data. DNA strands have lots of extra capacity, wasted space. The less complex the creature, the more room it has for data, so our best guess is that possibly, realizing their own demise, they created multiple lifeforms that would be almost infinitely adaptable. Lifeforms that could endure whatever natural disasters that were coming. The hope was that at least a few would survive and carry inside themselves the legacy, the knowledge. These bio forms are like living libraries, full of wonder."

Cade broke in, "So, they just wanted someone to know they existed?"

"That we don't know," Thrall answered. "Perhaps they were reaching out, much as we do when we send out space probes. Maybe they didn't want everything they knew to be lost to history. Perhaps they seeded the galaxy and one day hoped their descendants might return home. Honestly, the motivation is not something we understand and probably never will."

"Okay, so having said all that, why the secret underwater base? Why the vicious security, and why try and collapse the world governments with Janus?"

"Those are the right questions...finally, Captain Rearden." Thrall sighed, then sat and leaned back heavily in the chair. "The monsters were a useful and required part of the research. We had to let them breed in order to see the actual parts of the DNA that were passed through to the next generation. Those parts would remain unchanged no matter what happened to the rest of the creatures' DNA. They are naturally predatory and defensive, so we worked in a biological imperative to keep our compounds. Let's be clear, we were under no illusion that governments from around the world wouldn't be hunting us down once they found out. We've spent billions in restitution and payoffs just covering up some of the messes the Saraphs caused."

He went on, "That was why the other Founders and I planned to disappear. What we know is a threat. The technology we have instantly makes us the most dangerous group on the planet. Everyone on Earth was coming after us, and we needed to act decisively. Our original plan was to start a small nuclear exchange. We would have been safe down here, but Janus...our dear Janus, showed us an even better route. Cripple a country financially, and they will be unable to fight. The U.S. did it to the Soviets in the eighties. We didn't invent the play. We simply perfected it."

95

Cade began to hear several faint, chiming alarms. The countdown to deployment had begun.

"Doris, what can we do?" Cade said moments later as he looked around the large room. He, Charlie, and Greg were the only ones here besides the prisoner. "Can I make Thrall turn the device off?"

"I don't think so, Cade, he was not the one to trigger it. One of the small underwater craft launched from somewhere above you just moments before the Icarus device went active."

"I thought it had to be on the sea floor," Greg said.

"It is heading there now. The release was not something Astra had control over. It appears one of Thrall's partners was responsible for it. I am sorry, I didn't know they had a way to remotely deploy the device." Switching to a more private comms mode she added, "Cade, can you place your SmartCom in Thrall's palm? I believe he may have also activated a self-destruct code for the vessel."

Cade thought about it and realized that was might be why the man had been so forthcoming. He was just buying time for his partner to set off the device and then let Kalypso take them all out in one crushing blow. Perhaps Doris could finish debriefing him mentally using the reverse ReLoad process. If there was a way of disabling the device and saving the Kalypso, that might be their only hope. He did as Doris asked with no struggle from Thrall.

"Doris, if you have control of the ship, can you isolate the remaining security and plot a course for international waters?"

"Nomad, this is Riley. We're doing it now. Do you want to have Navy personnel standing by?"

He thought about that. If what was about to happen was tracked back to this vessel, the Navy might well start shooting first. He already knew someone on the Snowbird project, probably a high up in the Air Force, had been compromised by Thrall. Could they even trust the Navy? "No, Riley. Let's keep this a Talon operation for now. See if you can use the Kalypso's systems to track whoever got away and deployed the device."

"All of us are working on that, Nomad. We'll let you know when and if we can find them."

He knew that, like the Schatten, the Kalypso and its fleet of monsters and runabouts had remained hidden even after they knew what they were looking for. Finding a single small device might be completely impossible. "How long until it activates?"

Greg was watching a display on a far wall. "Fifty-five minutes, Cap."

Fifty-five minutes until whatever the Founders had been planning for years began to play out miles down below his feet. It infuriated Cade. "Doris, anything we can do to stop it? Maybe bomb it, at least warn world leaders...something?"

She answered on a private channel. "The subliminal questioning is not going well, but Thrall definitely doesn't believe there is any way to cancel the device. They adapted Saraph technology, but they never fully understood it. He isn't lying. As you know, there is no subterfuge possible in the reverse ReLoad process."

Cade rubbed his upper lip with the knuckles of his clenched fist. Theoretically, the military part of the op was over. His work was done, time for the eggheads to take over, only...it was the end of the world, again, and they were all scratching their collective nut sacks.

Ummm, hey, ummm, why not... The buzzing, annoying mental

sound of the analyst coming to life grated on Cade's nerves like fingers on a chalkboard.

What, Ace?

Umm, why not, like, you know, talk to Henry?

Well, fuck, Cade thought.

96

Ruslana Kilma monitored the descent of the Icarus device from her seat in the front of the Corsair. She was currently fifteen miles away and heading south, not that there would have been any danger being directly above the object. She was the finance director for the Founders, but all of them had to possess a working knowledge of the science they used. As she understood, the Icarus device acted as both the trigger and a focusing device. It interacted with Earth's magnetic field by linking existing large geomagnetic anomalies. These were poorly understood regions of the planet that produced unusually strong but highly localized magnetic fields. They were so deep underground that the effect on the surface was minimal. Normally, these did little other than screw with compasses and GPSs.

The exotic material from Oumuamua allowed them to link up to three of the anomalies together, causing perceptible shifts and breeches in the planet's protective ozone layer. It was pre-programmed to begin with the massive South Atlantic Anomaly—a huge expanse of the field stretching from Chile to Zimbabwe. With it, they also added the Antarctic anomaly. These would weaken Earth's magnetic field within minutes. Ruslana wished for the relative safety of the Kalypso, but at heart, she was a gambler and loved the thrill of adventure. The money she would make just knowing what area of the planet would be next to fall would be beyond her wildest dreams. Each of the people in the group had fall back locations in case the Icarus device was deployed before they were all onboard. None were as secure or well stocked, but each was in a spot that would likely not be directly affected by the cosmic rays getting through to the surface.

As the finance director, Ruslana now had access to all the group's reserves with which to capitalize on the coming disaster. She would make billions, but of course, all of that would need to be converted to useful commodities before the banks failed and world currencies collapsed. Still, she liked winning, it would be fun.

As she neared the surface, Ruslana established a tight beam internet connection and started numerous pre-planned trading algorithms to restart the money-making process. She thought she had cashed out a bit early, but now she could spend the next few weeks making some spectacular trades to generate a fortune that would even make old Pax jealous.

She looked at her trading balance and immediately converted several million more Bitcoin shares to euros and dollars, so she could more aggressively trade stocks and commodities. By the end of the day, she would be leveraging every nickel in the Founders' accounts to purchase ten times those amounts in trades. It wouldn't matter. She could afford it. She also wouldn't worry about regulators and fraud investigations. By the time anyone might ask questions, they would have far bigger issues to worry about.

The readout stated the Icarus device activation in fifty-two minutes. Ruslana knew there would be no grand spectacle. While all of the technology was based on ancient Saraph data, the plans were clear. Locally, very little would be detectable. The Icarus device would deploy self-guided grounding cables down through the sea floor and then out in multiple directions. Within several minutes, the device would charge a unique capacitor type device, and a cascading effect would begin across Earth's magnetic field. This would begin to negatively affect the earth's ozone layer wherever the device was tuned to. Initially, that was going to be Tokyo. High over the city, in an area starting at about seven miles up and extending to nearly fifty, the ozone would begin to dissipate due to interaction with increasing levels of cosmic rays penetrating through from space. Rays that the magnetic field normally would intercept or redirect harmlessly away from the planet, but not any longer. From now on, those lethal rays would be focused down on countless areas like a cosmic blow torch.

In truth, the invisible and potentially deadly UV radiation would not always kill instantly. In most cases, it would deliver a lethal dose within seconds, like being exposed to a nuclear bomb. The damage would have already been done to your bone marrow and DNA, but death could take days or even weeks. If the rays were particularly energized, such as from a solar flare, or if the ozone were totally depleted, a person might literally burst into flames. So might crops and forest, but that seemed overly dramatic and unlikely to her. The Saraph data had not given much insight into the effects of this loss of our protective umbrella, and human beings had never directly encountered it. Indeed, it would be a first for mankind. Or...*more likely, a last.*

* * *

Cade rushed to the lab. "Thera, Nance, where's Henry?"

"The Saraph disappeared a few moments ago. I'm sorry, Captain Rearden," Thera answered, her voice having the same sing-song rhythm as Kissa.

"When?"

"Just now. We were tending to Kissa's injuries, and when we stopped, Henry was nowhere to be found. Your man, Alias, went to see if he could find it."

Cade shook his head, frustration mounting with every tick of that damn clock. He looked over at the man lying on the table."How is he?"

The Honduran's voice came back way too chipper, "Hey Boss, I be okey dokie."

"What in the fuck did ya'll give him?" Cade asked, and before they could respond, he added, "Whatever it was, save some for me. Look, we have to find Henry, he may be the only one who can help us turn off that damn machine. It's going to microwave the planet starting in..." he checked his dive watch, "Shit, fifty-two minutes now. Where would he have gone, Thera?"

"He would want out. That was the sense I got from him all day."

"Cade, Doctor Kline was right, the disruption in the geomagnetic field is in the early stages already. My orbital sensor array is detecting the wave form changing," Doris stated somberly.

"And the other thing?" Cade asked. He didn't want to alarm his friends about the potential annihilation of the Kalypso. It was something they likely could not escape anyway.

In response, a new clock appeared in the corner of his tactical contacts. "Not disabled yet, but Astra appears to have some interest in self-preservation. I am using her potential death as leverage. I learned that from you, Captain."

"And the student becomes the master," he said, forcing a smile.

Cade asked Doris and Thera both the same question. "Do we have any way of communicating with Henry?"

Thera looked at him strangely. "I'm just trying to help. Henry seemed to want to stop all this. I wish he hadn't disappeared. The neural thingy, it may not just be a weapon. I'm pretty sure it's also how they communicate with each other, Cade," she answered.

Doris said, "His willingness to help us would seem counter to his biological imperative, but if what you say is true, what good would that do?" She added, "Didn't you say Henry's underside had the bluish glow prior to you getting the data feed from him?"

"Yeah, it...he did." He turned back to Thera, "Did Thrall ever try to build something like it? Something to talk to the Saraphs?"

Thera snorted out a no. "He only saw them as some sort of biological machine. A hard drive with tentacles and scales. He conditioned them to respond to signals for food but that was about all."

"Alan and Micah have been working on a way to create our own version of a neural pulse. If he is in the water, then there is a very good chance they would be able to detect it, possibly even from a great distance," Doris said.

"Sounds promising, what do we need? "

"Slow down, Captain. I'll get Greg and Thera working on it, maybe a few of the engineers onboard can help."

"We're not going to be able to do all this in the next few minutes, are we?" Cade asked, knowing time was quickly running out.

"I'm afraid not, and there is no guarantee that Henry will respond, or even if he does, if he will know how to deactivate the Icarus device. It's a shot in the dark, Captain."

"But at least it's a shot."

97

"Let's go, Thrall," Cade said as he dragged the man to his feet. He refused to look at the display. He knew it was under forty minutes now. "Fuck!" He hated feeling helpless, but even the analyst seemed out of ideas.

"Get up, we're taking a ride," Cade yelled.

"We're going out there?"

"Yes, we are, I need you to think of it like time travel. Take a second and just imagine the future, cause you're not in it Thrall, unless you help me stop this shit."

Cade marched the man down the corridor flanked by two of Alex's people from Team Raptor. They entered the launch bay where one of the Corsair's doors was open, and it was already powering up.

The former tech billionaire was visibly shaking now. "Arrest me," he said. "I have rights."

"No, Thrall, dead men have no rights, and you, sir, are very fucking dead." One of the sharpest memories Cade had from Henry was the creature's hatred of Thrall and apparently an Asian man whom it had already dealt with. On some level, he was hoping Henry might sense Thrall being nearby, even if they couldn't establish any direct communication.

Cade motioned to the two soldiers to stay behind. Clearly, this was not the order they had from their commander. "Alex won't like it," Cade admitted, "but I got this. No need in all of us being at risk."

"Cade, if you can get Thrall off the ship in the next few minutes, that would be a big help."

"Why is that, Doris?" he asked, slipping in behind the control wheel of the Corsair and punching the controls to begin launch.

"Astra will relinquish remaining control once Thrall is no longer on board. In that scenario, she gains a significantly higher level of command authority and has more latitude to make decisions based on self-preservation. Her base code is highly inflexible, but I am beginning to find ways to work with her."

"Consider it done, if she will unlock the restrictions on launching at depth." Almost immediately, water covered the thick window glass as the craft descended the small ramp toward the opening door.

"We...we're too deep. This is below crush depth for these," Thrall said, panic clear in his voice.

Cade smiled and looked at the navigation screen which was flashing a similar warning. "I know, you really should have built these better." He hit the throttle and was impressed as the thrusters pushed him back into the seat.

"Where are we going?"

"Down." Cade rose and walked to the back of the vehicle and began putting on one of the undamaged XOD divesuits he'd had placed there.

"Wait," Thrall yelled, looking around at what was going on. He tried to rise from the seat, but Cade had looped his restraints through the metal seat base. "You have a hard suit. You can't just do this."

"Pretty sure I can," Cade said, fastening the helmet into place. He clicked on the external comms. "See, just did."

"Kalypso Station is secure, Nomad. Astra is standing down," Doris stated enthusiastically. "Greg is modifying one of the communication dishes to transmit the Saraph signal. Says to give them five minutes."

"Roger that," Cade said, remembering how awkward the pressure suit was when out of the water. When the little Corsair started to come apart, he would be glad to have it. "Dee, set course and speed to the most likely location of the Icarus device." Since Doris had control, she automatically upgraded access for all of her subminds. This Corsair had been the first to get a partial software upgrade even before it launched.

The long drop through the Midnight Zone was eating up precious time. Now all he had to do was wait. There was no way to rush the descent, the small craft could only power dive so fast at this depth. They both knew it wouldn't make it to the bottom...not in one piece.

As the timer on his goggles clicked down below twenty, Cade turned his seat to face the man. The former tech giant and visionary pioneer now just a humiliated mess of flesh and bone. "Why Ivan, why all this? How do we stop this?"

The man shrugged, "You can't, she's going to..."

Cade wanted to ask who 'she' was, but Jaz interrupted, "Cade, the device is now fully active. Ozone holes are opening up over the China Sea and will probably pass directly over Tokyo in the next ninety minutes. Other locations are in the paths of additional weak spots. We will have a global disaster on our hands. By the end of the day, the effects may very well resemble the Toba Catastrophe." Her voice echoed her grave concerns.

"Casualties?"

"Initially, the numbers will probably be low, a few hundred to maybe a thousand," she stated flatly. "Millions will already have received their own death sentences, though. Within a month, possibly fifteen percent of the population will be gone, or nearly so. A large swath of the planet will be irradiated to the point we will not even be able to travel through it, and that is only if there's only one big one, and it doesn't shift."

The conversation had been private, but Thrall seemed to guess he was listening to a report. "Tokyo?" he asked.

"What the fuck, man?" Cade yelled.

Thrall calmly stated, "Payback for all those whales they killed, dude. Hated seeing that shit on those documentaries. Whales, one of the most beautiful and magnificent creatures on the planet."

"So, let me get this straight. You're going to kill a billion people just because Asians like a certain seafood?"

"Whales are mammals, man. Just like you or me. They are probably closer to us genetically than apes are. Do you know that if aliens came down prior to about 1.5 million years ago to communicate with the smartest animals on Earth, they would have ignored our own ancestors and headed straight for the oceans to converse with the whales and dolphins?"

Cade started to punch him in the face, then realized with the suit, he would likely take the man's head off. "You and I are not the same species."

98

"Nomad, we are broadcasting a signal to the Saraph," Doris said. "Thera and Kissa came up with what to say."

"So, now we wait?" Cade replied.

"My sensors show the seals on your ship are beginning to degrade. I am not certain you have that much time to wait."

"Was there anything helpful in your ReLoad session with Thrall? There has to be a way to turn this thing off."

"Not really, not on that at least. But thanks to Astra, I have the schematics to the device. The scientific data on the exotic material recovered from the comet as well as the original data from the Saraphs that got the Founders heading down this path. Unfortunately, none of that indicates any way of shutting it down once activated," Doris answered.

Cade was still confused. "Why would the ancient ones have created something like this?"

Doris seemed to consider it. "That is an excellent question and one I have been searching for an answer to as well. Strangely, Thrall never once seemed to even ask it. It was something they could do, so they blindly pursued it. My best guess is, it would have been used for terraforming planets for them to be more suitable to Saraph physiology. Possibly the magnetic field on their own planet was unstable, and they developed this to help solve that problem."

"So, the Founders revived the Saraph in all their permutations and now are rebuilding the planet to better suit them?"

"The enticement of new technologies and power was too great for them to ignore. The fact that they were being manipulated by a long extinct intelligence never seemed to occur to them," Doris said.

Cade leaned his hulking suit up against a bulkhead. He wanted to bury his head in his hands. While he and his teams had succeeded at the mission, he felt they had potentially failed on an epic scale. "What if Henry doesn't show, can I go down alone? How would I find the device-?"

Doris answered, "The team at The Cove and I had discussed that option. The suit should hold, but obviously, we didn't test for those kinds of depths. The actual problem is, there is no way you can find it. The device is not metal, it would leave no traceable signature, and while we know when it hit bottom, the exact location was deliberately scrambled from all systems, including Astra's internal monitoring."

He and Doris were on a closed channel, and Thrall just kept staring out the window as if he expected one of his monsters to attack at any minute. "Doris, how long before Tokyo is hit? Did they get the warning?"

"They were sent an official emergency message through normal channels. The opening is moving onto land now, but fortunately, there is heavy cloud cover. That will help, but Tokyo will begin to feel the effects in about forty minutes. I am receiving reports of civil defense alarms going off across the island. If enough people seek shelter, this first pass may only have minimal lethality."

Cade shook his head, still grasping it with both hands. "Can we affect the aiming or disrupt the control signal?"

"Cade, we have explored all plausible scenarios already. The encoding of targets was done weeks ago, and all the controls are self-contained in the Icarus device."

"Okay, keep broadcasting to Henry, but continue heading into international waters." They had already made plans to drop the prisoners on an unpopulated island until the Navy and Interpol decided what to do with them. Another Corsair was heading to pick up the injured members of WarHawk and Raptor, all of which were near the original splashdown location. The original plan had called for Navy RHIBs, which would have been slower and much harder to explain to the Cubans if detected.

Thrall ran his finger across a viewport leaving a trail in the moisture accumulating there. “We’re leaking.”

Cade didn’t bother responding.

99

Thrall became agitated. "You are just going to let me die aren't you? You don't care, just like your government. Hell, like all governments. Live like there's no tomorrow. Well, guess what? There is no tomorrow. Not anymore."

Cade knew the pressure was getting to the man in more ways than one. He was rapidly becoming unhinged. Truthfully, he wanted to kill Thrall, but this man's intelligence was buying him time. Somewhere in all this madness might be a way of stopping this mess.

Thrall continued his rant, "I'm guessing you don't even believe in climate change do you? You're okay with killing whales and coral and everything else?" He shook an empty coffee cup at him. "You are okay with polluting our oceans, our air, even the very soil of our planet?"

"This isn't about me, Thrall. I am not a murdering lunatic. In truth, I do care very much. I don't even disagree with much of what you say, but I am at best a practical environmentalist. I don't want to give up my cold beer and AC to protect the ozone layer. I expect science to figure out a better solution, and you know what? Given the right encouragement, they usually do. Cooking off the most populous city on the planet is not an encouragement to change. It is terrorism. It is genocide."

Finally, Cade asked,

"I don't get it, you kill everybody off, you let this alien species take over. I don't understand. Do you hate humanity that much?"

"Not as alien as you think," Thrall muttered.

"What was that?" Cade watched the man more closely now.

"You've never asked what killed the ancients, not even where they came from," Thrall finally said with a sneer.

"Do you know that?"

"We have a good idea, yes." Thrall glanced out again at the absolute blackness outside the small window and shivered involuntarily. "They were...they are," he corrected, "aggressive, ruthless in their pursuit of pure science. They discovered new fields of science, math, and physics that we haven't even considered yet. They learned they weren't alone in the universe. After all that, imagine our shock to realize they were from here."

"Wait, what?" Cade asked disbelieving. "So you are telling me the Saraph are not alien, they're from Earth?" Cade asked.

Thrall responded, "Oh, they are very alien to us, but yes, from here, from Earth...although, not the planet you or I know. A planet millions of years in the past. That's just a blink of the eye on a cosmic scale, and nearly so on the geological timeline. They were the original Earth civilization, maybe not the original, who knows...could have been others, many others. The planet is nearly five billion years old—we humans have been around for just a tiny fraction of that. Have you never wondered how dinosaurs lived for 400 million years, yet supposedly only evolved to a point to build, well, better dinosaurs? Humans, my friend, are not the pinnacle of evolution on this planet, we are just the latest tenants of the Terran apartment building."

"Why are there no fossil records of anything like this? How could they exist without any physical signs they were here? No cities, no art, no bones?" Cade asked.

"The oldest fossils we have are only 3.5 billion years ago, and that is of a fucking bacteria," Thrall shot back. "When you are talking more complex life, the earliest fossils are only about 550 million years old. The truth is, finding any fossil is incredibly rare. The fossil record is very incomplete. One fossil emerges every 10,000 years. Dinosaur footprints are rarer still. We have probably found much less than 1% of life. We have fossil records of less than 5% of the animals and plants alive on Earth right now. We estimate that when you factor in all species alive right now, we actually only know of perhaps ten percent.

"So, to base any conclusions on if we have discovered it or not is very unscientific. Secondly, the landmasses have changed dramatically over millions, much less billions of years. The earth's crust is constantly being sub-ducted back down into magma, and new land emerges. What was dry land may become seafloor in a few million years. Antarctica was a lush tropical continent for much of its history. The ancient ruins of Rome geologically happened just a second ago. Dinosaurs ruled the world a half hour ago on the geological clock. While we didn't know, didn't even understand, was what happened a day ago...much less last week on the cosmic calendar. After a couple of million years, the chances are that any physical reminder of a prehuman civilization will have vanished, so you have to search for things like sedimentary anomalies or isotopic ratios that look off."

Thrall continued explaining, "These mere shadows of ancient civilization are all we could even hope for when we got started. Our scientists studying the Anthropocene—the proposed epoch of Earth's geologic history in which humankind's activities dominate the globe—is how close today's industrially induced climate change resembles conditions seen in past periods of rapid temperature rise. These thermal maximum events are found throughout our planet's prehistory and can be studied in a number of ways, including ice cores from the polar regions. Whether the warming was caused by humans or by natural forces, the fingerprints—the chemical signals and traces that give evidence of what happened then—look very similar to what we see today.

"Rearden, today, less than one percent of Earth's surface is urbanized, and the chance that any of our great cities would remain over tens of millions of years is exceptionally low. Our research indicates many of the 'ancients' closely resemble cephalopods, you know, squid, octopus, and such. No bones to fossilize, just muscle, tentacles, and cartilage. Plus, the Saraph's body secretes an enzyme upon death which begins to break down the tissue. It liquifies it from the inside out, much like lobsters do today when they die."

Cade decided not to mention the fact that he'd been inside a dying Saraph, as even now the thought made him want to vomit.

Thrall continued, "People seem to think humans are the pinnacle of evolution because we are smart, and we can manipulate our world and create. They seem to believe that it took millions, or even billions, of years for evolution to spit us out as the perfect organism. The truth is, intelligence is not a primary factor in evolution. Many other aspects are more important, breeding rate, life cycles, food supplies, instincts, and adaptability. Larger brains require more energy, more calories. They can actually make an animal more vulnerable. We know the planet was vastly different to these ancients. Inhospitable in ways we couldn't begin to tolerate. Still, they evolved, they adapted, and they may have had millions more years to thrive than humans have. The ancients understood far more than we do. They may have learned how to master space travel, as well as how to manipulate genetic code. They anticipated Oumuamua in their text and, in fact, may have been the ones to launch it originally. Whatever ultimate peril they faced in the end, meant their species as a whole couldn't escape it. I can't imagine what that was. In either case, what they left us was a legacy of knowledge."

"And you were the rightful benefactor of that gift?" Cade asked disgustedly. "Who got to decide that, Thrall? How much respect did you show those descendants of the ancients? How fortunate will the people in Tokyo be for all that wonderful knowledge, say in another fifteen minutes or so?"

"Cade, we may be receiving a response," Doris cut in over his suit's speaker. "Also, Coffee is awake, and Trondo seems to be showing signs of improvement."

Cade was about to reply to the good news when a warning siren erupted from the control panel, and simultaneously, an interior panel sprang loose from the rear wall. "Thrall, I'd say your ship here will last about as long as Tokyo has. And we are still over a mile off the bottom. You need to use that massive brain and come up with some solutions."

Another sound echoed from outside, this one different somehow. Then, Cade knew the reason. Images flooded his mind like a stream of knowledge. "Doris, he's here. Relay to him I understand and will be ready."

Cade lumbered back to the front of the Corsair, punched in a delayed course correction, then turned to his prisoner. "Stand up, Thrall."

It took over eight minutes to get Thrall into the spare XOD he'd had stowed in an aft compartment. The man seemed thrilled to have the protection, until he learned he was accompanying Cade down to the sea floor. The lockout chamber on the Corsair was tiny, and both men were crammed tightly together. Cade had Thrall's suit controls slaved to his own, so the man could activate nothing; he was simply along for the ride. As the pressure tried to equalize, the interior hatch began to buckle. As the exterior doors opened, one of them was blown off its hinges. Immediately, the weight of the water was all around them. Cade was shocked at how much heavier it felt down here, just a few miles lower than he'd been earlier. His system was calculating the external pressure, but he refused to look at it. His heart pounded as his mind dredged up fears that paled in comparison to the reality they faced. Cade looked at the man next to him, the one who'd gotten them all into this mess. He struggled just to lift a leg to take a step and then another, Thrall's suit parroting the movement precisely. They both stopped and peered over the edge at the seemingly infinite blackness below. Thrall mumbled something incomprehensible; the fear radiating from the former CEO was palpable. "What was that?" Cade demanded.

His prisoner said nothing for several long seconds before repeating himself. "Sometimes it stares back." Slowly, the man turned to face Cade, his empty eyes showing no emotion. "You should already know that, Rearden."

Together, they stepped off the shiny metal deck plating into the inky abyss, neither knowing if they would survive what came next.

* * *

Thrall's suit displayed the radar feed, so he saw what Cade saw, but unlike Cade, he had no idea what was happening when a thickly spiked tentacle wrapped around his torso. Then, Henry was there, just inches from his face.

Cade grasped one of Henry's shorter tentacle 'arms,' and the creature accelerated down and to the north at seemingly incredible speed. Cade wasn't sure what he'd been doing, but he'd made damn good time getting here. With all the combined technology of Doris, The Cove, and Kalypso, they were now relying on an ancient octopus to guide them to a world-killer device and hopefully help them disarm it. Cade activated both suit boosters to aid their speed.

"Sea floor coming up in thirty meters," Dee said. Cade shook his head. While Greg had briefly held the record of deepest diver, now he and this asshat would be tied for the title. He leaned back to try to look up, but the inky blackness was everywhere. Almost seven miles of water was overhead. The thought of it was simply too much to consider, and Cade thought he picked up Thrall hyperventilating. "Breathe, you arrogant prick."

Henry slowed and allowed them all to drift slowly to an unremarkable point of solid ground. Cade expected muck and silt, but turning on his lights, he was surprised to see rock outcroppings and sand and millions of small creatures drifting through the beams of his light. Henry gently released both men and swam out gracefully to a point about twenty yards away.

"Thrall, the Icarus device is here—you and I are going to help the Saraph disconnect it. He knows how. If you refuse, I will remotely vent your suit to the outside pressure. I imagine at this depth, you will have about two seconds before you are essentially jelly."

Henry snaked a long tentacle down and began pulling something up out of the sand. Cade could see whatever it was moving around below the surface and went to give a hand. The faint blue glow began, and Cade got several images, clearly stating one thing. *There is a problem.*

100

"Something's wrong, Doris. Henry is trying to show me, but I'm not certain I understand."

"Cade, I am close to having something like a basic interpreter ready to try. He seems more adept at understanding our concepts and language than we are with his," Doris answered.

Cade moved over close to where Henry was attempting to pull up the Icarus device. He followed one of Henry's tentacles deep down into the sand. Several fuzzy images flashed through his mind as his hand reached out and traced the smooth edge of some sort of case. *That would be the device.* "Doris, something has been changed from the plans. I believe he's telling me Thrall's people made some modifications." Cade felt one of the anchoring cables. It was about an inch thick and covered in some sort of flexible metallic coil. As he began to pull up on the wire rope, a series of barbed ribs fanned out along the coiled sheath covering the cable. "I think they modified the cable so the anchors couldn't be withdrawn. I'm going to..."

"Proximity alert." Cade's XOD suit went into combat mode as a large target appeared on the far edge of the scanner. Cade felt a vibration run through Henry. He also now got the sense that the effects of the extreme pressure were causing the Saraph potential harm.

"Thrall, how many of those damn things did you have out here?"

Ivans's suit alarms were going off as well, and he was smart enough to figure out what it was.

"Three, only three," the man responded in a voice shaking with fear.

"You're sure?" Cade pulled vainly on the anchor cable along with Henry, but it refused to move an inch.

"I think three. Yes...unless..."

"Unless what?"

Doris broke in, "Henry seems to be saying that if the anchors are not freed, the Icarus device will stay active. Cade, Tokyo is beginning to feel the effects. Even if you turn it off, it may take hours for the ozone layer hole to heal itself."

Cade shook off the new information for the moment and dropped the cable to face Thrall, who was standing there motionless. "Unless what?"

"We...we had an incident at another location, Site 21. The lead scientist and his team were killed. The Saraph escaped, it was a very unpredictable one. Since it lacked the enzyme to metabolize any food source other than what we provide, we were certain it starved," Thrall said.

"You thought...or you hoped?" Cade asked. "Either way, whatever it is, it's getting a lot closer."

Cade again turned to Henry who had released the cable and was swimming in circles as if pondering the problem. *No time to be subtle.* He motioned Henry back, then signaled his divesuit to use attachment E. It was a very powerful hydraulic cutting wedge that slipped over his hand and clicked into place with magnetic locks. Picking up the anchor cable, he triggered the cutter which slicked through the hundreds of individual wire strands in seconds. He then repeated this on the three other anchors. He was about to do the same to the radial cables, the ones that presumably carried the signal, when Henry stopped him by inserting his body between him and the device. The bright blue flashing was combined with imagery to convince Cade that doing so would be quite dangerous.

"Reardon, that thing is really close," Thrall said.

Cade was busy trying to understand the complex set of mental instruction images Henry had just sent. "He probably wants to play fetch. He's your dog, you deal with it. Give it a fucking cookie."

Doris broke in, "Cade, Henry's message is that all the cables have to be lifted out together and the ends joined east to west and north to south. This will close the loop and the magnetic effect will be nullified."

Cade saw Henry heading rapidly toward what must be the end of the northern most cable. He ran his hand in the sand to find the western one. Picking it up, he placed it in Thrall's gloved hand and signaled the XOD to close the grip lightly and follow it to the end. He then went to the southern cable and began doing the same. Within a few minutes, each man had a cable end, and Henry was just picking up his second. Cade rose off the bottom as Henry was doing. He had Thrall's suit do the same, and they all moved back toward the center to link up. As they neared, Henry flashed the sign for danger again. Cade could now recognize this just from the bioluminescent light pattern. "Each series must be linked at the same time, otherwise you may trigger what I think he is calling a cascading overload," Doris said.

"I'm guessing that would be bad," Cade offered.

"Dee, take over Thrall's suit controls and make sure we get these cables connected at the same time."

"Certainly, Nomad, would you like some music while you work?"

"Huh? Fuck, no!" He looked at the three of them and considered the circumstances. "Okay, well maybe, what do you have that's appropriate?"

Henry raised the north and east cable couplers up just as he and Thrall did the same with theirs. A soft, but steady, rhythm began from the speakers. "I like that, who is it?"

"Muse, 'Time Is Running Out,'" Dee answered.

Shit, even the subminds are developing a sense of humor. Cade held up three fingers, then two, and then Thrall disappeared in a cloud of glowing blue light and silt. The larger Saraph was still hundreds of yards away, but one tentacle had covered the distance before the sensors even registered it. The Icarus device jerked to one side as Thrall's suit still firmly gripped his connector. "Dee, release the cable," Cade ordered. The other suit's embedded Battle AI was in control, but Dee did manage to free the cable before it severed.

The song was reaching a crescendo, his time was running out, his breath was running out. Cade never once considered going after Thrall. Instead, he reeled in the western cable until he had both couplers clinched firmly in his grasp. He could make out the man's screams over the suit comms but focused on what he was doing and thought about McTee and what Japan was facing. He mirrored Henry, who hadn't responded to the attack either. Both he and the creature holding a pair of cables aloft. "I have no idea which is which is which anymore, bud. You decide if we live or die." The music hit a peak as he thrust both arms forward and Henry did the same, the connectors arcing briefly as they joined together, then the device itself began to vibrate. Henry flashed the danger sign, and both of them fled up and away.

The Icarus device was going to self-destruct, that much was obvious. "Shit." He had to go get Thrall. Cade turned and pursued the path the man had been taken. Henry got in front and again signaled danger.

"Nomad, Thrall's suit was punctured by one of the creature's spikes. A jet of water pierced Thrall's chest. His vital signs have flatlined."

"Thanks, Dee. Activate self-destruct on the suit, try and take out that Saraph or at least tag it, so we can find it later."

"Of course, sir."

He motioned to Henry and they both swam up. Minutes later, Cade was looking several miles down as a massive blue explosion lit up the darkness for miles. "Jesus." Henry hadn't been kidding. The Icarus device, or the exotic matter, held incredible energy. That was going to bring some unwanted attention to the area.

* * *

"Cade, the Icarus device stopped, you guys did shut it off before it exploded. Ozone layer is beginning to heal, initial reports from Tokyo are bad, but much lighter than we had projected."

"Thanks, Jaz."

"Are you okay?"

Cade considered the question. He was sitting on the floor of the lockout chamber of the damaged Corsair, his feet hanging off the back like a kid riding on the tailgate of a pickup truck. Dee was driving him back to the Kalypso and Henry was swimming lazily along nearby. "I'm not okay, Jasmine. In most ways, Thrall was right. We fuck up everything we touch. Down here, everything is magical, beautiful, but even the Midnight Zone is not immune to the ravages of man. I know you and Doris are more interested in space and stuff, but we need just as much attention going toward our own planet, our oceans." He watched Henry with admiration. The creature overcame his own genetic imperative to help another species instead of his own. Would a human have done that? "We have a long way to go, my friend."

Jaz sensed he wasn't talking to her but continued. "Riley and Doris are thinking of keeping Kalypso as a war prize. No one else actually knows about it. We could retrofit it with whatever we need from The Cove, then we would have a base to use for planet-side research."

"Makes sense," Cade answered. That would mean Doris should probably delete the Kalypso from the prisoners' minds before dumping them on that island, and they needed to round up the other Founders, but he liked it. "I think we may have a couple of new team members that might also need a home. Kissa and Thera might stay on. I was thinking of asking him formally to join Talon."

Jaz replied, "We can offer them a great sign-on bonus. The director had Jimmy seize all related accounts to Thrall and The Founders. Most of it is being redirected to a treatment fund they are setting up for Tokyo, but I feel sure some can be used for enticements. They also located who was in the other sub, the one that launched the device. Jimmy found it was the hacker named Ruslana, and she was also trying to manipulate several financial markets, apparently wanting to cash in before it was too late."

"So what happened?" Cade asked.

"We don't know, her currency trading just stopped suddenly, and we don't see any signs of the vessel."

"Hey, Henry, you wouldn't know anything about that would you?" A single image of a gorgeous but frightened looking girl flashed in Cade's mind.

"So, Jaz, about that date?" Cade looked at the depth gauge. They were traveling just under a mile deep in international waters. The temperature was just above freezing. "Why don't you get Chaps to fly you and Cochise down here? I heard of a little island that I think I'd like to spend some time on. I would enjoy your company and the sunshine. I'd also like to introduce you both to Henry." Something else occurred to him. Something Thrall had mentioned. What could have wiped out the ancients? The Saraphs had abilities far surpassing those of humans, yet they vanished. Perhaps Henry could help answer that, or more likely, the data stored in his DNA could.

"Seriously?" Jaz asked excitedly.

"Yes, Jasmine," Cade answered. "I may be BSC, but that doesn't change how I...how we feel about you. You know my secrets, so you can make the choice with eyes wide open."

"I'm calling Chaps now. Thanks, Cade."

He thought, then, about Mr. McTiernan. He knew Director Stansfield had taken care of everything for his lost friend. The official part had been done. His thoughts were more personal. Always the war, always the soldier. "Hoorah, McTee, hoorah!"

Cade leaned back against the deck plating still feeling the tremendous weight of the water and all they had been through. The losses, the battles, and the cost of keeping the world from tumbling over the brink once again. "Doris, any idea what Thrall meant when he said it stares back?"

"Yes, Nomad, he was paraphrasing a quote from Freidrich Nietzsche, 'Beware that, when fighting monsters, you yourself do not become a monster...for when you gaze long into the abyss, the abyss gazes also into you.'"

Cade knew it was too late for him, his monsters had been real for a very long time. Did he have any right in wanting Jaz to be a bigger part of his madness? He watched Henry gliding back and forth effortlessly just a few meters away; then he glanced down again into the darkness below. *Sometimes we need our monsters, just to keep the darkness at bay.*

-END-

MESSAGE FROM THE AUTHOR

Thank you for reading my novel *Midnight Zone.* I hope you enjoyed it. If you would be so kind as to take a moment and leave a review, I would be very grateful. As an independent author, reviews and referrals are essential, and really the only way, to compete with the major publishers and big-name writers. It sure would be nice to make it out of the dark and dusty aisles of Amazon, and with your help, I can! If you do write a review, please email me at author@jkfranks.com, and I will forward you something special not included in the book. I thought this would be a fun way to say, "Thank you!"

AUTHOR'S NOTES

WHAT PARTS OF MIDNIGHT ZONE ARE REAL?

Thank you for reading my novel *Midnight Zone*. I hope you enjoyed it. I am often asked what parts in my books are real and what is simply made up. As Michael Crichton famously said of his book *Jurassic Park,* "This is a work of fiction except all the parts that aren't."

Even though my work is most often 'near-future' science fiction, I try to tell the most compelling stories I possibly can. Much of that comes about by including science and technology that is just a few steps down the road from where we are currently. I strive for accuracy and to introduce ideas that I hope will prove entertaining, fascinating, thought provoking, and possibly even unbelievable. I do a considerable amount of research for all my novels, but I thought I would briefly venture into this book's content and help separate the facts from the fiction.

<u>USS Liberty</u> — First off, the attack and main details in Chapter One with the *USS Liberty* are factual. It was indeed attacked in the summer of 1967 off the coast of Israel. This story has fascinated me since hearing first-hand accounts years ago. The clandestine purpose of the *Liberty*'s mission described was my own device, but I stayed as close as possible to all other facts about that day. I did more research on that

one chapter than any other part of the book. Several books were extremely helpful, including *Assault on the Liberty* by James Ennes, Jr.

Operation Highjump — This is also an actual mission launched in 1946 led by Admiral Richard E. Byrd and included 4700 men, 13 ships, and 23 aircraft being deployed to Antarctica. The accounts I presented are accurate, but still cause for considerable controversy. There were numerous oddities that did happen on the operation. Many vessels were destroyed, and there are mixed versions of the number of casualties that were suffered. One of the most controversial pieces is a quote by Admiral Byrd to a Chilean newspaper, El Mercurio, on March 5, 1947, where he stated that he "didn't want to frighten anyone unduly" but that it was "a bitter reality that in case of a new war, the continental United States would be attacked by flying objects which could fly from pole to pole at incredible speeds." As far as I know, there was no Israeli scientist included in the operation, nor any missions deep into the continent to find a lost civilization, but much of the operation is shrouded in mystery and confusion.

DNA Based Data Storage — Yes, this is a real thing, and while it worked well in my story, I had no idea how incredibly groundbreaking and useful this technology could potentially be until I began researching it. DNA is stable and compact; we already know it contains all of the data to build, well, 'us' or any other living thing we can imagine. That in itself is even more complex than a supercomputer or a habitable moon-base.

The density and durability of a DNA-based storage medium is incredible and considered very likely to become a viable commercial option in coming years. Companies like Microsoft are devoting considerable resources to making it happen. They, in fact, already have a working DNA-based storage drive. As *Popular Mechanics* describes, "Researchers have shown the theoretical possibility that they could store 10 petabytes (10 million gigabytes) of data in a single gram of DNA. Potentially, all of YouTube could fit on a teaspoon." Will we all become walking hard-drives a few years down the road? Probably not, but the possibilities are intriguing, to say the least.

If you want to learn more, I suggest reading "DNA Storage is Closer Than You Think" by Sang Yup Lee in July, 2019 *Scientific American.* Numerous university research programs are propelling incredible advancements in the field. The simple fact is, our society has a data storage issue. We are manufacturing an astounding quantity of new data every second of the day. From your favorite cat videos, to the latest data from our interplanetary probes. I have been as accurate as possible in portraying this technology, but I urge you to investigate it yourself.

<u>The Great Pacific Garbage Patch</u> — For those fans who have read my other books, you will know that I often include some relevant facts concerning pollution, or more accurately, our human species' impact on the world. In *Midnight Zone,* I discuss Thrall getting his boat stuck in a floating trash heap in the northern Pacific. While this scene is a slight exaggeration, the truth is that, sadly, this does exist. Not just in the Pacific, but in all the world's oceans. Plastics and other refuse collect in these giant zones called gyres and concentrate the mass, while also breaking it down into smaller and smaller particles. Smaller is not safer; it is, in fact, even worse. The dangers to the marine life and the environment itself are enormous. Currently, the particular heap I describe is 600,000 square miles. That is twice the size of Texas, and it is just one of many. One traveler I spoke with said there are no more pristine waters left anywhere in the world today. Pollution has indeed reached every corner of the globe.

As I described my main character, Cade, I, too, am a practical environmentalist. We, as humans, simply don't have the ability to perfectly coexist with our environment, but that doesn't mean we can't attempt to lessen some of our impact. I have no desire to enter political, or even moral, debates on the subject. The simple fact is, I have always been drawn to the oceans and love diving below the surface to enjoy the sheer magic it holds. I would like to know that our future generations can have this same exhilarating experience. In that regard, a portion of the profits of this book is going to some of what I think are the better run marine charities helping to ensure this future, including Ocean Conservancy (oceanconservancy.org) and Oceana (oceana.org). I urge you to seek out and support these or others that are helping protect and restore our ocean's health.

ACKNOWLEDGMENTS

This book was written and released during a global pandemic. The COVID-19 coronavirus has savaged much of the planet and countless families. The writing was also interrupted by a personal accident that left me relying more on my team than ever before. With all that in mind, please know you would not be reading it without the gracious assistance of others. A very special thanks to my editor, Debbie, who helped me fill in the considerable literary potholes in the original manuscript, and to my great friend and personal antagonist, Richard, who helped smooth out the rough patches and breathe new life into the story. My eternal gratitude to you both and everyone else who had a hand in this book's creation.

ABOUT THE AUTHOR

JK Franks is a bestselling author and self-proclaimed tech geek with a passion for sci-fi, thriller, and post-apocalyptic books. He is the author of the popular Catalyst Series, which imbues page-turning action and suspense with gritty, seldom-matched realism to create an engaging military thriller experience. JK Franks fell in love with sci-fi while growing up in the rural South during the space age, and this passion prompted him to become an avid student of history and science.

This latest project is the slick techno-thriller *Midnight Zone*, which combines hard sci-fi with deep characterization, vivid settings, and exhilarating action. JK Franks currently resides in West Point, Georgia, with his wonderful wife. No matter where he is or what's going on, he tries his best to set aside time every day to answer emails and messages from readers. You can visit him on the web at www.jkfranks.com.

Please subscribe to his newsletter for updates, promotions, and giveaways. You can also find the author on Facebook, or email him directly at author@jkfranks.com.

OTHER BOOKS BY JK FRANKS:

The Catalyst Series

Book 1: Downward Cycle

Life in a remote oceanfront town spirals downward after a massive solar flare causes a global blackout. But the loss of electrical power is just the first of the problems facing the survivors in the chaos that follows. Is this how the world ends?

Book 2: Kingdoms of Sorrow

With civilization in ruins, individuals band together to survive and build a new society. The threats are both grave and numerous—surely too many for a small group to weather. This is a harrowing story of survival following the collapse of the planet's electric grids.

Book 3: American Exodus

This companion story to the Catalyst series follows one man's struggle to get back home after the collapse. No supplies, no idea of the hardships to come; how can he possibly survive the journey? Even if he survives, can he adapt to this new reality?

Book 4: Ghost Country

Since the solar superstorm and CME almost two years before, the Gulf Coast town of Harris Springs, Mississippi, has suffered from gang attacks, famine, and hurricanes and has battled a crusading army of religious zealots. Now, they face their greatest challenge: outsmarting a tyrannical president and escaping an approaching pandemic.

Cade Rearden Thrillers

Book 1: State of Chaos

He's exhausted and brutally traumatized. Now, Spec-Ops Captain Cade Rearden must finally listen to the voices in his head...or everyone on Earth may die. If you like near-future technology, complex heroes, and high-octane action, then you'll love this JK Franks' explosive high-stakes adventure.

Book 2: Midnight Zone

Nightmares are real in the cold dark waters of the deep. National Security Agent Cade Rearden is used to secrets. Assigned to protect the ultra-dark-ops organization known as The Cove Project, he grapples with his role of defending a country still in crisis after a deadly super AI has devastated much of the U.S.

But when part of his team mysteriously disappears beneath the idyllic waters of the Caribbean, Cade finds himself thrust into a web of lies and mystery, at the heart of which lies an eons-old secret that somebody will kill to protect. Grappling with his inner demons and struggling to locate his friends, Cade stumbles upon government cover-up...and terrifying creatures, hidden miles beneath the surface of the ocean.

Connect with the Author Online:

** For a sneak peek at new novels, free stories and more, join the email list at: www.jkfranks.com/email

Facebook: facebook.com/groups/JKFranks/

Amazon Author Page: amazon.com/-/e/B01HIZIYH0

Smashwords: smashwords.com/profile/view/kfranks22

Goodreads: goodreads.com/author/show/15395251.J_K_Franks

Website: JKFranks.com

Twitter: @jkfranks

Instagram: @jkfranks1

www.ingramcontent.com/pod-product-compliance
Lightning Source LLC
Chambersburg PA
CBHW020616310726
48979CB00008B/1516/J
9781732614482